T0322223

THE SILENCE IN BETWEEN

www.penguin.co.uk

THE SILENCE IN
BETWEEN

Josie Ferguson

doubleday

TRANSWORLD PUBLISHERS

Penguin Random House, One Embassy Gardens,
8 Viaduct Gardens, London SW11 7BW
www.penguin.co.uk

Transworld is part of the Penguin Random House group of companies
whose addresses can be found at global.penguinrandomhouse.com

First published in Great Britain in 2024 by Doubleday
an imprint of Transworld Publishers

A CIP catalogue record for this book is available from the British Library.

ISBNS
9780857529695 hb
9780857529701 tpb

Typeset in 11.5/15pt Minion Pro by Jouve (UK), Milton Keynes
Printed and bound in Great Britain by Clays Ltd, Elcograf S.p.A.

The authorized representative in the EEA is Penguin Random House Ireland,
Morrison Chambers, 32 Nassau Street, Dublin D02 YH68.

Penguin Random House is committed to a sustainable
future for our business, our readers and our planet. This book is made
from Forest Stewardship Council® certified paper.

For those whose stories deserve to be heard

'Those who cannot remember the past
are condemned to repeat it.'

GEORGE SANTAYANA

BERLIN

WEST BERLIN

French sector

Brunnenstraße

1
3
4
6

Karin's house

Brandenburg Gate

Wilmersdorf

Unter
den
Linde

British sector

Checkpoint
Charlie

American sector

Waldfriede Hospital

Marienfelde

KM 0   5   10

Miles 0   5

EAST BERLIN

North Sea   Baltic Sea

Berlin

EAST
GERMANY

WEST
GERMANY

Volkspark Friedrichshain

Berliner Dom

Soviet sector

Harzer Straße

Teltowkanal, Johannisthal

1 Bornholmer Straße checkpoint
2 Prenzlauer Berg
3 Bernauer Straße
4 Lisette and Elly's apartment
5 The Resi
6 Friedrichstraße station

LISETTE

Now – Berlin, 12 August 1961

Any parent who says they don't have a favourite child is a liar. As Axel finally falls asleep in my arms, a bubble of milk resting on his upper lip, a tidal wave of love washes over me. I never had this with Elly. Not on the day she was born or on any day in the fifteen years since. Yet even the crippling guilt I feel at this fact is insignificant in comparison to this sensation swelling in my chest. What I feel for Axel is bigger than me, bigger than all of us. For a moment I let myself believe it is so big it will eclipse everything else, including the past and all that I've done.

I kiss his soft, feathery hair and stroke the red pinpricks in the crook of his arm where they've taken blood. He's so little; he shouldn't have already experienced pain. I clutch him a little closer and I vow to take care of him, to love him, to be better. I can't fail at this again.

A man pushes the door open with his shoulder, his arms full of folders, a stethoscope around his neck. The rim of a Styrofoam cup is gripped between his teeth. He drops the folders on the cluttered desk and drains the last of his coffee before sitting down opposite me.

'I'm sorry you've had to wait for so long,' he says, opening one of the files and sifting through the papers. A single sheet escapes and flutters to the floor. He reaches down to grab it with a liver-speckled hand and bumps his head in the process.

'Right, right, where were we?' he says, rubbing his bald patch where I imagine a weal is already forming. 'Yes, Frau Hartmann and Frank.'

'Lange.'

'What?'

'Frau Lange. And Axel.' I keep my voice to a whisper but the man doesn't seem to notice that Axel is asleep in my arms, doesn't understand it's taken me hours to get him to stop crying.

'Right, right. Let me just . . . yes, here they are.' He extracts a page from one of the folders and holds it under the desk lamp, squinting at the handwriting.

Gently I shift Axel's weight from one arm to the other and rub my gritty eyes. The room is blurry and the lamp seems to sway as if we're on a ship. I can feel a dampness between my legs, the blood leaking out of me staining my skirt.

'I'm afraid we're going to need to run a few more tests,' he says.

'But we've been here for . . .' I have no idea how long we've been here. From the fading light outside the window, I know the day is already dying, but I don't know what time it is, or even what day.

'We've a backlog, I'm afraid. But it doesn't look as though we need to be too worried. I just want to do a few extra tests. Just to be sure.'

'To be sure of what?'

'That it's not something more serious. Your baby's oxygen level isn't quite what we'd like it to be. You were right to bring him in. I suspect it might be to do with his heart.'

'His heart?'

A sob heaves in my chest, taking us both by surprise. Axel stirs in his sleep and I jump to my feet so I can rock him once more.

'Is he going to be OK?' I can hear my voice crack. I clear my throat and try again. 'He's going to be OK, isn't he?'

'Oh, yes. I have no doubt. He's – how old? Three weeks?'

'Five.'

'Well, there you go. If it were something more serious, he wouldn't have made it this far.'

I ignore the urge to push this man's folders to the floor and stamp on them. Instead I start pacing in front of the window, rocking and jiggling, rocking and jiggling. The movement like a physical mantra.

'Right,' he says, shuffling his papers. 'A nurse will collect Axel shortly. And perhaps you should go home and have a rest.'

I stop rocking. 'And leave Axel here?'

'Just for the night. Get some sleep, bathe, collect some things. Let your family know what's going on.'

I turn and look him in the eye. 'Absolutely not.'

'You've been here for over forty-eight hours and your body is still recovering from childbirth.' He looks pointedly at my skirt and my cheeks burn. 'Axel will be absolutely fine.'

'But I'm breastfeeding.'

'We have formula. You're an educated woman, Frau Lange. Very few women breastfeed these days.'

I clutch Axel tighter to my chest. 'I just . . . I don't think I can leave him.'

He glances at his watch and stifles a yawn. 'It will only be a few hours. As I said, we need to check a few things, keep him in for observation. You can't be with him until the morning anyway, as we don't have a room free. And your son needs clean clothes. Nappies, too.' He sniffs and raises one eyebrow. 'He can't very well wear that outfit another day.'

I finger the stained lapel of Axel's blue pyjamas. It releases a faint sour smell of curdled milk. In my hurry to get him here, I hadn't thought to bring an extra set of clothes. Heat rises up my neck in small, itchy welts. I'm failing again.

'I'm not sure. It feels . . .' I look down at Axel, his button nose, the frown that creases his forehead when he sleeps. His little fist is wrapped around my finger, his pink fingernails so delicate and small. I don't want to be separated from him, but if we're to be here for several more days, I will need to let my family know. My husband will be worried. Elly, too. And I should check on Mother. Not for the first time, frustration over the city's severed phone lines boils inside me. There is no logic to it. Why have an open border but forbid us from speaking on the phone?

He sighs. 'I'm a doctor, Frau Lange. I can guarantee Axel will be fine.'

I nuzzle my baby boy's perfect little squashed face and feel the heat of his small body. 'I live in the East . . .' I begin.

'As do I.'

'What if I can't get back?'

He waves a hand as if I'm a fly that needs swatting. 'Of course you'll be able to get back.'

He stands up and gathers his folders. I remind myself that this man is supposed to be the best. Better than any paediatrician in East Berlin, at least.

'I'll see you again tomorrow.' His voice is firm. 'We should know more by then.' He turns to go but then stops. 'He'll be fine, your son. There really isn't anything to worry about.'

And then he's gone.

Outside, the sky has turned a deep purple and the day's heat has retreated. Descending the hospital steps, I'm painfully conscious of my empty arms. Nothing about this feels right.

I look at my watch. I can be home in thirty minutes, back

here in two hours. My thoughts are a blur and I almost collide with a man bleeding from a deep cut on his forehead. His white fringe is stained red, and the left side of his face seems to be drooping as if it's made of melted wax. He clings to a small, pale woman with fleshy lips and oversized teeth.

I sidestep out of the way and steady myself on the banister. As I slide my hand down it, I feel the sudden sharp stab of a splinter embedding itself in the soft flesh of my palm. On the bottom step, I pause and turn back to face the entrance. The couple has disappeared inside.

'I'll be quick,' I whisper, as if Axel can hear me. 'I'll be back before you wake.'

I walk to the S-Bahn, stumbling a little on the badly lit pavement. With each step I take, I can feel the distance between Axel and me stretching like a taut rubber band.

I take a seat by the window in an empty carriage. Usually I love taking the S-Bahn across the city. Travelling from West to East Berlin is like moving back in time. Everything is more colourful in the West, the buildings are newer, the people happier. The moment the train crosses the border into the East, it's as if a light has gone off. The buildings are drab and pockmarked with bullet holes from the war; people walk cautiously in their broken-soled shoes and unfashionable clothes. Even the smell is different: cheap coffee and cigarettes.

Today I don't bother to look out of the window, I just rest my head on the vibrating glass and will my eyes to stay open. What I need is a piano so I can fold myself into its music, forget just for a moment that my baby is sick. But the music that once sat inside me was taken from me long ago and I will never get it back.

There are no spot checks on the train tonight – there usually aren't on the way into East Berlin, just on the way out, when *VoPos* sift through passengers' luggage to determine who's planning on 'fleeing the Republic'. There has been more of this lately, a steady trickle that has turned into a flood. Perhaps it's time to try again to persuade Mother to leave. For now, though, I just need to focus on Axel and getting him healthy.

As the train approaches my stop, the lights flicker and the engine groans. A group of teenage boys get on, their eyes glassy, a hint of whiskey on their breath. They don't wait for me to get off first and I resist the urge to shoulder them out of the way.

When I get home the apartment is dark and the smell of bleach hangs in the air; Mother must have been on one of her cleaning binges. Her thunderous snores are now reverberating around the apartment. I can hear the sharp notes of Elly's electronic keyboard, too, and if I had the energy I'd cross the hallway and tell her to have a bit more respect for the rest of the household.

I touch my breasts; they are already hot and heavy. I know the hospital has formula, that it's supposedly superior to what I have to offer, but if I hurry I can be back before Axel's next feed.

I find my husband asleep in our bed. When he's not plagued by nightmares, he sleeps as Elly does, deeply and silently. I climb in beside him. He stirs but doesn't wake. Beside me, the curtain flutters in the breeze, but the air is stagnant in here and our sheets are damp with sweat. He would want me to wake him, to let him know what's going on, but I will write him a note instead. I don't want to disturb him, not when he's sleeping so soundly. Instead, I curl myself around him and press my face into his warm back. The earthy scent of his soap makes me feel at home.

I close my eyes. Just for a moment.

~

I wake to threads of morning light seeping in through the crack between the curtains. My breasts feel like hot bags of sand crushing my ribs. Instinctively I reach out to touch Axel's back, to feel his chest's slow rise and fall, but he's not here. I kick off the sheets and look down at my deflated stomach as if I'll find him still in there.

Axel. He's in the hospital.

I look at my watch. It's almost six a.m. I've slept for hours, not minutes.

'Wake up,' I say, shaking my husband's shoulder.

'Hmm?' His eyes are still closed and he turns his back to me as if that will be enough to stop the conversation.

I start stuffing clothes into a holdall. 'I had to leave Axel at the hospital.' The moment I say the words, my throat burns. I didn't *have* to do anything.

My husband sits up, rubbing his eyes and propping his pillow up behind him.

'Is he OK? I've been so worried.'

'He's fine. They think. They just want to keep him under observation for a few more days. I came home last night to pack some things and then I was going to go back. I must have fallen asleep . . .'

'You look tired. Why don't you sleep some more and I can go to the hospital?'

'No, I've slept now. Didn't you hear me? He's alone in the hospital.' I pull a dress over my head. My hair snags in the zip but I yank it down, ripping several strands from my scalp. 'I need to get back there.'

'Lisette, breathe. You just said he's fine. Let me get dressed, have some coffee and then we can go together.'

He untangles himself from the sheets, stretches, then ambles out of the room. He can never do anything quickly and I don't want to wait for him to get ready. I rush to the bathroom and splash a handful of cold water on my face. I give my teeth a quick brush and then scan Axel's cot for his teddy. He hasn't

7

taken to it yet but maybe it will make the hospital feel more like home.

'Lisette.'

I know something is wrong just from the way he says my name.

I find him in the living room, his face pale, his hand on the radio as if he's trying to push the presenter's voice back inside. He looks at me, and his eyes seem to be drowning.

'The border,' he says, his voice so quiet I can barely hear him. 'They've closed the border.'

PART ONE

ELLY

1961

LISETTE

1938–46

1

ELLY

Now – Berlin, 13 August 1961

The unwritten music sits in my fingers tingling painfully. I need to release it but it exists only at the borders of my mind and I can't quite grasp it. I screw up the song sheet into a ball and throw it at the window, poised to start afresh, when a scream pierces my fragile bubble of concentration, a feral wail that echoes around the room. Then there's another scream, followed by a third. An entire orchestra of screams.

My body is still heavy with sleep and I stumble to the door, tripping on my mud-caked trainers.

Initially I think Mama must be hurt, but I don't see any blood when I find her crumpled on the living-room floor. Another of her 'moments', I assume, but this screaming is new. Usually she just sits there staring at the corner of the room – at the space where her piano once stood. Other times, she fixes her gaze on the same spot on the far wall. There's never anything there. But this screaming, that's not something she's done before.

Papa is kneeling beside her, his hands clasped together. His face is pale, his brow furrowed. The music I have assigned him – an overture with a steady, consistent drumbeat, reliable but with a hint of sadness – has become an erratic hammering. Mama's music is usually a storm – loud and angry, similar to the 'Allegro molto' in Shostakovich's Eighth Quartet. Now it's more like the whimpering of a dying animal.

Oma Rita stands in her nightgown a few feet away, her hand clamped over her mouth, her grey hair loose around her shoulders. I've rarely seen her hair down, free from the tight bun that usually holds it in place.

'What's going on?' I ask.

Mama's screams and sobs continue. Papa and Oma Rita seem to have been deafened by the noise. No one looks at me and the feeling of not being seen or heard is like a volcano inside me, ready to erupt.

'Why is Mama screaming? Why is everyone crying? Can someone please just answer me? I'm standing right here.' The room is so full of anguish I have an urge to jump out of the window just to get away from it all.

Mama closes her mouth and the screaming stops. The air becomes thin in the sudden silence. She lifts her finger. At first I don't know what she's pointing at.

But then Papa says, 'Listen,' and I do.

The voice on the radio crackles, static eating the man's words. I recognize the presenter, but his voice sounds more high-pitched than usual, as if he's being strangled.

'A fence . . . barbed wire? What's he talking about? When did this happen?'

'Elly, please, stop with the questions.' Papa is still crouched down beside Mama. 'There will be a way to cross,' he says. But I can hear he doesn't believe his own words.

'Come, let's go down,' he says, gently touching Mama's shoulder. 'We'll speak to them at the border. Explain.'

Mama won't look at me. She simply howls once more and it's then that I see the empty wooden cot in the bedroom beyond, the crumpled sheet poking out through the bars. I finally understand the full horror of the situation.

'Axel?' My voice is a whisper.

Papa looks at me, his eyes strained. 'He's on the other side.'

~

The street heaves with bodies, pushing and shoving and panting their stinking morning breath on each other. A few cars sit in the middle of the road, the throng too dense for them to pass through. One man beeps his horn repeatedly but the sound is smothered by the crowd. The air is thick with anxiety but it could easily be excitement, too. If it weren't for the stricken faces, the scene could be mistaken for a parade.

My armpits are damp, the bright morning sun competing with the heat of so many bodies. Everyone's songs will change for ever with today's news and, though I know it's only my imagination that creates the sound of their music, I still find the cacophony of panic deafening. At fifteen I'm too old to hold Papa's hand and yet I want to reach for it all the same.

There's a crescendo of noise and a large woman shoves past me. Her hair is piled messily on top of her head and the pungent smell of her hairspray catches in my throat. I stumble on the cobbles and when I regain my balance, my parents are gone. The air leaves me and my skin turns so cold I begin to tremble. I want to resist the surge of people but if I fall I'll be trampled beneath their feet. My fear grows bigger than my body, panic like a film over my eyes.

A hand grips my arm and I hear Papa's voice beside me. 'Your music,' he says. 'The music you hear that's only yours. Find it.'

I nod and close my eyes. I stop resisting and instead am carried forward as if the crowd is a riptide. I will the beat of my song to soothe the swelling of my heart. It usually works but today my tune becomes swallowed up by everyone else's and the anxiety is still a shimmering mass at the edge of my vision.

'OK?' Papa says. Mama strides ahead, pushing people out of her way. Papa hesitates; he doesn't want to abandon me but he won't leave her either.

'Better,' I say.

We cross the street, Papa finding gaps for us to slip through. As we catch up with Mama, I turn to see Oma Rita watching us from our window. Even from this distance, I can see how her skin stretches painfully over her cheekbones, her eyes hollow and vacant. She's probably the only woman in Berlin whose music will remain the same – a muddled melody that is almost hypnotic in its confusion.

'Papa, we shouldn't leave Oma Rita alone in the flat.'

He turns to look at me and blinks, his right eye slightly magnified by the thicker lens on that side of his glasses.

'Are you still wearing your pyjamas?' he asks.

'What? Yes. I didn't have time to change.'

'Stay close,' he says.

Ahead of us are fences, barbed wire lining the tops like jagged teeth. Soldiers stand stone-faced, trying not to engage with the hordes of people who are shouting at them, demanding answers and begging for passage.

We've come as far as we can, but Mama still tries to push her way to the front.

'What are we going to do?' I ask Papa, my voice faltering. 'How are we going to get Axel back? It has to be temporary, don't you think? Papa, you're not listening . . .'

Someone tugs on my pyjama top. I look down to see a frail, hunched woman. Her scalp glimmers in the sunlight through her thinning hair.

'I can't see,' she says. 'Tell me what's going on. What are they doing?'

'There are soldiers,' I say. 'Lots of them. Some are standing guard with guns. Others are ripping up the street. It looks as though they're piling up pieces of paving stones to form barricades.'

'Let me through,' Mama shouts. 'Please. Please. I have to get through.' And then she howls like a rabid dog. There are other people shouting too, but many are silent, standing motionless as they bear witness.

'This way,' Papa says. When Mama shakes her head and again tries to squeeze through the wall of bodies, he adds, 'We'll be able to see better from over there.'

We climb the steps of a nearby building. In front of us, there is a sea of bobbing heads. I reach out and touch Mama's shoulder but she shrugs my hand away.

'Where are the Western Allies?' someone cries. It's unclear whether he's asking Papa or God. 'Why aren't they here? Why aren't they stopping this?'

Finally, over on the Western side, a battered grey jeep appears. It pulls to a halt, whipping up a cloud of dust. Two uniformed men climb out wearing the distinctive red caps of the British military police. They stand at a safe distance from the border and we all watch them with bated breath. The older one, his body rigid, sucks on a cigarette, a deep frown marking his forehead. I imagine I can hear the pop of his jaw as he releases the smoke. The other man – younger and rounder, his belly stretching the fabric of his uniform – takes off his cap and twists it in his hands, bending it out of shape. Slowly he shakes his head and then they both turn away, bowing their heads to talk. I find myself straining forward as if somehow I might be able to catch the words passing between them, but all I can hear is my own uneven breath.

The older officer flicks his cigarette butt towards the border in a pathetic act of defiance, then they climb back into the truck, slamming their doors in unison. The engine stutters to life and they drive off, leaving another flurry of dust in their wake.

'Don't they care?' I ask. 'Where are the Americans?'

'They can't do anything,' Papa says quietly. 'No one wants another war.'

Mama begins to wail once more. She rocks back and forth, hugging her chest as if Axel is there in her arms. Papa and I exchange a look. Neither of us knows what to do. This is not who she is. Mama doesn't bend, she doesn't break – not in this way, at least. Today I don't even recognize her. I want to try to give her some comfort, reach out and take her hand, but I'm terrified she'll look at me and wish it was me on the other side.

~

As morning slides into afternoon, some people give up and trudge home. But more keep coming. Mama shifts between bouts of sobbing followed by persistent efforts to push forward, mumbling jumbled, hysterical words. Eventually my parents and I inch closer to the barrier until we are a mere metre away.

Papa attempts to speak to a stocky guard. The man stands with his feet wide apart, spine straight, a gun strapped to his chest. Sweat trickles down a damp strand of hair poking out of his helmet.

'Please listen,' Papa says, his voice steady but pleading. 'My son is in a hospital in the West. He's just a baby, a few weeks old. He's sick and his mother, my wife, came home last night just to wash, get a change of clothes, and then this . . . We need to cross, we need to get our son.'

The guard won't even make eye contact. He just moves his hand up so one podgy finger rests on the trigger of his gun. Papa retreats, his shoulders stooped. I want to try as well but Mama holds me back with a furious frown.

When darkness has settled for the night, we finally head home. Mama can barely walk. I imagine her grief like a man sitting on her shoulders, his weight driving her into the ground. Papa half walks, half carries her, and I follow a few paces behind.

Inside the apartment, Oma Rita is asleep in her chair by the window. She's snoring loudly, her head lolling to one side, a string of saliva stretching from her bottom lip to her chin.

'We'll try again tomorrow,' Papa says, lowering Mama on to the sofa. 'Once we've explained our situation, once they've organized a new visa system, everything will be OK.'

There are reminders of Axel everywhere – his small cot yawns empty; his play mat lies forlorn. He hasn't been with us long and yet it feels like we've never existed without him. Mama looks up at Papa with a glazed expression, as if her soul has already left her.

I go to the fridge and rummage around for something to eat. I take out yesterday's stew and reheat it on the stove, ignoring the globules of fat it spits on to my pyjamas, then dole out small portions on four plates. It looks unappetizing but it smells of yesterday when everything was OK.

Behind me I hear Papa repeat, 'It'll be OK. I promise you. We'll get Axel back.'

By the time I turn around, Papa is carrying Mama to bed, her long thin legs dangling over his forearm like a pair of empty tights. He comes back, closing the bedroom door gently behind him, then turns on the radio. The presenter's disembodied voice floats around the room.

'An "anti-fascist protection barrier"? Is that what they're calling it?' The volume of my voice rises with each word. 'They're not trying to keep the West out. Everyone knows that. They're trying to keep us in!'

Papa simply nods and joins me at the table. He picks up a fork and starts separating the carrots from the stew, piling them on one side with the focus and precision of a surgeon.

A sudden loud snort breaks the silence. Oma jumps up from her seat, her hands clenched into fists, her eyes wild.

'What was that? What's going on?'

'It's nothing, Rita,' Papa says, going over to her. 'You were sleeping. Do you want some food? There's some stew warmed up. And I've picked out the carrots for you.'

'No, no stew. I need to sleep.'

'OK. Come on, then.' His hand hovers near the small of her back, not touching it but close enough to make her instinctively move away.

'Where have you been? You left me alone.' Her voice trembles. 'I thought ... when you didn't come back ... Have the bombs stopped falling?'

'The war's over, Rita. It was over a long time ago.'

'Who are you? Where's Ernst?'

'You're tired. Let's get you to bed.'

She shakes her head and lets him guide her to her bedroom, but when she gets there she ducks inside quickly and slams the door, forcing Papa to take a step back. He stares at the closed door. Slowly he takes off his glasses and rubs the bridge of his nose.

'Papa, what are we going to do?'

He comes over to me and kisses my hair. I lean into him, breathing in his faint woody aftershave. My heartbeat begins to slow, the tightness in my chest easing.

'I don't want you worrying about this, El. We'll get Axel back. The borders won't be closed for ever.'

'Things have been so much better lately,' I whisper. 'With Mama.'

'I know. But everything will be good again, I promise.' He gives me a squeeze, then releases me gently. 'See you in the morning.'

I should do the dishes or at least pile them in the sink, but the very thought exhausts me. I clear the food away, though, scraping the leftovers into the rubbish bin, the gloopy stew sliding down the inside like a slug.

I trudge off to bed, not even bothering to change into clean pyjamas, but I can't sleep. The mattress is lumpy, the air humid. I want to play my keyboard, let the sound of the music mute the day's screaming chaos, but my limbs ache and I can't seem to move.

Through the wall, I can hear someone in Axel's room.

I force myself to get up. The lamp is off but the door to his room is ajar. I push it – the sound of a sigh in the night. Axel's cot now sits by the window, moved here from my parents' room. Moonlight shines down on to the empty mattress like a spotlight. The wardrobe is open and an avalanche of Axel's clothes has spilled out on to the floor. In one corner is a pile of stuffed toys – some used to be mine, the fabric worn, stuffing poking out; others are soft and yet to be loved.

In the other corner is a slouched figure, head bowed.

'Papa?'

He's so close but I can barely hear his music; his drumbeat has become slow and quiet, like the weak pulse of someone gradually fading away. Clutched in one hand and pressed against his face is Axel's teddy-bear sleepsuit. Papa's shoulders shudder, but his sobs are silent.

2

LISETTE

Then – Berlin, 9 November 1938

The night had already closed in and outside there was an icy wind that bit, but tonight nothing could ruin my mood. My hair was curled with a new hat pinned neatly atop it, and tucked into my purse were the Reichsmarks Mother had pressed into my hand as I left. I looked good – not beautiful, perhaps, but respectable and maybe, at a stretch, pretty. I walked along the tree-lined boulevards, my shoulders back. I didn't have a job yet, but I was no longer a schoolgirl. Instead of watching the world, I was becoming a part of it.

I crossed the street, narrowly avoiding a tram trundling past. Ahead, our local Jewish hatmaker was closing his store. He looked at me oddly. I gave a little wave but he fumbled with his keys, his hands clearly shaking. Maybe he didn't recognize me – I was no longer a child following Mother around while she did her shopping. Or perhaps the growing discrimination against the Jews had put him on edge. Lately Berlin had been twitching with a nervous energy. My friends Julius and Max said things were bound to get worse, but Father said everything would calm down eventually.

Gertrud was already at the club when I arrived, checking her reflection in a nearby shop window. She was always in search of a mirror, a window, the back of a spoon – anything that would confirm her immaculate appearance.

'Lisette! It is so good to see you,' she said, kissing the air in my vague direction. 'And don't you look beautiful as always.' She said this same line every time we met and it niggled at me like a stray hair tickling my face.

'Ruth and Karin are already waiting in the queue. Have you eaten?'

'No, I—'

'You have? Good, excellent. It's best not to drink and dance on an empty stomach. Goodness, one would think on an evening as cold as tonight, the doors would simply be thrown open and we would all be rushed inside immediately. I suppose they may want to make sure only the right sort is admitted.'

'I suppose,' I said, but I wasn't really listening; my eyes were on a group of young boys puffing on cigars, the smoke from their mouths curling up into the darkened sky.

'Come now,' Gertrud said. She pushed her way through the crowd, ignoring those who tutted. I followed dutifully, apologizing as I went, careful not to step on anyone's toes. As I squeezed into the queue beside Karin and Ruth, the heel of my shoe momentarily caught in a crack in the pavement. I grabbed a man's shoulder, more scared of falling and humiliating myself than adhering to social decorum.

'Steady there,' he said, holding my elbow as I freed my foot. I smiled and thanked him, but his attention was already on Karin.

'You're not hurt, are you, Lisette?' Ruth said, greeting me with a kiss on both cheeks.

'Lisette, I simply love what you're wearing,' Karin said. She gave me a dazzling but self-conscious smile – it was clear she knew people were watching her, captivated by her beauty.

The girls stamped their feet and blew into their gloved hands as we waited, but the excitement and my quiet anxiety kept me warm. As Gertrud dealt out gossip like a pack of cards, I searched for Julius's face. Knowing he would be here somewhere made my heart beat a little faster.

It wasn't long before Gertrud managed to persuade the doorman to let us in and we were ushered inside. Beyond the doors was a new world. The space was more extravagant than I'd imagined. The ceiling was made of reflective glass and mirrored globes hung down from it like diamonds. In the far corner, jets of water rose and fell to the sound of music, like a strange, otherworldly ballet. In another corner, there was a full-sized carousel, where fetching men and women rode ornate horses. It was early but the dance floor was already filling up. I longed to join the other revellers, to immerse myself in this new realm, but Gertrud was pulling me towards one of the tables. A group of men looked over at us. Ruth flicked her hair, Karin giggled uncontrollably and Gertrud frowned her disapproval.

'Come now. We must sit,' she said sternly. 'It's still early. Let us take our seats, have a look around, wait for someone to call us – each table has its own phone, you know – or perhaps someone might send us a note.'

'A note?'

'This,' Gertrud declared, taking the seat beside me and gesturing to a curved, snake-like contraption, 'is a pneumatic tube. If someone likes you, they can send you a message. And it's not just messages you can receive,' she continued, relishing our attention. She picked up a dark-red, leather-bound menu. 'You can order presents, too.'

A waitress appeared, her short hair arranged in neat waves, her lips a red rose. Gertrud ordered brandy for us all and it appeared almost instantly, presented with a flourish on a gold tray. Karin sipped at hers, warming the glass in her hand, but mine disappeared quickly, the subtle sweetness too much to resist. Gertrud ordered another round and while the other girls chatted, I took in the motorized glass dome above us, the revolving mirrored balls, feeling the music pulse through my veins. There was a jazz band playing and when the pianist took over in a spotlighted solo, my own fingers tapped out the song on my thighs. One day I hoped I'd have the confidence and the skill to be up there, playing with the best.

Karin received her first message, which appeared with a whooshing sound. Soon, I thought, soon it will be my turn. I waited patiently for the phone to ring or a message to arrive and shake me from the deep sleep of childhood. I was desperate to become an adult, and what defines you as an adult more than being desired as one? But the phone never rang for me and no message appeared, either.

'Isn't that Julius?' Gertrud asked after we'd been sitting there for well over an hour, poking an elbow into my ribs and nodding towards the dance floor.

I found his face in the crowd. It took only moments for the flutter that was born in my chest to grow and consume me.

'Yes, yes, it is,' I said, jumping to my feet, holding my hat in place.

'Goodness, Lisette, what are you doing?' she said, gripping my arm. 'Sit down. You like him, do you not? As more than a friend? In which case, you cannot simply bound over there like an oversized horse. Let him come to you.'

'But . . . I've known him for ever.' It felt wrong not to go over but I sat back down all the same. I didn't know the rules, and if anyone knew them, it was Gertrud.

'Right now, he sees you as a sister. You want him to start seeing you as a woman.'

'But how do I make him see me as . . . a woman?' I asked, a blush heating my cheeks.

'You need to behave differently around him. Be more aloof, sophisticated.'

I nodded, resisting the urge to ask her what that would look like exactly. I needed her help but Gertrud was not someone to whom I wanted to be indebted.

'Max is with him,' she said, taking off her white silk gloves and folding them neatly in front of her. 'They are as thick as thieves, those two. Look at them flirting with every woman in sight.'

I ignored the sharp pain in my chest, swallowed the hurt.

'Maybe it's best he and I just stay friends,' I said quietly, but even saying the words pained me. I gulped down more brandy, found some strange respite in the way it burned my throat.

'I heard Max is planning on becoming a doctor,' Gertrud said. 'I wonder if he would take a look at my knee.'

'Your knee?'

'Yes, it looks bigger than the other one. It's quite odd. I really do need a professional to take a look . . .'

Karin returned from the bathroom, her lipstick reapplied, her hat pinned neatly in place. Before she reached our table, a man approached her and, after a short exchange, they headed for the dance floor. Meanwhile, Ruth was busy talking to someone on the phone that was attached to a pillar beside our table.

'I am just going to powder my nose,' Gertrud said, standing up and smoothing down her dress in the process. 'You will be all right on your own?'

'Of course.' I buried my face in the menu as if it were the latest romance novel and I couldn't keep my eyes off the page, but after a few minutes, my attention turned back to Julius, who was twirling one girl after another on the dance floor, his glasses threatening to slip off his nose. None of the girls kept his attention for long, though, and soon he was clambering up on to the carousel, pulling Max up with him. There was only one free horse but Julius insisted they both climb atop it. Max hesitated then gave in. It was impossible to say no to Julius.

I looked at Max, the man who had taken my place. I liked him – he was funny and kind – but it used to be just me and Julius. And then, a few years ago, something had shifted in our friendship. It had been imperceptible at first but now it yawned between us – a void that couldn't be crossed. I wanted to regain the ease of our friendship, the jokes that only Julius and I shared, but when his voice had deepened and my hips had widened, our parents had encouraged us to find other friends. It made me feel like what we had was shameful, though I couldn't understand why. At first, we had laughed at our parents' words, promised each other that nothing would change. But it did. We grew up, and now I knew it wasn't just a friendship that I wanted, but something more.

Both Karin and Gertrud returned and ordered more drinks. Karin filled Gertrud in on the man she'd been dancing with and Gertrud listened intently, occasionally offering unsolicited advice.

I watched Julius, willing him to see me.

'Maybe undo a button, Lisette,' Karin said after a while, a giggle escaping her lips. 'If you want him to notice you.'

'Absolutely not!' Gertrud said, slapping my hand as it crept up to my collar. 'We are educated young women. We do not need to lure men in by acting seductively. Do not fret, Lisette. We will find you a suitable man eventually.'

I tried to ignore the spark of irritation that flared in my chest. No men had approached Gertrud either and yet no one was feeling sorry for her.

'Isn't it time to leave?' I asked, glancing up at a large clock on the wall and fanning my face with a menu.

'It is, actually,' Gertrud said, checking her reflection in her compact mirror. She pulled on her gloves and snapped her handbag shut.

'But they don't close for another half-hour,' Ruth complained.

'We do not want to be one of the stragglers,' Gertrud said, swallowing the last of her drink. 'Trust me.'

I glanced back towards the carousel, but Julius was gone and the dance floor was already emptying. As I stood, my stocking snagged on the chair. I bent down to inspect it and saw a small hole had appeared, revealing the deathly pale flesh of my shin. I straightened only to find my heel was wobbly, ready to snap.

As we stood in the queue to collect our coats, I held on to the wall to keep myself steady. The cigarette smoke, the brandy and the heat of so many bodies was making me feel slightly nauseous. It was a relief finally to step outside into the shocking cold.

'Lisette,' a voice said.

I turned to find Julius leaning against the wall, his nose pink, an unlit cigarette dangling from his lips the wrong way round. I saw now that his hair had grown since I'd seen him last – it was tousled, but in a deliberate way. Having longed to be beside him all night, now that I was, I couldn't breathe. It was as if he had stolen all the oxygen from the air.

'Hi,' I said, just as Max took the cigarette from Julius's lips and turned it around for him.

Julius smiled widely at me and the cigarette dropped from his mouth. He tried – and failed – to catch it.

'Have you been here all night? I didn't see you inside. Here, have a cigarette,' he said, taking the packet from Max. 'Join us.'

'We were about to head home,' Gertrud said beside me, offering a small frown.

'Don't go home.' His brown eyes, the colour of acorns, seemed glazed behind his glasses and his voice was a little too loud, even among the noisy crowd spilling out on to the street. 'Stay with us, Lisette. We'll walk you back.'

For me, there was no question. I gave Gertrud what I hoped was an apologetic look and took the cigarette from between

Julius's ink-stained fingers. Gertrud turned without a word, linked her arms demonstratively through Ruth's and Karin's, and disappeared.

Julius stifled a laugh as he lit my cigarette. 'Her mind is too old for her body, that one.'

I gave him a friendly push and then swung my hair in a way I hoped was alluring. 'She's nice really.'

'If you say so.'

'Is it your first time at the Resi?' Max asked, offering me a smile. There was something sympathetic about it, almost pitying, as if he knew how I felt about Julius.

'Is it that obvious?'

'Of course not,' Max said, leaning back against the wall, his dark hair flopping over his face. 'I've just never seen you here before.'

Max was shorter than me and sometimes it made me want to slope my shoulders, fold down into a smaller, daintier version of myself. He made me feel like I took up too much space.

'You live on Chausseestraße, right?' Max asked. 'It might be a bit far for us to walk from here. If those are the only shoes you have.'

He was right, of course. One shoe was on the verge of breaking, my feet ached and I couldn't fathom why I'd decided to wear heels when I already towered over everyone.

'No, it's fine,' Julius said, finishing his cigarette and looping his arm through mine. 'It will only take us thirty minutes.'

He tripped as we stepped off the kerb and we almost tumbled to the ground together, but Max grabbed his other arm, kept him steady.

The brandy protected me a little from the numbing cold, but the sky above us was black and endless and I felt light-headed. As we walked through Alexanderplatz, we met with the smell of smoke, the memory of a fire carried by the chilling breeze.

I'd never been in the square at night. During the day, it felt like the beating heart of Berlin, with swarms of people milling around – women hunting for bargains, plucking at garments and squeezing ripe fruit; men searching for work while children dashed between legs playing hide-and-seek; street performers dancing and singing for a few Reichsmarks. I had expected it to be eerily desolate at this time, but surprisingly large groups of men were moving through the square. Something didn't feel quite right. A man rushed past us. Elsewhere I heard a shout. Or was it a scream?

In the distance a great plume of smoke rose like a dragon into the sky. I turned to Julius to point it out but then I saw another spiral of smoke behind him. And then another. And another. Berlin was on fire.

Angry cries rose from a group of men directly ahead of us. They stood beneath the Berolina statue and it was as if she was gesturing towards them – look, see here! We should have turned, chosen another route, but we were drawn to the chaos. The men were shouting at something – someone – lying on the ground. The glow of a street light illuminated the men's faces. There was anger there. No, not anger – twisted, vengeful fury.

I tightened my hold on Julius's arm and was relieved to find Max had moved to my other side.

'Let's go,' he said, steering us away from the jeering mob, but as we left I turned my head. On the ground, partly obscured by kicking feet, was a young man. He held his head as boots cracked his ribs. One eye was swollen and blood from his split lip glistened on the cobblestones. For a brief moment, our eyes met.

'What's happening?' My voice was a whisper.

'Riots against the Jews. That's my guess,' Max said.

'What? Why?'

With his hand on the small of my back, Max led Julius and

me away from the square and on to a side road. But there were mobs there too. Soldiers, it seemed, their SA uniforms unmistakable. Further down the street, a man threw a rock through a shop window. Another distant scream pierced the air.

'A reaction to the assassination of Ernst vom Rath?' Julius said, pushing his glasses up his nose. He no longer seemed wobbly on his feet.

'The diplomat in Paris?' I kept my voice low. 'But what do the Jews in Berlin have to do with that?'

Max looked at me as if I was a naive child. And I suppose I was. I'd believed Father when he'd said that things would get better soon. Like so many, I chose to be ignorant of the events that were unfolding. I was like a small girl plugging my ears with my fingertips and singing loudly to drown out the voices of truth. I was present, yet stupidly unaware.

We navigated our way through the streets, broken glass crunching under our feet like crisp new-fallen snow. We passed another group of soldiers raiding a clothes shop. I kept my head down. We turned a corner and were faced with a Nazi Storm Trooper kicking an old man lying on the pavement. We stopped, too shocked to move. The old man was weeping, clutching his head where white strands of hair had been stained red by the blood seeping from a wound on his forehead. The Storm Trooper glanced up when he sensed our presence but he didn't stop his assault. He just smiled then carried on, as if he was doing a little jig. The old man rolled on to his side, tucking his knees into his chest. On his back, 'Jew' had been daubed in garish yellow paint.

'Stop.' The word slipped from my mouth unintentionally. Julius gripped my arm, and Max hissed in my ear. Before the Storm Trooper could react, they dragged me away.

'Just look straight ahead,' Julius instructed. Instinctively I disobeyed, but we had already rounded a corner.

29

'We need to get you home,' Max said. 'Now.'

'But we can't just do nothing.'

I couldn't tell whether Max was angry or scared. The outside world was colliding with my small, insignificant life and I was terrified, my heart threatening to burst through my ribcage.

Instead of slowing down, Max's pace quickened. I ripped my arm from his grip and stood defiant like a stubborn child. A look passed between the two boys – one I didn't understand.

'Max is right,' Julius said, but his voice was laced with regret. 'It's dangerous; we need to get you home. What's happening . . . it's . . . it's not our place to get involved.'

I looked from one to the other. I wanted to be brave. I wanted them to be brave too. But I wasn't. And nor were they.

Three Storm Troopers were heading our way, their steps heavy with determination, their faces dark with purpose. We crossed the street, kept our heads down, averted our eyes. The streets had become a war zone – broken doors, shattered windows, men with bruised and bloodied faces. Slogans had been smeared on the doors of Jewish shops. Smashed furniture lay on the pavements, broken chairs with legs askew like fractured bones.

We picked our way through the chaos, saying nothing, our lips sewn shut by the fingers of incredulity. On one corner a clothes store had been vandalized. I recognized the shop – I had bought my first pair of heels there on my thirteenth birthday. A smart black pair that had made me feel like a grown-up for the first time. I stopped, feigned pain in my ankle, and looked inside. Drawers had been pulled out and emptied, furniture splintered, hats destroyed. A mannequin protruded through a broken window. Snagged on one hand were the remains of a white curtain. It fluttered in the wind like a flag of surrender.

3

LISETTE

Then – Berlin, 9 January 1940

I sat playing the piano, ignoring the wind outside breathing through the trees, ragged, asthmatic and snagging on branches. For a moment I thought I could also hear knocking, then dismissed it as the wind, trying to get in. My fingers tingled with cold but I continued playing, savouring the melody like grains of sugar on my tongue.

'Was that the door?' Frau Weber asked, helping herself to her third glass of wine. It had been over four months since war had broken out and wine wasn't being rationed, but Mother and Frau Weber acted like it soon would be.

Frau Weber had been sitting with Mother all afternoon and, like Mother, she was dressed in her fur coat, hat and gloves as if on her way to the theatre. By her feet was a birdcage, big and dome-shaped. I couldn't understand why she insisted on dragging her annoying budgie with her wherever she went. Mostly he seemed distressed at being hauled around, his chirps anxious, his body swaying. Or perhaps he simply wanted to get out and use his wings.

I envied those wings. This life was not what I had imagined. A match had been struck on Kristallnacht and no one had dared blow it out, or perhaps they simply hadn't cared to. That small flame had become a blazing fire of hatred and now here we were, turning our backs to it, hoping we wouldn't also be singed by the heat. Jews were being persecuted, our men were going to war, and instead of playing the piano in an orchestra and travelling the world, I now spent my days pretending things were different.

The sound came again. An insistent rap this time, knuckles on wood.

'Yes, definitely the door,' Julius said, his fingers dancing on the oversized typewriter balanced on his knees. He was wearing so many jumpers that he looked like an overstuffed teddy, round and cuddly. Every so often he would slip off his gloves, push his too-big glasses up his nose and dip his fingers in a bowl of warm water he'd heated on the stove. Mother was too polite to remind him that the latest law decreed no heating of water during the week.

It was Mother who finally stood up, reapplied her red lipstick, then opened the door. When she closed it again, her face was white, her lips like an open wound. She had a letter in her hand, tears already lining her cheeks. My fingers stilled. I went over, took Mother's arm and guided her back to her chair.

She sat down, one hand clutching the corner of the table to steady herself. She placed the conscription letter gently in the centre, as if it might bite her if she was too rough with it, an animal with teeth.

'Your father won't survive it,' she said, her voice a whisper.

'Don't say such a thing,' I said. 'Of course he will. He survived the last war.'

'No,' she replied, 'he didn't.'

~

Hours later I stood on the street with Julius. The wind had died down and an evening mist stalked commuters on their way home. Behind me, the smell of Mother's *Sauerbraten* curled down the stairs towards me, its fingers enticing me back inside.

'Thank you for letting me work in your flat again,' Julius said, unlocking his bicycle. 'I promised I'd get this article in by the end of the week, but my father is constantly breathing down my neck at home. You know what he's like. I'm hardly going to get fired if my writing isn't up to scratch, since he owns the damn newspaper, but he doesn't want people thinking that I don't deserve this job. Every time I try writing in the kitchen, he hovers behind me reading over my shoulder, then pretends to look out of the window. Anyway, I've always felt more at home in your apartment. When you play the piano, it helps me focus. So, thank you. And, Lisette?'

'Yes?'

'I'm sorry about your father.'

I felt my cheeks redden. I hadn't been thinking about Father.

'Do you have a cigarette?' I asked, stopping him from leaving in the only way I knew how.

'Of course.' He rummaged inside his coat pocket, tapped out a cigarette, dropped it, picked it up, dropped it again, then finally held a new one out between inky fingers.

He laughed, showing his perfectly straight teeth like a row of beautiful ivory piano keys. 'I thought I would grow out of this clumsiness but it seems to be a permanent affliction.'

He lit my cigarette, cupping his hand around mine to protect the flickering flame. The touch of his fingers sent small ripples of heat up my arm. The cigarette caught but he didn't move away. He was so close I could feel his warm breath. He smiled, small wrinkles appearing around his eyes.

It was in moments like these that he could so easily have stepped forward, pressed his lips to mine. But he never did. Gertrud and Ruth thought Julius just didn't want to ruin our friendship. Karin said he was probably too focused on his job for romance – preoccupied with his desire to write the truth yet being careful not to draw too much attention to himself. I didn't know what to think.

'Are you scared?' I asked as he stepped back and lit himself a cigarette too.

'Of course.'

A crease appeared between his eyebrows. I wanted to lean forward, smooth the wrinkle away with the tip of my finger.

'I don't want to fight,' he said after a moment. 'I know that sounds cowardly but it's true. This isn't my war; I don't support the man who started it. And I certainly don't agree with his politics. Why should I give my life for him?'

He looked at me as if he expected an answer. I had none to give.

'I just wish someone would stop him.'

There was no one close enough to hear his words but my body tensed. It was dangerous to speak in this way. You never knew who might be listening, who was ready to report you. I worried about Julius, about his views, the thoughts he sometimes couldn't contain. He spoke to me freely but sometimes his words came out like lava spewing from a volcano. I worried that one day the pressure would become too much and he would say something in front of the wrong person.

I had learned to suppress my own views. My parents weren't members of the Party but many of their friends were, Frau Weber included. There were consequences to speaking up. I wasn't too young to understand that. Not any more. The war had woken us all up.

'But it's not just that,' he continued. 'I'm terrified of dying. I don't want to take my last breath on some battlefield far from home. I can't murder men that I have no personal grievance with. Nor do I want to be killed at the hands of someone who has no personal grievance with me. I want to live. I want to go to university, study literature, maybe become a proper journalist on a paper other than my father's – or, better yet, a poet!'

I looked up at the sky. Far above us, beyond the mist, a flock of birds was gliding on the last breaths of the retreating storm. I envied their freedom, their ability to flee.

'As long as journalists are needed, they might not call you up. Perhaps the war will be over before they get the chance?' I said.

'Perhaps.' But we both knew it wasn't true. It was a dance we all did, skirting around the truth.

'I need to go,' Julius said, glancing at his watch. He threw his half-smoked cigarette to the pavement and climbed on to his bike. 'I'll see you again soon?'

He was gone before I could reply.

The night was creeping in and I yanked at the collar of my coat, defending my throat against the winter's grip.

'Good evening, Lisette.' Frau Weber's voice cut through my thoughts. 'I just popped out for a few things. Would you mind helping me with these bags?'

'Of course,' I said. 'Sorry. I didn't see you there. Go upstairs, rest your legs. I can carry these up for you.'

'I'm not an invalid,' she snapped. 'You don't need to carry all of them. If you could take one or two, though, that would be most helpful.'

I smiled pleasantly, ignoring her tone. When I reached over to take the bags, her potent perfume tickled my nose. Standing too close to her was like sticking my face into a bouquet of musty old flowers; it was almost impossible not to sneeze.

The bags were heavy. Their weight had strangled her fingers and left deep red marks on her skin. She was small and wiry but she was undoubtedly strong. War widows usually were. We arrived at her floor and she fumbled with her keys. This time, I didn't offer to help.

'He'll never love you, you know,' she said, sliding the key into the lock.

'What? Who?'

'Your friend. Julius.' She turned to face me. 'I have seen how you look at him, but he doesn't love you. I am not saying this to be unkind. Quite the opposite, in fact. He is very fond of you, but I can see he doesn't have romantic feelings for you. You're like a sister to him. Oh, don't look at me like that. I am stating a simple fact, and once you have understood that fact you can move on, find someone else, save yourself the hurt.'

I had a sudden urge to shove her over the banister and watch her fall. An accident, is what they would say. An old woman wobbly on her feet.

'Your parents so want you to find a nice man. It is your duty to give them grandchildren, after all. Do not waste your time on someone who isn't interested, that is all I am saying. In fact, I have a lovely nephew I am going to introduce you to. I have a feeling you might be perfect for each other.'

~

I found my parents at the dining table, the conscription letter sitting between them. Mother's *Sauerbraten* was simmering on the stove, the smell of onions and cloves marinating the air. It seemed wrong to feel hungry, as if my body was letting me down. Soon Father would leave, become another soldier on a battlefield, and all I could think about was my stomach.

I thought of Julius too, of course. I always thought of Julius. Frau Weber's words were echoing in my mind, but I pushed them away. She was wrong. She was a stupid old woman and she was wrong.

Mother dished up our dinner and we sat down to eat. We didn't speak of the letter, but swallowed our thoughts along with the food. Between mouthfuls Mother filled the silence with trivial slices of gossip. She spent her days acquiring these morsels so she could offer them up each evening like small, mostly unwanted, gifts. I didn't care that Antoinette next door had had a frightful haircut or that Erna had accidentally served rotten meat at a dinner party. But that night we all needed some triviality and I felt momentarily grateful.

Father rolled up his sleeves, helping himself to another serving. I winced at the sight of his arms – they were blighted by raised bubble scars, still red and angry twenty years after the wounds had been inflicted. I had never known him without those scars and yet I couldn't help flinching each time I saw them. I had only read about the horrors of the Great War – Father never talked about the years when he had served, his time in the trenches, or the mustard gas that had eaten his skin. But the scars on his body and on his mind were forever present, however much he tried to hide them. Father was a powerful man, but at night he was reduced to a boy, crying and calling out for his mother. He was a walking contradiction – strong yet weak, kind yet cruel, looking towards the future but for ever stuck in the past. And in less than a week, he would become a soldier once more, thrown back into a war that might not return him.

'Lisette, will you play the piano for us? Something cheerful.'

'Of course, Father.'

Mother cleared the table, wiped the surfaces until they gleamed, and then settled down beside Father to listen to me play. I preferred to play alone, let the music envelop me in its grace, but after a few minutes it never mattered who was present – they would disappear and I'd find myself somewhere else, somewhere private.

Later, my fingers sore but my soul renewed, we were gathered around the fireplace. We still needed several layers of clothes to fight off the cold, but the food had warmed us a little and the fire crackled and spat with a magnificent heat. Father snipped off the cap of a cigar and then held a flame to it, puckering his lips around the end, making hollow popping sounds as he brought it to life.

Outside, the citywide blackout was about to start, cloaking Berlin in darkness. It had been over four months since Berlin had turned off its lights. Every night, it held its breath until morning, and I still wasn't used to it. Each evening I looked out of the window and faced the gathering gloom with trepidation. Occasionally I saw a flash of light from the S-Bahn or the glow of a cigarette dancing in the street like a firefly. But otherwise the darkness was complete – thick, heavy and suffocating. Some embraced the blackness, romanticized it, but the colour had been drained out of the city I loved and it simply made me feel lost.

Just as my parents were about to retreat to their bedroom, the siren sounded. Father stiffened; a small gasp escaped Mother's lips. A bomb had yet to fall on Berlin but each time I heard the alarm my chest tightened. I went over to the window and looked out at the night, half expecting to see a plane. We needed to go down to the basement but Father always resisted. Something happened to him when the siren screamed. A wildness appeared in his eyes and he became motionless – like a man turned to stone. If a simple siren could instil such fear in him, I wondered, how would he survive on a battlefield?

We heard footsteps on the stairs, our neighbours descending into the basement. I took Father's hand in mine, ignoring how it trembled, and led him to the door.

'It will be another practice,' I said. 'Nothing to worry about. But let's go down all the same. Frau Weber will appreciate the company, I'm sure.'

'Yes, she will,' Mother said, grabbing her hat and tucking a lipstick into her jacket pocket. 'Come now, Ernst. Let us go down.'

She took his other hand and together we led him like a small child through our front door and down into darkness.

Underground we found our neighbours huddled with gas masks hanging around their necks. One group of women saw the unexpected night-time rendezvous as an opportunity to catch up on gossip and play some cards.

'Join us, Rita?' one asked, but Mother glanced at Father then shook her head.

Herr Fischer from the third floor, our designated air-raid warden, had brought a bottle of whiskey down with him and he shared it with the other men. Father smiled cordially at them but he didn't speak; he didn't speak to anyone. Instead, he found himself a corner and sat there staring at the wall, his face white, jaw clenched, the candlelight casting ghostly shadows across his features. Mother engaged quietly in conversation with Frau Weber, who sat clutching her birdcage, the budgie hopping and chirping with excitement. I listened idly, if only to pass the time.

'There is no need to be worried,' Frau Weber said, fingering the Nazi Party badge pinned to the lapel of her coat. 'Berlin will never be attacked. We are completely safe. My nephew, Egon – he will be an officer soon, you know – he says we have plenty of anti-aircraft weapons to defend us.'

'Oh, I am not worried,' Mother replied, patting her hair to make sure everything was in place. 'Berlin will always be safe. I just find this so tiresome. We have already been through one war. Do we need to proceed with another?'

'We must trust in our Führer.'

'Must we?' I said, cutting in.

Mother looked at me sharply and I knew she would scold me later. Not being a member of the Party was one thing, but publicly criticizing it was dangerous.

'I mean, we all love the Führer,' I added quickly. 'Obviously. But no one wanted another war.'

Frau Weber sniffed as if I'd personally offended her. 'I am not sure politics is a suitable subject for a young lady.'

'I quite agree,' Mother said, the conversation over.

Some slept, but the fear and anxiety felt like a pair of hands squeezing my throat, and I knew sleep would never find me. I hugged my knees and pulled my coat around them, burying my face in the fur. Somewhere there was a leak, the sound of dripping water strangely accentuated. At one point I got up and, like a madwoman, started searching for it. Eventually I gave up, sat back down and closed my eyes. In my mind's eye, I could see my piano. I let my fingers drift over its keys. There was a tune I was composing for Julius but I couldn't quite get it right. It was too melancholic and I wanted something triumphant.

The sound of distant flak disturbed my focus. Images of trenches and bloody corpses invaded my mind. I looked over at Father, sitting there in the corner, stiff with fear. The bombs hadn't come, not yet, but one day they would. Though I feared a bullet might find him first.

4

ELLY

Now – East Berlin, 14 August 1961

Mama stands in the living room, her nightgown yellow at the armpits, her hair wild. She opens her mouth but not a single sound falls from her lips. She points to her throat as if that's where the words are sitting, her tongue refusing to bear them.

'Are you OK?' Papa asks, dropping his toast. Oma Rita frowns as he uses the tablecloth to wipe the crumbs from his fingers.

Mama glances around but she can't find whatever she's looking for. Instead, she touches her fingers to her cracked lips and then shakes her head.

'Can't you speak, Lisette?' Papa asks. 'Is it happening again?'

5

ELLY

Now – East Berlin, 17 August 1961

It has been three days since Mama stopped speaking, yet at night I can still hear her wailing. She has become a ghost haunting our apartment – I never see her, I only hear her cries. The screams seem inhuman, belonging to something possessed. Papa's grief is quieter, yet no less disturbing. Only Oma Rita remains calm, seemingly untroubled by the unfolding events. She simply sits, as always, by her window, watching and waiting.

Most days Mama goes out, trailing from one ministry to the other, queuing with hundreds of others, notebook in hand, her scribbles of desperation mostly going unread. It's the school holidays and I've offered to go with her, be her voice, but she just shakes her head. I can't help but be relieved. I want Axel back and I want to help get him back, but my presence just seems to agitate her.

'I don't understand,' I say, leaning against the kitchen counter. 'How does someone's ability to speak just disappear?'

Oma Rita shrugs and takes a sip of her tea, even though the air itself is crisping in the day's heat.

'It's not the first time,' she says after a moment, rubbing the lipstick from the rim of her cup. 'It's happened before. A long time ago.'

'How? Why? And how did she get her voice back again?'

Oma Rita doesn't answer. She places her teacup on a coaster and gazes out of the window. It's as if a memory has taken her hand and is leading her mind away.

'Oma Rita? O-ma?'

But still she doesn't answer.

I turn my back to her and pour a glass of water. I close my eyes and start humming *'Ein Schiff wird kommen'*. At first, it's a mere vibration on my lips, but soon it moves through my body, relaxing my muscles. As I reach the chorus, I have an urge to wiggle my hips, to sing the words. I long to stand by a harbour and see a ship, too. For something to take me away.

As East Germans, travel beyond Germany has not been an option for us for a long time, but Papa has always said that one day the restrictions will be lifted and we will be free. I want to see the world; I want to see everything there is to see. Now the barrier is here, I can't imagine that ever happening. If I think about it too much, my eyes grow hot and it feels like I'm drowning.

I sense someone behind me and I spin around, dropping the glass. It shatters on the floor, and small shards jump up and sting my bare legs. Mama is standing a foot away. The look she gives me is like a snake ready to strike.

'I'm sorry, I'm sorry,' I say, crouching to pick up the pieces. 'It just slipped. I was thinking about something else and . . .'

I see how she tries to rein in her rage, calm the hand which trembles with the need to slap my cheek. She closes her eyes, turns her head, draws in a deep breath of polluted Berlin air. Along with her voice, her music has been muzzled, too. The loud and angry song I imagine defines her has become muted. I never thought I'd miss it, but I do. The silence is unsettling.

With a pile of splintered glass in my hand, I quickly slip away so when her eyelids open I'll be gone – a fleeting bad dream she can forget.

'Elly,' Papa says, almost colliding with me in the corridor. His skin is grey and his shirt has been buttoned up wrong. 'I'm heading out. Will you stay here? Keep an eye on your mother? It took some persuading but she's staying home today.'

We both know Mama doesn't want me here, but I don't say the words. I simply nod and then ask, 'Where are you going?'

'The checkpoint at Bornholmer Straße.'

'Weren't you both there yesterday?'

'Yes, but ... we need to keep trying. Maybe the Brits or the Americans will do something soon.'

'I'm sure they will,' I say, giving him the words like a present, even though everyone knows that every hour that passes without a challenge from the wider world hints at the barrier's permanence.

I go to my room and dump the shards in the bin. I kick some clothes into the corner and throw open the window, letting out the hot, stale air. The courtyard below is empty of people, but the garden is in full bloom and even from this height I can smell the sweet, herby scent of lovage.

I lie on my stomach on the bed, swinging my legs and flicking through the latest issue of *Bravo*. My keyboard calls to me but I'm trying to be mindful of Mama – I know how she hates to hear me play. Oma Rita says Mama once played herself and a grand piano used to dominate the living room. It's gone now, though sometimes I know Mama still sees it. In her 'moments', I catch her looking at the empty space.

A knock on the front door stirs me from my thoughts. I look up, momentarily disorientated. As I cross the short distance through the living room, I notice how dirty the flat has become. A scent of decay tickles my nose. On the windowsill, a foot from where Oma Rita sits with a book lying unopened on her lap, flies buzz around a discarded sandwich. A trail of determined ants is marching across the floor. This descent into disrepair bothers me – if Mama or Oma Rita were in their right mind, the state of our home would horrify them.

Otto and Monika stand on the other side of the door. My hand goes to my unwashed hair and I attempt to comb it away from my face.

'Can we come in?' Otto asks.

I hesitate, glance at Mama's closed door, my eyes passing over all the mess.

'Or . . . we could go out?' Monika says, licking her cracked lips. I can see her resisting the urge to peer over my shoulder.

'Yeah, let's go out.' All the windows are open but there is no wind and the air is dead; I can't stay inside all day. I know I promised Papa I would, but I'll make sure I'm back before he is. It's not as if Mama will miss me. 'Give me a minute?'

I leave my friends in the stairwell, shutting the door but not letting the latch click. I pull out a red sundress from the pile of clothes on my bedroom floor along with a thick fabric hairband I hope will cover the worst of my hair. The dress is slightly crumpled and Oma Rita will think it too short, but it will have to do.

'Sorry,' I say as I join Otto and Monika on the landing. 'Things are a bit chaotic at the moment. Mama is . . .' I pause. 'Visitors are probably not a good idea.'

A shadow moves behind the peephole of my neighbour's door. Otto gives the closed door a demonstrative wave.

'*Guten Tag*, Herr Krause!' he shouts, ignoring my elbow jabbing him in the ribs. He grabs the banister and leaps down the stairs two at a time. Monika and I hurry after him.

'He's so obviously a Stasi spy,' he says, not bothering to keep his voice down.

'He's just nosy,' I whisper. 'And lonely, too.'

When we step outside, the heat hits us like a wall. The air is thick with the smell of brown coal and burnt metal, and the smoke from the distant steel mill hangs heavy around us. Further off, dark clouds gather, promising rain.

There used to be four of us, but Hans moved to Düsseldorf, in West Germany, like so many of our other friends. I miss him – we all do – yet we don't speak of him. It's an unspoken rule. When someone abandons us, we pretend that person never existed. It's easier that way, less painful.

Everyone's saying that's why they've closed the borders – it was the only way to stop people leaving. East Germany has been losing its citizens for years. How did we not see this coming?

'At least it's not cold,' Monika says, linking her arm through mine. I smile at her and pretend not to notice the fresh hand-shaped bruise on her arm, the dark-blue fingerprints marking her skin. We don't talk about this, either – the violence living in Monika's house, the rage her father can't always contain.

As we walk, I talk about anything and everything. My music blends with that of my friends and I feel lighter with each step. The song I have assigned Otto is fast, upbeat and determined, the kind of music that makes you feel like you can face anything – which is what we all need today. Monika's tune is a sweet and calm adagio, a touch of sadness clinging to the notes.

At first, we see few people on the streets. The new school term hasn't started and usually the cafés would be full, tables crowding the pavements outside. Instead, everywhere is uncomfortably quiet. We're a city in mourning. I correct myself – half a city. The worst half.

As we walk along the wide, cobbled boulevard, I notice a few scattered pieces of paper. I grab a dusty sheet. Though the ink is smudged, I can just make out some of the printed words:

Anti-Fascist Protection Rampart – protecting our population from fascist ideals.

'What is it?' Monika asks.

'That's what they're calling it – this barrier,' Otto says, shifting from foot to foot. 'They say they're trying to protect us, it's an act of self-defence, but they're just trying to lock us in.'

I drop the leaflet, stamp out the words with my shoe. As we walk on, I try to ignore the pieces of paper chasing our feet, the lies stealing our freedom. I start humming a song. Monika joins in and soon we're belting out the words.

'Seriously?' Otto says. 'Do you have to?' He doesn't bound ahead as he usually does, but eyes the side streets as though looking for an escape route.

As we near the border, more people appear and our singing fades away. The roads are crammed with citizens of all ages, united in disbelief. Beyond the crowd, the recently restored Brandenburg Gate rises up, twenty metres high. Between us and it is a scramble of barbed wire, an open mouth of razor-sharp teeth.

'What's going on?' I ask a bystander, but then I see it. A group of construction workers flanked by soldiers is building something; they're replacing the barbed wire with a wall of hollow blocks.

'I've heard some people have escaped,' Otto says, staring at the soldiers as if he longs this very second to make a break for freedom.

'Aren't they just rumours?'

'Our neighbour's son swam across the Spree yesterday,' Monika says. 'They shot at him but he wasn't hit. And I've heard some people are jumping out of the houses on Harzer Straße.'

'Those houses are being walled up now,' a man mumbles beside us. He is tall and broad-shouldered, half his face obscured by a hat he has pulled low over his forehead. To shield his face from the scorching sun or to hide his identity – it's unclear.

'One of the border guards jumped over a couple of days ago, too,' the man adds.

'Jumped over? The wire?' I ask.

He nods. 'I saw it. Just over there.'

'He wasn't stopped?'

'I think it took them by surprise,' he says. 'But they won't be caught out again. Soon there will be no way to cross. Not without getting a bullet in the head.' The man shuffles off and seamlessly becomes another faceless body in the crowd.

'We should have left months ago, years ago,' Otto says. 'When we had the chance.'

Beside him, I simply nod, the truth of his words almost too heavy to bear. Even though my parents have discussed leaving for years now, Oma Rita has always refused. We couldn't have abandoned her. And we never imagined it would come to this. We've always had to be careful with our words in the East – the Soviets and the Stasi ever-present, our phones tapped, informants on every street corner – but for me, it's always been this way. I've never lived in a world without them. For as long as I can remember the phone lines to the West have been cut, artists exiled, bananas as rare as a smile between strangers, but if we wanted to breathe freely, to listen to rock bands, to buy a fashion magazine, to speak to a relative abroad, we could just cross the border and be a tourist in the other half of our country for a day. Until now.

For a long time, we stand and watch and say nothing. I've never known Otto to stand still for so long and this change in him is disconcerting. My silence is probably equally unsettling to my friends. We don't move until we feel the first drops of rain, at which point the crowds begin to disperse, allowing us to edge a little closer.

The soldiers stand stiff-backed, machine guns held tightly against their chests. Behind them, the workers construct the wall in silence, pausing only to wipe the sweat from their brows. There are tears there too, but they aren't rubbed away; instead, they run down the men's cheeks, defiant, leaving clean streaks on otherwise dusty, dirty skin.

Above us, the sky is suffocating and the rain intensifies, but I don't want to go home yet. There's nothing to go home to. Not any more. Mama was never really a mother to me until Axel made her one. He opened a door in her and we were both invited in. As I stand and watch, an idea is forming. I can't stay here on the wrong side of the wall, waiting for the border to open. I need to get over to the other side. I need to bring Axel home.

6

LISETTE

Then – Berlin, 14 January 1940

'Well, they were Jews, weren't they?' Frau Weber said, sitting at our dining table, nursing a cup of strong coffee. By her feet, in its cage, her budgie hopped and squawked. I had an urge to grab the bird, throw open the window and release it.

'Were they?' Mother said, using a cloth to rub at an invisible spot on the table. 'That can't be right. We would have known.'

'Who?' I asked, helping myself to a slice of stale cake. I didn't want to be drawn into their conversation, but sometimes words just fell out of my mouth.

'The Beckers,' Mother said. 'Use a plate – I do not want to be picking up crumbs all afternoon. I found their key slid under our door this morning and a note simply saying, *Sorry*. They must have left in the night.'

'Good riddance,' Frau Weber said. She fiddled with her Nazi Party badge as if her life depended upon drawing attention to it. 'Definitely Jews. It wasn't common knowledge, of course, but he certainly looked Jewish. I suspect they have scurried off to England or some such place. You'll find more tasteful tenants soon enough.'

'In these times? I very much doubt it.'

'Don't worry about finding new tenants,' Father said, appearing from the bedroom. He touched Mother gently on the shoulder. 'Everything at the factory is going well. The one good thing about this war is that everyone needs locomotive parts. And you'll also receive my monthly salary from the army. Everything will be all right. The war won't last much longer.'

Mother reached up to hold Father's hand in place on her shoulder. She hated the touch of others – she said the intimacy it reflected was distasteful – but now I saw her embrace it, closing her eyes for a few moments. Father had diminished in the weeks since the war had started. He was thinner, paler, weaker. He didn't talk about his fears, but his body revealed everything he was trying to hide.

I wanted Frau Weber to leave, let my parents have their last day together, but she remained oblivious to everyone else's needs. Her small frame somehow dominated the room, her sickly perfume an assault. Along with her incessant chatter, her smell gave me a headache.

There was a knock on the door. Too late, I remembered I was scheduled to give a piano lesson to one of our neighbour's daughters. Teaching was not as much fun as I had thought it would be; most of the children I taught had no talent and were simply fulfilling an obligation to their parents, but I was desperate to save up some money. The war wouldn't last for ever and, once it was over, I wanted to get my own place. If I was ever to become a professional pianist, I needed to be able to practise at all hours of the day.

'That'll be Krista,' I said, rising from the sofa. 'A new student. I'm sorry. I should have cancelled.'

'No, no, it's fine,' Mother said. 'Your father and I will go out for a walk.'

'In this weather?' Frau Weber said, sniffing loudly. 'I have never heard anything so ridiculous.'

When Mother didn't invite her to join them, she let her cup clatter into its saucer, the remaining coffee sloshing over the edge. She gathered her things as though in a hurry and then waited tight-lipped as I opened the door.

In the corridor I found a girl, tall for her eight years of age, smartly dressed in woollen stockings and with two tightly braided pigtails framing her face. She was so typically German it almost made me laugh. Frau Weber shoved past, her budgie screeching, ignoring the tall, blond man who was leaning against the opposite wall. He had smooth, unblemished skin, his eyes like polished chestnuts behind his glasses. When he saw me, he held out his hand and gave a lopsided smile. He reminded me of Julius.

'*Guten Tag*. I'm Wilhelm. This is my sister, Krista. We were at school together. Maybe you remember me? I am sure you don't. I was a year younger. *Am* a year younger. Wilhelm, that's my name.'

I laughed and his cheeks flushed.

'I'll pick Krista up in an hour?'

'I can get home on my own,' Krista said, rolling her eyes.

'No, it's fine,' he said, his thick hair flopping forward. The kind of hair that would feel soft between fingers. 'I'll be back in an hour.'

'See you then.' I smiled at him and watched him go.

Back inside the flat, Krista wandered around the living room, tracing her right index finger across the furniture as if inspecting the apartment for dust.

'He likes you,' she said, not bothering to keep her voice down, and despite myself I felt the twitch of a smile.

'Shall we get started?' I said, gesturing to the piano. Behind me, my parents slipped out of the front door.

'Will it take long?' Krista asked, tucking her skirt in neatly as she sat down. 'To learn?'

'That depends on you. Do you have a piano at home that you can practise on?'

'Of course. Papa says there is no point learning something unless you are going to be the best. Papa says that takes practice.'

'You live in the building next door, don't you? You have a little sister too?'

She scrunched up her nose as if the very word would taste unpleasant on her tongue. 'Yes. Gisela – she's awful. She never leaves me alone but Papa says I have to be nice to her. He says one day she'll be my best friend, but between you and me, I very much doubt that.'

'You sound very grown-up for an eight-year-old,' I said, hiding a smile with the tips of my fingers.

'I'm almost nine. It's my birthday in two months – the twentieth of March. Papa says I was born at three a.m. but Mama says, "He wasn't there, so how the hell would he know?" I've seen you with a man on the street before – he's very handsome. Is he your boyfriend? I've seen you down in the air-raid shelter, too. They say "air-raid shelter" but it's just a basement, isn't it? You sit beside your father – he always looks scared.'

'Shall we get started?' I asked again.

'Yes, let's.' She flicked her pigtails over her shoulders and sat up straight, as if she was about to perform in front of a packed auditorium. Her eyes narrowed in concentration, her fingers – long and slender – poised above the keys. For the rest of the lesson, she listened silently and responded obediently. While my other pupils plonked away with no respect for the sounds they were producing, Krista gently stroked the ivory keys, intrinsically understanding their power.

She reminded me of myself at her age. I envied her youth, that time when things felt uncomplicated. I felt stuck on the cusp of adulthood, unable to cross the threshold entirely. My friends were leaving me behind. Most had boyfriends, some had jobs, and I'd never even been kissed. I was consumed by thoughts of Julius. It was not just his love I wanted. I needed to possess him, for him to be entirely mine. I should have been trying to meet a suitable man. After all, my parents said a German woman's most important function was to bear children. It was one of the few Nazi ideals that they agreed with. But no one could really compare to Julius; he was my addiction.

'Are you OK?' Krista said, her words slicing into my thoughts.

'What? Goodness. Sorry. I was miles away. We should finish for today. Did you enjoy it? Would you like to come back?'

'I would *love* to come back. I'm not good yet, but Papa says it's befitting for a girl to play the piano and I think I could become quite good at it. Don't you think?'

'I do, actually. You have the hands for it.'

She smiled widely, the way only a young child can smile: uninhibitedly. Her teeth were crooked with a big gap between the front two, but she hadn't yet reached the age when she felt the need to hide them.

'Papa says your father has been conscripted,' she said, making her way to the door.

'He has. He leaves tomorrow.'

'My papa will probably be called up soon. Wilhelm, too.'

I nodded. I didn't want to lie to her. It was only a matter of time. Just like the Grim Reaper, war would catch up with everyone eventually. And now that Father's time was up, it wouldn't be long before Julius's time came too. I didn't know how I'd survive it.

7

LISETTE

Then – Berlin, 18 August 1940

'Come in, come in,' Frau Weber said, throwing open her door, her budgie squawking and dancing in his cage behind her. She planted a dry, wispy kiss on my cheek, marking my skin with a bloom of orange-red lipstick that I'd need to scrub away later.

I had never actually been inside her apartment. The scent of musty flowers was pungent, already irritating my nose, and I now saw why. On every surface sat a crystal bowl of potpourri – most were overflowing with dried rose petals and what looked like wood shavings, some had orange and lemon peel in them, too. I wondered what scent she was trying to mask. Other than the smell, the flat was nothing like I had expected. The furniture was tasteful and the walls were filled with the most beautiful art I'd ever seen. Every painting or drawing depicted some form of water – lakes, rivers, the ocean – and most were either at sunrise or sunset, when the sky was an explosion of pinks and purples. The flat was so full of colour it was like walking into a rainbow. I spun in circles, taking it all in.

'These are beautiful,' I said, unable to keep the hint of incredulity out of my voice. 'They're all by the same person, aren't they? Who's the artist?'

She looked at me strangely, frowning and tilting her head. 'Me, of course.'

'You're an artist? But . . .'

'Stop dithering,' she said, her words slicing mine in half. 'Come and meet my nephew.'

Mother had arrived earlier and was already standing in the living room beneath the candle chandelier. Seven agonizing months had passed since Father had left but she still had the habit of checking over her shoulder, looking for him wherever we went. She smiled when I came in, gazing past me. When she saw the empty space, she looked away, then drained the rest of her wine in one gulp.

In the past few months Germany had invaded Denmark, Norway, Luxembourg, the Netherlands and France. We had seen images of our military marching down the Champs-Élysées, hanging a swastika on the Arc de Triomphe. So many Germans were filled with pride at this sight – finally, the injustices of the Treaty of Versailles were being rectified – but that wasn't how I saw it. For me, Paris was a city of love, not violence and hate. I had dreamed of playing in the Salle Pleyel alongside Casadesus and Stravinsky, but there were never any soldiers in my imaginings, no Nazis in the audience, and certainly no Aryan-only ensembles devoid of talented Jewish musicians. When would it all end? When would Father come home?

A young SA officer strode across the room, his ugly brown uniform a dirty smudge ruining the vibrant artwork surrounding him. He was a small, rotund man, like a tick full of blood, but he held his body erect, his spine rigid with superiority. He looked at me in the way one might admire a jacket in a shop window. As if I was something to be possessed, flaunted. He was the complete opposite of Julius in every single way.

'My name is Egon,' he said. 'Heil Hitler!' He swiftly raised his arm in a Nazi salute, barely missing my right eye. I lifted my own arm half-heartedly.

Mother joined Frau Weber in the kitchen. Egon sidled closer. The evening's stifling heat had painted his face crimson, and drops of sweat formed in the fine lines on his forehead. He was at least a head shorter than me but it seemed not to bother him in the slightest.

'It's such a pleasure to meet you, Fräulein. You are even more beautiful than my aunt described.' His voice was surprisingly shrill for someone who clearly wanted to flaunt his manliness.

'I hear your father is part of the North African campaign, bravely fighting for our country,' he continued, undeterred by my obvious indifference to his presence.

Perhaps he thought I was being coy.

'The war is going well, so I can assure you your father will be home soon. Hitler is a great leader and will steer us to victory.'

He took a gulp of wine, then wiped away the dribble that escaped his mouth.

'Hmm,' I replied, avoiding looking at his face. Instead, I drank in the paintings that adorned the walls.

'I've actually met him. Hitler, I mean. Many times, in fact. A true hero.'

He was like a little boy craving approval and I wasn't sure how to react. His attention was unnerving, especially as my heart belonged elsewhere.

'Egon,' Frau Weber called from the kitchen. 'Please escort Lisette to the table. Dinner will be served momentarily.'

Egon smiled at me, the smile of a hungry predator eyeing its prey. I had thought him unpleasant but harmless, a chubby schoolboy playing dress-up in a soldier's uniform, but that smile hinted at something else – an unwavering belief in his own authority in this world, a conviction that he could take what he wanted.

Frau Weber served a steaming casserole, which hardly cooled us down in the oppressive heat, but the beef was delicious, the smell alone nourishing and the quality better than anything we'd eaten since the beginning of the war. The advantage of having an SA officer as a nephew, I assumed.

'Auntie, this is simply delicious,' Egon said, before turning his attention to Mother. 'Frau Richter, my aunt has told me you are also a fine cook.'

Mother smiled, her cheeks flushing. There was a smudge of lipstick on one of her front teeth. I couldn't tell whether she was genuinely blind to his sycophantic ways or if she was choosing to flatter him. We all knew that being acquainted with someone powerful could be advantageous.

'Like every good German, my nephew has a great appreciation for food,' Frau Weber said, her voice loud and puffy with pride. Her budgie, now perched on her shoulder as if the dinner party were his to host, chirped his approval.

I could feel Egon's stare, his hungry gaze making me nauseous. He shovelled more stew into his mouth.

'How long are you on home leave?' Mother asked.

'Only two weeks,' he replied. 'But things are going very well at the front. Soon victory will be ours.'

His voice irked me, like a fly buzzing around the room. My hand tingled with the urge to swat him.

'Oh, I didn't realize you were actually fighting at the front,' I said. 'Your aunt hinted that your job was more . . . clerical?'

He shifted in his chair, pulled at the collar of his uniform. 'Every soldier's job is part of the war effort,' he said. 'I can assure you my job is not clerical.'

'Oh,' Frau Weber said, 'I am sure I never said *clerical*. Egon's not on the front – he's not quite built for digging trenches. Are you, dear? But he is very important in the Party.'

Egon pursed his lips, looked down at his now-empty plate. For a moment, I thought he might cry. It was a bizarre sight, his shame as clear as the stupid Party badge on his lapel. Fleetingly, I pitied him.

Frau Weber's bird chose that moment to poo on the table, green slime marking the pristine white tablecloth. Mother immediately dipped her napkin in her water glass and scrubbed away the stain.

'Who's a silly boy?' Frau Weber said, sticking out a scrawny finger. The bird hopped up on to her hand and she lifted it to her face, where it proceeded to peck at her dry lips.

Mother gave me a subtle nod and I began to clear away the dinner plates. I stacked everything by the sink and searched for a dish brush and a tea towel. Behind me, I heard Egon pour himself another glass.

'It must be hard remaining in the city,' he said, stifling a burp, his brief humiliation all but forgotten. 'But, as I've assured my aunt many times, Berlin will never be bombed. You're safe here. We have countless anti-aircraft missiles. Göring himself said that no enemy bomber can reach Berlin.'

'That is such a relief to hear,' Mother said. 'Isn't it, Lisette?'

I didn't bother replying. As a journalist, Julius was privy to more information than the rest of us and he said it was merely a matter of time before Berlin was bombed; we needed to be prepared. I'd said as much to Mother, but she was wilfully blind.

There were other things Julius told me, but I never repeated them to Mother. He would get arrested for telling anyone. It was illegal to criticize the Nazi government; even telling a joke about Hitler was regarded as treachery. But that wasn't the only reason why I didn't speak up about the horrific things that he claimed were happening. I didn't say anything because as long as the words remained inside me, I could deny the truth of them.

'You only need to worry if you hear the flak going off,' Egon continued. 'Which you never will.'

He was so bloated with faith and fervour I wanted to pop him like a balloon. Instead, I placed the plates back in their cupboard and announced it was time to go home.

'So soon?' Frau Weber said. 'Egon brought chocolates.'

The promise of chocolate was almost too much to resist but I couldn't bear to spend one more minute in their presence.

'I really do have to go,' I said. 'I have an early piano lesson with a student tomorrow.'

'If you really must go,' Egon said, folding his stained napkin and standing up, 'perhaps, at some point, I could come by with the chocolates? I would very much enjoy hearing you play the piano. Music is one of my great joys.'

I doubted he knew his Schubert from his Chopin, but before I could make up an excuse, Mother jumped in.

'Lisette would love that, I am sure.'

No reply felt like the most suitable response so I gathered my things and took Mother's arm. I would drag her out of there if I had to.

Exhaustion and wine had made me sleepy, and when Egon brushed my buttocks with his chubby fingers as I slipped out into the corridor, I was too slow to slap him away. He leered at me as he closed the door. I feared he thought I'd enjoyed his roaming hand.

'Goodness, that was quite rude of you, bustling us out of there,' Mother said as we made our way down to our own apartment. 'We have to be careful, Lisette. Things are going to get worse before they get better. Rations are tightening. It is summer now but winter is just around the corner. And Egon – he is not so bad.'

'He's an insufferable Nazi,' I whispered. 'You're always spending time with Party members – why don't you join yourself?'

Mother slid the key into the lock. Inside, the apartment was
stifling, and she threw the windows open, but it did little to cool
the air.

'You know I do not agree with their vision,' she said, pouring
herself a glass of water. 'Neither does your father. And I do not
want to be part of an unfair system where lazy people are treated
better simply due to their political affiliations.'

'And yet, you have no problem affiliating yourself with those
very people.'

I knew I was overstepping, even as I said the words, but the
alcohol had loosened my tongue.

'We need . . . friends.' She kept her voice measured but a vein
pulsed at her temple. She took out her handkerchief, held her
glass up to the light and wiped the smudged lipstick from its
rim. 'Especially those in high positions. Even those whose politics we may not agree with.'

There was little point in arguing with her. While at times her
words provoked my anger, she always remained calm and reasonable. It was infuriating, arguing with someone who was
always in control.

'I'll see you in the morning,' I said, placing my heels in the
shoe rack, making sure they were aligned just the way Mother
liked them.

'Lisette, wait.'

'Yes?'

She sighed. Not an irritated sigh, but a weary one.

'You forget that I have lived through one war already,' she
said, her eyes shining. 'I was the same age you are now. You have
never felt real fear or real hunger. Not like I have. You have
never experienced what starvation can do to a body – and to a

mind. I lost five babies before I had you. The sorrow almost killed me.' She blinked rapidly but one tear still fell.

I nodded but stayed silent, not wanting to break this fragile moment.

'We have to take help where we can find it,' she said. 'We need to survive this. You and I.'

8

LISETTE

Then – Berlin, 25 August 1940

A week later, I woke to screaming sirens and barking flak. I rushed to the window and saw the searchlights dancing drunkenly in the cloudy sky.

Mother ran into my room, her face ashen, eyes wide. Above us we heard the rumble of a plane's engine.

'Quick.'

I grabbed our air-raid bags while Mother grabbed her hat, then, sliding our hands along the wall, we descended the stairs into the cellar.

That night, no one was playing cards, no one gossiped. Fear was a person and he joined us in the dark. Our neighbours huddled together, some trembling, some with their eyes squeezed shut, others muttering words of prayer.

Mother and I tucked ourselves into our usual spot, me in a corner and Frau Weber along with her screeching bird to Mother's left. Though we had all tried to make it cosy, it was cold and damp in the basement with a distinct smell of rot. Somewhere, I suspected, a rat lay decomposing.

'Lisette, can I sit with you?' My eyes were still adjusting to the dimly lit space but I recognized Krista's face.

'Of course.' I shifted a little to make room for her. She squeezed in beside me and then pulled my arm over her shoulder so she could rest her head on my chest. I could smell the fruity soap on her skin, the oil her mother combed into her hair. I laid my blanket over her knees and tucked it in tight. With no siblings and no close cousins to speak of, I had very little experience with younger children, and I found her embrace solidifying, calming. Apart from Egon's wandering hand, it had been a long time since I'd been touched. I knew Mother loved me but she was not the cuddling type. I had assumed I didn't need the touch of others either, but Krista's warmth made me feel almost safe, if only for a moment.

I glanced over at Krista's mother, afraid she would disapprove, but she simply nodded gratefully, her lap full with Krista's sleeping sister. Wilhelm sat beside her. He smiled at me with such warmth it made me blush. Now eighteen, his conscription letter had arrived the previous week – one more thing I refused to think about.

I looked down at Krista. I couldn't help but imagine a future child of my own – a beautiful girl with my eyes and Julius's nose. A small human who would love me far more than I loved myself.

'Mama says Papa will come home one day. He will, won't he?' Krista whispered to me. I stroked her hair; it was the first time I'd seen it loose, free from her braided pigtails.

'Of course he'll come home,' I said. Because sometimes a lie is necessary.

Eventually Krista began snoring softly, her legs folded over mine, her warm body pressed against my chest. I found it impossible to sleep, though; I could never get used to the sound of sirens – it was as if the city itself was crying.

Previously, when the alarms had wailed and howled, we would hurry half-asleep into the basement and then sit there bored until dawn. That night was different. We could all hear the planes roaring overhead, the distant rumble of bombs falling.

Göring had been wrong. Egon had been wrong. The war had finally found us.

9

LISETTE

Then – Berlin, 6 July 1941

Krista was having a lesson with me when Julius showed up at my door, his spectacles foggy from the humid air, his hat clenched between his hands. She didn't go home; instead she retreated to my bedroom to give us some privacy. Even she recognized the look on his face, the reason he had come.

'Don't say it.' Already I could feel the tears creeping from the corners of my eyes.

'I must,' he said. 'I'm leaving. It seems my luck has run out.'

'Russia?'

'They haven't said, but I expect so.'

'And there's nothing that can be done?'

'No.' His sigh filled the room, the flat, the world. 'My time has come.'

As we had both known it would. We had lived through another year of war, nights filled with fear as bombs whistled through the sky above us, too often finding their target; another year of hoping it would all come to an end; another year of me waiting for Julius to see me as a woman he could perhaps love instead of just a friend. We saw each other often and he never spoke of anyone else, but sometimes a thought or memory would tug at the corner of his mouth, lift his lips into a smile, and I worried that he might love someone else – that perhaps, somewhere in Berlin, there was a woman who made his heart sing.

'When?' I asked, my throat hurting with the strain of speaking as if everything were normal.

'Tomorrow. Max too. We're in the same unit.'

I gestured for him to sit down on the sofa, then fled to the bathroom. I bent over the basin, gripping the sides, taking deep breaths that would never be sufficient to quell the tsunami of sorrow rising within me. I'd known this day would come, I'd prepared myself for it as best I could, but it was futile.

'Sit with me,' he said, when I returned blotchy-skinned and trembling. 'I can't stay long. My mother wants me home. But sit with me. Just for a minute.'

I sank into the sofa beside him. He pulled me into his chest. His shirt was damp but he smelled of soap and cigarettes.

'I'll write to you,' he said, his words getting tangled in my hair.

'You'd better.' I tried to sound stern but I ended up sobbing, my body convulsing with anguish.

'Hey, hey,' he said, lifting my chin. 'I'll be OK. I'll come back. I promise.'

His fingers traced my jawline, his touch as soft as a feather. He wiped away my tears, then tucked a damp strand of hair behind my ear. I held my breath, kept my body still. He kissed my hair, stroked the nape of my neck. The air was warm, but the tips of his fingers were cold. A shiver of longing fluttered down my spine. My chest seized as if I couldn't get enough air into my lungs. I pulled away, just so I could look at him and memorize his face – his brown eyes, the colour of autumn; his straight teeth; the small red dent on the bridge of his nose underneath his glasses.

And then we both leaned in, our lips brushing together.

'I'm sorry,' he said, pulling back. 'I shouldn't.'

It was barely a kiss, over much too soon, but it had happened. It had finally happened.

'Don't be sorry.'

He took off his glasses, rubbed his eyes.

'I have to go,' he said, standing up. Behind him, beyond the window, the sky was fading towards evening, the sun losing its strength.

'Don't go, please don't,' I said, trying to keep the desperation out of my voice. 'Stay. Just a little longer.'

He opened his mouth and I knew he wanted to tell me something. That he loved me? Or that he didn't? He blinked, shook his head.

'I'll write as soon as I can.'

And then he swept through the front door, letting it click softly behind him.

'What can I do?' Krista asked when she found me staring at the door, listening to the echo of his footsteps on the stairs. When I didn't answer, she took my hand and led me to Father's armchair.

'I'll get you some water,' she said. 'You look like you might faint.'

She was just a young girl; she'd never experienced romantic love or the heartache that could be born from it, but she'd watched her papa and brother leave – she recognized the fear etched on to my face.

I closed my eyes and touched my lips with the tips of my fingers. They still tingled, the memory of Julius's mouth imprinted on them. How could life be so cruel, granting me what every atom in my body had longed for but paired with Julius's departure – the very thing I had feared most?

The kiss embodied hope and it would sustain me through the dark months I knew were coming, but what if Julius never returned from the war? Would his body survive it? Would his soul? I understood what the horrors of war could do to a man. I had never known Father before the Great War, but there was no denying he had become a broken man after it.

'He's young, he's strong,' Krista said, handing me a glass and sitting down beside me. 'He'll come back.'

Someone else had given her those words – her mother, perhaps. Those same words were being recycled all over Germany, all over the world.

10

LISETTE

Then – Berlin, 18 October 1941

'They're leaving,' Frau Weber said as I greeted her in the stairwell.

'Who?'

'The Jews, of course.'

I was going down and she was heading up, but her words stopped me like a fierce gust of wind.

'What do you mean?' I asked.

'Hordes of them are being marched through the streets as we speak. I saw them with my own eyes. Good riddance is all I can say.' She sniffed and a fleeting look of distaste passed over her features.

I hesitated on the stairs, considered turning back, but curiosity nibbled. This was what the Nazis wanted – the Jews gone. My chest burned. I knew what Party members were saying – that it was the Jews who had made us lose the Great War, they were money-grabbing vermin, determined to poison our culture. I knew many Germans felt disgusted by them, but Julius had opened my eyes to a different view. And I still remembered Kristallnacht like it was yesterday; I still remembered that old man's face as he was being beaten and the horror it evoked in me.

So, then, perhaps it was best they left – maybe then they would be safe at last? I didn't know where they were being deported to, but surely it would be better for them than staying here? The hatred towards them had only increased since Julius had been sent to the front. Just last month a new decree had been issued that prohibited them from using public transport and now they were being forced to wear a yellow star on their clothes. At first the persecution had been slow but steady, each new law a subtle small step. But now I could see the bigger picture, the extent of what had been done to them over recent years, their rights gradually stripped away. And, as if embarrassed, we had all looked away. For the first time, I felt relieved Julius was fighting in Russia. Unlike everyone else, he wouldn't have been able to stand by and watch while innocent people were being evicted from their homes. He would have said something, done something, without considering the consequences.

Outside, the sky was grey. It was starting to rain but I didn't bother to fetch my jacket. I grabbed my bicycle and, holding on to my hat, cycled towards the closest Jewish neighbourhood.

When I got to Große Hamburger Straße, I finally saw them – a huge crowd of people branded with their yellow stars, wet from the rain, being herded along by soldiers. They looked tired, worn out. And scared.

I climbed off my bicycle and began to push it instead, keeping parallel to them.

They walked past St Hedwig Hospital, where a tapestry of autumnal leaves climbed the exterior wall, and then they were marched on towards the Jewish cemetery, where they joined a larger crowd.

My gaze fell on an old man with sunken eyes, arms like sticks and wrinkles so deep they looked like scars. He clung to the arm of a younger man – his son, I presumed. They had the same high cheekbones, the same tufty eyebrows. The older man seemed bewildered, lost. Behind him, a mother carried a toddler in a pair of pale-blue pyjamas. The boy's cheeks were pink and his head was lolling, as if he had just woken from a nap.

The mother looked at me. 'Fräulein! Take him. Please.' The wind carried her voice towards me, delivering the words like an unwanted gift. I could see the fear in her eyes, the way it moved beyond her, something she couldn't quite contain.

I wanted to help, but my courage failed me. I didn't answer. I turned my head.

By now, other passers-by had gathered to watch what was happening. Many stood and gloated. I'll never forget their faces. Some were jubilant; the Jews were leaving and this meant we would get more of whatever there was to have. Some seemed indifferent – the plight of others barely impacting their day. For them, the crowd was simply a minor inconvenience, like the rain. Easily avoided, quickly forgotten.

The woman called out to me twice more, and twice more I turned my head, my face hot with shame. And then, driven forward by a soldier's threats, she was swallowed up by the throng.

Evil demanded little of me – it merely asked me to remain silent, to do nothing. And I complied.

~

I cycled home slowly, my head a blizzard of thoughts. Where would they be taken? They were Jews, yes, but they were Germans, too. I told myself again that surely they would be better off elsewhere. That it would be better for them in the long run. I couldn't have taken the boy. A child should never be separated from its mother.

I parked my bicycle outside our building and removed my hat, shaking off the water that had gathered on the fabric.

I felt unimaginably tired as I climbed the stairs to the flat. Inside I found Mother by the open fire, dusting the photographs on the mantlepiece. Shadows crept up the wall behind her. She nodded when she saw me but then turned back to her cleaning. I sat down by the piano, hoping if I played gently Mother wouldn't complain. I played out my anxiety, I played until the strange feeling in my stomach dissipated. And then I went to bed and I let the Sandman steal the rest away.

11

ELLY

Now – East Berlin, 21 August 1961

I flick through Mama's leather address book, its pages yellow and flaking with age. Finding the address I've been looking for, I write it down on a scrap of paper and then tuck that into my bag. I glance at my keyboard and my stomach aches. I've packed and unpacked a dozen times, but there will never be enough space for it.

I look at my watch. It is hours until nightfall. The afternoon stretches lazily like a cat, uninterested in the passing of time, ignorant of my need for it to speed up.

The air is hot and sticky but I don't want to open the window and let the sweet floral smell of home drift out. I pace up and down, my mind a swarm of bees. I close my eyes and remind myself why I'm doing this. I remember the weeks before the barrier, when Axel came into our lives and Mama softened around the edges, her love for him somehow igniting her love for me. There was a lightness to her step, her music no longer a raging storm, her 'moments' few and far between. For once, we felt like a family, and knowing we could have that again – that I can make it happen – stops my heart from exploding out of my chest.

Mama is in her room. Yesterday her visa application was rejected and she spent all night on the phone, dialling the hospital's number. Papa sat beside her, there to speak for her if somehow she got through. The lines to the West have been cut for almost ten years now, but she kept trying anyway, twisting the phone cord around her fingers, cutting off the blood.

There has been no letter, no word from the hospital. Our post from the West has always been both censored and sporadic, but at the moment, it seems nothing is getting through at all. We don't even know if Axel is alive.

I open her door as quietly as I can, but it swings out of my grasp and the handle thuds into the wall.

'Sorry,' I whisper, but she doesn't stir. She's lying on the crumpled sheet, facing the wall, a dead woman breathing. I crawl on to the bed like I used to do as a child. I have an urge to fold myself around her, breathe in the citrus smell of her wispy hair, pretend it's a good day. Instead, I touch her shoulder.

'Mama? Can I get you something to eat?'

She stiffens but then reaches out and squeezes my hand. She doesn't turn to look at me but this touch is enough. I lie beside her for as long as I dare, blinking away my tears and listening to her laboured breathing, willing her song to return.

Back in the living room, Oma Rita shifts in her chair by the window, the quiet, hopeful tinkling of her own melody everpresent. 'Are you making lunch, Lisette?'

'It's Elly.'

'Elly?' I can hear the confusion in her voice but I don't bother to explain who I am.

'I'll make you a sandwich,' I say. 'Just cheese?' I've learned that too many options stress her out. Her mind is already muddled without the burden of decisions.

'That sounds lovely.'

She looks at me strangely when I hand her the plate. I can see her studying my features, searching her memory for a clue. She won't ask me who I am, though. It must be unsettling to find a stranger in your home. I used to explain each time, guide her back to the present with crumbs of information, but not any more. If I don't make it back, at least she'll easily forget me.

'I was hoping you could play me a sonata,' she says, nibbling suspiciously at the bread, 'but it seems the grand piano is missing.'

'There hasn't been a piano here for a long time,' I say. 'Shall I open a window, let in some fresh air?'

'Goodness, no, the bird will escape.'

'The bird?'

'Frau Weber's bird. She would never forgive us.'

'Do you need anything else?' I ask, crouching down beside her. I touch her hand gently but she snatches it away as if I've pinched her. No one likes to be touched in this home and yet it's something I crave.

'*I* do not need anything, but I am certain that our allotment needs tending to. I want it to look nice for when Ernst returns.' She pats her hair and smooths her skirt, as if she's expecting him to appear at any moment.

I don't have the heart to tell her the allotment garden is gone, that for months she didn't go and so eventually Mama stopped paying the rent for it. I don't tell her that her husband is gone too, that no one has seen him in almost twenty years.

'I went to the allotment this morning,' I lie. 'It's looking beautiful, so there's no need to go again today. We could go down into the courtyard, though? Do some weeding, pick some fresh flowers for the table?'

As she goes in search of her hat, I dig out some gloves and the pruning shears.

Without looking at her, I say, 'I'm going to go away for a while, Oma.' I try to keep my voice measured but it catches in my throat. 'A few days. Maybe weeks. I'm not sure.'

She stands by the door watching me. She doesn't answer but I can tell she's listening.

'I promise I'll come back.'

I join her and with a papery-dry hand she cups my face. With her thumb she wipes a tear from my cheek.

She'll forget, as she always does, but perhaps my promise to return will stay somewhere locked inside her. Even a promise forgotten is a promise made.

~

Later, once the night has crept in, I lie fully clothed on my bed, pinching myself to stay awake. I watch the curtains flutter in the hot, dry air and listen to the sound of Oma Rita snoring in her room across the hall. Even with her door closed, her snores reverberate around the apartment. I find the sound strangely comforting and I wish I could box it up and take it with me, a reminder of home I could keep in my pocket.

It's almost two a.m. I shouldn't delay any longer. It's now or never.

I make my bed – at least this might make Mama smile – and place the letter I've written on top of my keyboard. It's time to go, but I can't help stroking its lid one last time. This keyboard is the only item I'll miss. The keys are smudged with use and the sound is not as pure and sharp as it once was, but it feels like my soul is contained inside. I tell myself I'll be back. Then I sling my bag over my shoulder and quietly slip out of my room.

In the hallway, I stop outside my parents' room. I place my hand on the rough wood of the door and whisper a silent goodbye. I hear the bed creak, a body shifting in discomfort. Quickly I back away and leave the apartment.

Outside, the air is warm, the sun's heat still trapped in the pavements. I've never been out alone at this time and the quiet is unnerving. I climb on to my bike and cycle slowly through the streets, ignoring the way it makes the cobbles jar my body. Every so often I catch a waft of the sewers. They say the only thing worse than summer in Berlin is winter in Berlin; it's true, but only marginally so. The city stinks in the summer – not only because of the sewers but also the rotting stench from all the household rubbish that's been left out in the heat, attracting flies which then lay eggs that hatch into writhing maggots. In winter, it gets so cold the hair inside your nostrils freezes and the air burns your lungs. In the autumn, it rains, and spring is too short. I want to live anywhere but here, but first I want to see the world – the beaches of Greece, the French Alps, New York City with its glittering lights and dazzling freedom.

It's not long before I see a group of soldiers. There are at least four of them and they're leaning against a wall, smoking. I swerve into an alleyway, dismount. Before I can stop it, my bike clatters to the ground. I don't know if they'll decide to investigate the sound. But even if they do, there's no curfew; there hasn't been one since 1953. There's no law against cycling around the city at night. I've done nothing wrong. Not yet.

I don't wait to find out, though. I slip into the shadows and then slide my back along the wall of an apartment building.

I approach Bernauer Straße from the south. The street appears to be deserted apart from two soldiers sitting underneath a tree. One has a cigarette burning between his fingers, a speck of glistening gold. The other is slightly slumped and it's clear he's sleeping.

I'm sweating and shaking. My legs ache with an uncontrollable urge to run. But I need to do this. I have to do this. I think of Papa in the corner of Axel's room, I think of Mama's missing voice.

The front door of the building I'm looking for opens easily, with an almost imperceptible click, though it feels as if I've rung a bell. I wait, hold my breath. Nothing happens. Inside, the paint on the walls is peeling, the steps crumbling in places. The stairwell is wide and too grand for the state of the building. Slowly I climb the stairs. I hear nothing, but I imagine my very breath is echoing off the walls like a scream.

I stop at the third floor. It's been almost a year since Hans and his family fled west and there's a chance new people have moved into his flat, but I doubt it. Like so many buildings that were hit by bombs during the war and still haven't been repaired properly, this house isn't safe. And who wants to look out of the window every day and see West Berlin only a few metres away; a place where things are better, where people aren't merely existing but living?

I'm ready to throw my weight against the apartment door again and again until the hinges give, the wood splintering, but when I try the handle, the door swings open. It can't possibly be this easy.

Inside the apartment, curtains cover the windows and the darkness is so deep and complete that it takes several minutes for my eyes to adjust. The living room is large but empty, the wooden floor a little uneven. It's just a shell now and it's difficult to remember what it was like when it was a home. There's also a strange smell here, one I can't quite place. It's disconcerting.

Through the fabric of my bag, I feel the contours of the rope. There's nothing here that I can tie it on to. Why didn't I think of this before? Worst case, I jump.

I take a step forward and the floor groans. Are there neighbours downstairs? Will they wake? Call the soldiers? I stand still, steady my breathing, and listen to the night. But the longer

I wait, the more I risk being caught. Perhaps speed is better than stealth. I take another step, pull the curtain aside.

A brick wall.

I yank aside the other curtains but behind each one is a wall where a window should be. I touch the brickwork, feel the tacky surface beneath my fingers, and I realize that the musty, earthy smell is that of drying cement.

I should have known. They bricked up the houses on Harzer Straße a week ago. It was only a matter of time before they did it here as well. I'm too late.

'Who's there?' The voice is deep and grating but it wavers with uncertainty, as if he's the one who's scared.

I don't move a muscle.

'I can see you.' The voice is fiercer now, more sure of itself. 'I know why you're here. You're not the first.'

He steps into the room, the door to the corridor swinging open behind him. Moonlight from a small skylight out in the hall shines down on him. It's still dark but I can see that his skin is smooth and unblemished, his nose sharp but slightly crooked. When he flicks on a torch, his eyes are the bluest I've ever seen. He's young, twenty perhaps. His *Grenztruppen* uniform is unmistakable, even in this light.

In his other hand, there's a gun. He raises it, points it at my heart.

Terror glues me to the spot, fills my mouth so no words can escape. I wait for a bullet to tear through my flesh, but nothing happens. The soldier and I just stare at each other.

He's so close I can hear him breathing. And all I can think about is Monika's neighbour who was shot at as he swam across the Spree. The border guards have their orders. Shoot to kill – that's what everyone's saying.

Several agonizing seconds pass and yet neither of us makes a move. Inexplicably my nose starts to itch, then there's the tell-tale tickle of a sneeze about to erupt.

He takes another step forward and then he lowers his weapon.

'You're just a girl,' he says. His German is perfect but I can hear the harsh lilt of Russian lurking underneath. 'You shouldn't be here.'

'I got lost,' I say, trying to keep my voice steady. 'I'm staying with my aunt, but I got confused. This isn't her building. It looks the same. They all look the same at night. I'm lost, that's all.'

He doesn't believe me. I can tell by the way he tilts his head, by the way a smile pulls at the corners of his mouth.

'So, I won't find a rope in your bag or a make-do parachute?'

The sneeze I've been trying so hard to withhold finally bursts forth, surprising us both.

He laughs. It's such a strange, out-of-place sound that the terror that was consuming me releases its jaws just a little.

It's then that I hear his music. It's unlike anything I've heard before – a beautiful melody with a steady, strong beat. It's made up of a whole orchestra – I can hear solemn violins; airy, whistling flutes; even a soft but powerful trombone. His song is a complex symphony with so many layers it fills the room and pulses through my veins, merging with my own song. It can only belong to someone kind, I'm sure of it.

I know he can't hear our songs colliding but I can see that he senses it, the way a deaf person can perceive music through its vibrations. Something unknown passes between us and, for a moment, everything falls away and I've forgotten why I'm here, what it is I'm doing.

There's a noise behind him and his music ceases. Heavy footsteps on floorboards, the swinging light of a torch. I'm pulled back to my presence in a forbidden apartment in the dead of night. My escape attempt gone wrong.

The other soldier is shorter but broader, with a wispy moustache and a huge, unruly mop of dark hair.

'Andrei,' the man says, and then more words spit from his mouth, a barrage of harsh syllables. Another gun aimed at my chest. I don't understand the orders he is firing out but I can guess.

'It's OK, Boris,' Andrei says in German, his voice smooth and calm. 'This is Ida. She's my girlfriend. I've told her not to visit me here, but . . .' He shrugs. He holds out his hand and without thinking, I take it. And then I press my head into his chest, pull his arm tighter around my shoulders.

'Sorry, Boris,' I say, keeping my voice soft. 'I couldn't sleep and I knew Andrei was on patrol here tonight. I just wanted to see him, to . . . give him a kiss.'

Boris looks from me to Andrei and then back to me again, his moustache twitching. He says nothing but I can almost hear his thoughts, the questions he's asking himself. His gun is still raised, his finger on the trigger.

'Boris, please, lower your gun. You're scaring poor Ida.'

They're wearing matching uniforms so their rank must be the same, but it's clear that Andrei is the one making the decisions. I pray today won't be the day Boris finds his voice.

'I should go,' I say. 'I don't want either of you to get into trouble.'

I let go of Andrei's hand and move past Boris slowly, as if he's a mousetrap I need to tiptoe around, knowing that at any moment he could snap me in two.

Just as I reach the door, the butt of Boris's gun nudges my hip. 'Did you get it?' he asks.

'Get what?'

'Your kiss.'

A laugh, too high-pitched to be natural, escapes from my mouth. 'Um, no, I didn't, actually.'

I turn back, flick my hair, and before I have the chance to panic and change my mind, I grab Andrei's collar and pull his face down towards mine. My lips find his. My first kiss.

I leave the building without looking back, but before I reach the street corner, a hand grabs my shoulder. I swing around, ready to fight or scream.

'You can't leave without giving me your real name,' Andrei says. He moves under a street light so I can see him better. He's handsome, there's no denying it, but he's also a Soviet border guard. The enemy. I look past him but the street is empty, Boris nowhere to be seen.

'Thank you,' I whisper. 'Thank you for not arresting me.'

'Or shooting you,' he says with a smile.

'Are those your orders?'

'For those who attempt to escape? Yes.'

I don't bother denying my intentions. 'Well, thank you for not shooting me, then.'

I turn to leave, but he stops me once more.

'Your name?'

I should lie but I don't. 'Elly. Elly Lange.'

12

LISETTE

Then – Berlin, 19 May 1943

The war dragged on and our rations diminished. The bombs were relentless. Cologne had been almost flattened, millions had been left homeless across the country, and there were whispers on the streets that our army was in a stalemate against Russia. The US had joined the war. We were losing. And we all knew it.

I spent my days worrying about Julius and Father. Wilhelm and Max, too. Julius sent letters weekly and I cherished them. They weren't love letters but they proved he thought of me and that gave me some comfort. He wrote often about Max and I was glad he was not alone in the trenches. Though he wrote detailing the mundanity of war, the waiting, the cold nights, I could sense the fear hidden behind each word, the sadness tucked into each letter.

'From Julius, Egon or my brother?' Krista asked as I folded the letter and slipped it gently back into its envelope. She sat behind me on the sofa brushing my hair. The floor was hard and I shifted uncomfortably but I loved having my hair brushed; it made me feel like a small girl again. When I was little, Mother would stiffen and hold her breath when I forced a hug on her, but she had shown her love in other ways – brushing my hair being one of them. Eventually I had stopped trying to climb on to her lap, even though occasionally this loss left me feeling weightless. Sometimes I found myself bumping into people on the street, just so I could feel alive. I never knew why Mother hated the feeling of skin against skin, but I learned to accept her limitations and I longed for the hours when she would sit running a brush through my hair, whispering fairy tales into my ear, spinning my hair into silk.

Krista was always trying to cuddle me. She had become the little sister I'd always dreamed of having.

'It's from Julius,' I said, his name always paired with a smile, a skipped heartbeat. 'Did I tell you he wants to be a poet one day? Even his letters seem poetic – I love the way he strings the words together.'

'You should ask him to write you one – a poem,' Krista said.

Frau Weber blustered back into the room, returning from the bathroom. In greeting, her budgie let out a loud shriek then clawed the bars of its cage. She had grown thinner; we all had, even her stupid bird.

'I assume you have heard the news,' she said, sitting back down at our dining table. '*Judenrein*,' she declared. 'Finally, Germany is free of the Jews.'

She sounded strangely triumphant, as if this was due to her efforts alone.

'Hmm,' Mother said, wandering over to the window. She'd fallen into the habit of sitting in Father's armchair for hours at a time, staring out of the glass, searching the street below for Father's face. Her last three letters to him had been returned unread and the unknown weighed heavily on us both.

'Where do you suppose they've gone?' I asked, trying to keep my voice light. 'The Jews?'

'I don't much care,' Frau Weber replied, plucking lint from her jacket.

I tried not to think of the rumours that had leaked through the walls about the fate of the Jews. Whispered gossip spoke of awful things, barbaric acts. I tried to shut my ears to it, but every night, just as I was falling asleep, I saw that woman with her son – her pleading eyes, his pale-blue pyjamas – and I would wonder: what had become of them?

'Two braids or one?' asked Krista.

'As many as you want,' I said, pulling my knees in towards me.

'One of our neighbours doesn't have a painting of Hitler on her wall,' Krista said, making conversation. 'Mama says everyone should have one in their home.'

'Maybe it fell down,' I suggested. 'Maybe it's at the shop getting repaired.'

'That's shocking,' Frau Weber said, cutting in. 'Which neighbour, I would like to know? I shall report them immediately.'

She fingered her Nazi Party badge as if drawing strength from it.

'I don't think that's necessary,' I said in the sweetest voice I could muster. 'I'm sure Krista's mother will remind them of its importance the next time she visits.'

'I don't remember who it is, anyway,' Krista said, sensing the tension in the room. Her mother had insisted she join the *Jungmädelbund* but I knew she hated it. She was twelve now, awkward in her growing body; too tall, as I had been, and bullied relentlessly by the other girls. While joining the Hitler Youth probably made her peers feel important and gave them a sense of belonging, I knew Krista felt increasingly cut off. She came to our apartment often, not just for piano lessons, and I found I enjoyed her company. More so than the company of my own friends, who lately I'd drifted away from. Their teasing about my seemingly unrequited love for Julius had left me feeling inferior to them. I wanted to tell them about the kiss, to prove Julius might love me after all, but something stopped me. It felt too sacred and too fragile to be voiced out loud.

'This coffee is not good,' Frau Weber said, her hands cupping Father's favourite mug.

She was right, it wasn't. It smelled weak, strange, and I'd let my own cup grow cold.

'It's *Ersatzkaffee*,' Mother said, her voice weary. She returned to the table and filled her own mug. 'It is made from acorns and barley seeds.'

'Will it never end?' Frau Weber said, poking a gnarled finger through the bars of her budgie's cage. 'These rations, this war.'

She used to place the cage on the floor by her feet but lately she'd given it pride of place on the dining table. The yellow bird hopped over and pecked at her wrinkly knuckle. Frau Weber complained all the time, her whining tugging at my already frazzled nerves, but I was sure she quite liked our current situation. Berlin had become a city of women. With everyone's fathers, husbands and sons gone, the women had banded together and Frau Weber was no longer as lonely. Until our men came home and proved otherwise, we were all war widows.

There was a timid knock at the door. The budgie whistled in excitement. We exchanged relieved looks – the Gestapo were known to bang loudly, break the whole thing down; this was someone else, someone not looking for trouble. I knew Egon would soon be home on leave but he always knocked then strode straight in, shoulders back, stomach out, never waiting for a reply.

I went to the door, forgetting my hair was now twisted into six ridiculous-looking braids.

At first I didn't recognize the bony, bearded man standing before me, but then he pushed his glasses up his nose and gave me a hint of a smile.

Time moved forward, then back, collapsing in on itself.

I couldn't move, terrified it was only a dream and the slightest tremor would make him disappear.

'Lisette.' Hearing my name from his lips made it real. He was here; he was alive. His cheeks were hollow and his eyes, magnified by his glasses, were wide and haunted; I could almost see in their depths the things he must have witnessed. His shoulders were hunched, his swagger gone, and there were no ink stains on his fingers. But he was still my Julius. And he was here.

'Well, invite him in, dear girl,' Frau Weber said. 'Don't just stare at him.'

'Of course, of course,' I said, grabbing his hand and pulling him quickly inside. I led him to the sofa and sat him down, as one would a child. Krista jumped up and at some point she must have left, but I didn't notice.

'What can I get you? Coffee? Schnapps? I can't believe you're here. Food? You must be hungry. How long are you home for? Some bread? Or just water?' My words stumbled over each other like the feet of a drunken man in the street. 'No, no, don't get up. You rest. I will get you all of those things. No need to decide. You're here. You're home.'

To my dismay, I found I was crying. I forced myself to look away – he didn't need to see my silly tears.

As Frau Weber reintroduced her bird to Julius and then proceeded to batter him with questions, I busied myself in the kitchen. I made more coffee and then rooted around in the cupboards for something sweet to give him. He was thinner than when I'd last seen him, and his skin was sallow, as if the colour had been bled out of him.

'Perhaps we should go for a walk? Leave these two to catch up?' Mother said, touching Frau Weber lightly on the shoulder. I shot her a grateful smile and ignored Frau Weber's displeased frown. Before she could protest any further, Mother lifted the birdcage, grabbed their jackets from the coat stand and opened the door, practically pushing Frau Weber through it. Before she slipped out, Mother gestured to my hair, reminding me I looked like Medusa with my head full of snakes.

I quickly released the braids. Usually Julius would have teased me, but he didn't seem to notice. I handed him the coffee but he placed it on the table without taking a sip. I suspected the slightly stale *Stollen* would also remain untouched.

I stood awkwardly, shifting my weight from one foot to the other, unsure of what to do, where to sit, what to say. After too many words, I now had none.

'Will you play the piano for me?' Julius's voice was quieter and softer than I remembered. 'Sometimes, in the trenches at night, I would close my eyes and imagine I was here listening to you. And now, finally, I *am* here. I would so love to hear you play.'

'Of course.'

It was always Julius I played for, whether he was there or not. Having him actually present made my fingers light with joy. My body and the instrument became one, until I was no longer sure if I was playing the piano or it was playing me. I performed all the tunes I'd composed for Julius over the years – the ones that cried with melancholy as well as the ones that sang with hope. Every time I turned to look at him, he sat with his eyes closed, a small smile on his lips, and, in those moments, I was the happiest I'd ever been.

I could have played for hours but I wanted to talk to Julius, too, see his beautiful face, and so finally I let the music drift out of the open window and I closed the piano lid.

'Thank you,' he said, opening his eyes. 'Come – sit with me. Tell me what's been going on.'

I wanted to sink down beside him on the sofa, take his hand in mine; instead I perched on an armchair opposite him.

'How are you?' I asked.

His shoulders sagged, his spine curving with sorrow, and I wished I could stuff the words back into my mouth. Clearly he was not OK. Clearly he never would be.

'Fine,' he said, the lie pushing us apart. 'Tired, but I'm all right.'

'And Max?'

His face brightened a little. 'He's alive. I honestly don't know how I would've survived all this without him.'

'Good. I'm glad you haven't been alone.' I stood up and busied myself tidying away his untouched coffee. The afternoon was sliding into evening, the light shifting across the room. The breeze that breathed through the apartment was cool, threatening a chilly night.

The front door swung open and Mother appeared. Behind her, I heard Frau Weber climb the stairs to her own apartment, her footsteps slow yet determined.

'You will stay for dinner, Julius,' Mother said, a statement not a question. 'I will prepare the guest room, too.' And, like a gentleman, he agreed.

As I laid the table and Mother cooked – the stew bubbling on the stove, the succulent smell filling the apartment – Julius and I chatted quietly. It didn't take me long to realize it was more than just his appearance that had changed. My vibrant, dynamic man had become withdrawn, despondent. The fire in him was gone; only fading embers remained.

After dinner – the most extravagant dinner we had eaten in months – Mother left us alone and I sat with Julius in near darkness, a flickering candle keeping us company.

'What's it been like?' I asked. 'The war?'

'It's been . . . it is . . .' He shook his head.

'Please talk to me,' I said. 'It might help. You can't keep it all inside. I'm here. And I can listen.'

He sighed, pushing his glasses up his nose. He pulled a

crumpled cigarette packet from his pocket and extracted the last one. I passed him some matches but he struggled to light one. His hands shook and the flame wouldn't catch. Gently, I took the match from his hand and lit it for him.

'There are things I've seen that can't be unseen,' he said, sucking hard on the cigarette. 'I'm not particularly religious but I've always believed in God. Until now. I knew war would be ugly but, Lisette, it is so much worse than I imagined.'

His voice was so quiet I had to lean closer to hear him.

'The cold we experienced this winter was unbearable,' he continued. 'I can't describe the horror of it. And when people are desperate they do terrible things.'

I poured him some wine and he drank as if it were water. He then sat back and began to speak.

'We were gaining ground but then winter came and the tide turned. The Russkis are used to the snow, the blizzards, the intense cold, but we couldn't stand it. It hurt to breathe. They started pushing us back and we had no choice but to retreat. We found a town and we needed shelter. I'm a good man. But I allowed things to happen. I just wanted to be warm again.'

He drank more wine. It stained his teeth like blood. As he spoke, he looked past me, as if he could see the scene unfolding right there in the room. His cigarette lay momentarily forgotten, its smoke shifting and swirling, responding to the breath of unseen ghosts.

'We spread out and went in search of houses where we could warm up, rest. One of the officers ushered us into what can only be described as a large hut. But there was a fire and it was warm. The women and children who lived there . . . He made them leave. They screamed and cried and begged but he held a gun to the youngest child's head. They had no choice. They went out into the snow. It must have been at least minus forty. The kind of cold you can't survive long in. We stumbled over their bodies the next morning. Along with hundreds of others.'

He began to cry. The tears slid easily from his eyes and he made no attempt to wipe them away.

'We destroyed villages, killed thousands, but it's that family I can't stop seeing. Can't stop hearing. We were told they were our enemies, pitiful sub-humans, but they were just people. Civilians.'

He turned to look at me then, his face like crumpled paper. I wished I could smooth away the creases.

'I can no longer look at myself in the mirror, Lisette. I don't know who I am.'

I removed his glasses, placed them on the coffee table and took his face in my hands.

'*I* know who you are,' I said, looking into his eyes. 'You've been my best friend for years. I know you. And you *are* a good man.'

I wiped a tear from his cheek and folded him into my arms, let him sob on my shoulder. I wanted to take his guilt from him, wrap it up and bury it somewhere it would never be found.

We sat like that for a long time, two bodies welded together by his grief. For all his sadness, I couldn't help but feel some joy. He was here with me, in my arms. And then he lifted his face and our lips found one another. His beard tickled my chin and I could taste the saltiness of his tears, the wine on his breath. I pressed myself against him, my body on fire. I moved his hands into my hair, fused his lips to mine. Could he feel my hunger? His eyes were closed but I kept mine open; I didn't want to miss a single second. I didn't care that Mother was a few feet away in her bedroom; he and I were all that existed.

And then he pushed me away, sat up. The spell was broken, the moment snapped in two.

'I can't, Lisette.' He stood up, avoiding my eyes, straightening his clothes. 'I'm sorry. There's someone else . . . I'm so sorry.'

The weight of his words crushed me. I reached over to him once more, tried to find his lips with my own, but I felt his hands on my shoulders, gently pushing me away. He may as well have punched me.

I had loved him half my life, but he loved another.

13

LISETTE

Then – Berlin, 3 June 1943

Clutching our dwindling weekly rations to my chest, I pushed the door open with my bony hip. Inside, I found Mother scrubbing furiously at an invisible stain on Father's armchair, her hands red, the skin on her fingers peeling. The smell of bleach was acrid; I could taste it on my tongue. She groaned as if in great pain and her face was wet with tears. I dropped the bags by the door, the contents spilling across the hardwood floor.

'What is it? What's happened?' I crouched beside her, took her damaged hands in mine.

She lifted her face and I could see it; I didn't need her to tell me. 'Father?'

She nodded and then whispered, 'They have declared him missing in action. Somewhere in Tunisia.'

'But not dead?'

'Missing. What does that mean?' Her voice splintered, her head lolling forward as if it was too heavy for her neck to bear.

'Perhaps he's been captured?'

'Yes. Captured. That must be it.' The suggestion was a gift she grabbed on to with both hands. If I'd known how much the hope would make her suffer, I would have taken back my words, thrown them straight out of the window.

'Yes,' she repeated. 'Not dead. Captured.' The scrubbing stopped, the tears subsided. Within minutes she stood up, smoothed back her hair and wiped her cheeks. Her poise was restored so quickly I thought she had momentarily been possessed.

'What happened to the shopping?' she said, seeing the mess by the door. 'Goodness, let's get this cleared up straight away.'

I followed her and then knelt down beside her to help, all the while watching her face, waiting for the tears to reappear. My own heart felt heavy in my chest, my eyes stinging, but I remained stoic. Together we closed the door to the truth, locking it out in the cold where it would surely be forgotten and eventually die a quiet death.

'Is that the time? We must get ready – we are expected at Frau Weber's in an hour.'

'Let's cancel. Please? I don't want to see Egon. I'm not interested in him. But he simply won't give up. And . . . after the news today . . . let's just be us two tonight.'

I could see the internal battle play out on her face. Mother was never rude; manners were more important than emotions. But she was depleted. We all were. There was a shortage of food, water and basic supplies. The bombing raids were constant, the progressive destruction of our city, the shrapnel-scarred buildings, impossible to ignore, and we lived in perpetual fear that our home would be next.

Julius was gone now, back at the front. Father was missing.

'OK,' Mother said. And with those words, her composure evaporated, her shoulders slumped, and if I had not taken her arm and led her to the sofa, I doubt her legs would have held her up.

'Will you play the piano for me?' she asked. 'I do love it when you play.'

'Of course.'

Night would soon be creeping in and I knew that all that awaited us was an abyss of darkness, but when I sat down to play, I could think of other things. Of Julius and that kiss which would for ever be imprinted on my soul. As my fingers danced over the keys, I relived that moment. He had said there was someone else, I had heard the words, but I didn't quite believe them. Perhaps he feared he'd die in the war and didn't want my consequent sorrow to destroy me. When I played the piano and let my mind wander, I saw our future children, the life we would live, the happiness we would create.

As long as I had my music, I knew Mother and I could get through this. Father would be found, Julius would come home, the killings would stop. The war would end.

14

ELLY

Now – East Berlin, 29 August 1961

The envelope sits on the table, my name written in meticulous script. The address is missing so it must have been hand-delivered. The fact it's unopened means Papa was the one to receive it; in this house, he's the only one who believes in privacy.

I open it in my room, sitting on the bed, my palms sweating. The Stasi would rip the front door from its hinges, not send a letter, but I can't tame the galloping horse in my chest.

> *Fräulein Elly Lange, I would very much like to see you again.*
> *I will be on patrol along Teltowkanal, Johannisthal, this afternoon. I hope you will come and see me.*
> *Liebe Grüße,*
> *The soldier who didn't shoot*

My chest is still heavy, my hands still damp, but a different feeling washes over me – one I don't recognize. It starts in my toes and quickly reaches my face, flushing me with warmth. Perhaps I'm getting a fever.

I carefully rip the paper into minuscule pieces. Then I throw them ceremoniously into the toilet, a handful of confetti, and flush the words away.

As I leave the apartment and climb on to my bike – recently retrieved from the alleyway I abandoned it in – I tell myself I can't meet him. And why would I want to? Anyway, I have plans for today. Time is running out and I need to find a way over the border. Today is a reconnaissance mission and nothing good can come from a friendship with a Soviet soldier.

I try to look casual – just a teenager out on her bike, humming a melody. The heat is oppressive; this morning's rain has done little to cool the city. Steam rises from the wet pavements as if the earth itself is smouldering. Expertly I dodge the potholes filled with dirty rainwater, swerving like a drunk.

I cross the wide boulevard of Unter den Linden and then cycle through the Gendarmenmarkt. Papa says it was once the most beautiful square in Europe, but it lies in ruins now. It's been sixteen years since the war ended but there is still rubble in the streets, and buildings bear the marks of bombs and bullets. Living in Berlin is a constant reminder of what was done all those years ago, the need for us to be punished. All my life, soldiers have roamed the streets and the city has been divided. I hate that I'm German; I hate that I, too, carry our nation's shame on my shoulders. I was born after the war; the guilt shouldn't be mine, and yet it is.

I've dreamed of leaving this city, escaping the past that hangs over it like a brewing storm. I want to see oceans, mountains, rainforests teeming with life – not these crumbling buildings. I want to taste freedom, the kind of anonymous freedom that can only be achieved far from here. But what if I never get out? What if this wall really is permanent and I'm stuck here for ever?

I cycle past Checkpoint Charlie and see the desperate crowds. I imagine their songs but instead of an orchestra of music, it's a chaos of frantic noise. People still gather here every hour of the day, begging in vain for passage, my parents somewhere among them.

I need to go further afield, find a weak spot. They can't man every inch of this metal curtain.

I cycle aimlessly, heading south, keeping as close to the border as I can without raising suspicion. I'm not aware of time passing, only the sweat on my brow and the hunger tapping on my stomach. It's not until the murky water of the Teltowkanal appears in the distance that I realize I've cycled all the way to Johannisthal. Now that I'm here, something else propels me forward. I dismount my bike. My skirt snags on the pedal and I hear it rip. Mama will be angry; it's the third skirt I've ruined in so many months. *YOU'RE SO CARELESS*, she'll write, the words scrawled in capital letters because her voice is still missing and she needs to shout. I'm careless, noisy, messy, incapable of clearing up after myself. I'm all those things and yet sometimes I wonder whether the role of the inconsiderate teenager is something I've fallen into. Something that has been expected of me, so it's who I've become. I don't know why but Mama wants to hate me, and sometimes I want to give her a reason to.

I abandon my bicycle in the high, damp grass and stroll down to the canal. I'm trying so hard to look casual but each movement feels accentuated, like I'm a clown at the circus. I hope I won't see Andrei – I'm not here to see him; this is part of my scouting operation. The Teltowkanal is the perfect place to cross over to the West.

The usually calm water is disturbed by patrolling motorboats and guards are stationed along the sides. Some are smoking, others chat among themselves, but they're all alert, their arms heavy with guns. It's summertime; people should be lounging on the banks, swimming in the water, but instead we're imprisoned and the canal is just one of the bars on our cage.

'Elly Lange.'

He's leaning against a tree, a cigarette dangling from the corner of his mouth. He's in uniform but his hat is askew, the laces of his boots untied. His gun lies abandoned by his feet. He tilts his head, the same way he did a few nights ago, and when he looks at me my breath catches in my throat. A part of me knew I was heading here.

I hear the steady, strong beat of his music and I realize I've been aching to hear it again. It's a melody that shouldn't just exist in my mind. I need to trap it and learn how to play it.

'I was hoping you would show up,' he says, taking one last drag of his cigarette before grinding it out beneath his boot. 'I'm on a break. Join me?'

My body is already shifting towards him before I consciously make the decision to move. Perhaps a friendship with him might be useful.

'Thank you,' I say, 'for the other night.' I struggle to meet his eyes. 'Andrei, right?'

I shift from foot to foot, a childish dance. Suddenly I'm painfully aware of my unbrushed hair, my ripped skirt, the fact I'm carrying my schoolbag and not the trendy but completely impractical clutch bag Papa gave me for my fifteenth birthday. Obviously I don't care what he thinks, but if I'm going to befriend him, perhaps I should make more of an effort with my appearance.

'Do you often kiss boys without knowing their name?' he says, a smile playing on his lips.

Standing this close to him, I can see his eyes are even more striking in daylight – a splash of cerulean blue in a world being bled of its colour.

'Only soldiers,' I reply.

He laughs, raises his eyebrows, and I find myself laughing too.

We wander down to the footpath by the water's edge, falling into step. It's barely wide enough for both of us, and my arm brushes against his as we walk. It feels like we've been here before.

'So, Elly Lange, how are your escape plans going? Were you planning on swimming across the canal today?'

There's no one within hearing distance but I still feel a sharp pinch of fear. This man has the power to throw me in prison or get me sent to a juvenile correctional centre. I need to tread carefully.

'Seriously, though, why?' he says. 'You would risk dying for a better life? East Berlin isn't so bad.'

'Says the Soviet soldier who can leave whenever he wants.'

'I can leave here,' he says. 'But I can't travel. I'm only allowed to return home. Here is better.' He turns to look at me then, a sadness in his eyes. 'Trust me.'

Two soldiers pass us on the path. They're older than Andrei so we're the ones to step aside. They nod at us, give Andrei a knowing look, and I feel my face flush. I'm relieved to be so far from home, in a place where I'm unlikely to bump into someone I know. The Soviets are our enemy. We're no longer at war with them but they patrol our streets and now they're our captors. Mama would be furious if she saw me now, my friends horrified. I know this, yet I can't bring myself to make an excuse and leave.

'My brother – he's just a baby – he's in a hospital on the other side. He was born too early and they think something is wrong with his heart. Mama was with him in the hospital but the night the barrier went up she was at home. She came home just for the night. It was the first time she had left him.' I look at him, study his face for a reaction. 'That's why I need to cross. I need to bring him back.'

He doesn't seem shocked; he simply nods. We're not the only

family who've been separated. I imagine as a border guard he's already heard countless such stories. Perhaps he's immune to them now and the devastation this blockade has caused.

'So, you want to find a way over? And then ... come back again?'

'Yes.' I hesitate, look over my shoulder. 'I mean, I know that sounds ridiculous, but yes, that's what I want to do. Wouldn't you? My parents are distraught. Obviously. Mama's stopped talking and Papa ... I just don't think they can survive this. Axel – that's my brother's name – he's just a baby. He needs to be with Mama. With us.'

'And why is that your responsibility? To get him? To risk your life?'

'Who else is going to?'

Andrei stops and extracts a cigarette from the packet in his breast pocket. He offers it to me but I shake my head. On the bank beside us, rubbish has been caught in the reeds, and there's a film of green on the water that smells strangely soap-like.

I haven't asked a question, but he turns to me then and says, 'OK, Elly Lange, I'll help you.'

I leave him on the bank and go to retrieve my bike. I can feel his eyes on my back as I walk away. But he's not the only one watching me. Boris ambles towards me, swinging his gun. His shoulders are sloped and his head bows forward, like a bull ready to charge.

'Ida,' he says. He comes right up to me, uncomfortably close, his feathery moustache twitching. His breath smells of raw onions and I resist the urge to take a step back. 'Disturbing Andrei again?'

'Just for a few minutes. He was on a break.'

'He's always on a break.' With one chubby finger, he strokes his gun as if it's some kind of pet. 'You should be careful. Of

Andrei. If you want a soldier boyfriend, there are far better ones around.' He puffs out his chest, reminding me of the manky pigeons that strut through the park scavenging for leftovers.

'I'll bear that in mind.'

I sidestep past him and pick up my bike. I'm about to climb on, but something catches my attention further up the canal. The reeds quiver but it's not the wind. Something big is sliding on its belly down the bank. Absurdly, I think it's an alligator and I clench the handlebars, my nails digging into the rubber grips. I glance over my shoulder.

Boris has seen it, too.

The water ripples and the duckweed floating just beneath the surface stirs. I don't see the man slip into the canal – the reeds are obscuring my view – but I see the back of his head just before he dives down. Boris lifts his gun, charges forward. Andrei hasn't noticed; he's twenty metres away, walking in the other direction, his hat tucked underneath his arm. I open my mouth to warn the man in the water, but nothing comes out. Boris is at the edge now, scanning the slow-moving current. The butt of his gun is pressed against his shoulder, his finger on the trigger. There's no way the man can hold his breath and swim the breadth of the canal underwater, but I keep watching the other side, praying that's where I'll see him appear – safe, free.

The first shot is a sharp whistle.

Water sprays upwards.

A mass of dark, wet hair. A head. Shoulders. A swish of splashing arms.

'Don't shoot,' the man screams. 'Please don't shoot.'

He dives down once more. The water is too murky to see anything beneath the surface so Boris starts shooting indiscriminately. Andrei has disappeared but three other soldiers rush to join Boris, their guns raised. My legs are blocks of ice, my heart two sizes too big.

A briefcase bobs to the surface and the man appears once more, gasping for breath.

'*Da drüben* – over there!' a soldier shouts.

Boris looks clumsy, his weight a hindrance, but he swings his gun expertly.

Aims.

Shoots.

The bullet connects with the man's shoulder. He should duck back down, swim on, but inexplicably he turns to face his executioner. Later, I'll imagine that I saw the bullet fly through the air, heard the moment it connected with the man's skull, the skin on his forehead scorching, the ragged entrance wound a bloody ring. But all I really see are his eyes, wide and scared. And then he's gone. His body sinks to the bottom of the canal, no imprint of his life on the surface, just a small, spreading red stain.

15

LISETTE

Then – Berlin, 8 March 1944

Gertrud caught up with me as I left the market, a bag of mouldy vegetables pressed against my chest like a newborn baby. The wind had teeth and everyone kept their heads down, getting their rations then heading swiftly home. We were no longer being bombed only at night. No time of day and no place was safe any more. Berlin had been reduced to rubble and unexploded bombs littered the streets. Our military had suffered major defeats, the siege of Leningrad was over, the Red Army was advancing from the Eastern Front and the Allies were closing in from the west.

'Is Egon visiting today?' Gertrud asked, falling into step beside me.

'I think so,' I said, distracted by the food in my bag. My hunger was a growling beast; the harder I tried to silence it, the louder it snarled.

'Not this way,' she said, grabbing my arm. 'The whole street is gone. We'll have to go around.'

'Are you coming to mine?'

'Well, yes. We made a plan.' She frowned. 'Don't you remember?' And then, 'Egon said he would try to bring chocolate . . .'

'He did, didn't he?' I felt a smile form on my lips. It stretched my dry, flaking skin and I imagined the sight would scare a small child. I didn't want to see Egon but his presence pleased Mother and the promise of chocolate was too tempting to resist.

'Perhaps it's time you gave Egon a chance,' Gertrud said, helping me over a mound of broken bricks. The snow had melted to dirty slush, leaving them slippery, and I would have lost my balance if Gertrud hadn't gripped my elbow. She was surprisingly strong and I was glad of her company. It had been almost six years since the war had started and the city was full of hungry, desperate people; it was better to be two.

'He has been trying ever so hard,' she continued. 'And he's not so bad, is he?'

'Actually—'

'Yes, I quite agree. A distinguished soldier. And from a decent family, I hear.'

'He's not Julius,' I said simply.

'Well, obviously not. But' – she shrugged – 'beggars can't be choosers.'

It had been sixty-three days since I'd received a letter from Julius. Each morning Mother and I both watched the letterbox, waiting for the whoosh and the metal clang that never came.

'I've been meaning to ask you,' Gertrud said. 'I've got this rash. It's here on the back of my neck. I'm worried it's meningitis. Would you mind taking a look?'

'I'd rather not.'

'Yes, you're quite right. Not here in the street. I'll show you when we get to your apartment.'

Up ahead, Krista bounded towards us. 'Lisette, Lisette.' She'd grown taller in the last few months, but thinner too; it looked as though she'd been stretched like a piece of dough.

'Look,' she said, halting abruptly in front of us. 'I've got new boots.' She lifted one foot at a time, moved them this way and that. The boots were a deep burgundy, clunky and too big for her, but they had good thick soles and would be the envy of all the neighbourhood kids.

'They look great.'

'Thank you.' She smiled widely, showing her oversized, gappy teeth. 'Can I come and play the piano this afternoon?'

'Not today. Gertrud here is coming over. Tomorrow, though.'

She glanced at Gertrud shyly. 'OK. See you tomorrow.' She threw her arms around me in a brief squeeze of affection then bounded off again without a backward glance.

'Gosh, what an annoying girl,' Gertrud said, taking my elbow once more as if I needed a guide to lead me home.

'Krista? Not at all. She's really sweet. One of our neighbours and—'

'Oh, well. Good on you . . .'

'Good on me for what?'

'Well, goodness, I don't know. Having the patience, I suppose.'

Ahead of us, an old woman was carrying a bag of belongings. The weight of it forced her to walk almost doubled over. As we watched, her bag fell to the pavement. Pots and pans and clothes spilled out of it. She had a familiar look of shock on her face, a look that belonged to someone whose home was gone, ripped apart by a falling bomb.

I rushed forward but Gertrud held me back, shaking her head. 'She'll ask for help,' Gertrud whispered. 'Help we can't give.'

On her knees, the woman began gathering her things together. No one else helped her either, and I wondered where she would go, how long she would survive.

'We should've helped her,' I said, once we'd turned a corner.

'We barely have enough food for ourselves. We can't take in strays.'

'Next time it might be us.'

~

'It's clear our enemies are becoming desperate,' Egon said as I paced the room.

I couldn't stop thinking about my hunger – its fingernails scratched inside my stomach, its voice a hollow drum. Our rations had diminished over the winter months and the air wheezing out from our coal-starved stove was pathetically tepid. My stomach cramped and I shivered constantly, but then the bombs came and the hunger and the cold were no longer what I feared most.

'Yes, I quite agree,' Gertrud said, stoking the fire to life, poking it like she was trying to rouse a dead animal.

Egon stretched his arms out across the back of the sofa and rested his boots on the coffee table. 'They know they're losing the war.'

'Or it is *we* who are losing the war,' I said.

Gertrud looked up sharply. 'Lisette, don't say such things.'

'Enough talk of war,' Egon said. 'It's not befitting for charming young ladies such as yourselves. And, as promised, I have come bearing gifts.'

He placed a decorated tin box on the table. It had a deep lid with a recessed line around the top and a raised design depicting a couple embracing. The words *A woman never forgets the man who remembers* were embossed in cursive text beneath it. The very sight of the box made my mouth water. It had a similar effect on Gertrud. Though she was immaculately dressed, the war was taking its toll on her too. Exhaustion had bruised the skin beneath her eyes and her sharp shoulder blades looked like clipped wings beneath her dress. Egon seemed to be the only energetic, undamaged soul in Berlin. While the rest of us were wasting away, his jowls still jiggled. And while others finally began to falter, he remained forever faithful to his Führer. His fingernails were chewed to the quick, though, and his podgy fingers were red and cracked. Perhaps, I thought, there *was* something eating at his soul.

'Here, take one,' he said, offering me the box. I opened it but the paradox of choice overwhelmed me. I stared at the chocolates stupidly. What I really wanted to do was stuff them all greedily into my mouth before anyone else got the chance.

'Try the toffee one,' Egon said, picking his teeth with a dirty fingernail.

I plucked it out, popped it in my mouth and tried to resist swallowing it whole. I kept my eyes closed and savoured the smooth, creamy chocolate, the tacky toffee that stuck to the roof of my mouth and coated my teeth with a sweetness that was almost too pleasurable to bear. My jaw ached with the unfamiliar effort of chewing, but I never wanted to stop.

I started to pace once more, my mouth now intolerably empty.

'Lisette. Please,' Gertrud said. 'Stop marching around. You're making me feel dizzy.'

'Sorry.' I forced myself to perch on the windowsill, the frost-covered pane stinging my back. How long could I wait before taking another chocolate?

'I've actually been feeling dizzy quite a lot lately,' Gertrud said. 'I'm starting to worry there's something seriously wrong. It's impossible to find a good doctor these days. Someone who actually knows what they're doing.'

'It certainly is,' Egon said. 'And bouts of dizziness aren't something to brush aside. I have connections – I'll ask around and see if I can find a good physician for you.'

Egon puffed out his chest like a bird preparing for a mating dance. Gertrud beamed. I suddenly recalled how irritating I found her.

'"Healthy female workers between the ages of twenty and forty wanted for a military site,"' Gertrud read from the newspaper resting on her lap. 'We should apply, Lisette, don't you think?'

'Well—'

'Yes, I quite agree. And the wages are good, plus there's free board.'

'Let me see,' Egon said, reaching out to take the paper. Dark patches had formed around his armpits and the sickly smell of sweat filled the space between us.

'Ah yes, this is at Ravensbrück – where I work.'

He smiled at Gertrud and her face seemed to brighten.

'You should definitely apply. The guards live in the most beautiful cottages with balconies overlooking a forest and a lake. I'm sure you would adore it there, and I could even put in a good word.'

'That would be wonderful, Egon,' Gertrud said, biting into another chocolate. 'We all must help the war effort. It's our duty, after all.' This last bit was for Egon and, if I had been in any doubt before, it was now abundantly clear a romance was brewing between the two of them. For a brief moment, I felt a tickle of betrayal. But then I looked over at him – his beady eyes, his small lips that were swallowed up by his cheeks whenever he smiled, the sweat glistening permanently on his upper lip even on this cold afternoon – and I remembered how much he repelled me. Gertrud was more than welcome to him.

'You will apply too, won't you, Lisette?' she said. 'The rations will be much better.'

'I'm not sure.'

'Why not?'

There were rumours. And though I tried to refuse them any

space among my other troubling thoughts, they swarmed in my mind like a group of persistent, stinging bees.

'Well, Ravensbrück,' I said, 'it's a . . . labour camp, isn't it? For Jews?'

'Not just Jews,' Egon said, biting into a chocolate. 'Other criminals, too.'

'I've heard things. About their treatment.'

'Goodness, you can't believe everything you hear on the Berlin grapevine,' Gertrud said. 'It's just enemy propaganda. Isn't it, Egon?'

I could feel the weight of his hesitation on my own shoulders. I worried the truth lay in that brief silence.

But then he said, 'Well, of course. The Jews are perfectly happy among their own. I dare say they prefer it. And soon they will be resettled elsewhere. A few months of hard work never hurt anyone.'

His words didn't set my mind at ease. So much more was going on than what we were being told. I was sure of it. I could still see the face of that mother who'd called out to me on the street, the little boy in her arms. Stories of atrocities were trickling into Berlin, following us around like shadows. It would have been easier to ignore them but I couldn't. Others – through fear, ignorance or sheer selfishness – chose to look at the sun so the shadows fell behind them, unseen but still present.

'Come on. It will be so much fun working together.' Gertrud was persistent but half-heartedly so. This job would give her and Egon's romance a chance to blossom; she knew I would only be in the way.

'No. I can't. I don't want to be . . . a part of it. Anyway, I can't leave Mother alone. Not when Father . . . I just can't.' I took two more chocolates, swallowing them without savouring them this time. With a stab of panic, I wondered how many we should save for Mother.

I twisted around and looked out of the window behind me. It was early afternoon but these days a smoky darkness hung persistently over the city I'd once loved. Berlin had been mortally wounded. The roads had gashes in them, buses and trams were no longer running, the streets were full of rubble, and the constant fires cast a gloom as if the sun had abandoned us. Opposite, I could see an empty space. A pile of beams and bricks and twisted metal where a building had once stood. The house beside it was devoid of its roof, and another was missing some walls – Berlin was becoming a city full of doll's houses, the facades of buildings stripped away so we could all peek inside.

How long until our building also fell to its knees? How long before death found its way to us too?

16

LISETTE

Then – Berlin, 18 March 1945

I sat on the edge of the Spree, letting my feet dangle, listening to the music of gurgling water. I pretended it was another time, another life. The grass was damp and cold and it would leave a stain on my skirt but I didn't care. It was so wonderful to be outside and away from everything.

I lay down, closed my eyes and took a deep breath, ignoring my scratchy throat, the dust irritating my eyes, the smell of smoke. Instead I focused on the birds, the babble of the fast-flowing river and the promise of spring. The zoo was destroyed, Café Kranzler flattened, but they couldn't take the Spree.

Though I tried to empty my mind, I found myself worrying about Mother. I shouldn't have left her alone at home – she seemed to be shrinking and fading before my eyes; her clothes hung loose, her cheekbones were sharp, and most days her hair remained loose and unbrushed, her lips devoid of colour, which somehow distressed me most. Krista was probably looking for me, too – I had promised her a piano lesson – but I needed to take a moment to breathe.

I felt the first bomb before I heard it. The ground vibrated as if it was trembling in fear. My heart skipped a beat and I opened my eyes. Above me, dozens of planes were swooping and shooting. I had to run and find cover. But I couldn't move.

Another explosion rattled the earth and still I didn't budge.

Our apartment building was too far away. I needed to find somewhere closer. But my mind wouldn't work; my thoughts were too scrambled.

I wanted to crawl but I forced myself to stand. Friedrichstraße. The station had already been bombed; surely it wouldn't be again. I began to run.

The bombers streaked through the sky, banking left then right. I heard the flak guns from the towers. There were teenagers operating them now, children much younger than me – that's what we'd heard. Weapons manned by the Hitler Youth as all our men were at the front. Did those kids know what they were doing? Would they be capable of protecting us?

The streets were a sea of rubble. I tripped over some bricks, fell to my knees. A sob rose in my chest. Shock waves of bombs shook the ground and I watched in horror as a building further up the street collapsed in a roar of falling concrete. I scrambled to my feet, my hands and legs wet with blood. But I felt no pain. A cloud of dust encircled me.

'This way.'

A woman's disembodied voice and then the touch of someone's hand in mine.

Blind, I stumbled and fell once more, but the hand pulled me up, yanked me forward. My eyes were full of grit, my throat burned, my lungs heaved with the effort of each breath, but I forced myself to keep moving.

We were descending some stairs. And though I couldn't see them, I could feel the press of moving bodies both in front of me and behind. I steadied myself against the solid brick wall to my right. If one person lost their footing, we would all tumble.

The stairs came to an end and I knew I was on the U-Bahn platform. I could feel the open space even though it was filled with a tide of people who were carrying me along with them.

When I reached a wall, I pressed myself against it, slid down and staked my claim. Pulling my knees into my chest, I waited for my breathing to slow, for my heart to stop thumping.

The air felt cooler down here, the dust no longer choking me, but it smelled strongly of urine and sweat. There was another thundering roar and the walls shook. A shiver passed through the spine of the station. The crowd fell silent, as if the enemy might be able to hear us, as if our silence might save us.

Another explosion, closer this time, and I ducked my head instinctively. I thought of Mother, of Krista. I hoped they were in the basement, prayed they were safe. And I thought of Julius, somewhere at the front. Father and Wilhelm, too. Alive – because they had to be alive.

Time seemed interminable. Beside me a small boy cried softly as his mother murmured in his ear. 'And Alice,' she whispered to her son, 'had never seen a rabbit with either a waistcoat-pocket or a watch to take out of it.'

On my other side, an old man sat with his head bowed, his arms resting on his knees. He was wheezing and his whole body trembled. I took his hand, held it firmly in my own. For me or for him, I wasn't sure.

'It will be over soon,' I said. 'Soon.'

I closed my eyes, shut out the sound of the war raging above us. And then I heard something else. Music. The shaking, reedy sound of a harmonica. And then someone began to sing. A young woman's voice, pure and beautiful. '*Es geht alles vorüber,*' she sang. 'Everything will pass, everything will come to an end.' Her voice held and then let go of each note, allowing them to drift gently into the air like delicate feathers. 'Every December will be followed by a May. Once the war is over, the soldiers will come back home.'

The bombs kept on falling, the ground continued to shake. But for a while, the music was all I could hear.

~

I emerged from the ground, dusty and dazed, earlier than my instincts told me would be safe. But the sky was clear, the planes gone. For now. We looked like corpses released from our underground graves with vacant eyes and grey skin. The world was strangely silent.

I guessed it was late afternoon but there was no way of knowing for sure. I picked my way through broken brick and cement. I don't know how long it took me to get back home. I would turn a corner to find a whole street gone, craters where buildings should have stood. There were bodies, too, but I averted my eyes, kept my focus on the fractured road ahead. The smell of burnt hair was something I didn't dare dwell on.

When I finally got back to Chausseestraße, I had to climb a mound of debris. As I reached the top, several bricks came loose and tumbled down in front of me. I slid a few feet, my hands scrabbling to grip on to something stable, the crumbling cement causing a small avalanche of dust.

I stood up, digging my knuckles into my eyes, desperate to see. Was it still standing? The dust settled and a moan escaped my lips. And then tears of relief sprang from my eyes. Our home was still there. The whole front of the building next door had been torn off – I could see inside each apartment, the house like a body without skin, its organs on display. But our house was untouched.

'Lisette, Lisette,' a woman screeched, running towards me. At first, I didn't recognize her, but then I saw her eyes. Krista and Wilhelm's mother – Patricia, that was her name.

'Have you seen her?' She grabbed my shoulders, shook me violently. 'Answer me. Have you seen Krista? Was she with you when it started?'

'With me? What? No, I . . . I haven't seen her.'

She began to wail.

'She went to look for you,' she sobbed. 'You were supposed to have a lesson. You weren't home. So she went to look for you.'

'We'll find her,' I said, trying to focus. 'She'll have gone for cover when it started. She's a smart girl,' I added, as if her intelligence could somehow have staved off a bomb.

Around us the walking dead continued to clamber out of basements, shielding their eyes against the sudden light or perhaps the destruction all around them.

Suddenly, Patricia fell silent. I followed her gaze to a mound of rubble piled high on the other side of the street.

And then I saw it. A burgundy boot. And beside it, pallid and small, a foot. Without thinking, I walked over, crouched down, pulled the foot from the wreckage, expecting a leg, a torso to follow, but there was just a foot. A child's foot, pale and dusty, and still vaguely warm. As I held it, it grew cold like a porcelain doll. There was no blood on it, just dust. Further up I saw the back of a head, two blonde plaits, and I knew. I knew.

~

Mother found me an hour later, still cradling Krista's foot. It was as if I myself had been ripped apart by a mortar, crushed by those stones. She wasn't my child, nor my sister, yet the grief felt unconquerable. I couldn't even imagine the tidal wave of emotions her mother was going through. She'd collapsed and been led away by some neighbours, her cries still echoing down the street.

I'd heard of other children dying and there were rumours of children murdered by my own country's army, but it was the death of this child, a child I knew and loved, that showed me what an awful world we lived in. The guilt of my own involvement had been muted until this point, buried under the broken bricks of my own denial. We were bystanders, not perpetrators. But in that moment, I realized we were all guilty. And we would be punished.

17

ELLY

Now – East Berlin, 10 September 1961

Mama has been standing in the living room staring at a spot on the wall for twenty minutes now. Since Axel's separation from us, she's been doing this more frequently. I don't know if she's lost in a fog of memory, or whether her mind just goes blank. Either way, she disappears and only Papa is able to coax her back. But Papa isn't here.

I glance at the clock – it's almost ten a.m. I don't want to be late but I don't feel right leaving her when she's like this. Oma Rita is here but that's not particularly reassuring. Eventually Mama will snap out of it, act as if nothing ever happened, but with her voice gone and her music muted, I'm worried about her.

'Mama?' I take her hand in mine and tug gently. Her hand remains limp, her feet two blocks of concrete. Irritation swells inside me. I'm risking everything for her and yet she can't pull herself together enough to move from this square of faded carpet.

I tug again, a little harder this time. I can feel my armpits growing damp, my newly applied make-up starting to slide.

'It's the blood,' Oma Rita says from her chair by the window. The sun is streaming in through the glass and dust particles circle above her head like a strange living halo. 'That's what she's looking at. The blood on the wall.'

'What blood?'

'It's always there. I've scrubbed and scrubbed but it's seeped into the plaster.'

With both hands, she pushes herself up and out of her chair. Oma Rita isn't that old but lately her movements have become stilted. I suspect the same would happen to anyone who never goes anywhere. The courtyard is usually the furthest Oma Rita will venture, and even that's rare; she doesn't seem to realize this flat has become a prison of her own making.

'Music sometimes helps,' Oma Rita says. 'Not the piano, of course. Definitely not the piano. But singing. I think that's what your father does.'

'He sings to her?' I've never heard him sing. I'm pretty sure he doesn't have a musical bone in his body. Then again, when Mama is being like this, I usually retreat elsewhere, let him deal with her. It isn't normal – these moments of hers – I know that much, and usually I don't want to make the situation worse with my presence.

Oma Rita steps in front of Mama, blocking her view of the wall and whatever it is she's looking at. She's on the verge of taking Mama's arm but she stops short, her hand hovering an inch from Mama's lifeless fingers. She begins to hum a tune, something I vaguely recognize but can't quite place. The gesture is so intimate I find myself taking a step back, averting my eyes.

The melody is beautiful – calm yet uplifting – and I commit it to memory, vowing to play it later on my keyboard. Mama blinks once, twice, then shakes her head. The spell is broken.

'It is OK, Elly. I have her,' Oma Rita says. Without touching her, she guides Mama to the sofa. Mama looks dazed, as if she's just woken from a deep sleep. It's odd seeing their roles reversed. Perhaps one day I'll be the one being led.

'Off you go,' Oma Rita says, sitting Mama down then ushering me towards the front door. 'Don't keep him waiting. Lisette will be fine.'

'Him?' A blush creeps up my neck.

'You're meeting a boy.'

It's a statement not a question, and I don't deny it; she'll forget soon enough. 'What makes you say that?'

'For starters, your hair is brushed and you're wearing make-up. You're always hungry but you haven't eaten anything today. And I know that look. I've *had* that look. Just be careful. Men are tricky creatures.'

She smiles at me and in this rare moment of lucidity, I can see the woman she once was – the person she is – behind the confusion and memory loss that so often keep her fragmented. I'm tempted to stay awhile; I don't know when she will next be this present. But the clock is ticking and the soldier who didn't shoot is waiting for me.

When I arrive he's already nabbed a table outside in the shade of a tree, a large slice of chocolate cake sitting untouched in front of him, a cigarette in one hand and a book in the other. His long legs are stretched out, crossed at the ankles. He's wearing his uniform, clean but creased, and his hat sits on the table. He looks happily at ease.

The corner café is busy but the tables beside him are empty; no one wants to associate with a *Grenztruppen* border guard, especially a Soviet one. The weather is turning, too; the days are shortening, the leaves starting to yellow and curl. The days are getting cooler and the nights are starting to bite. Soon we'll all be huddled inside, hiding from winter's chill.

I take a moment to observe him. His nose is a little crooked, as if he once broke it and it never set properly. I keep telling myself I don't find him attractive – I would never find a Russki handsome – but it's impossible to deny it. Since it happened, that kiss has never been far from my mind, however much I try to ignore it. It was my first kiss, so it's understandable I'm struggling to forget it, but it meant nothing. I'm fascinated by his music, though, and I know that's also why my thoughts keep returning to him.

Even though I'm far from home, in a neighbourhood I rarely come to, I look around and make sure I don't see anyone I know. I tug my hat down and tuck my hair in before strolling over to him.

He smiles when he sees me. He has a dimple on his chin. It makes him look younger, kinder, less dangerous than I know he is. Every night, just as my consciousness begins to slide away, I remember the man in the canal. Andrei was not the one who shot him, but it could have been him. I can't let myself forget that.

He grinds out his cigarette in an overflowing ashtray and stands up, pulling out the other chair, its metal feet scraping the pavement with an unpleasant screech. It's something no one has ever done for me before and I can't help but laugh. He frowns and I worry I've offended him.

'Elly Lange, it's good to see you.' I love how he says my full name, as if it's the most beautiful name he's ever heard and not the boring middle-class German name of a nobody.

'I'm sorry I'm late,' I say, sitting down. 'Have you been waiting long? Mama was . . . she needed me for something. And then I had to do the dishes, make some food for my grandmother, finish this tune I was writing. And there was a rat in the kitchen. And then . . .'

'There was a rat in your kitchen?'

'Well, no. But there could have been. I mean, there were droppings.'

Andrei laughs and, behind it, I can hear his music again. Its solid, unwavering beat calms my pounding heart as I pretend to look at the menu. I listen to the way our tunes converge, twist around each other until they become one song. The new melody it creates is beautiful and I never want to stop hearing it. I wonder what he sees or hears when I'm present. Can he sense the strange connection we have? Is that why he wants to help me?

'Have you been here before?' he asks, waving at the waiter to get his attention. 'Prenzlauer Berg is my favourite part of Berlin. It's the least . . . destroyed.'

I shrug. 'It's still grey and ugly like the rest of this city.'

He smiles. 'So where would you rather be?'

'Anywhere but here,' I say. 'Wouldn't you?' But it's not true. Right now, there's nowhere else I'd rather be. Perhaps I'm already feeling nostalgic for East Berlin because I know I'm soon going to leave it. 'New York, maybe. Somewhere creative and colourful. Somewhere that no type of music is a crime.'

'You're musical. What instrument do you play?'

'The piano. Well, the keyboard. That's what I want to do when I'm older. Compose music, travel the world playing in an orchestra. Or maybe a band.' I blush but he smiles at me and tilts his head.

'I hope you manage it one day.'

'Me too.'

The waiter comes, a bespectacled boy with bad skin but beautiful brown eyes and floppy hair. He reminds me of Otto and guilt pinches me. Otto, Monika and I have never had any secrets – our friendship has existed as long as we have – but suddenly I'm keeping from them not only my plans to escape but my friendship with this soldier.

The waiter clears his throat, waits for my order. I can see his disapproval; I can hear it in his music – the short, jumpy, staccato notes that make up his song. He glances at Andrei who seems oblivious to this boy's hatred. The waiter doesn't say the words but I know what he's thinking – a Russki soldier and his German whore.

'She'll have a coffee,' Andrei says. Ordering for me is the kind of thing Mama does, her impatience too much to bear in the face of my indecision. Perhaps it's a trait they share or maybe he just wants to get rid of the waiter.

I nod, though I know I won't drink it. Stupidly, I chose a white blouse today and there's no way my shaky fingers won't result in a spill.

'What are you reading?' I ask, picking up Andrei's book, once the man has gone back inside.

'Actually, it's for you,' he says. 'I've already read it – I think you'll like it.'

I'm equally touched and confused. We don't know each other. How could he possibly know what kind of book I might enjoy?

'*On the Road*. What's it about?'

'Music, poetry, freedom. Read it quickly,' he says, giving me a wink. 'The GDR will ban it soon enough.'

Without consciously wanting to, I find myself relaxing. I want to sit here all day in Andrei's company, discover everything there is to know about him. Knowledge is power and if I'm going to use him to achieve my goal, I should find out everything I can about him. I need to do it quickly, though. My heart beats like a clock, a constant reminder that time is running out. We have no idea how Axel is, or if he's even alive, but if I am to have any chance of getting to the West and bringing him home, then I need to act now. Apartment windows on the border have already been cemented up, the barrier is turning into an unscaleable wall. Soon there won't be any escape routes left.

The waiter arrives with my coffee and then retreats without a word. I glance over my shoulder, look past Andrei as well. There's no one close enough to hear me speak but I whisper all the same. 'You said . . . when I saw you last . . . you said you'd help me.'

'I did,' he says, leaning towards me and lowering his voice.

His eyes are the colour of the sea – shades of rippling green and dazzling blue. I feel like I might fall into them.

A pigeon swoops from the tree, a handful of leaves fluttering down in its wake. The bird, dirty and scrawny, settles on the next-door table, eyeing the untouched slice of cake. Andrei offers me a fork but I shake my head. He shrugs and helps himself. We're discussing something that could have us both killed yet he's a picture of calm.

'My mother used to make the most amazing chocolate cake,' he says, taking a bite.

If it wasn't for Andrei's uniform, my sweating palms, the waiter's eyes boring into me from behind the counter inside, it would feel like a date.

'There was always more icing than cake,' he continues, taking another bite.

A crumb sits on his lower lip and I have a bizarre urge to lick it off.

'It's strange how a taste or a smell can transport you home,' he continues.

'When were you last there? Home? You must miss your family.'

'It's been a while. But I have family here too. My father's stationed in the city. My cousin as well. I didn't want to be a soldier but it was the easiest thing to do. Less hassle. And my father insisted. He's not a man you argue with.'

'And you like it here? Berlin?'

'I like it more now.'

He smiles, a row of perfect teeth. I find myself smiling too, grinning stupidly like the schoolgirl I am. The Russkis are ruthless, cruel. I know this; I've been told a hundred times. They invaded our country and never left, burrowing themselves into our city like maggots infesting human flesh. I shouldn't trust Andrei – he's one of them; his partner blasted a hole through a man's head without a second of hesitation. I know I shouldn't trust him, but I do. His music alone confirms his kindness. Otto and Monika think I'm crazy when I talk like this, that I can't trust the music I hear in people, but it's never failed me. If they could hear it too, they'd understand.

'I need to get back soon.' They're not the words I want to say. There's a strange battle raging within me, but I have a plan, and I need to stick to it.

I glance over my shoulder again. I almost check under the table.

'What are you thinking?' I whisper. 'Where can I cross?'

He doesn't move – his shoulders remain relaxed, a smile still playing on his lips – but I see the way he also scans the space around us. He's more cautious than he appears. As he should be – as we both should be.

'I think your best chance is to wade through the sewers,' he says finally. 'The sewer system was created before our occupation and there are no barriers between East and West. It won't be pleasant, I grant you, but I think it could work. But we need to plan.'

'What planning do we need to do? Couldn't I go today . . . tonight? Surely it will only be a matter of time before this route is discovered? I don't want to miss my chance.'

'You're impatient, Elly Lange. And impulsive.'

He laughs but not unkindly. Pushing the remains of the cake aside, he lights a cigarette, closes his eyes and draws in a deep breath. 'First, I need to get my hands on a map of the sewers. You can't go down there blindly, splashing about in—'

'Shit?'

'Well, yes.' He laughs again. 'We need to figure out where you should climb down and where you should climb up on the other side. It's an intricate system; you could get lost down there. And then there are the people here – your family, your friends.'

'What about them?'

I feel a presence before I see anyone. The air stirs, shifting to make room. Beside me, Andrei stiffens, balances his cigarette in the ashtray, the smoke rising and swirling between us. He takes my hand, perhaps to reassure me or maybe to stop me from bolting. Someone appears from the alleyway a few metres away and then moves behind the tree, dry leaves crunching softly beneath their feet. A man. He must be in his fifties, broad and tall but with an obvious slouch. With him is a small, rat-like dog with tufty white fur. And yes, he could just be a man walking his dog, but he's too close and it doesn't feel safe any more.

The man glances up and our eyes meet briefly. Do I know him? Have I seen him before? Then he moves away, crosses the street, the little dog trotting after him, struggling to keep up.

Andrei stands up and tosses some Marks on the table – more than we can possibly owe for our drinks and cake. 'Let's go,' he says, taking my hand once more. He walks quickly and I almost trip but he catches me around my waist, which makes my heart stumble instead. I follow him down a side street where the cobbles are uneven and my slingbacks keep slipping off my heels.

'Where are we going? Was that man a . . .?'

'I think he was just someone walking his dog. But I've learned to always trust my instincts. If something doesn't feel right, get out.'

We turn another corner just as it starts to rain. At first it falls lightly, a vague dampness in the air, but then I hear the menacing growl of an approaching storm and great baubles of water begin to fall from the sky, drenching us in seconds. We run down Schönhauser Allee and duck under the S-Bahn bridge just as a train rattles overhead. The space is open but we stand by one of the concrete piles and the sheets of rain on either side of us give us some privacy.

We're alone.

Andrei is standing so close to me that I can feel his heat, see drops of rain trembling in his hair. My clothes are sodden, but I imagine the water evaporating off my warm skin, the molecules escaping and mixing with his.

'So . . .' I say, leaning back against the pillar, feeling its round bumps press into my spine. 'You don't think he was a Stasi informer?'

'Probably not, but we need to be careful. Here we can talk.'

I nod, look down at my feet, anywhere but his face. He pulls out his cigarettes, rummages in his pocket for his lighter. It's a Zippo and, when he pulls it out, I can see his name is engraved on it. I can't help wondering who gave it to him.

'You said – before – something about my family and friends? What about them?'

'They don't know about your plan, do they?'

'Of course not. They'd try to stop me.'

'Well, yes, I imagine losing one child is bad enough . . . So, you are just going to disappear?'

'I'll leave a note, explaining. Let them know I'm coming back.'

'People will wonder where you are,' he says. 'Questions will be asked; the Stasi will be informed. Your family interrogated.'

'I . . . hadn't thought about that,' I say, shaking my head, feeling my face grow hot. Had I honestly thought I could just vanish and no one would wonder where I'd gone?

'You're in school, no?'

'Yes, the new term starts tomorrow.'

I try to focus on what he's saying, but his eyes are such a

strange shade of blue and I can see now there are rings around his irises that are a shade darker, almost purple. I look away; I need to listen. What he's saying is important – this is why I'm here.

'The best thing would be to wait until your half-term holiday, but I know you'll think that's too long. My suggestion is that you tell your friends a relative in another city is sick, that you have to go and visit her. You'll need to mention it somehow to the informant in your building.'

'The informant in my building?'

'There's a Stasi informant in almost every building in Berlin,' he says. And even though we all know this to be true, hearing it said out loud so matter-of-factly makes me shiver. This is why everyone wants to leave. How can we ever be happy, ever breathe freely, when we are always being watched?

'Herr Krause,' I say. 'He lives opposite us. It'll be him. He's hardly subtle about it.' I'd always thought him harmless – annoying and nosy, yes, but ultimately harmless. Now I understand the full weight of his power, everyone's potential power – to denounce.

'Obviously you can't tell your family your plans beforehand but, when you go, make sure you leave them a note explaining the lie you've told everyone else.'

I nod, already imagining the moment they discover I'm gone, the fury Mama will feel, but perhaps the hope, too. Because I'm doing this for her. She'll understand that. And I won't – I can't – return unless I have Axel with me.

'Assuming you do manage to find Axel, how were you planning on explaining his reappearance?'

I pull my lips over my teeth, look down at my feet.

He grins. 'Don't worry. Actually, I have an idea. You can leave that with me.'

My eyes burn. 'Why are you helping me?'

'Honestly,' he says, 'I'm not entirely sure. I know what it's like to be separated from the ones you love. Perhaps that's it. And there's just something about you, Elly Lange.'

With these words, he narrows the gap between us and tilts my chin upwards. Our eyes meet. The moment stretches, folds and then implodes. For a moment, I think he'll kiss me. And I know the distinct, earthy smell of rain, the cigarette smoke and the sound of a train clattering overhead will for ever remind me of it. But then he takes a step back and smiles. There's a heavy feeling in my chest. It feels like disappointment, but I know it must be relief.

18

LISETTE

Then – Berlin, 2 April 1945

There were few people out on the road, but we were running out of food and I had to collect our rations. I pushed my bicycle through the deserted, dusty streets. I worried about the lack of clouds in the sky; even through the smoke, I could see patches of terrifying blue. Silently I begged for rain and cloud cover so we wouldn't be seen by enemy planes.

The air was acrid, the neighbourhood broken, Berlin ruined. Krista gone. Why couldn't they leave us alone?

Krista.

A stab of loss and guilt cut through me, puncturing a lung. Krista was dead. And it was my fault. I knew it; everyone knew it. Almost everyone. Wilhelm didn't know it yet, but soon would.

'But where were you?' Mother had asked. 'You were supposed to give her a lesson that day.' What could I have said? I was lounging by the river . . . I needed space? And now Krista was gone. Because of me.

I joined a queue of dishevelled Berliners. Our rations had been cut again but no one was grumbling about food; we were hungry, but our main distraction was fear.

'They're coming,' the woman in front of me said to her friend. She was short and I found myself leaning against the brick wall so I didn't tower above her.

'Berlin will never fall,' her friend replied.

I absorbed the woman's words but all I could hear were Krista's mother's howls. All I could see was Krista's foot.

'Look around you,' I said, suddenly furious at this stranger's denial. 'Berlin has already fallen.'

The woman turned and looked at me sharply. Her eyes were small, her face a map of wrinkles. She took her friend's arm and shuffled forward. I wanted to seize her head between my hands, dig my fingernails into her scalp and shake her, make her see the truth. We were losing. We were dying. And if the rumours were true, we deserved this.

'She's right,' the smaller woman whispered. 'Berlin's destroyed and the Soviets are coming. Did you see those photographs? Of the East Prussian village? They raped and murdered all the women. Little girls, too.'

'An exaggeration, probably staged,' her friend cut in. 'Germany won't surrender. We *can't* surrender.'

'We have no men left to defend us.'

'Enough. It will be fine.' But then she added, 'If we must, we will hide.'

The line lumbered forward. A plume of smoke moved across the sun and I shivered in the shadow of it. Suddenly, there was a commotion ahead. A flurry of whispers travelled along the queue.

'Refugees,' someone said. 'At least twenty.'

And then I saw them. A group of women and children stumbling towards us, the youngest hanging off their mothers like baby monkeys, the older ones clinging to each other's torn shirts. Like a cloud full of raindrops, they moved as one, expertly avoiding the piles of bricks and keeping their distance from the crumbling facades of bombed-out buildings. They stopped outside the shop, eyeing the empty window display, and then turned their attention to us. Their faces were streaked with grime, their shoes worn thin. The day wasn't hot but they were sweating with the effort of dragging their tired, starving bodies across the country. The smell hit me like a crashing wave. The ladies in front of me visibly recoiled, turning their heads so they could avoid eye contact, but an old man who'd just collected his rations stepped forward and spoke.

'*Guten Tag.*'

He was old and weak but several of the refugees flinched and took a step back. One girl buried her face in the folds of her mother's skirt and began to cry softly.

He lifted his arms, showed the palms of his hands – a sign of peace – and said, 'Where have you come from?'

The oldest woman was the one to speak. 'Do you have any food?'

An exchange – food for information. The man hesitated and I was ashamed by the relief I felt that I didn't yet have anything to offer.

'Just a little,' she said. 'For the youngest.'

Her face was bruised and one of her front teeth was missing, a bloody gap in its place. I was suddenly overwhelmed with the feeling that I was her and she was me. I was looking at my future self.

Slowly the man opened his leather satchel, pulled out a hunk of bread and ripped off a small piece. He handed it over with an apologetic shrug. 'We don't have much ourselves.'

The woman jumped forward and snatched it, as if afraid the man might change his mind. She handed it to one of the other women, who carefully divided it up among the youngest children. The bread was gone in moments but the children continued to stare wide-eyed at the man's bag. If he'd been alone in the dead of night, I didn't doubt the whole satchel would have disappeared before he knew what had happened.

'We've come from East Prussia. Königsberg.' The woman embedded herself once more in her group.

'We should have left sooner,' she continued, tucking a dirty strand of hair back underneath her scarf. 'We became trapped. There was nothing to eat and there were only bad choices left. If we'd stayed, we would've starved to death. We could have tried to get to Pillau, but the only way was across the frozen Vistula Lagoon and the ice was already starting to thin. We decided to cross the front lines instead, to go past the Soviets. We made the wrong decision.'

She took a deep, shuddering breath, then shook her head, shaking the memory away.

'Has Königsberg fallen?' the man asked.

'Not yet,' she said. 'But it will. Soon. Berlin, too. Our days are numbered.'

She turned then to the women in the queue and glanced at me as well. 'You should leave. The Soviets are . . . angry.'

'They won't want me,' the short woman said. 'I'm too old.'

A noise escaped the refugee's mouth. A grunt or a bitter laugh, it was difficult to tell. 'I'm older than you and it didn't stop them. It's not about pleasure. It's about revenge. Our army, the Nazis, have done terrible things. Despicable things. And when the men are missing, it's the women who are made to suffer.'

'Propaganda,' the small woman's friend repeated, but this time her voice faltered.

'Do what you want. But they're coming, and when they get here, you'll wish you'd left.'

'Absolutely not,' Mother said when I returned to the apartment and told her about the refugees. 'We are not leaving.'

She was scrubbing the wallpaper, a soapy bucket by her feet. The smell of bleach had seeped into the walls, the carpet, the furniture. Every morning I woke with stinging eyes. She used to clean the apartment from top to bottom every fortnight, now she did it several times a week. With no money for gloves, her hands became raw, yet she seemed oblivious to the discomfort. I'd become used to her unruly hair – though I missed the tight bun she used to have, never a hair out of place – but it pained me to see her once-beautiful hands, which had always been adorned with rings, now looking like the hands of a poor washerwoman. None of us looked the way we used to – even Frau Weber's bird had shrunk, its squawking half-hearted – but Mother's diminishing affected me most. I needed her strength and resilience, her faith that all would be well.

'I hope you did not get too close. These refugees carry diseases. Diphtheria, typhus.'

'I kept my distance,' I said. 'But you're not listening to me. Why can't we leave?'

'Because your father might come home any day now.' Furiously she scoured one of the flowers patterned on the wall as if it were a child's drawing rather than part of the wallpaper. 'He would be devastated to return and not find us here. And, anyway, we would need a travel permit, which we do not have.'

'The Soviets are coming,' I said. 'And when they come—'

'Nonsense. Berlin cannot fall. It just . . . cannot. Now stop it. I will not talk about this again. This is our home. We are not going anywhere. Besides, Frau Weber is too old to be traipsing across the country and we cannot very well abandon her.'

I left Mother to her imaginary stains and went to sit by the piano. My hands trembled but they stilled the moment my fingertips touched the ivory keys. I played softly, the tune a whisper, but Mother huffed.

'Must you?' she said. 'It gives me such a headache.'

'It's all the bleach that's giving you a headache,' I muttered, but I retreated to my room all the same.

The air in my bedroom was stale, but an open window would let in the smoke. Defeated, I lay down on my bed, closed my eyes and took deep breaths. We were all irritable, scared, starving, but I reminded myself that we were still alive. Unlike Krista.

Krista. The memory of her face was blurring, like a photograph being burned, the edges slowly furling until all that would remain was ash.

I began to hum the tune of my latest composition. In my mind's eye, I could see my fingers moving over the piano keys, the music rising in the air as if it were something physical. I held on to the image; I let it caress me until I felt a little calmer and I could breathe again.

19

LISETTE

Then – Berlin, 16 April 1945

I woke from a fitful sleep to the sound of distant thunder, but outside the sky was clear of any clouds.

Bombs.

The Soviets were coming.

I threw open my bedroom door, my body shaking, my mouth dry. I found Mother peering out through the faded red curtains in the living room, the material clutched in her hands. She was wearing her nightgown but while mine was creased, hers looked newly ironed, as if she'd just put it on. Beyond her the sky was dark but every few seconds it lit up: explosives punching holes into the dying body of Berlin.

I rushed over to her. I wanted her to take charge, to tell me what we should do. Instead, she simply said, 'They are coming.'

'We should go down to the basement.'

'No, not tonight,' she said. 'If the building gets hit ...' She shrugged. And I felt it, too – even through my terror – a despondency. What was the point in hiding, crouching like vermin in a dirty, uncomfortable basement? If we died, we died. Perhaps it would be for the best.

We stood side by side gazing out. Fear tried to push its way between us but Mother took my hand.

'You were right,' she said. 'I am sorry.'

The tremors became more forceful and soon the vibrations were so strong a painting fell from the wall, crashing to the floor. I swallowed a sob, but forced myself to stay standing. Another quake made the building shudder and our phone began to ring. It rang and rang and then clattered off its hook, swinging against the wall like a hanging body.

I looked out into the fiery darkness and thought of Julius. Was he fighting the Russians in the east, retreating into Berlin? Had he waved a white flag and was now a prisoner of war in a labour camp, sick, starving and beaten daily? Had he deserted and was in hiding? Or was his body rotting in a trench somewhere? I pushed this last image away; if he were dead, I would know it. He would come home, he had to, otherwise there was no point in living.

I knew Mother was looking out and having the same thoughts about Father. She still believed he was alive somewhere – a prisoner of war or perhaps lying in a field hospital suffering with memory loss. But however strongly she believed this to be true, I was equally sure he was dead. I had already grieved for him in my own private way. And I was glad he wasn't here to see how one man's madness – and the complicity of others – had brought his beloved country to its knees.

Briefly I wondered too if Father and Julius had been involved in all the awful things we'd been hearing about. They'd been given no choice but to fight for their country; they weren't Nazis – I knew that – and yet . . . I pushed the thought away. I knew Julius; he was a good man. He would've surrendered the moment the opportunity arose.

Our front door flew open and for a moment I thought the Red Army was already here. But then Frau Weber charged in, her budgie's cage pressed against her bosom. She was sobbing and her bird was screeching. I wanted to push her back out, irrationally fearing the noise would bring the Soviets straight to our apartment door. She looked demented, like an old woman escaped from an asylum. Her bird kept flapping around the cage, flying into the bars again and again.

I waited for Mother to comfort her but she did nothing. She didn't even turn around. Eventually I went over to Frau Weber and led her to the sofa. I prised her fingers from the cage and placed it on the floor. She was drowning in fabric, her night-gown now several sizes too big.

'Towels,' she said. 'We need towels.'

'Why?'

'If we wrap them around our heads, we can survive even if there's a direct hit.'

'That's ridiculous—'

'Just get some towels!' she shrieked.

Mother still hadn't moved, so I found some towels and dumped two on Frau Weber's lap. She wrapped one around her head and covered her bird's cage with the other. I left her to it and rummaged around in the cupboard under the sink. I extracted Father's bottle of schnapps – the one Mother had been saving for his return. I poured all three of us a glass, gulped my own down before pouring myself another, then handed the other glasses to Mother and Frau Weber. I sat down beside Frau Weber, patting the old woman's knee absent-mindedly. She was still crying, her towel turban bobbing up and down. Mother stood by the window looking bewildered. It was happening, just like everyone had said it would.

As the sky wrestled violently with the dawn, turning the clouds blood red, I switched on the radio. The broadcast of the Red Army's approach paralysed us. Mother joined me and Frau Weber on the sofa and we sat together, motionless, as if carved out of stone, quietly listening to the news as it unfolded. No one made a sound, not even Frau Weber's bird, but our silence pulsed with fear like a fragile, beating heart. I knew Germany's defeat would tear into our lives, ripping us all apart at the seams.

It was hours before anyone spoke. Frau Weber was the first to break the silence. 'Can we leave? Is it too late?'

I was perched on the piano stool. It wasn't the time to play but being near the instrument gave me some comfort. In our flowing nightgowns and in the grey morning light, we looked like a confused trio of ghosts.

'It's too late,' I said, trying to keep the anger out of my voice. Why hadn't Mother listened to me? 'You heard them – the Red Army is closing in from the east and the Allies are approaching from the west. There's nowhere for us to go.'

'Maybe we should get some cyanide?' Frau Weber said. 'The Hitler Youth were giving it out. Suicide will be better than defeat.'

'It's not defeat we should fear,' I said, thinking of the refugees. 'They'll want revenge.'

'Revenge? Revenge for what? We haven't done anything!' Frau Weber's voice sounded like a whimpering child. But just as a child so often does, she knew the truth. We all did.

'Jews have been murdered, goodness knows how many . . . women, children, the elderly.' A wave of nausea almost swept me off my feet. 'Soviet villages razed to the ground. We can't pretend any more. It's been happening and we're guilty.'

'No. It's not true,' Frau Weber cried.

'It is,' Mother said, her voice devoid of all emotion.

Frau Weber stood up and stamped her foot. 'Propaganda. Lies.' Her bird began to squawk in support and the towel slipped from its prison. It hopped angrily up and down on its perch and I had to resist the urge to kick its cage.

I walked over to Frau Weber and took her by her shoulders. 'Stop it,' I said. 'Just stop it.'

Frau Weber began to wail then, her cries as loud as any siren. So I slapped her. A hard slap across the cheek that left a glaring red mark. The silence that followed was deafening.

'You hit me,' Frau Weber finally said.

'I'm sorry.' And I was. I'd never hit anyone, however much the urge had sometimes possessed me. 'But you have to be prepared,' I said. 'You have to know what's coming.'

'But we haven't done anything,' she repeated, quieter this time. 'We're just women. We can't be punished for what the men have done. For what our leaders ordered.'

'They don't care,' I said. 'And we *are* guilty. We did nothing. And in doing nothing, we gave our consent.' It wasn't until I said it that I fully realized the truth of those words. Again I thought of that woman, the toddler in her arms. The way she had called out, begging me to take him, and how I had turned my head, ignored my conscience. Yet she was just one of many. Their blood was on my hands. The blood of all of them. And Krista's, too. I stood by. I didn't do anything.

I did nothing.

20

LISETTE

Then – Berlin, 17 April 1945

'What do you want for the clothes?' the woman asked, approaching me as I crossed Torstraße. Apart from the piano and some of Mother's most precious jewellery, I was selling everything we had left. Carpets, clothes, clocks, china. I'd piled them into an old pram. One wheel spun drunkenly and it tilted at a funny angle, but it worked.

'Flour, herring, bacon,' I replied. 'Any food you have.'

The Soviets had encircled Berlin, that much we knew. Though the full truth of the assault evaded us, we knew they were getting closer; soon they'd be making their way through the city, fighting street by street. There was nowhere we could go. Our only choice was to hide, try to survive. But to do that, we needed food.

'Let me see,' the woman said, stepping forward and rifling through my things. Her face was streaked with soot, her hair a scarecrow's nest. She plucked Father's wool jacket from the pram. I'd had to sneak it out of the apartment, knowing Mother would never allow me to sell it, even in these dire times.

'Looks warm,' the woman said, stroking the interior. 'Our apartment's gone, we've lost everything.'

I simply nodded in reply; I wouldn't be swayed by sob stories. Food was what we needed and I'd only part with Father's things if this woman could provide some. Gertrud had taken the job at Ravensbrück a year earlier, joined Egon in overseeing whatever horrors were unfolding there, and, though I hadn't seen her in months, her hardened attitude had rubbed off on me. We couldn't help everyone; we had to take care of ourselves.

'Food,' I repeated. 'Do you have any?'

Reluctantly the woman nodded. She led me to a bombed-out building, the remaining walls blackened where flames had once licked the masonry. She wanted me to climb over a hill of broken bricks and shattered glass, but I refused to leave the pram.

'OK, stay here. I'll be right back. Please don't go. The nights are still so cold and my daughter needs that jacket.'

I waited amid the dust and destruction, reading the messages scrawled on a section of wall. *Alwin, our home is gone but we're all right*, one said. *Find us at Tante Ruth's*. Another said, *Josef, my Josef. We can't stay. We'll go to Flensburg. Meet us there. Your Elisabeth*. We thought ourselves lucky that our home was still standing, but perhaps losing everything would have been a blessing. Perhaps then Mother would have agreed to leave. I felt a wave of terror as I stood there trying not to think about what the future might hold.

By my feet was an old metal frame. The image held within it was too burnt to decipher but I remembered this building – a cinema had once stood next door. I wondered whether I'd ever again experience the simple joy of watching a film, the thrill of being transported elsewhere.

I heard footsteps, glass crunching.

I spun around and saw an old man, completely bald with dark liver spots covering his hairless head. He stood staring at me, his eyes bloodshot, his lips parted as if his tongue was swollen and too big for his mouth.

'Klara,' he said. 'Come here. I've been waiting all day.'

'What? No, I'm not—'

'Don't talk back to me, girl. I won't have it.'

He took a step forward and I found myself recoiling.

'Give me that pram back,' he said, spittle flying. 'I told you to come straight home.'

'The pram is mine,' I said. 'And I'm not Klara. I don't know you.'

He lunged forward and grabbed at the pram, but there was no way I was going to let go.

'Give it to me.' He yanked hard, his eyes locking on to mine.

I pushed him then, a firm shove on his bony shoulder, and he scrambled away like a rat scuttling back to its hiding place. He was gone as suddenly as he'd appeared, and if it hadn't been for my ragged breath, the thumping in my ears, I would've wondered whether it had happened at all.

I was about to give up waiting and head home empty-handed, when the woman finally returned. Behind her was a small girl – not much younger than Krista – with short, scraggly hair tucked beneath a hat and red, scaly arms which she kept scratching. She watched me with wide eyes and I feared for her. Would her youth spare her? Krista's death still tormented me but I felt some relief she wouldn't be here for whatever was to come.

The woman handed me a small cloth bundle. I unfolded it gently and found a hunk of bread, not yet stale, some bacon, two eggs and even a pouch of flour. It wouldn't quieten the hunger pangs – I wanted more – but I could see the woman had little else to offer. She had children; she needed to survive, too. I rewrapped the package and tucked it into the front of the pram, away from prying eyes. I lifted the jacket to my face, breathed in Father's scent one last time, then handed it over.

'*Bleib übrig* – survive,' the woman said. It was our new way of saying farewell. She gave me a slight smile and then retreated back to her makeshift home hidden beneath the wreckage.

I continued on my way, moving into the middle of the wide boulevard where there was less debris so it was easier to manoeuvre the rickety pram. The faint sound of artillery was constant and I wished I could gauge its distance, somehow figure out how long we had. Was it hours, days, weeks?

Around me, smoke hung in the air like the ghosts of those who'd been taken.

I tried not to think of Krista.

Every shop I passed had been looted or bombed. The only stores left untouched were those selling alcohol. We'd been told drink would impair the enemy so we should let them have it; it was clear this was a rule made up by men, the safety of women inconsequential. If Mother had not been anxiously waiting for me at home, I would've taken a brick and smashed every last bottle.

Near the ruins of Monbijou Palace, a crowd had gathered. The palace had been completely gutted so perhaps people felt it was safe to assemble there. There was a strange logic in believing a site wouldn't be bombed twice. Most were trading goods, others exchanging gossip – stories of what we could expect in the coming weeks. The people I passed whispered in a way that somehow felt violent – as if the words themselves were arguing.

I stood apart from the rest, waiting, shifting from one foot to the other. I hoped I looked approachable. I wasn't sure of the rules, but perhaps no one was. I unpacked a few items and spread them out on the ground, attempting to ignore the smell of charred flesh that wafted in the air.

A woman who looked plumper than most approached me. She nudged a large cooking pot with the toe of her boot.

'Please,' I said. 'Do you have any food? I have good china, a pair of smart women's boots, a small carpet . . .'

Her clothes were sooty but they were tailored and her dark

hair was neatly pinned back underneath a stylish hat. I recognized her – I didn't know her personally, but I was sure she had mixed in my parents' circle. Before the war she had had money.

'Hmm,' she said, moving on from the items on the ground and now rifling through my pram. 'These boots, yes. And I do need some clothes.'

A boom echoed across the ruins.

Collectively we shrank, holding up our arms to protect our heads. The clouds were on fire and ash rained down on us.

The time to leave was now.

'I'll take the boots and all of the clothes,' the woman said, quickly hauling the items into a small cart that sat by her feet. She passed me a mouldy fabric bag. It felt heavy and I peered into it. Inside was a small net sack with a few dirty potatoes. I was about to move them aside and see what else was on offer but she snapped, 'There's more than enough food in there to cover this. Cans of meat and condensed milk. Butter, too.'

Another explosion shook the earth, forcing me to my knees. Near by, the remaining facade of a small building began to crumble and then slid to the ground in one deafening crash. When I glanced back up, the woman was gone.

I closed the bag, hauled it on to the pram; I didn't want to stay another minute in this wasteland. We weren't safe anywhere but I felt a strong urge to get home. At least there I could play my piano; and if I was going to die, I would do so lost in its sound.

When I got home, Mother was in the kitchen peeling some potatoes for dinner. Frau Weber sat on the sofa, a drink in her hands, her budgie out of its cage and perched regally on her shoulder. If our food ran out entirely, we could probably eat him. Though I doubted there was much flesh on him, just feathers and bones.

Both Mother and Frau Weber had towels wrapped around their heads like turbans.

'How did it go?' Mother asked. 'What is it like out there?'

'People are bartering in the streets,' I said, joining her in the kitchen. 'I didn't need to go all the way to Alexanderplatz.'

The potatoes on the counter were small and wrinkly with patches of green. Some had tiny sprouts growing from them: small fingers desperately seeking out the earth. I poked one, scrunching up my nose when my finger broke through the slimy skin.

'Did you find any food?'

'Some, yes.' I went back to the hall and collected my wares. I placed the food pouch and the heavy bag on the dining table. While I unwrapped the pouch, Frau Weber hobbled over and opened the bag.

'There's nothing in here,' she said, her face turning a sickly shade of white.

'What? Of course there is.' I stretched over and dragged the bag across the table towards me. I pulled out the small sack of potatoes. Beneath it, all I saw were a couple of bricks.

'You didn't check . . .' Mother said.

'I . . . I . . .' But there were no words to excuse my folly. I'd been so careless. No one was trustworthy; I knew that. And yet, I'd been tricked by the woman's nice clothes, distracted by my desire to get home. And then that building had collapsed . . . But I should have checked.

Frau Weber crouched down, yanked off her towel and began to pull at her long grey hair, moaning repeatedly, 'We're going to die, we're all going to die.' I could hear the panic rising in her voice as if it were something physical.

Mother said nothing. She just stood watching me, twisting a dishtowel in her hands, her knuckles turning white.

21

LISETTE

Then – Berlin, 27 April 1945

We ripped small strips from a bedsheet and tied them around our arms – both left and right, just to be sure. Then we hung the sheet from the front window, watched as it quivered in the smoky wind. White shirts, tablecloths and bedsheets adorned the facade of every building that was still standing on our street. We all hoped it would be enough.

There was a sudden storm of gunfire. The sound ricocheted around the apartment like a lone bullet, but then moments later it was quiet and we could hear the birds singing once more.

In Berlin, people were saying the optimists were learning English and the pessimists Russian. I was a realist; I didn't bother learning anything. It would be the Soviets who got to us first – they'd already breached the city's borders – and knowing a few words of Russian would make little difference if they were out for revenge.

Once the white sheet was secured, the weight of the closed window holding it in place, I took down the mandatory picture of our Führer from the wall. I lit the fire and then watched as it burned, the flames slowly eating his face. Frau Weber refused to look, turning away as if I'd personally offended her.

'Your Party badge,' I said, gesturing to her lapel. Her fingers flew up to her throat then settled on the pin. The look she gave me was hateful, as if I'd suggested throwing her bird into the fire – which had, in fact, crossed my mind.

Slowly, she unpinned it. It sat in the palm of her hand, so small and seemingly insignificant.

'It will not burn,' Mother said. She sat with her shoulders hunched, wearing a blank, dazed look. Her face was clean of make-up, her hair flat and unstyled. She looked like a different person – the kind of woman who didn't care about her appearance, a woman of whom she herself would disapprove. And she wasn't acting like Mother, either. I wanted her to instruct me on what to do but instead the situation had paralysed her.

'No, it won't,' I agreed. 'Shall we bury it? Swallow it?'

Suddenly I felt panicked by its mere existence. If we threw it out into the courtyard and a Russki found it, would they shoot every last tenant in our building? I'd promised to go to the Tiergarten and collect some more wood; perhaps I should take it with me and bury it among the shrubs. But what if the Red Army came before I managed to get there? When they arrived I needed to hide, not be out on the streets with a Nazi badge in my pocket.

'Let's bury it. Now,' Mother said. 'Though, we should do it at night. Is it night? Or is it morning?'

We'd been spending less and less time in the cellar – there seemed little point – but even above ground, it was difficult to tell the difference between night and day. We were hungry and scared, and the smoke choking the city kept us in perpetual darkness. In the past twenty-four hours we'd heard bullets rebounding off houses, so close by that the fighters must only have been a street away. I'd never heard or seen a tank, but I knew that's what we could hear in the distance – the dull clunk-ing sound of heavy machinery, the vibrations rumbling through the streets.

'What's that?' Frau Weber said, gripping my arm, her ragged nails digging into my flesh. 'I hear something.'

Footsteps echoed in the stairwell. All three of us ducked behind the sofa. I gripped Mother's hand; it was slick with sweat. I closed my eyes – embracing the childhood belief that if I couldn't see whoever it was, they wouldn't be able to see me. Beside me, I could hear Frau Weber's rasping breath and then the scrape of her dragging the birdcage across the floor towards us.

The door of the apartment flew open, its hinges letting out a screech.

I kept my eyes closed and my head down. Whoever it was stumbled down the hallway, tripping on tired feet. Or perhaps he was drunk.

'*Hallo? Ist jemand zuhause* – is anyone home?'

His footsteps grew closer and then I sensed him standing over us.

I opened my eyes and looked up. He was only a boy, a dream of a moustache darkening his top lip. And he was wearing a German uniform.

My muscles relaxed a little, some of the tension from my body releasing itself in the form of a sigh. I nudged Mother who opened her eyes, too. I stood up, then helped Mother to her feet.

'He's German,' I said to Frau Weber, whose eyes were still squeezed shut.

'Water,' the boy said. 'Please.'

His adult-sized helmet was too big for his head and he kept having to push it up. Mother and I exchanged glances. His pres-ence could get us all shot.

'Please,' he said again. 'Just some water and then I'll be gone.'

I rushed over to the kitchen, grabbed an unwashed glass –

even though it bothered Mother, our water was too precious to waste on washing up – and scooped some water out of our pail. I handed it to him and he gulped it down. I filled the glass again.

'There's a hydrant on Behmstraße,' Frau Weber said, sniffing distastefully. Her forehead was a mess of seams, a child's sewing project gone wrong.

'Behmstraße has already been taken,' the boy said quietly.

He looked from Frau Weber to Mother to me. I knew he wanted to ask us to hide him, to save him. He was just a child – no older than fifteen. Too young to die in another man's war.

'Sit down,' I said. 'I'll get you some food.'

'Absolutely not,' Frau Weber shrieked, stamping her foot like a petulant child, her fear forgotten. 'We don't even have enough for ourselves.'

I ignored her. The food was mine and Mother's to give, not hers. I glanced at Mother but she said nothing, and so I led the boy over to the dining table and sat him down. I prised open a tin of meat I'd found a few days earlier inside the carcass of a nearby building. The silver metal had winked at me in the dwindling light. When I'd uncovered several more tins of both meat and vegetables, I'd found myself crying. As I gathered them up and hid them in the pram, I hadn't allowed myself to think about the owners, had refused to imagine their rotting bodies hidden somewhere beneath my feet.

Now, I spooned a few chunks into a bowl and handed it to the boy. His eyes widened and he licked his cracked lips. He shovelled the food into his mouth, denying himself even a single breath between spoonfuls. It was all gone before I could sit down beside him.

'How long until they get here?' I asked.

'Not long,' he said. 'An hour, perhaps. Maybe two.'

He was visibly shaking and I had to stop myself from taking his hand and promising him shelter.

'I am sorry,' Mother said, her voice quiet but firm. 'It is time for you to leave.'

'Of course he should leave!' Frau Weber said, flapping her hands. 'We should never have allowed him inside in the first place.'

'We didn't *allow* him inside,' I said. 'He came in on his own.'

'You *gave* him food. That we need. He's a dead man walking. What a waste.'

I almost hit her again; the truth was so unnecessarily cruel.

'She's right,' the boy said, standing up, his eyes glistening. 'Thank you for the water and the food. I'll leave you now.'

He stumbled to the door, drunk with exhaustion and despair. Before he left, he turned and gave me a faint smile of gratitude, then said, 'When they come, don't hide in the basement. That's the first place they'll look.'

~

'For goodness' sake,' Mother said. 'Do as I say.'

'I can't just leave you here.' But I didn't step down off the ladder.

'Of course you can. There is not enough space for both of us up there. You do not need to worry about me. I am too old; they will not want me.'

'You're not even fifty.'

'Please, Lisette. We have run out of options. You were right; we should have left when we had the chance.'

Frau Weber sat motionless, the birdcage in her lap, her budgie blinking its beady little eyes. She had finally stopped talking. She'd also stopped wearing the stupid towel.

Outside we could hear cheering, the sound of drunken men singing. Darkness had wrapped itself around Berlin but the air was full of jubilant cries.

There were screams, too.

I climbed the last few steps, the rusty old ladder wobbling under my weight even as Mother steadied it with her hands. I pushed up and slowly lifted the cover of the crawl space. Stale air drifted out and there was a flurry of dust. I glanced behind me once more. Mother nodded. And then I climbed inside and slid the cover back into place, shuddering as the light was smothered.

The space was so small I could only sit with my head bowed; it would have been easier to lie down but then it would have felt like I was in a coffin, earth below and above, the air slowly running out. There was a smell of decay and rotting wood. Something scuttled over my foot and I stifled a scream.

Breathe, I told myself. *Just breathe.*

I forced myself to think of my piano, pictured my fingers sliding over the keys. I listened to the music I'd tucked safely inside me, let myself imagine Julius sitting behind me, listening while I played. Julius. Where was he? I was too old to believe in fairy tales but I allowed myself the fantasy of him suddenly appearing, carrying me down from my hiding place, saving me.

I remembered that Julius and I used to come up here as children. Most apartments had crawl spaces, but Julius's didn't and he was fascinated by ours – a place that was too small for adults but big enough for secrets. We had hidden all kinds of trinkets among the abandoned suitcases and old clothes. Julius had kept books and scraps of paper up here – though he refused to tell me what he'd written on them. I'd kept small, smooth pebbles from the garden that I'd decorated with crayons. We would lie side by side in the dark and Julius would tell me stories of kings and queens, pirates and Vikings.

A scream. Mother's scream. And then the sound of heavy boots, the voices of men.

They were here.

I slid on my belly towards the cover, a worm burrowing through the dirt. There was a thin sliver of light and I pressed my face to it, peering down into the room below. I could see Frau Weber cowering in the corner, Mother standing in front of her, her arms outstretched like Jesus on the cross. The men – five of them – stomped around the room, pulling out drawers, kicking over chairs. Their shabby brown uniforms were stained and ripped. Even from where I was crouching, I could see their boots were falling to pieces and they had lengths of string instead of gun slings. Absurdly, each soldier was wearing several watches on each arm.

Harsh, foreign words flew around like thrown objects. One soldier found the schnapps under the sink. He swigged the remaining liquid straight from the bottle. Even through her mask of terror, I could see Mother wrinkle her nose in disgust. It was then that one of them grabbed her, ripping her shirt as she feebly tried to bat him away. His eyes were bloodshot, his balance slightly off, but he was strong.

I couldn't watch it. I couldn't let it happen. I should have stayed hidden; I knew that. But I also understood I would never forgive myself if I was a bystander in this – the destruction of my own family.

I slid my fingers into the crack and lifted the cover. The men were too drunk to notice the ceiling opening above them. The ladder was gone, hidden somewhere in Frau Weber's apartment. And so I jumped. I didn't mean to land on one of the men but he must have moved just as I let myself drop. I tumbled down on top of him and he shrieked like a small child.

There was a roar of laughter, interrupted only by Mother's cries. The man who'd grabbed her was now pulling her by her hair, dragging her towards the bedroom. Another soldier started pawing at me as I lay on the floor, my ankle throbbing. With drunken, fumbling hands he tried to pull off my skirt.

And then I heard Frau Weber shriek as she launched herself on top of the man who'd pinned me to the floor. She clawed at his scalp, his face, his eyes. Her screaming voice was like a ghoul's, her fury untamed. Somewhere close by I could hear her budgie screeching too. It was a war cry, a call to battle.

'Get off her,' she screamed. 'Get off. She's just a child.'

I saw the shadow of the man before I saw his face. It was as if he was darkness itself. He plucked Frau Weber from the soldier's back as though she weighed nothing at all. Her arms flailed and her legs thrashed. He threw her across the room like a discarded piece of paper scrunched into a ball. She hit the wall and then crumpled to the floor. The other soldiers fell silent.

I watched as everything played out in slow motion. Frau Weber pulled herself to her feet, her legs visibly shaking, but the rage was still there. She was scared but she was also furious. Before she had a chance to launch herself at the man, he pulled a pistol from his jacket. He didn't hesitate as he cocked the gun.

And then he blew a hole through Frau Weber's head.

22

ELLY

Now – East Berlin, 23 September 1961

A flicker of hope has stirred in me. The plan has been set in motion; today is the day I will leave East Berlin.

When I get to Volkspark Friedrichshain, Andrei is already there waiting for me. He's sitting on a bench, his long legs outstretched, his eyes closed, a cigarette dangling from his lips. I envy how laid-back he always seems. Since I made the decision to escape, my heart has been erratic. And whenever I'm with Andrei, it skips a beat entirely.

Last week autumn blew in with a violent storm and, though the rain has ceased, the warmer days are gone. I look around the park, listen to the songs of the few people who have ventured out. I scan every face, but have to be careful doing so. Showing any fear will make me a target.

Last night Monika called and I could hear a clicking noise on the phone. Someone was listening. Perhaps they always are. Monika could sense it, too; I noticed by the way her music slowed as we talked, shifted from one movement into another. She wanted to discuss our homework but once the clicking started, our sentences became carefully composed and in the end I cut our conversation short.

I lean my bike against a tree and then push my hands deep into the pockets of my jacket. The wind picks up, prickling my skin and chasing leaves through the park. As I sit down beside Andrei, bumping my hip against his, he opens his eyes. I have a strange need to touch him, for our bodies to be in contact. Does he recognize that I'm manipulating him? I have to believe that if he thinks I like him, he won't betray me.

He slips his arm around my shoulders and I let myself sink into him – just a little, just to keep up the act. His distinct smoky smell burrows its way into my damp clothes.

'Will you miss me, Elly Lange?'

I want to say no, but my mouth won't let me lie. 'Yes,' I say. I will miss him. Not because I feel any real emotions for him – obviously not – but for a Soviet, he's not all bad.

'You don't need to go,' he says softly. 'It's not your job to bring your brother home.'

'It is,' I say. 'I can't explain it. It's just something I need to do. Mama is broken, her voice gone, and this is the only way to fix her.'

'Making it over to the other side will only be the first of many hurdles. You know that, right? What if Axel is still too sick to leave the hospital? What if the route we've chosen becomes impassable for some reason and you can't make it back the same way? Once you've crossed, there will be no way for us to make contact. Everything that goes in and out is checked. There are so many things that could go wrong.'

'I know. I'll figure it out.' I don't know how. And thinking about it too much hurts my chest.

A girl my age walks past. I shift along the bench, distancing myself from Andrei. I can't bear the way she looks at us, her disapproving stare popping the bubble of our friendship. I want to tell her that we're not a couple. I would never be together with a Russki.

As she passes I can hear her music. It's decisive, unwavering; it belongs to someone who abides by the rules. It reminds me that she'll sleep safely tonight while I will not.

'You're still ashamed of me?' Andrei says. He's only half joking; I can hear the hurt tucked just out of sight.

'I'm sorry, it's just . . . if my friends knew, my parents . . .'

There's a burning sensation in my eyes. I try to blink it away.

'Let's walk,' I say, jumping up, vowing not to pull away from him when the next person passes. Unless, of course, it's someone I know.

The grass is already muddy and our boots squelch on fallen leaves that have started to decay, turning into mush. Some trees are still clinging on desperately to a few speckled yellow leaves, but soon winter will come; I can almost feel its icy breath.

'Mama and Oma Rita built this hill. Did I tell you that?'

'Built it? How can you build a hill?'

'They were rubble women after the war,' I say. 'They moved a load of the rubble to this park and made it into a hill.'

'Really? I never knew that.' He lights another cigarette, closes his eyes and inhales. 'So, this whole hill is made of rubble?'

'Yes. Weird, isn't it?' I try and fail to imagine Mama as a young woman after the war, carrying buckets heavy with her country's defeat. Imagining Oma Rita here is even more difficult. Every day she wears her Sunday best, her hair pulled back in a neat bun, a splash of red lipstick on her thin lips. She feels at home in the garden, her gloved hands in the earth, but even gardening she manages to do in a ladylike way. Sometimes a streak of dirt will mark her forehead, but it always looks as if she has smeared it there deliberately, for authenticity's sake. Following orders and hauling bricks wouldn't have suited her.

I also can't imagine Mama and Oma Rita teaming up as two corresponding links in a chain. They seem so out of sync, like two people forced to be dance partners who keep stepping on each other's toes. Were they ever close? They must have been for Mama to have stayed with Oma all these years. It's not a secret that Mama has always wanted to move west, or out of Germany altogether, but Oma Rita has refused, adamant that my grandfather will one day come home.

'They had such different lives,' Andrei says. 'Our parents at our age.'

'I know. I ask them about it sometimes – the war years – but none of them will say much. Papa never wanted to fight, I know that. He said the war ate up bits of his soul. People forget that not all German soldiers were Nazis. And conscientious objectors faced the death penalty, so it's not like he had a choice. Even those who made defeatist statements could be sent to a camp.'

I can hear my voice becoming defensive, a distinctive pleading whine. I know this is the argument we all give for the actions of our parents. *They had no choice. They didn't know. Not all Germans were Nazis.* I really do believe Papa, though. He's the kindest person I know. And I've heard his music – there's no meanness in it, no violence.

'I'm sure your papa is a good man,' Andrei says.

I'm embarrassed that I need to hear this from him, but I do.

'History is written by the victors,' Andrei continues. 'Churchill said that, I think. The things that happened were horrific, but a whole nation can't be bad.'

'And here we are again,' I say. 'Life should be easy, fun. Shouldn't it? But Berlin's been divided, Axel is stuck in the West, and instead of hanging out with my friends, planning my future, I'm—'

'Spending time with an incredibly handsome Soviet soldier.'

I laugh. 'If you say so.'

A huge branch has fallen on the path ahead of us. It's wet and starting to rot. I suspect if someone kicked it, it would reveal a family of woodworms eating their dinner. I don't need help climbing over it but Andrei offers me his hand and I take it.

'I'd like to meet your family one day,' he says, holding my hand a second too long.

My cheeks burn. I don't know what to say. He makes it sound as if we have something more than friendship, something long-term. He makes it sound as if he doesn't know that my whole family would disown me if they knew I was in contact with a Russki.

A flock of pigeons swoops down and Andrei suddenly grabs my arm, pulls me in the other direction, as if the birds are missiles and we're their target.

'Sorry, sorry,' he says, his focus still on the birds that have now settled in a tree. He lets out an embarrassed laugh. 'I . . . don't like birds.'

'You're scared of birds?' He's a soldier, a body built like Superman, and the calmest, most collected person I've ever met, and yet a flock of pigeons has left him visibly shaken.

'Not *scared*,' he says, moving back on to the path, his eyes still fixed on the tree and its threatening inhabitants. 'I dislike them. They're . . . dirty. And their beaks. They peck.'

'I'll protect you,' I say. I grin and he smiles at me sheepishly. 'They say the best way to get over a fear is to face it.'

'It's not a fear—'

'If we locked you in a room with a bunch of birds, you'd come out cured.'

'I'd come out with no eyes. They would have pecked them out.'

'So, you don't want to try it?'

'Can we talk about something else, please?'

I bump my shoulder into his. 'Sure.'

The path starts to climb steeply and my breath quickens. Andrei slows his pace to match mine.

'Tell me more about the songs you hear. It's fascinating.'

'Well . . . it's difficult to explain.' And it is. But I'm also worried about what Andrei will think. It's not something I talk about much. When I was little I thought everyone heard the melodies surrounding them. It was only when I mentioned it to Papa that I realized this wasn't the case.

'It's like each person has been assigned a piece of music,' I say, choosing my words carefully. 'Sometimes I hear whole orchestras and other times just a singing voice. They say some people think in words, others in images. I have those too, but mainly it's music.'

'I'm not sure what I think in . . .'

'If I say "cat", do you see a cat in your head or is it the word?'

'I hear the word. No, maybe I see the cat, too. But definitely the word is there. Do some people think just in images? They just see the cat?'

'Apparently. We assume everyone thinks in the same way we do. That we all see the same things. But maybe my red is your blue. There's no way of knowing.'

'It must be noisy in your head. With all that music.'

'Yes and no. Mozart said that music is not in the notes but in the silence in between. I think that's where our souls are – hidden in that silence.' I feel my cheeks heat up. I'm not making any sense.

'You're interesting, Elly Lange.'

I laugh but it comes out as a yelp. 'I don't know about that. I tried to tell Mama about it once and she got so angry. No, not angry exactly. Scared. It was strange. I've never mentioned it to her again. You must think I'm weird.'

'Weird isn't necessarily bad. Weird can be wonderful. No one wants to be the same as everyone else.'

'So you *do* think I'm weird?'

'No, just wonderful.'

He says it so simply, as if it's a fact. I go still.

'Thank you,' I say eventually.

161

We start walking again. His hand brushes mine and I hold my breath. For a moment, I think he might lace his fingers through mine, but then a dog barks and the moment passes.

In the distance, a woman is walking her overweight Labrador. As the dog pees against a tree, she demonstratively turns to look in the other direction as if she wants to give it some privacy. Other than her, there's no one else in sight.

'We need to go over the plans for tonight,' I say, dropping my voice just to be safe. 'What time are we meeting?'

He sighs; he's still hoping I'll change my mind.

'Three a.m.,' he says finally. 'It should be quiet then. The evictions on Harzer Straße aren't going well, which is good for you. Everyone's focus will be on that neighbourhood. The GDR is giving promotions and pay rises to anyone who foils an escape, so all the guards and *VoPos* are hanging around, waiting for their moment.'

'I thought the windows had all been bricked up?'

'Not all of them. The ones higher up haven't been.'

'Have any of the tenants jumped?'

'Not yet. But someone will. There are already people in the West urging them to jump – shouting that they'll catch them.'

'A promotion and a pay rise . . . Aren't you tempted?'

I'm only half joking. I trust him, yet he is the enemy.

'No, Elly Lange, I'm not tempted.'

We go over the plan once more and then I ask him if we can just walk and talk about other things; I want to pretend for a little while that my life could be different. We climb up to the top of the hill and take in the view. The sun dips in the sky, the clouds no longer holding it up. A mist is settling over Berlin but the trees are a rainbow of autumn colours and it's good to be reminded that there's still some beauty in this half of the city. I've wanted to leave ever since I can remember, but I've been happy here. It's easy to forget that.

23

ELLY

Now – East Berlin, 23 September 1961

'*Guten Tag*, Herr Krause,' I say, trying not to sound too relieved. 'It's good to see you.'

I've been loitering on the street for almost thirty minutes. I was worried he was already gone. He's a creature of habit and every Saturday evening he goes out for his weekly food shop, his battered shopping trolley trailing after him like a pet. I wanted to speak to him before, but I couldn't risk him mentioning something to Papa, as that would have ruined everything. By waiting until the last opportunity, though, I almost missed him.

'How are you?' I ask, blowing into my cupped hands, my breath escaping as billows of mist. 'I haven't seen you in a while. Are you well?'

'Just fine,' he says. His eyes sit like black beads in their sockets, lifeless and doll-like, watching me suspiciously. Standing this close to him, I can see small hairs like spider's legs growing on his earlobes. They seem to quiver in time to his music. His is a strange song – just a slow drumbeat paired with a piano solo. It's repetitive and dull. I've experienced music that scares me before, but this is different. It sounds like the notes are being played by someone half-heartedly, by someone who doesn't like music at all, a person who doesn't like anything much.

'Good, good,' I say. 'I'm fine, too. Well, obviously not fine. It's a difficult time and . . . Papa's cousin is sick . . . She lives in Leipzig.' I sound nervous. I've prepared these words in advance, sewn them carefully together in the hope that they will fit, but my lips are clumsy. 'I'm actually going to see her tomorrow, stay with her awhile.'

'Don't you have school?'

'Well, yes, but she's not well. She needs my help. You know how it is. Family. I'm going there. Tomorrow, actually. I'll be gone for a while. Probably.'

He nods but it's paired with a raised eyebrow, a thick, hairy caterpillar arching its back. I hope it denotes disapproval and not suspicion.

'Anyway,' I say, 'it was nice seeing you.' And then I slip past him, through the building's front door and up to our apartment, my seed sown.

Inside, I find Papa in the kitchen making dinner. The apartment smells of garlic and fried onions. A stew simmers on the stove and the counter is a mess of chopped vegetables.

'Elly, there you are. Where have you been?'

'Just out with Otto and Monika.' The lie slips so easily from my mouth. 'We went for a walk. And then got some cake.'

Slowly Papa takes off his fogged-up glasses and cleans each lens on his jumper. He's aged so much in the past few weeks. New wrinkles line his face and he looks shorter, too, as if he is carrying a great weight that has compressed his bones.

'Can I help?' I ask.

'Thanks, Elly. I'd like that.'

He continues to chop and sauté. I clean up his mess, gathering the papery onion skins and the severed ends of carrots and dumping them in the bin under the sink. I know this recipe, I've helped him prepare it countless times, but I still ask him to explain each step. This apartment has never felt like home, but he does.

Mama won't miss me, I think, but Papa will. And if I fail – if this suicide mission turns out to be exactly that – Papa will have lost both his children. I don't know if he'll ever recover.

The day finally settles. Across Berlin I imagine everyone getting ready for a deep sleep while I pack and unpack my bag. I unfold the song sheet tucked into my notebook and stare at Andrei's tune. It's still unfinished. I can't quite get it right. Even though my mind is full of the night and days that lie ahead of me, this incomplete song is like a splinter I can't remove, however much I pick at it.

I slip it into my pocket and then sit on my bed, watching the hands of the clock move slower than they've ever done before. It's still not time to go, but I hear someone crying in the living room. I leave my impatience behind and step out into the hall.

The hardwood floor is cold on my bare feet, the autumn chill making itself at home. The apartment is dark but the familiar sounds of night – Oma Rita's loud snores, the tick-tock of the grandfather clock – are comforting.

Mama must hear my approaching footsteps, the creak of the floorboards, but her weeping continues as if there's no stopping her tears. She stands in the middle of the room, staring at the space where I know her piano once stood. The curtains are drawn and the moonlight casts a pale glow. She's wearing her white nightgown, embroidered at the neck, and her hair is loose and flowing.

I wonder what it is that haunts her. Axel is missing, of course, but it's more than that. Why did she stop playing the piano? What happened all those years ago for her to lose her voice the first time? Papa's hinted that Mama's past was difficult – the war years, her father's disappearance – but what does that have to do with her piano? And why has her sadness not stayed in her past? Why has it followed her here, like a stalker, preying on her in the present?

'Are you OK?' I ask, still standing in the hall, not daring to cross the threshold. 'Well, obviously you're not OK. But . . . can I do anything? Make you some tea? Wake Papa?'

Her sobs subside but it takes several minutes before she turns and faces me. When she does, her face is white, the same colour as the moon behind her, but her cheeks are marked with lines of mascara that make it look as if she's been crying blood.

She looks confused, the same look Oma Rita so often has, as if she doesn't know who I am. As if she's living within a memory. So many secrets reside in this apartment, hidden in corners, folded between clothes, whispered between my parents – places I'll never be able to access. The reason she hates me being one of them.

She steps out of the moonlight and into the shadows. I want to say something. Force a hug on her, tell her I'm going to fix this, fix her – but I don't do anything at all. I think she'll slip past me, oblivious to my presence, but suddenly she stops and pulls me into her arms. The unexpectedness of it takes my breath away. She holds me in a tight embrace, so close I can feel her heartbeat and smell the faint citrus scent of her hair. And then, just as quickly, she releases me and is gone.

24

LISETTE

Then – Berlin, 28 April 1945

Afterwards, once the soldiers had left, Mother and I clung to each other in a corner of the living room. I couldn't remember the last time she'd held me in her arms. I knew the touch of others bothered her, but our bodies were no longer our own. We had separated them from our souls – or at least I had, and perhaps she felt the same. I could vaguely sense a burning between my legs and something wet and sticky was smeared on my thighs, but otherwise I couldn't feel anything at all. It was as if the pain was someone else's. A person that wasn't me.

The men had departed with the first threads of dawn. Frau Weber's body lay a few feet away, her blood splattered against the wall like a round, red sun. Her eyes had turned cloudy, almost opaque. I wished Mother would go over and close them.

My mind felt strangely empty. Images of what had happened tried to penetrate my vision but I wouldn't let them in. They swirled and twisted, knocking on my skull, but I chose to fill my brain with music instead. Heller's 'Warrior's Song' – slow but strong. My body was weak, but I needed my mind to find strength. I tried to fold myself into that music. I'd embody it; that was how we'd survive.

'We need to take her outside,' Mother said, her voice a strangled whisper.

By our feet was the birdcage and inside Frau Weber's bird sat quietly. Did he understand she was gone? He kept stretching his neck repeatedly as if he was struggling to breathe. I hated the constant noise he usually made, but his silence was worse.

'Lisette. Did you hear me? We need to take her outside.'

I waited for my words to come together, to form into something coherent, but they flailed and flopped like fish drowning in the air.

Instead I let the music overcome me, the tune vibrating on my lips, and finally I found the energy to stand.

It took us another hour to steady ourselves, but once we were both up and standing, Mother brushed herself off and took control.

'We will bury her in the park.'

'Is it safe outside? What about the soldiers?'

'They will have moved on. The whole of Berlin has not fallen yet. They are taking the city street by street. They might come back. But not during the day. For now, we are safe.'

'Are you sure?' How could she know this? I wouldn't allow myself to dwell too much on her last sentence – the 'for now'. I couldn't face what that meant.

With bruised, broken bodies, we carried Frau Weber down on to the street. She was surprisingly light, a mere bag of bones. We had all diminished since the war began but it had been so gradual. Now I noticed the gauntness of Mother's cheeks, her bruised arms like sticks. I looked down at my own deflated body; my breasts had become small, swollen mounds, like two infected mosquito bites.

We found the pram in the alleyway and carefully folded Frau Weber's body into it, her legs dangling over the side. Mother collected our garden spade from the courtyard and tucked it under her arm. Outside, small groups of women and children had gathered. They nodded at us as we passed. Most had obvious cuts and bruises, all looked haunted. No one seemed surprised by the sight of a dead old woman in a pram.

The bodies of soldiers – both German and Soviet – were strewn across the streets like bundles of discarded clothes. I tried not to look at them but their dead, milky eyes followed us everywhere. There was no need to bury Frau Weber; we could have just left her among the ruins with the rest. But she was one of us and she deserved better.

When we got to the park, we saw it was full of flowers and the scent of lilacs briefly masked the smell of everything else. Spring had softened the ground and though it took time to dig a shallow grave, the gruesome task distracted me from replaying the horrors of the previous night.

Finally satisfied with its depth, we lowered Frau Weber's body into the hole and scattered handfuls of dirt on top, then shovelled in more earth to cover her up as best we could.

'She tried to save me,' I said as I laid flowers on the grave. 'She died trying to save me.'

'She would have wanted it that way.'

'That doesn't make any sense,' I said.

'She died trying to save someone she loved. What better way is there to die?'

'She didn't love me. We hated each other.'

'Of course she loved you. She has been around since the day you were born. She has known you all your life and she has no children of her own. She has – had – a sharp tongue, but she always cared about you.'

I swallowed hard, my chest burning. I looked down at my

dirty hands. Frau Weber's blood had mixed with the earth and embedded itself under my fingernails. I knew it would be a long time before I tried to wash it away.

~

'Did they get you?'

Frau Roth was old and astonishingly ugly. Her two front teeth were missing and she had a large hairy mole in the middle of her forehead that looked like a target. She had scared me as a child and even now I found myself taking a step back in the stairwell, grabbing the banister to stop myself from tumbling down.

'Well, did they?' she asked. When neither of us answered, she shrugged and said, 'Better a Russki on top than a Yank overhead.'

'Are you OK, Frau Roth?' Mother asked. 'Is there anything we can help you with?'

'Of course I'm OK. I'm alive, aren't I? At my age, I never thought a man would want to get into these knickers. But the Ivans aren't picky.' She opened her mouth and cackled, her laughter bouncing off the bare walls.

Mother flinched and wiped a drop of Frau Roth's spittle from her face.

Frau Roth leaned towards her and lowered her voice, as if I wouldn't hear her even though I was only a foot away. 'They got her too, didn't they? I can tell. Make sure she douches. She's a skinny thing these days, probably hasn't had her period in months, but you can never be too careful. Douching with oil or vinegar is best, but anything will do.'

She nodded, agreeing with herself, and then shuffled past us down the stairs, patting my cheek on the way.

Mother pushed open our front door. I hovered on the threshold, memories of the previous night rushing towards me. I never wanted to set foot in our apartment again but there was nowhere else to go.

So many times I'd imagined making love to Julius, running my hands over his naked body, playing the piano on his skin. My body would heal; I knew that. But it would never forget.

As I stood frozen in the doorway, the world tipping from side to side, Mother began to tidy the apartment. She picked up the chairs, straightened the sofa, swept up the broken glass. The wall was still covered in blood, the stain blooming like a flower, and I couldn't stop staring at it.

Mother came over to me, looked me in the eyes. 'I am sorry this happened to you,' she said firmly. 'But we will survive this. We need to survive it. Father will come home. Julius and Wilhelm, too. This war is almost over. What happened last night, what will most likely happen again . . . we will bury it, forget it, move on. That is the *only* way. Do you understand?'

All I could do was nod. And then I went to my room and slid to the floor. I thought about what Mother had said, studied her words as if they were resting in the palms of my hands, where I could feel them, touch them, see if they were real.

What will most likely happen again . . .

I closed my eyes and searched for the music that would save me. I imagined my fingers moving over the keys, my hands slow and steady, Heller's 'Warrior's Song', crisp and clear, reverberating through my veins.

25

LISETTE

Then – Berlin, 30 April 1945

A truck sat outside our building, its engine idling, a grumble of impatience. The driver was a woman – though I didn't realize it at first. She was stocky with a wide nose and forehead, and her short hair was tucked away under her hat.

'You,' she said, her Russian accent thick. 'Your name is Lisette? The piano player?'

Water sloshed out of the bucket as Mother and I lowered it to the pavement. She'd wanted to come with me, afraid of letting me go out on my own.

I looked to Mother; I didn't know what the right answer was.

'I do not have time to deal with liars. Do you play the piano or not?'

Still I didn't answer.

'I assume that is a yes. Get in.'

When we didn't move, she took out her gun and pointed it at my head.

Seeing I had no choice, Mother said firmly, 'I must accompany her.'

The woman hesitated for a moment then gave a brief nod.

We climbed in, ducked our heads, conscious of people watching us.

'The General wants a piano player. One of our men saw a piano in your apartment and your neighbour told us you play very well. We are celebrating, *da*? You will be the entertainment.'

She sneered as she said it. Alongside my fear, I felt a wash of unbearable shame. It sat within me like some sort of parasite, devouring me from the inside.

The soldier and I were probably the same age. I wondered how the war years had been for her. Had hating and killing come easily to her, or had she needed to learn that role? As a soldier, had she been treated with respect, or did the Ivans treat all women as objects?

I clutched Mother's hand as we drove through the mess of streets, past flaming ruins and scared, starving people in ragged clothes. Slowly the city fell away, buildings were replaced with budding trees and overgrown grass, and the smoke-heavy air cleared a little. Grand villas appeared on either side of us. This used to be a Jewish neighbourhood and I tried to stop myself from wondering where the owners were now.

'Here,' our driver said. She parked the truck in front of a large, imposing house with concrete pillars at the entrance and a wraparound balcony looking out over a small lake beyond. An abandoned rowing boat lay upside down on the shore, a broken oar lying beside it like a fractured limb. I could hear voices and raucous laughter before we even opened the truck doors. My legs carried me forward but my mind was screaming at me to turn around.

Inside, the space was opulent. The furniture was extravagant and luxurious – the sofas were red velvet and the marble floor seemed to glitter. Those who had once lived in this beautiful house were gone, but they'd left little pieces of their souls – books that had inspired them, paintings that breathed life, furniture that defined who they once were: regal, hopeful, defiant. But it hadn't helped. They'd been rounded up, stripped of everything, and this building was all that was left.

The soldier led us into a large living room filled with people. The smell of unwashed bodies and stale alcohol hung in the air. I had expected only soldiers but there were German women too, hiding their shame behind glasses of brandy and plastered-on smiles. They looked up when we came in but then quickly averted their gazes. On one of the sofas was a dark-haired girl who could not have been older than sixteen. Her lips were a gash of red. Purple bruises decorated her arms. An officer had his arm draped over her shoulders, his hand resting on her breast. She reminded me of Krista.

I sensed someone watching me and I knew it had to be him – the General. He sat in a velvet armchair, his legs crossed, a smouldering cigarette pinched between thin lips. His eyes were slate grey, his features sharp. His hair was thinning but he wasn't entirely unattractive. There was an intensity to him that was unnerving, though. His gaze still on me, he poured himself a glass of water from a jug that sat perspiring on the table beside him. The air felt thick and hot.

'The piano player,' he said, the words broken by his accent.

Which neighbour had given my name? Had it been a betrayal or was it supposed to be a gift?

He stood up, clapped his hands and the room immediately fell silent. Even the men whose speech was slurred, their eyes unfocused, stopped talking and gave their attention to the General – out of respect or fear, I couldn't tell. He spoke softly to them. Russian is an ugly language but he managed to bring some music into it. And then the female soldier who'd picked us up appeared beside me and gripped my arm, hard enough to leave a bruise. She guided me over to a grand piano that sat in the corner. It was beautiful and looked expensive but I didn't want to play it. I didn't want to be there at all.

I sat down on the stool, closed my eyes and felt the keys with my fingers. I imagined I was at home, the rest of the room falling away. I played Debussy's 'Clair de lune' – Julius's favourite song. I didn't want to sully it by playing it among the enemy, but I also needed Julius beside me and this was the only way I could feel as if he was.

When I finished I looked up to find the General slowly clapping his appreciation. He gestured for me to sit in the armchair and then slipped in behind the piano. His hands were delicate, his fingers long. When he played, people couldn't help but listen. I was good but he was better, and he wanted me to know it. Once this fact had been established I was instructed to return to my position and entertain the men for the rest of the evening.

Soon I was dizzy with exhaustion and the cramp in my hands spread into my arms. Still, I played on. Gradually the soldiers around me drank themselves into a stupor, and one by one they began to fall asleep.

'If you make your daughter behave, I will protect you both.' The General, leaning towards my mother, did not try to speak quietly; he wanted me to hear. 'Me. Or ten of my men.'

My fingers hovered; I held my breath.

'No. Take me instead.' Mother's words were a whisper, a pathetic croak.

He laughed, a humourless bark, and I felt like I was sinking into the floor, my body heavy with defeat.

'One or ten. You choose.'

I didn't see her nod, but I felt it with my body, her betrayal a knife between my shoulder blades.

She appeared beside me, touching me lightly on the shoulder. 'He is a musician like you,' she whispered. 'He will be kind, I am sure of it. It will be over quickly. Just think about something else.'

As he led me upstairs, Mother sat perched on the edge of a sofa, her hands scrunching the folds of her dress. She watched as we went but I refused to meet her eyes. I didn't want to see the pathetic apology they would offer.

A four-poster bed with lace curtains dominated the master bedroom. The room was neat and the sheets looked clean but a musty smell of mothballs permeated the air. One of the wardrobes stood ajar and inside I could see elegant dresses hanging forlorn, waiting in vain for the owner who would never return.

He was strangely gentle at first and I did what Mother said – I closed my eyes and thought of something else. Soon it would be over.

But then I felt his hand around my neck, his fingers crushing my windpipe. I tried to pull his hand away, my fingernails digging into the flesh of his arm, but he was too strong and I flailed beneath him, panic rising like a flood. The more I struggled, the tighter he squeezed. His face swam. Black spots moved across my vision.

I was dying. This was where it would all end.

Just before I passed out, my eyes bulging, all the breath in me gone, he smiled, shuddered and then let me go.

26

LISETTE

Then – Berlin, 2 May 1945

The news reached us through jubilant shouts on the streets, whispers on the stairwell, and printed letters on every newspaper littering what was left of the pavements, and yet it was still hard to believe. His death should have been long and agonizing, bloody fingernails ripped from their beds, burnt and bruised limbs wrenched from their torso. Instead, it was violent but short. A gunshot to the head, with the woman he loved by his side. A bunker full of evil. And then nothing. The Führer dead.

27

LISETTE

Then – Berlin, 5 May 1945

'Vodka,' he said. He only ever commanded, never asked.

Mother scurried to the kitchen and returned instantly with the half-empty bottle, her smile a thin crack across her face. She placed the bottle carefully on the coffee table, sliding a coaster underneath it.

The General eased himself into Father's armchair – as if it was his own, as if he'd always sat there. He watched me with his flat, slate-grey eyes and I found myself wilting beneath his gaze.

Most of the other soldiers had left, the General tired of entertaining his men. Though his right-hand man lay asleep on the sofa, snoring deeply, his stinking breath permeating the air around him. I knew what their retreat meant. Nausea rose in my chest.

Of all the men that could have been our protector, he was the worst. There was no kindness in him. No hint of compassion or regret. I knew he could speak German but he rarely spoke to me directly, as if I was too far beneath him to warrant any speech. I was nothing. Merely a body to entertain him.

He tapped his cigarette into an ashtray and an errant flake of ash floated to the floor. I saw how Mother took note, already adding it to the list of things that needed to be swept away later. I felt a sudden, violent surge of hatred towards her. Every time the General came, she offered him a seat at our table and supplies from our larder, even though one of his minions usually brought food and drink. Each night, once the General had taken me to bed, I would hear Mother entertaining his officers with her basic Russian. I wasn't a child when war broke out. And when my innocence was stolen from me, I wasn't a child either. But I'd expected more from her. Each night when he forced himself upon me, the tinkling of her strained, polite laughter was another violation.

'Piano,' he said. But not to me. 'Cheery song. Hitler dead. The war almost won. We should celebrate, *da*? *The Marriage of Figaro* or *Ruslan and Lyudmila*. You know Glinka, yes? Papa of Russian music.'

Perhaps this was why she'd thought he would be kind – his superior knowledge of classical music. If we'd been in another time or place, I might have been impressed by him. There were so few men who really appreciated or understood the greatest composers. Though I doubted he had a soul.

Mother turned to me and gave what I suspected she thought was an encouraging smile. Obediently I moved over to the piano. My beautiful piano. After that first night, the General had insisted on always coming to our apartment rather than bringing us to the mansion he had sequestered. By invading our home, his domination over us was complete. I'd thought that what had happened to me the night the Russians arrived was the worst thing I'd ever have to go through. But those men were drunk and clumsy and quick. I was an object they had used and then discarded. With the General, it was different. He wanted to have someone to humiliate, to control, to break. He wanted someone he could bring to the edge of death and then allow to live. Each night was worse than the one before.

I moved my fingers over the keys but struggled to think of something upbeat. The piano was an extension of me but I was floating aimlessly in an infinite ocean, waiting for the waves to overcome me and the water to fill my lungs. I could only play the song of someone drowning.

I heard the ashtray hit my forehead before I felt the pain shooting across my temple. Slowly I took my fingers off the keys and brushed away the ash that had landed in my hair. My head throbbed like a heartbeat. I bit my lip to stop myself from crying.

'Something cheery,' Mother whispered in my ear, her voice pleading. And I obeyed. Because my core impulse was to survive – it was the same for all of us. I wished for death, yet unwillingly I defied it.

'Warrior's Song' now flowed through my fingers, its majestic rhythms invigorating, the notes lifting me up and transporting me elsewhere. It made me feel weightless and I knew as long as I could find comfort through playing my piano, I could survive anything.

At the end of the piece, I lifted my fingers from the keys, stretched them out before wiggling them and then flicking them to expel the cramp.

'Why stop? I not give permission to stop playing.'

He stood up, taking his glass with him. It left a stain on the table – a ring of darkness that would never disappear, no matter how much Mother scrubbed at it later. He moved over to the piano, standing so close I could see each wrinkle marking his tanned leathery skin.

'Play. Now.' Impatience crept into his voice. I tried to focus my attention but panic rose in me like bile. I could feel my heart throbbing in my neck. I remembered his hands around my throat and I didn't know if I could go through it again.

He placed his glass on the piano lid. Then, without taking his eyes off me, he took out a knife from the waistband of his trousers. He ran his finger along the serrated edge. He was a coiled spring of violence, a venomous snake waiting to strike. And yet, still, I couldn't play.

He held the handle and then stabbed the knife down into the piano lid.

Slowly he carved his initials into the wood. He might as well have been slicing into my flesh, branding my soul with his name. Because I was his. I understood that now.

28

LISETTE

Then – Berlin, 6 May 1945

I woke to find the General gone and Mother standing over me, an indiscernible look on her face.

'I made breakfast. There is bacon and eggs.'

I rolled over and faced the wall.

'Do not be like this. Soon they will be gone . . .'

'And you'll miss them.' I threw the words over my shoulder like objects, wanting them to hit their target. 'I hear you every night, you know. Laughing with them. Joking.'

'What would you have me do? Be rude to them? Ask them to leave? I know they are our enemy. I do not enjoy having these dirty men at my table, their dirty souls in my home. And you . . . I am just trying to keep us alive until—'

'You let this happen,' I said. 'I will never forgive you.'

She opened her mouth. Closed it again. I stared her down and finally she retreated. I went back to looking at the wall.

War had taught me that we were alone in the world. We were all selfish and cruel. I was no different.

Later, I found her at the dining table sterilizing a needle and cutting some thread. Behind her, Frau Weber's bird sat on its perch, watching. It had been virtually silent since her death and I was surprised it had survived at all.

'What are you doing?'

'That wound on your head needs attention,' she said. 'Let me stitch it. Please?'

I fingered my forehead and found a swollen lump. My fingers came away wet and sticky. Wordless, I pulled out a chair and sat down beside her.

Her brow furrowed in concentration as she prepared the first stitch. I tried not to wince as I felt the needle puncture my skin and the thread tug at my flesh. Then she began again. It took only a few minutes and then she put the needle down, nodded and gave a satisfied mumble at her handiwork. Tentatively I touched the stitches on my head – the bump, the warm skin.

'I am sorry,' she said quietly, using a tissue to wipe away a trickle of blood above my eyebrow. 'I am really so, so sorry.'

29

LISETTE

Then – Berlin, 20 May 1945

I trudged through the broken streets, weighed down by two pails of water. My shoulders ached with the effort. I'd spent so many hours in the water queue that I had started to hear the rusty squeak of the pump handle in my dreams.

I climbed over a mound of debris, struggling to keep my footing. Around me the dust lay thick like a coat of paint. Above me, hanging from bombed-out buildings, Soviet flags flapped their dominance in the wind. Blood-red with some strange symbol, they weren't unlike the Nazi flags they'd replaced. Why did men find power so intoxicating? Why couldn't we just be left alone to live?

Russian soldiers had spread throughout Berlin like an indelible stain. Two cycled past me, wobbling all over the place. Their friends cheered each time they fell.

'Fräulein,' one shouted. 'Come teach us.'

Since Hitler's death had been announced and Germany had surrendered, the Russkis had been in constant celebratory mode. Summer had almost arrived, but still they were here. In my memory, Berlin summers were always twinned with the faint smell of rotting food, of rubbish waiting on the street to be disposed of. But during the war, no morsel of food went uneaten and once the corpses had been removed, and the dead horses had been carved up by civilians for their meat, the air was disconcertingly free from the stench of decay. Instead, it was the women who were rotting, from the inside out. I felt humiliated and dirty. Each time I walked down the street, I felt as if everyone knew just by looking at me that I'd been defiled. Contaminated.

'Fräulein! Why so sad?'

A soldier, dirty and dishevelled, cycled around me. He was better than the rest of his friends, managing to maintain his balance with ease, but then suddenly he hit a brick, flew over the handlebars and landed with a grunt in front of me.

I stopped and placed the buckets on the ground while I waited for him to get out of my way. I was careful not to spill any water – I'd queued for two hours and had earned every drop.

The man stood up and brushed the dust from his trousers. The palms of his hands were scratched and bleeding. He frowned and then licked the blood away.

Behind a nearby wall shredded with bullet holes, I could hear children's laughter. There were orphans everywhere. They roamed the streets, looting and stealing and causing havoc. There was a time when I would have felt sorry for them, but I had no sympathy left to spare.

'I help?' the man said, moving to take hold of the handles.

I shook my head, jumped between him and the buckets.

Another soldier, sitting on a pile of bricks near by, was smoking a cigarette and watching us. He spoke to the bicycle man in a flurry of harsh syllables. All I recognized was the General's name. I'd been branded. They all knew who I was. The General's whore. Berlin had become one big brothel, but none of us was paid.

The bicycle man lifted his arms in surrender and backed away from me. I tried to tuck in my pain, like a shirt that was too long, hiding the fraying edges. I worried that with one more tug I would wholly unravel, my nakedness complete.

I turned back to my buckets only to discover a small boy, hair the colour of fire, lapping up the water like a stray dog.

'Get away,' I said, smacking him around the head. 'Get your own.'

He stood up, laughed loudly, and then kicked the buckets over before darting off in the other direction.

I closed my eyes, tried to steady my breathing. Hot tears fell. I furiously rubbed them away.

The cycling soldier approached me once more.

'Sit, Fräulein,' he said, picking up the empty buckets. 'I get.'

This time he handed me something. It was a Belgian chocolate bar.

'For Fräulein,' he said and smiled. I didn't know where he could possibly have got hold of it and I didn't care. I could already imagine the taste of it on my tongue and the smile Mother would share with me when I broke it in two and handed half to her.

'Sit,' he repeated. 'I back soon.'

I watched him as he walked away, this fleeting moment of kindness like the sighting of a rare butterfly fluttering in a snowstorm.

30

LISETTE

Then – Berlin, 22 May 1945

Mother found me in the courtyard, digging in the dirt. Our allotment had long since been destroyed so we attempted to grow whatever we could closer to home. The courtyard now smelled of wild garlic, the tomatoes were almost ripe and I'd found one lone cucumber hiding among the vines. It was too early to eat the vegetables but I knew that if I left them another day, one of our neighbours would probably steal them for themselves. If they did, I wouldn't blame them; I'd do the same.

Mother crouched down beside me and helped me pluck away the weeds, dusting the soil off her body every so often. She had gone back to wearing respectable clothes, her shoes were polished, her lips stained red, her hair in a tight bun. I knew she must have used some of our precious water to wash her face but I couldn't begrudge her that.

'Are you OK?'

There were no words that could describe how *not* OK I was. I no longer recognized myself in the mirror. Loneliness had curved my spine and sadness had turned my voice to gravel.

Some days I found I couldn't speak at all. There seemed little point; I had nothing worth saying.

'Talk to me,' Mother said. 'I want to help, if I can.'

I heard the guilt in her tone. But her guilt couldn't help me. Nothing could.

'I'm . . . I'll be . . . fine.' I strung the words together slowly like beads on a necklace, but the thread was almost invisible, the holes too small.

'The General will be gone soon,' she said. 'I heard him saying as much to one of his soldiers. And your father will come home. And Julius. You will see. Everything will change.'

Her words should have filled me with hope but they didn't. I just felt numb.

'Frau. Fräulein.'

One of the General's soldiers appeared in the courtyard. The same woman who'd driven us to meet the General that first night.

'Follow me.'

She touched the strap of her gun, a subtle warning to hurry. Quickly, I gathered the vegetables I'd picked, put them in my bag, and then tucked it under my arm out of sight. Mother and I got to our feet and trailed behind her through the front of the building and out on to the street. The pavement was full of our neighbours as well as many more people we didn't recognize. Over the past couple of weeks, German refugees who'd previously fled to other countries had been forced to return. Each day thousands arrived in Berlin.

A soldier stood on a pile of rubble, a loudspeaker in one hand, rattling out information from a piece of paper.

'*Zuhören!* Listen!' he shouted. His Russian accent was strong but his German was surprisingly good. 'Tomorrow all men and women – fifteen to fifty-five and capable of work – must report to the *Rathaus* for labour duty. It's time to clean up your disgusting city.'

I was sure that last part wasn't on his sheet.

We knew already what we'd be asked to do. The rumour mill had been in overdrive the past few days. First, anything valuable left in Berlin would be loaded on to carts to be taken to Russia, and then we'd be ordered to start clearing the rubble from our streets.

Behind me, I heard the female officer's voice. 'Fräulein,' she said. 'Piano is safe. The General has . . . saved it.' She gave me a faint smile, a small peace offering. She expected a thank-you. The General would expect one, too.

I turned away, pretended I hadn't heard, and then Mother and I climbed the main stairs to our apartment, the familiar dread knotting my stomach.

Inside, half a dozen soldiers had already gathered. They were rooting through our drawers, lifting mattresses, removing paintings from the walls. There was so little to take – we'd already sold most things that were worth selling – but they were like vultures plucking the last rotten flesh from the carcass that was our home.

We stood by the door and did nothing. I could feel Mother trembling beside me at the realization that the General's 'protection' only went so far. As the men carried several beautiful dresses and her last remaining jewellery out of the door, I heard her swallow a sob. We'd buried a few things of value in the courtyard, but why hadn't we thought to bury all of it?

A short, skinny soldier with buck teeth and unruly hair picked up the birdcage. He poked his finger through the bar, jabbing Frau Weber's budgie in the stomach. It pecked at him and he laughed. As he tried to carry the cage out of the door, I blocked his way.

'Please. Leave the bird. He's not a nice bird. You won't want him. I promise. But he belonged to our friend. I need to look after him.'

The man looked at me blankly. It was obvious he didn't

understand German but he understood my stance. I wouldn't let him leave with the bird, that much was clear. Finally he shrugged, handed me the cage and grabbed an ornament from the bookcase instead.

'You hate that bird,' Mother said quietly.

'I know. I really do.'

As promised, the piano remained untouched. Once they'd left, closing the door behind them almost apologetically, it dominated the room. It had been my most prized possession but now it sat like some great monster threatening to swallow me whole.

I looked at the poor bird in its cage. I opened the window, coaxed it out, and set it free.

There was a knock at the door. It opened before either of us answered.

'Both still here,' the General said. 'Good.'

Behind him, men descended the stairs, Frau Weber's paintings tucked under their arms. I couldn't imagine those beautiful watercolours adorning the Russkis' walls. They had murdered her and now they were trapping her soul inside their homes. I regretted not taking them and burning them all. She would have preferred that.

'Orders have come,' he said, directing his words to Mother. 'The city soon divided. Controlled by Allies. Some troops remain here in our segment, but is time for me to return home. I thank you for . . . hospitality.'

Mother nodded and then retreated, as if he and I were in love and she thought we would want some privacy. Perhaps that's what she'd told herself. Maybe she assuaged her guilt with a million little lies.

I backed up against the piano; once a life raft, now an

obstacle. The General took a step forward. His body pressed up against mine.

'Sometimes when I meet someone,' he said, 'I hear their *muzyka* – their song. When I met you first, yours was a string *kvartet*. But played by old musicians – once good, possibly excellent, but now defeated. Like your country. Now, all I hear . . . one lonely cello. Some strings broken, the others have been *sorvannyy* – plucked – too hard. Ready to snap.'

He squeezed my shoulder and then leaned forward to whisper in my ear, his rancid breath hot on my skin.

'I will miss you, Fräulein. Though I think you will not forget me. I find comfort knowing every time you sit to play the piano, you will think of me.'

I turned my face and looked at the wall, refusing to meet his eyes.

And then he was gone.

I stood motionless, staring at the closed door. I tried to ignore a hundred threads twisting and knotting in my stomach, creating a ball that would never unravel. I felt a thick cloak around me, shutting out the light, muffling my voice.

'Lisette?'

I couldn't look at Mother. I knew she would expect me to be happy now, to shrug off all that had happened and embark on the road to forgetting. But I would never forget.

I moved past Mother and extracted a knife from the kitchen drawer. Then I scratched out the initials the General had engraved on the piano lid. I scratched and scratched. I dug out big chips of wood as if I was gouging out his eyes. But it wasn't enough. I picked up the poker from the fireplace, walked back to the piano and lifted it high above my head. Then I brought it down with as much force as I could muster. Mother shrieked. I struck the piano again and again. At first nothing happened – just a few dents, but then the wood started to splinter and the beautiful keys rose up like a wave of white horses before collapsing and falling to the floor. There was a cacophony of broken sounds as the piano strings popped and snapped. But I continued, the piano's dying screams filling the room.

When my piano finally lay in pieces, I crumpled to the floor.

My piano was gone and the music that had always sat within me was gone too. It was not until later that I realized my voice had disappeared with it.

31

ELLY

Now – East Berlin, 25 September 1961

I leave the flat, resisting the urge to look back. I don't need to commit it to memory; I'll make it home again.

As I pick my way down the uneven cobbled street, shadows appear on every corner. I tell myself not to be scared; I've done nothing wrong. At least, not yet. I could simply be on my way home from one of the discotheques. Officially they're supposed to close by one a.m. but I know some have special permits. I kick myself for not memorizing one of their names.

I cross through a park and the wrinkled leaves under my feet taunt me. *This is a mistake*, they say. *You won't survive.*

Andrei is where he said he would be, smoking a cigarette, leaning against a car. It's a *VoPo* car, *Volkspolizei* emblazoned on its bonnet in dark green. Even though I know this is Andrei's friend's car, the sight of it still stops my heart.

The wind picks up litter and swirls it around as a fine curtain of rain sweeps down the street. I make my way over to Andrei slowly, scanning my surroundings, but there's no one in sight – the city is sleeping. He straightens up as I approach and then unexpectedly he pulls me into his arms. Briefly I press my face into the scratchy material of his uniform jacket. He smells of smoke and something sweet. I feel a sudden pain in my chest and I pull away. At best, something akin to a friendship has formed but, just like an animal raised in captivity, it's not something that could survive in the wild.

'Put these on,' he says, passing me a pair of boots.

They're wading boots, ones that will reach halfway up my thigh. I can already see they're too big, made for a man with wide feet and thick calves, but I'm grateful all the same. I take off my own boots, squish them into my backpack, and then pull the other ones on.

'Are you ready?' He takes my face in his hands. We're so close our noses are almost touching. Though I try not to, it's impossible not to remember that first kiss.

'As ready as I'll ever be. I mean, no one could possibly be ready for something like this. It's too . . . but, yes. I mean, I'm ready.'

'Stay,' he whispers, so quietly I'm not sure he's said the word at all. 'Please stay.'

'I can't.'

He nods and the fact that he somehow understands this makes me never want to leave.

I step back on to the kerb as he opens the car door and climbs inside. He drives it over the manhole cover and then climbs back out.

'We need to do this quickly,' he says. 'After you.'

I get down on my hands and knees and crawl under the car, dragging my backpack with me. There's so little space I worry we won't both be able to fit but moments later Andrei is beside me. In his right hand is a hook which he uses to prise up the manhole cover. Together we slowly slide it across the road, the metal screeching, the weight of it almost too much to bear. The sound is so loud it might as well be a siren.

That is when we hear it.

The hum of an engine. Skittering gravel.

Andrei holds a finger to his lips. I grip his other hand, squeezing it until I'm sure the blood will stop flowing. I can hear the car's sputtering engine. It's close, almost upon us.

Andrei's scared too – I can see it in his eyes. It's the first time I've ever seen his confidence falter. If we're caught, there is nothing we can say that will explain why we're crammed underneath a car, a gaping hole in the road between us. They'll drag us out, bundle us into a van, and then they'll torture us. Or, if we're lucky, they'll shoot us on the spot.

The car slows down as it approaches. I lock my eyes on Andrei's, trying to find comfort in their blue depths. I can taste petrol on my tongue.

And then the car rolls on and we're alone.

My face is wet and it's only now I realize I've been crying. A sob escapes me but it's a strangled cry of relief.

'Now,' Andrei says. 'Before it's too late. He might come back.'

There's no time to change my mind. I swivel around, bumping my head on the underbelly of the car, and then lower myself down into the hole, my feet pedalling until I find the rungs of the ladder. Andrei passes me my backpack. I swing it over my shoulder. I give him one last look but before I start my descent, he takes my face in his hands. He presses his lips to mine.

Without thinking, I kiss him back. The kiss is quick and hungry and I don't know if my shaking legs and the heat in my chest are due to the kiss or the fact that half my body is dangling in the entrance to a sewer and I might not live to see tomorrow.

The moment expands and stretches. The world becomes small.

It's just us here.

After what seems like for ever but also no time at all, our lips part.

'I'll be waiting for you, Elly Lange,' he says. And then he's gone.

The drain cover fills the hole above my head and my world tumbles into darkness.

~

My skin feels hot. I am clutching the ladder more tightly than I need to, suddenly scared I'll slip and fall. If I break a leg, no one will find me before it's too late. I want to get out my torch but I need both hands. The darkness is so complete it feels like I'm descending into the very depths of hell. I almost expect to feel the heat of flames licking at my feet, but it's cold down here and the further down I go, the colder it gets. It's quieter, too, the sounds of the city becoming muffled and distant.

The rungs stop and my feet find something solid. It doesn't feel entirely stable. I must have hit the sewer grate. Holding on to the ladder with one hand to keep myself steady, I pull out the torch from my jacket pocket and turn it on. The space is small and the walls around me are crumbling. The grate beneath my feet is brown and rusty. I move to the side and try to lift it. I can't see a padlock or anything keeping it in place but it won't budge. I'm going to die down here.

My forehead is slick with sweat and my fingers are already cramping. I need to calm my beating heart, but panic is an enemy squeezing my chest. I tug and I tug at the grate, and finally it gives just a little. I brace one foot against the wall and yank on it with all my strength. With a sudden snap, it lifts off, jerking me backwards, my shoulder painfully scraping against the wall.

I grip the torch between my teeth, then think better of it and shove it in my bag instead. Halfway down the next ladder, the stench hits me. I try to breathe through my mouth but the smell is a taste too and I find myself gagging. A few more steps and then my foot dangles. I can hear liquid flowing, the skittering sound of rats in the distance. The air is impregnated with filth. It's gritty on my tongue; it coats my skin like slime. I knew the piss and shit of millions of people would be horrific, but I wasn't prepared for this.

If I hesitate any longer, I will lose my courage. And so, I jump. I land in the river of shit, some of it splashing up into my face. The liquid comes up to my thighs and I am so incredibly thankful for the sewer boots Andrei gave me. I start to wade and almost lose my balance, but my hand shoots out and finds a damp wall. Am I going in the right direction? Did I turn as I fell? Andrei made me memorize the map, but the image flickers in my mind like a TV screen with a lost signal.

Now I can use my hands again, I swing my backpack on to my chest and rummage inside for the torch. I find the switch and flick it on. It looks as if the walls are moving. I don't understand why. I take a step closer. It's not the wall moving but hundreds of cockroaches scuttling away, scared by the light. I recoil, losing my grip on the torch. It plops into the sewage but I can still see its beam. I reach down for it, turning my face away as I feel for it with my fingertips. The smell is unbearable. My fingers find something solid. I grasp it and stand back up, the dripping torch in one hand. My whole body heaves and I vomit over and over again.

Finally, when there's nothing left in my stomach, I shine the torch in both directions. The tunnel ahead looks identical to the one that lies behind me – paths leading to the right and left. What did I expect? A sign saying *West Berlin this way*? I have to assume I'm going in the right direction. What other choice do I have?

I count my steps but my mind keeps wandering and I lose track. Did we calculate the distance correctly? It's better I go too far than not far enough but there will only be one manhole cover that's been pulled aside ahead of my arrival. I don't know who's helping me other than it's a friend of Andrei's. And I find myself wondering again whether I've been right to trust him. I won't be able to lift a manhole cover on my own. If his friend doesn't do what he's promised to or I can't find the right lid, will there be someone to hear me shout? Or will the sound of traffic muffle my voice? Panic rises in me once more and I try to focus on Axel – his tiny fingers, his wide eyes – and Mama – her gaunt face, her muted voice, her stifled song. I'm doing this for them.

A splash. Too big to be a falling rat. A flicker of light in the distance.

Someone else is down here.

I turn off my torch and stand as still as I can. My breathing sounds unnaturally fast and loud, so I try to slow it down, inhaling the stink. I swallow the urge to vomit again.

'*Hallo?*' A man's voice, gruff and distant. '*Ist da jemand* – is someone there?'

As slowly as I can, I wade over to the side of the tunnel. I press my back against the wall. Something scuttles over my face and it takes all of my willpower to hold in the scream.

There shouldn't be anyone down here. I don't know the schedules of those who work in the sewers but surely no one should be splashing around in the middle of the night. Unless it's a border guard. The driver of the car that passed us before I climbed down – maybe they put out an alert. Perhaps there's a whole army down here looking for me.

'*Hallo?*' The voice comes again. Torchlight swings towards me, missing me by inches. I can't hear the man's music – all I can hear is sloshing and gurgling and a thumping sound in my ears. I imagine he's not a human at all but a Minotaur, with the head of a bull and horns that will rip through my stomach. I can't tell if he's getting closer or further away but he's definitely in this main passage rather than in one of the smaller ones off to the side.

Sliding my back across the wall, I take a right turn, then move as quickly as I can without making too much noise. I feel along the wall, another right turn and then a left. I stop and I wait. It feels as if the walls are closing in on me – but I can no longer see the stumbling, waving beam of a torch. For the moment, I'm safe.

I wait longer than I need to, counting the minutes. Water trickles down the wall on to my neck; something skitters past my ear. I bite the inside of my cheek, squeeze my eyes shut. I try to find my music but can't.

Right, left, left – I'm trying to remember Andrei's instructions, the map we both memorized. Which is right and which is left? I turn in a circle, then press my back against the wall once more, trying to keep myself steady. The darkness is so complete down here – it crowds in around me like a horde of ghosts. For a bizarre moment it feels as though I'm upside down. But I keep going, my hands feeling the way. I don't know if I'm heading in the right direction, but I'm able to recognize when I pass a turning – there's always a brief draught and the stench isn't as strong for a fleeting moment.

Here. The ladder should be here but it's not.

My body convulses with a sob and the sound echoes. My limbs feel heavy, my hands numb.

My mind is lost somewhere in this maze of darkness.

32

LISETTE

Then – Berlin, 4 September 1945

I wrapped a scarf around my head and tucked in my hair. I put on a pair of Father's old boots. They were much too big for me but none of my shoes would do. I stuffed them with paper and accepted the discomfort.

The war was over – the atomic bomb had wiped out most of Hiroshima and Nagasaki, the Japanese had surrendered, the Allies had moved into our city, joining the remaining Soviets – and, along with our fellow Berliners, Mother and I crawled out of our bombed-out building like hedgehogs emerging from hibernation. Finally, we could live again, but we didn't yet know what kind of life it would be. I didn't think Berlin could rise from its ashes but many were hopeful. And clearing the destruction was the first step. In some districts, there were no streets left, just mounds of rubble like anthills. On the roads, weeds had begun to push their way through the broken concrete, nature already beginning to reclaim its space.

Shielding my eyes, I stepped out into the blazing sunshine. The wind was like the waves of a fever but I rolled up my sleeves and let it breathe across my skin. Once my eyes had adjusted to the light, I saw a poster had appeared on our building. It was an image of one of the concentration camps, a mound of skeletal bodies positioned like logs on a bonfire. Underneath it, the words *YOU ARE GUILTY OF THIS*. Mother glanced at it but then looked away, unwilling or unable to take in the horror of it.

We walked through the broken streets, avoiding craters and keeping our distance from buildings that looked on the verge of collapse. There were similar posters everywhere. I forced myself to look at each one.

At the time, had I known?

Only last week, Mother had agreed with Frau Roth that we civilians had been kept in the dark. I told myself it must be true; we wouldn't have allowed it to happen if we'd known. No human being could have known and chosen to say and do nothing. It wasn't possible.

And yet it was.

I struggled over a pile of bricks that had not yet been shifted from the centre of the road. I held out my hand to Mother but she shook her head. Around us the jagged forms of destroyed buildings looked like mountains against the expanse of blue sky.

Our task of clearing the city felt hopeless.

We passed an abandoned, scorched tank. First we had seen it burn, then we saw flowers placed in its gun as if the barrel were a vase. Now it was covered in Soviet propaganda posters mixed in with fly-posters advertising dance classes, like an absurd work of art.

I joined the group Mother and I had been assigned to, avoiding meeting anyone's eyes, though that did not stop a woman from approaching me.

'I'm Margarethe,' she said. Her face was gaunt, her hair long and plaited. It was impossible to discern her age; she could have been twenty or sixty. 'Which sector do you live in?'

'She cannot speak,' Mother said, then added, 'We live in the Soviet section.'

'Oh, bad luck. I'm in the American section.' She said it proudly, as if she had divided the city herself and made sure which section she was in.

A female Soviet soldier, with a wide nose, large breasts and small yellow teeth, ordered us into a line. 'It's simple, *da*?' she said. 'Fill bucket. Pass down. Put on truck.'

The strongest-looking women were positioned at the top and the bottom of the line. I was tall but the war years had made me thin and gangly, so Mother and I found a spot in the middle. Margarethe squeezed herself between us.

The women at the top began filling tin buckets with brick and slowly these were passed down the line. At the bottom, a group hauled the contents into the back of a truck.

'This is not a job for a woman like me,' Mother grumbled to no one in particular.

Despite my advice, she was not suitably dressed. She wore a wide-brimmed hat with a fancy feather on top and heeled shoes – the heels were low but I could see she found it difficult to keep her balance. Her dress was at least made of breathable fabric, but while the rest of us wore dirty, ragged outfits, hers looked newly washed. She had even painted her lips with her favourite red lipstick before we set out, as though she was on her way to a ladies' lunch.

'Why can't you speak?' Margarethe asked and then laughed. 'Lucky for you, I'm a talker. It's the only way to get through the days,' she added. 'The hours will pass quicker with me by your side, I promise you. We'll be doing this for a long old while. Better than digging graves for all those poor souls, though. I would choose this heat and dust over that any day of the week. And maybe our men will come home soon. Don't you think? It's definitely time. The soldiers who fought the Brits and Americans, at least. The POWs in Russia will probably never come home. Do you have a sweetheart? Did he die? Is that why you won't speak?'

I closed my ears to Margarethe's constant chatter. I found if I focused on ignoring her voice, it would grow quieter until it faded away, as if she was on the radio and I'd turned down the volume.

The heat sizzled but there was something satisfying in work that made me sweat. I enjoyed, too, how my hands stung with blisters and my muscles burned with the effort of lifting and passing, lifting and passing. I'd been numb ever since the Soviets had arrived four months ago and experiencing any sensation in my body at all felt almost rewarding.

'We look just like the *Trümmerfrauen* the media want to promote, don't you think?' Margarethe said. 'They've made it sound like we're all desperate to help the clear-up effort. I only did it for the promise of higher rations.'

'I wish you hadn't,' Mother muttered.

'What was that?'

'Nothing.'

The female soldier had positioned herself by the truck, throwing unhelpful instructions at us every few minutes while she smoked cigarette after cigarette. 'Faster, *da*? Too much in bucket. Too little in bucket.'

The dense, intense heat of the day was oppressive and the work was brutal. Unlike Margarethe, the women in the Soviet section hadn't been given any choice about clearing the streets. We weren't prisoners and yet it felt like we were. The city needed to be cleared up and who else was there to do it? For months there'd been chaos – no food, no transport, no electricity – but, slowly, things were getting better. At least, that's what we were being told.

'Have you sorted out your medical certificate yet?' Margarethe asked, wiping her sweaty brow with a dirty rag she produced from her pocket. She'd finally understood her badgering wouldn't elicit a word from my mouth and directed her chatter at Mother instead.

'What certificate?'

'You can't get your food stamps without a doctor's certificate stating you're clean of any sexually transmitted diseases. Quite shocking, don't you think? Though the men will be back soon, so it's probably just as well. I got mine yesterday. The clinic was overflowing – I had to wait five hours. I didn't get home until well past dark.'

'But why would I need to get tested?' Mother said, placing her hands on her hips, refusing to take the bucket Margarethe held out to her. 'I have not been with any man since Lisette's father left.'

Margarethe laughed and I didn't dare pull out my notepad and scribble that she had. Mother was not the only one who denied vehemently that she'd been violated by the Russians. But, with her, it was as if she genuinely believed it. Some days she refused to leave the apartment and I'd come home to find her confused. She'd look at me strangely as if she wasn't entirely sure who I was but was much too polite to admit it. Only the day before, I'd found her in her best dress, silk gloves on, and her fanciest hat pinned neatly in place. She was waiting for Father to take her to the opera and couldn't understand why he was late.

When the sun's brightness was a little less penetrating, the soldier finally shouted, 'Home, *da*. Tomorrow again.'

The truck full of bricks rumbled away, bouncing along the uneven street. I looked up at the mound we'd been dismantling.

My body was sore, my muscles ached and my hands were raw, but it seemed like we'd barely made a dent.

Margarethe handed me a cup of cloudy water that she'd scooped from a bucket being passed around. I drank from it greedily before refilling it and giving it to Mother, who perched beside me on the remnants of a wall.

I pulled out my notepad and wrote, *We should go to the doctor. Get the certificate.*

'This not-speaking thing is getting tiresome,' she said, refusing to look at the notepad when I tried to hand it to her. 'There is clearly nothing physically wrong with your voice. Is it a choice, not to speak?'

I shook my head. I couldn't explain it because I didn't understand it either. I would open my mouth but my throat would constrict and no sound would appear. If I tried, I felt as if the air was being sucked out of my lungs.

I stood up and shoved the notepad under her nose. She frowned as she finally read the words then shook her head. 'I have told you. There is no need for me to see a doctor.'

Come with me, I wrote, sitting back down. *You need to see the doctor anyway. You've been muddled lately. And you haven't been sleeping. Maybe he can prescribe something to help. Also, we need those certificates to get our rations. That's what everyone is saying.*

'Fine,' Mother finally said. 'If I must.'

The first clinic we went to was so overcrowded the queue stretched the length of the street. We joined it, unsure what else to do.

'Go to Helmholtzplatz,' the woman in front of us said. She was as thin as a broom and yet carried a skinny boy asleep on her hip who must have weighed as much as she did. 'There's a clinic there. It's not as busy. I would go there myself but it's too far to walk with this little one.'

'*Danke*,' Mother said while I nodded my thanks.

It was a long walk, but we needed those food stamps. There were no longer wounded and dying soldiers in the streets – or the corpses of those who hadn't escaped a building before it was hit – but it was not uncommon to see the body of someone who had succumbed to hunger.

Ahead was a field of rubbish, writhing with maggots and flies. We had no option but to wade through it. Mother closed her eyes and took a deep breath, then kicked her way through the mess. I'd been feeling nauseous for weeks. It was the lack of food, perhaps. Or maybe dysentery or typhoid fever had finally found me, like so many others. The sight of the maggots was too much to bear and I doubled over, throwing up on Father's boots.

Mother said nothing. She just turned around, gave me a rag to wipe my mouth, and then kept on walking.

The woman had been right. The clinic by Helmholtzplatz was less busy but we still had to wait for two hours to be seen. First we waited on the street. Then we squeezed into a waiting room that was overflowing with women of all ages. Most stood or sat in silence, but some chattered as if they were on a night out and were keen to catch up on the week's gossip. Mother stared at the floor, her face blank. I listened in to snippets of conversation.

'Her husband came and then left again,' one woman said, her hair the colour of dirty snow.

'But why?' her friend whispered.

'He couldn't accept that she'd been with a Russian.'

'As if she had a choice.'

'Well, exactly.'

'She shouldn't have told him. When my Fritz comes home, I won't be saying a word. They're fragile, these men. And what they don't know won't hurt them.'

Like water dripping from a faulty tap, our men were slowly

trickling back into the city. I had yet to see anyone I knew but every day I hoped that Julius might knock gently on our door. I knew he would go back to his mother first, but then he would come and see me, I was sure of it. All I could do was pray he wouldn't be one of those who returned only to disappear into the cracks of the city, broken and defeated.

'Richter? Rita Richter?'

A young woman, presumably a nurse, scanned the crowd as if our names would be pinned to our chests. I waved at the woman and then nudged Mother out of her stupor.

I was called next after Mother. I took a step back when I found a man in the doctor's office. He was old and hardly threatening, but hadn't we women suffered enough without being prodded and poked by a male doctor?

'Come in, come in,' he said, giving me a tired smile. His glasses sat slightly crooked on his nose and his blue eyes looked grey in the day's fading light.

'Let's do this quickly, shall we? Just hop up on that bed there.'

I closed my eyes and pretended I was elsewhere. It was something I'd become exceptionally good at. I didn't feel his hands on me or the closeness of his body. His words, 'All done', brought me back into the room as if I'd been woken from a deep sleep.

I pulled up my knickers, yanked my skirt back down, then sat on the chair opposite the doctor. The nurse was hovering by my shoulder.

'No diseases so I can give you your certificate. However,' he said, leaning forward and touching my hand gently, 'I think you might be pregnant.'

I looked at him stupidly. Even if I could have talked, I wouldn't have been able to find the words.

'Perhaps you've had some symptoms? Nausea? Tender breasts?'

When I didn't say anything, he glanced at the nurse for help.

'You could . . . get rid of it. If you want,' the nurse said.

'A pregnancy . . . interruption . . . is illegal, of course,' the doctor added quickly, 'but the current circumstances mean that it's something we can do. If you want.'

When I didn't reply, he added, 'We'll let you think about it. Though, don't wait too long. My guess would be you're already four months.'

The room felt unbearably hot. Now I knew it existed – this thing, this foetus – I could feel it in my stomach: a war wound that would never heal. It would grow inside me, a disgusting parasite, and then it would live with me, an unwanted guest, forever reminding me of the General and what he had done.

The nurse moved to the doctor's side of the desk and whispered something.

'Ah, yes. You are Frau Richter's daughter. Correct? I saw her before you.'

I could hear the relief in his voice at being momentarily reprieved – he could talk about something else.

'Your mother told me she's been feeling confused. She's experiencing memory loss and struggling to carry out familiar tasks. Have you noticed this too?'

I nodded.

'It's possible her symptoms are due to stress – trauma – or she could have early-onset dementia. She is still relatively young, but we know that vitamin deficiency triggers it to progress faster, and in the circumstances . . . Do you know what dementia is?'

I nodded again, but I wasn't really listening. There was a buzzing in my ears. Sweat trickled down my back and I wrung my clammy hands together. I could see my life unravelling, one stray thread at a time, and there was nothing I could do to stop it.

33

LISETTE

Then – Berlin, 9 September 1945

We arrived early; the office hadn't yet opened, but it was already busy. The outside walls were plastered with photos and descriptions of those who were missing – parents, friends and children whose disappearances had ripped a hole through those who were left.

We shouldn't be here, I wrote. *Father isn't displaced. He's missing in action.*

'Displaced – missing. It is the same thing,' Mother said.

Many of those who crowded around the office had lost their homes, but most had been imprisoned in the Nazi concentration camps or forced labour units along with their relatives. Shame forced my head down and rounded my shoulders. This was no place for us. No place, either, for the enemy growing within me.

'I have already been in to register him,' she said, extracting a faded photograph of Father from her bag. 'I just want to pop this up.'

She squeezed past a group of elderly women and stuck the photograph on the wall. Father looked young in the photo, handsome even. I committed the image to memory. I doubted I would see it again; within hours someone would pin their own photo over ours.

'Soon he will be found,' Mother said, making her way back towards the street. 'Don't you think?'

Sometimes I suspected she liked the fact that my voice was gone, as it meant there was no danger of me uttering a brutal truth she didn't want to hear. There were some things I did want to write down, but the permanence of words on paper was too much to bear. I wanted to explain that I couldn't be in the flat alone, that when I was there the memories closed in on me like the walls of a collapsing building – Frau Weber's lifeless body, her blood on the wall; the General at our table, on our sofa, in my bed; the empty space where my piano had once stood. I *did* write every single day that I wanted to move. She point-blank refused, as if her memory had erased all the horrors that had happened there.

'We must be here when Father gets home,' she'd say. 'When he returns, he will want to live in the flat he was born in, the flat where we raised you. You must understand that, Lisette. Leaving is not an option.'

And then she would take my pages and throw them in the fire, the flames consuming my words. If I persisted, she would leave the room. I had my silence and she had her denial.

We turned on to Unter den Linden. It was one of the first boulevards to be cleared of debris and it was refreshingly open and empty but for the Allied military vehicles driving up and down. Most of the buildings were still standing, though chunks of their facades had been damaged so they were now a patchwork of different shades, like peeling skin on a burnt back.

Ahead of us, two soldiers sat in a parked truck, their windows rolled down, elbows jutting out. Behind them was a huge poster of Stalin, red Soviet flags flanking it on either side and a star positioned above his head. He wasn't entirely dissimilar to

Hitler with his megalomaniac stance and his stupid moustache. What was it with these men who wanted to plaster their image everywhere? Their obsession with being bigger and better than those who preceded them? Their need to prove their manliness through hatred and war?

The soldiers in the truck smoked and laughed while they watched us walk by. I felt their eyes on my body. I wanted to make myself smaller. I wanted to scrub at my skin until it was raw, to scour out my insides too. It was as if everyone knew just by looking at me. A fallen woman, that's what I was. A Russian whore. And soon it would become even more obvious. My belly was already curving in defiance of my denial. Every day I woke hoping to find blood on the sheets, a ripping pain in my stomach, but the thing growing inside me was stubborn and cruel. Every day I grew weaker, while it grew stronger.

The doctor said I can get rid of it, I wrote to Mother the day I found out. *I wouldn't be the only one.* I wrote the words quickly and shoved the page under her nose.

'The decision is yours,' she said. 'But . . . perhaps . . . there has been enough death?'

Her last sentence hurt. I knew what she was saying, the truth that was stitched into those words. Krista. Frau Weber. But also, all the Nazis' innocent victims. Could I be responsible for killing another soul? If I'd found out sooner, when it was too small to be a thing, then maybe I could have done it. But my stomach was already growing round and I could feel it wriggling inside me; I'd already felt its first violent kick. If I got rid of it, would it be one more thing that haunted me?

'Is that your friend Gertrud?' Mother gestured at a woman heading our way but on the other side of the street.

I nodded. It was. I was sure of it. She was walking purposefully but with her head down, a large suitcase in each hand. I couldn't see her face but I recognized her walk, the way her shoulders sloped in a certain way. I'd thought of her often in the preceding months. We all now knew the truth of what had happened at Ravensbrück, the thousands who'd been murdered inside its perimeter. Both she and Egon had worked there, their guilt was indisputable, and yet it was difficult for me to align this truth with the friend I had once known. That Egon was capable of such horrors didn't surprise me. He was a weak, self-conscious man who craved power and respect. Bullied by his peers, controlling and torturing the persecuted would have come easily to him. But Gertrud? Yes, she was overbearing and bossy, but she wasn't evil. She was like me, I'd thought. She'd wanted a husband, a family, a healthy, happy life. How did she become a monster?

'Gertrud?' Mother shouted. 'Gertrud?'

Gertrud stopped, looked up. Our eyes locked. Her hair was different – her blonde locks had been dyed dark brown – and she'd put on some weight. Did she know that made her stand out? We were a nation of starving people and those with more flesh on their bones always looked suspicious.

I held up my hand in a half-wave.

'*Es tut mir Leid.* Sorry,' she said. She looked over both shoulders. 'My name isn't Gertrud. You must have mistaken me for someone else.'

And then she hurried off in the other direction, disappearing around a corner.

'Well, that was rude. It was her, was it not?'

I couldn't decide whether to nod or shake my head. I chose the middle ground and shrugged. There had been talk of trials being held for war criminals. I suspected there was a warrant out for Gertrud's arrest, and that would be the last we'd ever see of her.

As we turned on to Chausseestraße, lightning suddenly ripped the sky in two. Moments later thunder shook the ground as if an earthquake had struck. And then came the rain. It was a heavy tropical rain, the kind that comes after weeks of unbearable heat, and it drenched us in seconds. We ran through the street, flapping our arms as if that would somehow stave off the water.

Outside our building, before I had the chance to duck inside, Mother stopped me. She looked up to the sky and spread out her arms, gesturing for me to do the same. I tilted my head back, my fingers reaching and searching for the wind above my head. The torrent blinded me. I closed my eyes and let it wash down my face. My clothes hung heavy, the weight of them comforting. I breathed in the scent of rain falling on dry, dusty pavements and I listened to the song of water in the gutters. I was transported back to another time, a better one. And then I heard the strangest sound: Mother's laughter. I wanted to laugh too but silence still sat inside me, refusing to surrender – yet, briefly, it did allow a smile to form on my lips. It was a sensation I hadn't felt in months. I was so angry with Mother for so many reasons, but in that moment, I loved her with all my heart.

34

LISETTE

Then – Berlin, 10 September 1945

During the night, the storm howled through the apartment, water puddling by the shattered windows, forcing us to pull Mother's mattress into the hallway where the rain couldn't reach us. We slept side by side, huddled under a pile of blankets like children.

The sun had not yet risen when we woke to the sound of someone knocking. I untangled myself from the covers, rubbing the crusty sleep from my eyes. Mother was already in front of the mirror, straightening her nightgown. She quickly fixed her hair, swept lipstick across her lips and then went to the door.

Neither of us recognized the man who stood on the other side. His cheeks were hollowed out, his face decorated with dirt. His clothes were mere rags, streaked with dried blood. The man's hair was long and straggly, damp from the rain, his beard patchy. On his forehead was a deep gash that oozed infection.

Mother recoiled instinctively. Before she had the chance to close the door, I stepped forward and touched her arm. I would no longer turn my head away in the face of someone else's suffering. Mother nodded, understood.

'Do you need something?' she asked. 'Food? Water?'

He looked at her and a whisper of words fell from his lips, but they were too quiet to decipher. He coughed and tried again.

'Lisette,' he said. 'Rita.' Our names were not a question. He knew us.

I stepped forward, my legs trembling, and looked into his deep brown eyes – eyes the colour of acorns.

Julius.

My Julius.

I pulled him into my arms and cried into his neck. His clothes were wet and he was shivering. I could smell the rain on him, but something else, too: the scent of despair. I remembered the last time I had seen him. My stuttering madness, the tears, his confession, and, later, the kiss. That had been more than two years ago but it felt like yesterday. He'd finally blown back into my life, as if the storm itself had carried him in.

'Lisette,' he said again. Hearing my name on his lips made me cry even harder. He was alive. And he was here.

Mother hovered near the doorway. When I turned, I saw the disappointment lining her face. He wasn't Father.

'Julius, it is good to see you home,' she said. Then she retreated to her room, dragging her mattress and the blankets behind her like a great white sledge.

Outside, the sun now broke through the blackness of the night with fractures of colour. I took Julius's hand in my own and pulled him into the flat. I led him to the sofa and he collapsed into it. He looked up at me, pushing a hand through his scraggly, unwashed hair.

I took the pad of paper from the coffee table and scribbled on it, *I'll get you something to eat and some water. My voice is gone. I'll explain in a minute.* I ripped off the page, handed it to him and then went to the kitchen. I rooted around in the cupboards for some food and settled on a crust of bread spread with a thick layer of lard, then went to find him clean clothes, heated up some water and fetched a cloth.

He wasn't asleep when I returned but his eyes were closed, his head resting on the back of the sofa. I helped him take off his clothes, tried not to cry when I saw how thin his arms were, how his chest was caved in, each bruised rib sticking out like the bars of a xylophone. He was a mere shadow of the man I had known. But my Julius was in there somewhere.

I sat beside him and gently washed the cut on his forehead and the dirt from his body. I trimmed his beard, cut his hair, and then helped him into Father's clean clothes. They hung off him in great swathes of fabric; he looked like a child playing dress-up.

'Why can't you talk?' he asked finally.

I picked up the pen and paper but I didn't know what to write. Why couldn't I talk? I still didn't know. I'd stopped trying because I couldn't bear the feeling that came with any attempt – like my bones were being crushed, like the air around me was devoid of oxygen.

I'm not sure. I just can't. It's difficult to explain. My voice will come back. I just need some time.

He nodded and it felt as if he really understood, as if the fact I was mute was completely reasonable.

'Sometimes I don't want to talk either,' he said. 'What is there to say? Everything just seems pointless.'

But you're home.

'I'm home, but it feels like only my body is. Part of me is gone. It's lying dead in the trenches beside Max.'

Max?

'He's gone. I held him in my arms as he died.'

His voice was empty of all emotion, as if he was reading the words from a script. Perhaps he had pushed his devastation outside his body so it existed as something separate, in a place where it couldn't kill him.

I closed my eyes and I could see Max's face, his floppy hair, his easy smile.

'I tried to save him . . .' Julius said, 'but I couldn't.'

I didn't know what to write to that. No words would ever help him deal with such a loss. The memory of Krista's and Frau Weber's deaths still stabbed me in the chest daily. The guilt and the sorrow that lived in our home. And I wanted it. Why did I get to live and they didn't? I never wanted the pain of their deaths to disappear. I deserved it. We all did.

I leaned forward, took his hand in mine and squeezed it gently. I noticed the new wrinkles in his face, a fresh scar on his cheek.

'What happened to your hands?' he asked, turning them over.

I looked down at my chafed fingers and blistered palms. I was surprised to find there was still skin left on them. The first few days of moving rubble, the pain had been crippling. But I'd become used to it. Even pain can become ordinary.

We're Trümmerfrauen. We spend our days clearing the debris.

I felt a strange sense of pride in writing the words, but it was fleeting. We were different now, the women of Berlin. Some, like me, would never recover, whereas others seemed more confident, stronger. They'd survived, and not only had they survived but they were rebuilding Berlin with their own bare hands. We'd always been told our job was to make babies, to be good housewives, but it was clear we were capable of achieving so much more. Daily, I wished I could be one of these 'new' women, carving out something different from the rubble we'd been left with. A different me would've gone in search of my music, never giving up until it had been reunited with my soul.

That Lisette would have discarded her futile dream of marriage with a man who didn't love her. She would have found an orchestra instead, left Germany and travelled the world, knowing she could do anything. She could survive it all. But that wasn't me.

And Julius was here. Perhaps he did love me after all.

'Your mother is doing it too?' A smile twitched at the corner of his mouth and I rewarded it with my own.

Yes. You should see her, though. High heels, silk gloves. The other women laugh at her but she doesn't seem to notice.

'Your father?'

Missing in action. He's dead. I know it. But Mother refuses to accept it.

'I'm sorry.' He looked me in the eye. 'Sorry is such an inadequate word . . . It's something we just say to everyone now. But I hope you know I care and that I'm here if you want to talk about it.'

What about your parents?

I looked down at his weathered, bony hands. Hands that were made to write poetry, not carry a weapon.

'My father died somewhere on the Eastern Front,' he said. He took off his glasses and rubbed at his skin, as if trying to wipe the sorrow away. 'I arrived in Berlin yesterday. Our apartment is gone. The whole building is . . . and the ones on either side. I was told that those hiding in the basement when the buildings collapsed all died. A woman told me they could hear people stuck down there, underneath all the wreckage, but by the time they managed to dig them out, they were all dead.'

His words were hollow with grief. I squeezed his hand again because that was all I could do.

'What happened when the Soviets came? Did you . . .? Did they . . .?' His voice was quiet and I couldn't meet his eyes. It was all the answer he needed.

'Sorry . . . You don't need to tell me. It's none of my business. I'm so happy you're alive. I was fighting on the Western Front when I finally got the chance to surrender. I was taken by the Americans. We were put in a camp. It was . . . awful. But the thought of you gave me hope . . .'

My heart leaped in my chest.

'I know about the other camps. The Jewish ones and what happened there. Where I was . . . it was horrific, but what they went through . . . it doesn't bear thinking about. How did we get here? Why did our country – our people – do such despicable things? I should have refused to fight. I might have been executed but that would have been better. Much better than knowing I was a part of all this.'

I nodded. I felt it too. That guilt, the shame. Why hadn't we done more to change the course of history?

What now? I wrote. I was asking a million questions in one. What now for him? What now for us? What now for our society? Our future?

'Could I perhaps stay here for a while? With you? I need to be with a friend right now.'

Friend. A word that hurt more than any other.

When I saw you last, you told me you loved someone else. Where is she?

He sighed, closed his eyes for a moment, and then whispered, 'Gone.'

Who was she, what had happened to her? But I also didn't want to know. I didn't want to remind him of someone who wasn't me.

Of course you can stay. Stay for ever.

There is something I need to tell you, though.

He nodded then waited expectantly. It took me a long time to evoke the courage I needed to write it down. The thing growing inside me was something I tried not to think about. I expended so much energy on ignoring it that transcribing the fact felt like a betrayal of myself. Once the ink dried, the truth of the words would be impossible to ignore.

I'm pregnant. I don't want to keep it. But I think I have to.

Tenderly he pulled me into his arms. I rested my head on his chest and listened to his heart beating, breathing in his musty scent. He stroked my hair. A cold morning wind blew in through the space where the window had once been, but I felt warm and safe in his arms.

'Marry me, Lisette?'

My breath caught in my throat. I didn't move. I was so terrified that his sentence was made of glass and I would shatter it into a million pieces.

'I know we're just friends,' he continued quickly, 'but I do love you in my way. Let's keep this baby. Let me be its father. We can build a life together – a happy one. We can create something wonderful and beautiful after all this horror. At least we can try?'

There was only one answer. The hands squeezing my throat released me. And one simple word was born.

'Yes.'

35

ELLY

Now – West Berlin, 25 September 1961

I see a chink of light. Just a weak, grey glow high up and in the distance, but it's definitely there. I splash through the muck, no longer caring that someone might hear me. My legs burn with the effort, my arms flail. I have to get out.

A ladder. Above it, a shaft of light. I grab a rung, feel the cool metal on my skin. The rungs are slippery and when I lift my feet out of the disgusting water, there's a sucking noise as the gunk releases me with puckered lips. My hands are shaking and the weight of my wet clothes drags me down. I can't help imagining falling backwards and plunging into the river, drowning in the repulsive sewage of Berlin. But this can't be the way I die.

I take my time, pausing before reaching for the next rung. I focus on my song. I've found it again. It vibrates within me like a different kind of heartbeat.

Above, I hear the faint hum of early morning traffic. My plan had been to crawl up and out while it was still night, but it seems dawn has come early. If I haven't gone far enough, or at some point made a wrong turn and have ended up walking deeper into East Berlin, then the daylight will prove fatal. But the manhole cover above me is askew – this has to be the right one.

I squeeze my fingers through the gap, take a deep breath and then push. The weight is almost too much to bear, and the screech of metal on the pavement is impossible to avoid, but inch by inch I manage to slide the cover across. There's a rush of fresh air and I'm flooded in light. The air tastes different – it feels different – as if there's more oxygen on this side. The belly of a truck is above me but there's just enough space for me to crawl out. As quickly as I can, I roll to the side, haul myself up and then I'm standing on the road.

I am reborn in West Berlin. Now I just need to find Axel and make it back.

36

LISETTE

Then – Berlin, 13 February 1946

I remembered the sensation of ripping, the feeling of Julius stroking my hair. I remembered the blood, the repetitive shouts of the midwife to *drücken* – push – and Mother's confused and terrified face each time she came into the bedroom. At one point I thought she might have come in and held my hand – I recalled gripping bony fingers between my own and my childhood nickname, LiLi, being whispered in my ear. But I couldn't be sure.

I thought the pain would never end, I was sure I'd die so that this horrible thing could live, but somehow, finally, it was over. Now I lay tangled in clean sheets, my limbs both heavy with exhaustion and light with relief.

'You're awake.'

I turned to see Julius sitting in a chair, a small bundle cocooned in his arms. Outside it was dark, the curtains only half drawn. On the bedside table, a warm light bathed the room in a cosy glow.

'It's a girl,' he said. 'A beautiful, perfect little girl. Are you ready to meet her?'

I wasn't. I never would be. But I had known this day would come and there was no point in delaying the inevitable.

I nodded and pushed myself up into a sitting position, my back resting against a mound of pillows. My stomach had deflated a little but it was bigger than I expected it to be, still a cumbersome weight around my middle.

He handed the baby to me, gently supporting her head until I was holding her securely in the crook of my arm. She opened her eyes, looked at me and then let out a pathetic whimper. She was so small and fragile. If I threw her against the wall, she'd be dead in an instant.

I'd heard people speak about the sudden and overwhelming love mothers felt when they held their children for the first time. I looked at my daughter's wide-set eyes, the straight, sharp nose I knew would one day grow into his, and felt no love at all.

'Do you want to try feeding her?' Julius asked, a few hours later, perching on the edge of the bed. 'Would you like me to give you some privacy?'

'No. Stay. Please.'

Like no husband I'd ever heard of, Julius had been present throughout the birth, seen more than a man should ever really see. Asking for privacy now was pointless. Also, I didn't want to be alone with her.

I released my breast and let her latch on. She did so expertly, as if she'd had the practice. The pain in my nipple was sharp and sudden, like a thousand stabbing needles, but after a few moments it passed. She sucked greedily, her face pink and puckered with frustration.

'What shall we call her?' Julius asked as he stroked her greasy head. She had a slick of dark hair but otherwise she was completely bald. For months Julius had been trying to make me think of names – one for a boy and one for a girl – but I had refused, skilfully steering our conversations back to safe ground, somewhere the earth didn't threaten to crack and crumble beneath my feet.

'You decide.'

He pursed his lips, annoyed at my ambivalence. We'd known each other all our lives but it was only over the past few months he'd come to understand me more than anyone else. It was equally wonderful and terrifying.

'I *have* been thinking about it,' I lied. 'But I just can't make a decision. You decide. Whatever name you choose will be perfect.'

'OK.' He pushed his glasses up his nose. 'I like the name Elly. What do you think?'

I tasted the name in my mouth, let it roll off my tongue. 'Elly. Yes, let's call her Elly.'

I looked down and found she'd fallen asleep, her mouth open, her pale-pink gums on display. The tears came suddenly and easily, stinging my eyes with their insistence.

'It's OK. I'm here.' Julius stood up and tucked Elly back into her cot.

I hated crying in front of him. After the General left, I'd sworn to be cold and unbreakable, a fortress against any more hurt, but this tiny, helpless baby had brought me to my knees.

'It's the hormones,' Julius said, but not unkindly. He sat down beside me and I rested my head on his shoulder. 'These first few days are always difficult for new mothers. You're doing really well.'

I attempted to swallow a sob. 'I'm not doing well. And it's not the hormones . . . It's her. I . . . don't love her. I can't.' The confession shocked me. I'd thought it a hundred times but now I'd spoken the words aloud, had admitted the truth of it.

'I want to.' I spoke quickly, as if I could make these new words overtake the ones before. 'I really do. She's just a baby. Even if she's his, she's innocent. But . . . but when I look at her, all I see is him.'

Julius was silent for a long time. I wondered if he was preparing to leave. How could he stay with someone who hated her own child? I held my body still, kept my head on his shoulder and listened to him breathing.

'It's understandable.' His words were slow and measured. 'I don't doubt that one day you'll love her. It'll just take time. And that's OK. In the meantime, I will love her enough for the both of us.'

PART TWO

LISETTE AND ELLY

1961–2

37

ELLY

Now – West Berlin, 25 September 1961

I emerge from the side street in clean clothes – my dirty ones, along with my boots, discarded in a rubbish bin. I unfold the page with the address from my pocket. I know it off by heart but it gives me something to do with my hands. I can't shake the feeling I'm being watched. But this is the West. There are no Stasi, just happy, free civilians going about their day. The West Berliners look different from East Berliners. It's been less than two months since our city was officially severed but the dissimilarities between the two halves have existed far longer. The people passing me are dressed more fashionably – they're more at ease in themselves. And their music is distinctly different, too. Most people's songs here are more up-tempo and carefree. Not everyone's, of course – there will always be people who have demons regardless of where they are – but in general their music is lighter. Even here in the shadow of the barrier, people's lives have gone on.

Making my way down the street, I pass commuters and children on their way to school, the youngest dashing between people's legs in a game of tag. I envy their innocence, their inability to understand what's going on outside their small existence. I think of Axel. It's been almost two months since he was separated from us. Has it damaged his little soul, losing his mother so suddenly? They'll be taking care of his body at the hospital, but will they be looking after his spirit too? A few streets, but also a whole world away, Mama and Papa will be waking up. They'll think I'm being lazy and sleeping in but soon one of them will check on me and discover my note. Papa will be sick with worry, Mama will be furious, but perhaps they'll be hopeful too.

It takes me over an hour to walk to Charlottenburg. I could have taken the S-Bahn but I need to save my Deutsche Marks – they won't stretch as far in the West. Schaumburgallee is a quiet, pretty street, lined with trees still clinging on to their mottled leaves. The houses have large bay windows and wide steps leading up to the front doors.

I take off my hat and tug my fingers through my hair. Although I've changed into a dress, appearances are everything, as Oma Rita would say, and I realize that even with clean clothes on, I still reek and must look a mess. I tie my hair up and tuck it under my hat, then fix a smile on my face, climb the steps and ring the bell.

A balding man with cloudy eyes opens the door. Hair sprouts from his earlobes and his lips are discoloured as if he's eaten too many blueberries.

'What do you want?' He scowls at me and I find myself shrinking.

'I'm looking for Karin.'

'What do you want with her?'

'Well, I . . . perhaps I could talk to her?'

'I don't recognize you. I've never seen you here before.'

'No, it's probably been a while since I was here last.' I offer my most charming smile.

'I suspect she's busy,' he says curtly.

'Is she out? Should I come back later?'

He shrugs and I don't know what else to do but retreat back down the steps. I was sure Karin would be my best shot. Hers was the only name I vaguely recognized from Mama's address book. They were friends once – good friends. But it's clear this man won't let me past the threshold. The irony of escaping under the Wall but not being let into someone's house once I got here isn't lost on me.

'Fräulein,' the man says as I reach the last step. 'This is number twelve. Karin lives at number seventeen.'

He bares his teeth in what might be a smile but looks more like a grimace and then slams the door with an almighty bang.

I approach number seventeen cautiously. When I glance back at the old man's house, the curtain twitches and I know I'm being watched. The East is full of spies – maybe the West is, too. I can't afford to make another mistake.

When I reach the front door, I can hear someone inside – the patter of small feet and the heavier, tired ones of an adult. It takes so long for the door to swing open that I wonder whether the bell is working. I hover my finger over the button but then a shadow appears and there's the sliding click of a bolt being pulled back.

'*Hallo?*' Her dark hair is loose, there's a dry crust of food on her collar and she's balancing a toddler on one hip, but the woman is strikingly beautiful. She has huge eyes but otherwise small, delicate features. She reminds me of a doll I had as a child. 'Can I help you?'

'Yes, hello. Are you Karin?'

She nods, her hand still on the door-frame. With wet, sticky fingers, the toddler plays with a strand of her mother's curly hair.

'I'm Elly. You don't know me, but you knew my mother,

Lisette. That was her name. *Is* her name. I found you in her address book. I'm sorry just to show up on your doorstep. It's rude, I know, but perhaps I could come in and explain?'

My words trip over each other and I know I'm making little sense. Karin wrinkles her nose and I can tell she's wondering whether the smell is coming from me or the child she's carrying.

'Mama?' A boy's voice, loud and impatient.

Karin sighs and opens the door a little wider, giving me just enough space to squeeze past her. Her music is a tangle of instruments. I wonder if her song has always been like this or whether motherhood has jumbled it into a chaotic but happy symphony.

'Take a seat in there,' she says, gesturing to the living room. 'I'll be back in a moment.'

The room is large and bright, the floor scattered with toys, the walls adorned with photographs. The mayhem is comforting. I have no evidence for this, but I think perhaps messy people are rarely unkind.

It's another fifteen minutes before Karin finally reappears, the toddler still hugging her hip.

'Right, sorry,' she says, setting her daughter down on the floor and positioning herself on the armchair, crossing her legs at the ankle. She perches rather than sits, as if ready to spring into action if one of her children demands it. 'The mornings are . . .' She shrugs and laughs. 'Elly, you said?'

'Yes, Elly. Elly Lange.'

'Lange? Wow. So Lisette married Julius? I always thought . . . we always thought.' She laughs and shrugs again. 'Mila!! What is it? Please stop yanking on my dress. Look, your dolly's over there. Sorry – where were we?'

She waits for me to speak. I've practised what to say but now the words evade me. Above us comes the thunking sound of running feet. Mila tugs once more on her mother's dress. Karin

232

sighs but then lifts her daughter on to her lap and strokes the girl's chubby cheek, breathing in the scent of her hair. They relax into each other and I can hear the way Karin's music slows and envelops that of her daughter. I can't help but wonder if Mama ever held me like this – with pure, unadulterated love. I have no memory of her doing so but there's an ache in my chest as if my body remembers it.

'So . . .?' she says. 'Lisette. How is she? I haven't seen her in years. Not since before the war. I moved out to our country house and we lost touch. I only recently returned to Berlin. ERICH!! I CAN HEAR YOU. LEAVE YOUR BROTHER ALONE. The countryside is much better for children, of course, but I missed the life of the city.'

'Were you good friends?' I ask. 'My mother and you?'

She lets out a tinkling laugh. 'We met at school. There were four of us who spent time together. Lisette was always a bit awkward in herself, but I really liked her. We were an odd group, I suppose, but . . . yes, we were good friends. I actually don't know why we lost touch.'

Mila tugs on Karin's hair, looks at me pointedly, and then whispers loudly, 'Stinky.'

A blush creeps up Karin's neck and she clutches her throat as if trying to catch it.

'I'm sorry,' I say. 'It's me. Well, my bag. And me, I suppose. We live in East Berlin. I was there . . . this morning.' The words spill out into the room like red wine on a white carpet, the implications silencing us both.

Mila squeezes her nose between two chubby fingers. Karin just stares at me.

'I have a brother,' I continue. 'His name's Axel. He's just a baby – a few months old. When the barrier went up and they closed the border he was in Waldfriede Hospital, here in West Berlin. We were all at home when it happened. Mama too.' I know I'm rambling, but I'm so scared she'll kick me out before she's heard the whole story and so the words keep coming. 'Mama's devastated. We all are. But she's stopped talking. She literally can't speak. And I don't think she could survive losing him. I went through the sewers last night. I need to find Axel.'

'The sewers?'

'Yes. I waded through.' I laugh but it comes out as an awkward grunt.

'I should call my husband,' Karin says, standing up. Mila tries to cling to her like a koala, but Karin disentangles her and places her on the floor. 'He'll know what to do.'

'No, no,' I say, grabbing her hand. 'Please don't do that.'

'It's OK. You're safe here.' Her voice is soothing and I expect it's the same tone she uses to calm her screaming children. She squeezes my hand and I'm so grateful for this small kindness that I want to cry.

'You don't need to worry. You made it over ... under ... which is quite incredible. But there are procedures. Refugees need to register at Marienfelde. You'll get a residence permit. And, of course, I'll help you with whatever else you need.'

'No, you don't understand,' I say. 'I'm not staying. I need to find Axel but then I'm going back. I need to find him and take him back to East Berlin.'

They're arguing in the other room. They haven't raised their voices but the walls are thin. The violins of Karin's melody have taken on a screeching quality, like the bows are straining and the strings are too taut. Her husband Oskar's music is underscored with a steady, firm beat but I can hear it waver. I don't know who is on my side. Perhaps neither of them is. Maybe they're simply arguing about whether to throw me out today or tomorrow.

I've washed and Karin has lent me another dress but I can

still smell the sewer on me. I suspect Mila can too. She sits in the far corner playing quietly. Every few minutes she sniffs dramatically and throws me a scowl. She must be two, three at most, but she glowers like an old witch.

The front door closes with an apologetic sigh and moments later Karin strides into the living room. She goes over to Mila, strokes her head, then settles on the armchair. 'Right,' she says, slapping her knees. 'Let's make a plan. You don't want to register as a refugee?'

'No, I can't. If I get back into East Germany, no one can know I ever left.'

'Yes, that makes sense, of course. We're part of the West but the Stasi still has tentacles here. And the GDR surrounds us, so we need to be careful.'

'We?' I can't hide the relief that washes over me from hearing this one simple word.

'Let's not get ahead of ourselves.' Her words are measured but she offers me a genuine smile. 'My husband is a rule follower. So am I, I suppose. But you're Lisette's daughter. I'm hardly going to just hand you over to the authorities. Finding your brother and then making your way back to East Berlin, though . . . it's . . .'

'Crazy?'

'Yes. And I don't think you fully understand the risk you're taking. The fact that you made it over here – that you weren't caught – is a miracle. I don't want to be condescending, but you're still a child. I won't just let you risk your life again. I can't imagine what Lisette and Julius are going through. And now to have lost their other child, too . . . but you can't go back.'

'I have to,' I whisper, but I say it only once. There's little point arguing with her; when the time comes, she won't be able to stop me. Right now I just need her to help me find Axel – the rest will come later.

'For the time being, you can stay here with us and we won't insist on you registering at Marienfelde. This afternoon, we can go to the hospital and with any luck locate . . . Axel. Was that his name?'

I nod and wipe away the tear that has crept down my cheek. 'Your husband? Is he OK with me staying?'

She waves a dismissive hand. 'Oskar? Of course. He'll be fine. He's hardly the one who makes the decisions. When you've carried four children for a man, he knows who's in charge.'

She laughs her tinkling laugh again. I don't know why I chose Karin's name out of all the names I found in Mama's address book, but it's clear I made the right decision.

38

ELLY

Now – West Berlin, 25 September 1961

'The hospital was never hit during any of the air raids,' Karin says, making a sharp right turn, causing me to brace one hand against the car window while holding on to Mila tightly with the other.

'It's quite amazing, actually, considering the state of the rest of the city. After the war, I planned to move back to Berlin. I was so bored of the countryside. But seeing the devastation was heartbreaking and there was really nothing to come back for. It was a wasteland of rubble, so depressing.'

'Did you see my mother when you came back?'

Mila wriggles in my lap and tries to prise my fingers from her waist. She would clearly be much happier sliding around in the back seat, but Karin asked me to hold on to her.

'I meant to contact her, of course, to see if she was still around, but' – she shrugs – 'life happened, I suppose.'

She makes another delayed turn which is met by the blast of someone's horn. She waves her hand out of the window and I wish she'd keep both of them on the wheel instead.

'Has your mother ever mentioned our old friend Gertrud?'

'I don't think so.'

We leave the city behind and drive through Grunewald forest. The trees lining the road on either side are still green but at their feet lies a colourful carpet of newly shed leaves. I was last here only a few months ago with Otto and Monika, a couple of weeks before the barrier went up. Seeing a familiar path we cycled down, remembering how Otto had wobbled from side to side while singing loudly out of tune, hurts my chest. Do they know yet that I'm gone? I never told them the lie I offered Herr Krause. Monika would have believed me but Otto would have badgered me with a million questions and, at some point, I would have tripped up. When I get back – because I have to get back, there's no alternative – Otto will forgive me quickly but Monika will be angry in that quiet way of hers. She'll see my silence as a monumental betrayal. Not just regarding my plans to flee but my whole friendship with Andrei, too.

'Of course, I suppose she wouldn't mention Gertrud. Not now.'

'Why? Who was she?'

'Just someone we used to know. There were rumours . . . later. After the war . . . Never mind. Here we are!'

Karin reverses into a parking space, not even bothering to check her rear-view mirror. I hear the angry screech of metal scraping against metal.

'Oops!' She lets out a small, embarrassed laugh. 'That will have to be our little secret. I'm sure it's just a scratch. That car looks old anyway.'

Mila has become limp and heavy in my arms. I look down to find she's fast asleep. There's a bubble of snot coming out of her nose. It grows and shrinks in sync with her breathing.

'Gosh, isn't she just beautiful?' Karin says. 'You'll need to carry her, if that's OK. Waking her now would be a disaster.'

She climbs out of the car and then comes over to my side to

open the door for me. Mila is heavier than I thought and it's difficult to carry her, but her heat is comforting.

'Mila's the reason I have three boys, of course,' Karin says, striding ahead, the gravel crunching under her feet. 'I wanted a girl so I just kept trying until I got one. I love the boys with all my heart, of course, but there's something about having a mini-you. I expect Lisette feels the same. A mother–daughter relationship is so special.'

I nod, glad that carrying Mila in my arms gives me an excuse not to speak.

The hospital grounds are sprawling but Karin seems to know exactly where to go. If I'd gone to another person's house, someone who wouldn't have helped me, what would I have done? Had I really expected the nurses would just let me leave with Axel? Over the past few weeks, Andrei kept trying to talk to me about my plans – what exactly I was going to do once I made it over to West Berlin – but I couldn't look that far ahead. I worried talking about it would jinx it, too; I just needed to get here and then figure it out. Which seems naive now.

The automatic doors swing open. The smell of bleach with undertones of something not entirely unpleasant greets us like an old friend. The corridor is strangely quiet, the linoleum floor squeaky beneath my shoes.

'Right, the paediatric ward should be in this wing, just up the stairs,' Karin says. 'I'll find the doctor I spoke to on the phone and then we'll take it from there. I think it's best I do this part on my own, though. Why don't you sit in the waiting room with Mila? Don't look so worried. Oskar is a powerful man and I have my connections too. We'll figure this out.'

She seems so confident, but I'm starting to wonder whether I'm not the only one who's being naive.

I take a seat in the near-empty waiting room, relieved to move Mila's weight from my hip to my lap. As I settle in the chair, she stirs in her sleep and wraps her arms around my neck. I pray she won't wake.

A nurse sits by an information desk at the far end of the room but she glances only briefly at me before returning to the book resting in her lap. Hiding beneath the acrid smell of bleach that reminds me of Oma Rita is an aroma of wood polish. With nothing to do but sit and wait, I look out of the window, which has a view over the pristine hospital grounds. If I listen carefully I can hear the faint whistle of the wind in the trees, or maybe it's the distant sound of babies whimpering. Otherwise, it seems unnaturally quiet in here. Shouldn't a hospital be full of staff rushing around saving lives? One man in the far corner looks particularly out of place. When I glance at him, he ducks down behind his newspaper. He's dressed like every other man here – slacks and a fedora hat – but something about him just doesn't look right. His spine is too rigid, his presence too dominating. I haven't even been missing for a day yet – there can't possibly be anyone looking for me – but I have a niggling fear that refuses to listen to logic.

Mila lifts her head. She rubs her face with pudgy little fingers. Her eyes focus. For a moment there's a stunned silence. And then she starts to scream.

~

The drive back to Karin's is silent. Mila is lying on the back seat, the soles of her feet pressed up against the window. She's awake but depleted from all her hysterical screaming at the hospital. Karin and I are both lost in our thoughts. It's not until we turn on to Reichsstraße, the grand houses flanking us on each side of the wide street, that Karin finally speaks.

'Three months. It's not too long to wait.'

But it *is* too long. Even a day seems too long. How are my

parents going to explain why I'm away for months on end? The lie I offered about visiting Papa's sick cousin in Leipzig will only hold for a matter of weeks at best. And there's no way of getting a message to them. They'll think I died trying to cross. Or worse – they'll think I made it but decided to stay in the West. I'd like to think Papa knows that's something I'd never do, but time will wear down that belief eventually.

'Is he really too sick to leave?'

'He's stable and he's going to be fine. He just needs to put on some weight before they can release him. I'm sorry you didn't get to see him, Elly. He looks well, though, and he's been healing nicely since the operation.'

'So there was a hole in his heart?'

'Yes, but they've fixed it. He's going to be OK.'

I have no reason to doubt her, but without seeing Axel's face, feeling the weight of him in my arms, it's difficult to believe that he *is* actually OK. I should have insisted on seeing him.

Karin manoeuvres the car into a spot across from her house. And I get that feeling again – of something being not quite right. The day is growing older and an impenetrable mist clings to the ground. Commuters are returning home from work and I scan the face of each one as we cross the street, looking for anyone who might be taking an unusual interest in me or the house.

No one looks suspicious. But at the same time, they all do.

39

LISETTE

Now – East Berlin, 25 September 1961

While Julius prepares lunch, I wander barefoot around the living room, picking things up, putting them back down again: a dusty book I've been trying to read for years; one of Elly's dirty mugs, the coffee dregs hardened on the porcelain; Axel's birth certificate – the only proof I have of his existence. My milk has run dry, my stomach has deflated; already there is no evidence left on my body that I'm a mother.

Forty-three long days have passed, a thousand lost moments with my son. I've seen darkness before but this pain will kill me. My face is wet but there's no end to my tears.

I pick up the phone in the living room and dial the hospital's number. The lines have been cut for a decade – it's ludicrous even to try, but I do it anyway. I hold my breath and say a prayer but, just like every other day, I'm met with silence. I try four more times, convincing myself I might have dialled incorrectly, but there's nothing.

It's almost midday and Elly's still not up. How can she sleep so soundly while her baby brother is alone, separated from his family?

'She was probably up late playing her keyboard,' Julius says, cutting a loaf of bread into irritatingly uneven slices.

I'll go and wake her, I write, flashing my pad of paper at him.

'Let her sleep,' he says but then shrugs.

I knock hard on her door and then go inside without waiting for an answer. Elly can sleep through anything; the knock is entirely for Julius's benefit, as he believes above all else in privacy.

Inside, the curtains are drawn, the room dark and musty. It's unbearably hot, too. Why hasn't she slept with the window open?

I hate this room. The original peeling floral wallpaper has been stripped away, replaced long ago with a hypnotic yellow pattern. All the original furniture was disposed of, too. The smell is distinctly different as well, yet I'll never forget what happened in this room. The memory is a stain, refusing to be washed away no matter how hard I scrub.

I ignore the ghost in the corner, the face I'll never forget. I stomp over to the curtains and fling them open. I struggle with the latch on the window but finally it releases and I let in some well-needed fresh air.

I turn around, ready to shake Elly from her slumber. But the bed is made and Elly is gone.

40

LISETTE

Now – East Berlin, 7 October 1961

I sit on the bench while two fat pigeons waddle on the ground by my feet, searching for crumbs. I tug at the collar of my coat and rub my hands together. I forgot my gloves and my fingers are turning blue but I can't go home; I can no longer be in the flat. It's been two weeks since I found Elly's bed empty. Axel is gone and now Elly is too. My home is where my children are and they're not there.

I take out her note from my pocket and brush my fingers over the ink, trying to draw out the emotions she felt when she wrote it. I've read and reread Elly's letter until I can recite each word, but still I can't grasp what she's done. I tell myself she made it to the other side, but I don't know this for a fact. She could be dead. They both could be. How did this happen? How did I *let* this happen?

I think back to the weeks after Elly was born. She was always a watchful and quiet baby, but needy too. At night she would only sleep with her head on my chest; no other position would do. It felt as if she only found peace when I was suffering. In the middle of the night, when I knew the rest of the city was soundly asleep, the exhaustion and loneliness of being forced to sit still and stare into darkness was other-worldly. My life had become a hazy mess of feeding and crying – me more than Elly. She demanded so much from me. More than I had to give.

Growing up, I had always thought I'd play the piano for my children, that the music would lull them to sleep. But Elly's father ruined that dream for me, too. And staying in our flat in the East hasn't helped me heal. It's a prison of memories. Sometimes, still, when I come home from a walk, the memories physically knock me to the floor. I have always been so desperate to move, but Mother has continually refused. The doctors say she needs familiarity and stability. They diagnosed her with early-onset dementia but I didn't believe them at the time. I didn't believe her. Some days I still don't. Pretending she can't remember means she doesn't need to bear the guilt; she can make-believe it was someone else who sold her daughter to protect herself. She should have spent the rest of her life trying to make amends. Instead, she's retreated into the distant past, a place where she has yet to commit a crime against me. A place where we both exist as whole, undamaged people. A place where Father is still alive.

A storm has battered Berlin and the park looks bruised and broken. Leaves have been torn from their branches and a few trees have been ripped from the earth. The destruction makes me feel a little better. Though my nose is dripping and I can no longer feel my toes, I vow to stay here until the world turns dark.

'Lisette.' Julius appears in front of me, a scarf wrapped around the lower part of his face. 'I've been looking for you. Please come home.'

I shake my head, refuse to meet his eyes.

He sits down heavily beside me. He takes my hands and lifts

them to his lips, breathing hot air on them before rubbing them between his gloves.

'You'll get sick if you stay out here.' His glasses fog up when he speaks but he doesn't wipe the condensation away. 'Maybe that's what you want?'

I shrug, extracting my hands from his. I couldn't care less either way.

'It's not just you who's lost them. You know that, right? They're my children too. I'm hurting as much as you are.'

But he's not. How could he be? He didn't carry them in his belly, didn't feed them from his breast. And none of this is his fault. It is mine and mine alone.

'I found a book in the fridge earlier,' he says. 'And a towel in the oven. Rita's getting worse and I can't look after her on my own. I need to go back to work next week – I've taken all the leave I can. You have to be at home. No more hounding people at the ministry, no more wandering aimlessly around the park.'

I take out my notebook, rummage in my coat pocket for a pen. *I'm not giving up on them*, I write.

'I'm not asking you to. We'll keep applying for visas, but hassling the ministry isn't going to make a difference.'

You don't know that.

'I do. I'm not asking you to abandon hope. I'm just asking you to come home.'

He stands up and offers me his arm. I don't have the energy to argue with him.

'And there's something else,' he says as I force myself to stand. 'Herr Krause has been asking questions about Elly. I've told him what she asked us to say, but he's suspicious, I can tell. Yesterday, when my foreman called, I heard clicking on the phone again. They're listening. It won't be long before they come to our door.'

41

ELLY

Now – West Berlin, 28 November 1961

'We have to oppose the proliferation of nuclear weapons,' Peter says, anchoring his glasses on his substantial nose. With a spoon, he scrapes the last of his mother's *rote Grütze* from his plate, the berries painting his lips red. 'There is talk of a nuclear power station being built right here in West Berlin. We need to organize a protest.'

Hannelore rolls her eyes, but I lean in, resting my elbow on the table, my chin in my hand. 'I completely agree,' I whisper, my voice as low as the sea. 'A nuclear weapon could annihilate our entire city.'

It's only us in the flat and I've been in West Berlin for two months already, but I'm still not used to the nonchalance with which West Berliners speak of things deemed dangerous in the East. I used to examine each word before I let it fall from my lips. I looked over my shoulder so often that I developed a crick in my neck. Even in my own home, it always felt like someone was listening. That tickling fear hasn't disappeared and if I'm to return to the East, I hope it never does. That fear can save you.

I hope right now that fear is saving my parents.

'Yes, yes,' Hannelore says, her voice unnecessarily loud. While Peter's music is a happy, confident blend of boogie-woogie piano riffs and the warm, resonant sounds of a hollow-bodied guitar, Hannelore's song is a confused mash-up of genres that sometimes is simply a ceaseless torrent of noise that makes my head pound. 'But can't we talk about something more cheerful? These political discussions each night are wearing me out.'

She stands up to clear the dishes before turning to me. 'You don't need to be so polite, you know. You can just tell Peter to shut up when he's boring you. That's what I do.'

'No,' I say, too quickly, 'I'm not bored in the slightest.'

She fills the sink with water, the steam rising like wisps of smoke. She looks at me over her shoulder. 'You know my brother is gay, right?'

'What? No. Yes, I mean. I know that. I'm not ...' My words come out as if they are drunk – flailing and staggering.

Peter winks at me and they both chuckle, their laughter loud and unapologetic.

'You're too easy to tease, Jutta.'

Jutta. Some days I forget this is a borrowed life, a life that has a time limit on it. Jutta is now my name. It hasn't been long but when I wake, for the length of a breath, I really believe I am Jutta. It would be so easy to stay on, to wear this person's skin, and be happy here with my three new nephews who adore me and a little niece who most definitely doesn't. I go to school, I hang out in bars listening to music forbidden in the East, I have friends, and there's a real, exciting future – one with travel and opportunities – that could be mine if I just choose it.

But I made a promise. And even if that promise lies inscribed on a piece of paper on the other side of the Wall, I remember it. I remember who I gave the promise to. I remember, as well, the soldier who didn't shoot. I've tried to forget Andrei but I hear his music every day. Right now, I'm stuck here – Axel is still in the hospital and the sewer covers have been sealed shut – but I can't forget my goal, even if some days I want to. And just like so much else in this borrowed life, these friendships are a lie, my motives dishonest.

'I'd better head home. I promised Karin I'd help with the kids tonight.' I turn to Peter. 'Would you mind driving me?'

'Sure.' He pushes his bulky frame away from the table, the chair one loud scratch on the hardwood floor.

Outside, I stick my chin into the fake-fur collar of my jacket and brace myself against the wind. It keeps picking up the snow and flinging it around in flurries. I follow Peter down the street to his car, pushing my gloved hands deep inside my pockets.

His car is absurdly small and when he folds himself into it, his knees almost come up to his chin. He readjusts the seat while I fiddle with the knob of the heater. I hold my hand over the vent but it coughs at me once and then there's nothing.

'It's not working,' he says, manoeuvring the car out on to the narrow street. 'Schaumburgallee is only five minutes away, though. We should survive.'

'Thanks for taking me.'

'No problem. Thanks for being Hannelore's friend. Sorry, that's a strange thing to say, but she doesn't have many.'

I try to swallow the guilt but its bitterness coats my tongue. My friendship with Hannelore is no accident.

'Can I ask you something?' I ask.

He gives me a sidelong glance. 'I really am gay. Hannelore wasn't joking.'

This time it's my turn to laugh, but then I take a deep breath and drop my voice to a whisper. 'I've heard rumours ... that you might be helping students in East Berlin get over here to the West?'

It's almost imperceptible, the way his body stiffens; I need to tread carefully.

'Who did you hear that from?' He fixes his eyes on the dark road ahead, the beams of the car's headlights slicing through the icy mist.

'No one in particular.'

Several moments pass in silence. He glances in the rear-view mirror, and I do the same, half expecting a car to be following us, but the street is empty, the snow muting the sound of distant traffic.

Finally, he says, 'There are a lot of us – those who want to help comrades in the East. You'll find students in every bar in this half of the city discussing escape routes for East Germans.'

'So it's true?'

He sighs, a hard puff of white air. He leans forward, peering through the dark windscreen, then pulls into a parking space. The wheels squeak into the compacted snow at the edge of the tarmac. He turns off the engine and I can hear the wind outside – it sounds like the whoosh of a thousand arrows in flight. I hold my breath.

Peter turns to face me, his eyes studying me with an intensity that is unnerving.

'You want to help?'

'Not exactly,' I say.

And then I tell him everything.

42

ELLY

Now – West Berlin, 2 December 1961

'Will I be seeing you at the Eden Saloon later?'

'Not tonight,' I say, 'I promised my aunt I'd stay home with the boys.'

'Then I suspect we'll see her there later instead.' Hannelore laughs. Her teeth are so white they seem to glow underneath the street light.

'Probably.' Though thankfully I know 'Aunt' Karin has other plans.

I give Hannelore a wave and then head off in the opposite direction, but instead of turning towards Brixplatz, towards 'home', I take the tram down to Wilmersdorf. My lies to Hannelore no longer incite guilt; I've become surprisingly adept at stretching the truth, and Peter's one condition was that we wouldn't get his sister mixed up in our plans.

I try not to slip as I step down off the tram. It's starting to snow again and the road is icy. The streets are busy even in the sub-zero temperatures, and it's a relief to step into the warmth of the bar. I take off my hat and dust the snow from its brim. The air is thick with cigarette smoke, and in the corner there's an enormous fireplace with a roaring fire. Live jazz music floats in from another room but in here conversation dominates. Though the place is busy, it's not packed, and while it looks like a bar for an older crowd, with its deep sofas and peeling leather armchairs, most of the clientele are students.

'Jutta, over here!'

Peter is sitting in prime position with his back to the fire, surrounded by the small group I'm here to win over. He's wearing his glasses today and, not for the first time, I wonder whether he actually needs them. Though significantly larger, he's strikingly similar to his idol Buddy Holly and the spectacles complete the look; it wouldn't surprise me if the lenses were just glass.

The group, who are mostly about five years older than I am, turn to face me and all of them are smiling. Except for one. Instinctively I know this is Franz; Peter has warned me about him. Watching me cross the room, his grey eyes are as hard as concrete. I will my hands to stop shaking. Franz is short but he has large features with fleshy lips and a bulbous nose. His hair is long and I suspect he has grown it to cover his slightly protruding ears.

Peter makes room for me and I slip on to the sofa beside him. I greet his friends with the most genuine smile I can muster.

'Here she is,' Peter announces, draping one arm over my shoulder. He waves at the barman with his other hand and within minutes a pint of frothy beer appears in front of me.

'We were just discussing Castro's speech last night. Franz here believes the Americans will step in. That they'll do anything to stop the spread of communism.'

'I thought,' says a strikingly handsome man with carefully combed blond hair, 'Castro wants Cuba to become a socialist state, not a communist one.'

Peter nods at him and smiles encouragingly, his music quickening just as I expect his heartbeat is. This must be Knut, the man Peter is infatuated with.

'They're the same thing,' Franz cuts in.

'Actually, there are stark differences,' Peter replies. He puts his elbows on the table and steeples his fingertips together. 'They share certain beliefs, of course – mainly the advocation of public rather than private ownership – but socialism is more flexible. Individuals can still own property, for example, and they support a more democratic approach.'

'Yes, but Castro did say that his end goal is communism.' Impatience wriggles into Franz's voice. The others exchange glances. There's only one other woman in the group – a stocky Black American, who speaks German with only a hint of an accent.

'You're right, my friend,' she says, 'he did.' She has wide eyes and an intense stare. Her music is cool and flows like a stream. There's a strong yet soothing quality to it and I find myself warming to her immediately.

'Thanks,' Franz says, giving an appreciative nod. 'It seems perhaps Dina and I are the only ones who have actually listened to Castro's speech. I'm telling you, the US will join the war in Vietnam. They've been gearing up to it for years. They won't stop at just training South Vietnamese soldiers and sending in a few thousand troops to support them. Soon they'll be conscripting young Americans and there will be a full-scale war. The Soviet Union will be next, you'll see; the Iron Curtain and then the Wall . . .'

'Surely not,' I say. Jutta is less talkative than Elly – mostly I want to blend into the background – but a leopard can't paint over all of her spots. 'Perhaps Cuba. But Vietnam? It's across the globe from the US. Why is Vietnam such a threat?'

'Because if communism wins there, then it will spread across the rest of Asia.' Franz drinks the last of his beer and stifles a burp. His music is more complex than the others'. Angrier, too. The piano dominates and his song reminds me of the controlled rage of Bartók's 'The Chase'. He's quite unpleasant, but something darker than disagreeableness lurks within him; I don't trust him.

'They want to nip it in the bud,' Dina adds.

'I agree it's possible, but they would never attack the Soviet Union,' I persist. 'No one wants another world war. We're all still recovering from the last one. And the Wall? It's not going anywhere any time soon.'

'Well, *that* I think we can agree on,' Peter says, lowering his voice. 'It's why we're here, after all.'

43

ELLY

Now – West Berlin, 3 December 1961

'Well, they seemed to like you yesterday,' Peter says, driving slowly through the deserted streets. The windscreen is a mess of furious wipers and a swirling mass of white. 'Though trust is the most important factor. But men always trust women. It tends to be their downfall.'

'I'm not sure Franz is particularly keen on me.'

'Leave Franz to me. He roars like a lion but he's a pussycat. You'll see. He's actually the one I've known the longest.'

'Are they all on the same engineering programme as you?'

Peter laughs. 'Goodness, no. Knut is an actor. Well, he wants to be. He's incredibly talented, though. He really is.' He pauses, a blush creeping up his thick, stubbly neck. 'What was I saying? Oh, yes. Franz is studying medicine and Dina is going to be a great architect one day, though all she really wants to do is paint. Sebastian hasn't committed himself to any one course yet – he's trying them all out first. And Albert . . . literature, I think. And now we have you – our musician.'

'You've never even heard me play.'

'I can tell you're good.'

He spins the wheel and we slide rather than turn into a parking spot.

'How did you know to seek me out?' he asks, turning to look at me. 'That I was . . . involved . . .?' He tries to make the question casual but I can hear the uncertainty in his voice.

'Hannelore,' I say. 'She made some comment at school. About you wanting to save the world, but first you were going to start by bringing down the Wall, or at least getting people over it.'

'When she said that, were you friends with her already?'

I hesitate. I am not proud of my actions, but I have come this far and I can't lose his trust now.

'No . . . I became friends with her so I could get to you. You know my situation. Ever since I arrived, I've been trying to figure out a way to get back home. But I genuinely like Hannelore. My friendship with her is an added bonus.'

He nods slowly. I bite my lip, wait.

'OK,' he says finally. 'Thanks for being honest.'

He turns off the engine, pulls on his gloves.

'Are we here?'

'We are.'

I peer out into the dark street. The street lights are like spotlights but all they reveal are snowflakes dancing to a silent song.

'And where's "here"?'

'You'll see.'

I climb out of the car, bracing myself against the chill. It must be the coldest day of the year so far and it hurts to breathe.

'It's not far,' Peter says, coming round to my side and looping his arm through mine.

I scan the street ahead and glance over my shoulder. Warm lights shine in the windows but I can't see anyone on the road. That doesn't mean there's nobody peering out from behind a curtain, though. The Stasi move like ghosts and the border is under their control. If they want to have agents on this side of the Wall – and why wouldn't they? – then those shadows are already walking among us.

We struggle forward through the snow, our heads bowed against the wind. I can't see the name of the street – the sign on the corner is covered in a thick layer of frost – but when we turn right the looming watchtowers of East Berlin appear. It's dark and the visibility is too poor to see if there's anyone up there watching us, but I know that there will be; the towers are manned twenty-four hours a day.

'Brunnenstraße?' I grip Peter's arm. It's the only way I can stop myself from turning and running in the other direction. We're on the Western side, I tell myself. We're safe. But every time I see the barrier, I'm overwhelmed with fear and longing. My family. Otto. Monika. Andrei. All so close and yet unreachable.

Peter nods.

'But it's so close to the border,' I whisper. 'The watchtowers are right there.'

'Even one more street away could add three months. The closer the better.'

'Won't they get suspicious? Seeing all of you going in and out?'

'We go in through the basement of the residential building next door. Dina actually lives in that building. And there's nothing wrong with visiting a friend.' He smiles and I can see he's proud of what they've achieved so far. But pride can be dangerous, too.

'That's the one.' He gestures to an abandoned building across the street. 'It's set to be demolished next year.'

We step down off the snowy pavement and cross the road.

'What do you do with the dirt?'

'It's easier if I show you.' With a flourish, he opens a door and I follow him in. The staircase is lit but it's dark in the hallway where we stand stamping our feet to dislodge the snow from our boots.

'I almost forgot,' he says, taking off his glasses and wiping them, 'I haven't told the others about your brother. I've just said that you want to get back to your family in the East. A baby is not something they'd be happy about, for obvious reasons.'

'When are we going to tell them?'

'When it's too late for them to do anything about it.'

Peter leads me down the stone steps into the basement. A bare bulb hangs from the ceiling, its dull glow casting shadows around the room. Stacks of junk are piled up against the walls – old suitcases, broken furniture, boxes overflowing with musty clothes – but the floor has been swept clean. Leaning against the far side is a cracked mirror. A fragmented version of myself looks back at me. My cheeks are red, my nose runny.

'Follow me.' Peter pushes the mirror aside to reveal a gap in the concrete, a hole that's just large enough for a grown man to crawl through.

He disappears and, through the looking glass, I follow.

The other basement is much smaller than the one we've just left, or perhaps it only seems that way. Implements are strewn across the room but there's organization to the chaos. There are wheelbarrows and buckets; shovels, picks and hammers, as well as tools that I've never seen before. Old flour sacks full of soil stand in one corner, a dirty sunken sofa in another, and, over by the far wall, there's a great gaping hole in the ground.

'And here it is.' Peter spreads his arms as if basking in sunlight. 'Here is our tunnel.'

I pick my way over to the hole and peer down. It's a small vertical shaft and there's a ladder leading into it, though in the darkness it's impossible to tell how far down it goes.

'Almost ten metres deep,' Peter says, reading my mind. He stands beside me, hands on hips. 'We had to dig straight down first until we got to the water table. Otherwise, we'd risk the whole thing flooding. Now we're digging forward but at a slight angle, which makes it a bit easier to remove all the soil and rock.'

'And how long is it? How much further do you have to go?'

'So far we've dug out about eighty metres. We measure it every few days to make sure we're on track. And your second question should be: how much further do *we* have to go? Your first shift starts tomorrow.'

A pale glow appears beneath us. There's the echo of a cough. Someone is climbing the ladder, their breath a wheezy rattle. I know it must be one of Peter's group, but there's something strangely terrifying about waiting while a faceless being climbs towards you out of a dark hole in the earth.

'Damn, it's unpleasant down there.' Dina clambers out and collapses on the threadbare sofa, its springs groaning under her weight. 'Water,' she demands, waving her arm.

Peter doesn't look as if he's going to respond so I pick up the half-full water bottle that's sitting on a small wooden table and pass it to her.

'Thanks, Jutta.' Dina takes the water from my outstretched hand. She drinks the whole thing down in one go and then lies back on the sofa and closes her eyes. 'Though I suppose that's not your real name, right?'

I glance at Peter but he's busy fiddling with some kind of short-range radio.

'What makes you say that?'

'You just don't look like a Jutta.' She sits up, tilting her head. 'You're turning red.'

'It's hot in here.'

She laughs. 'Sure it is.'

'Peter said you live next door,' I say, changing the subject. 'Don't you go home between shifts?'

'I'm just having a quick break. I can only handle short stints down there. You'll see – it's pretty damn awful. So,' she says, bringing her legs up on to the sofa, 'tell me more about you. Peter says you got separated from your family when the Wall went up. He says you want to go back? Why don't you try and get them over here instead? I mean, you don't really want to live in the East, do you?'

'No, I don't. Not really.' I sit down on a stool opposite the sofa. It's wobbly so I have to lean forward to redistribute my weight. 'But my family won't leave. My grandmother especially. She's . . . she just won't.'

There's something about the way Dina looks at me that makes me want to tell her everything. She's the kind of person who really listens. But I stop myself from spilling the complete truth. Peter's right – it's best they find out about Axel when it's too late for them to say no.

'If we could somehow make you shorter and change your skin colour, you could just take my passport and walk across.'

'Of course – you've got a foreign passport, haven't you? You're the one who's been scouting the site on the other side?'

'Yup.'

'It's your boyfriend who's there? You're doing this for him?'

'Yes and no. Ulf – my boyfriend – wants to escape the East and I want that too. But I'm not just doing this for him. There are so many people who want to cross. And my role is pretty important.' She says this as a fact, without a hint of self-importance. 'In time, hopefully we can recruit more foreigners to help us, but at the moment it's just me.'

'How often do you cross?'

'Not as often as I'd like. Going over to see Ulf just draws attention to him. Having an American girlfriend, he'll most definitely be under surveillance. I don't want to jeopardize everything we're trying to do here. That's why we've decided he shouldn't cross over with the first group.'

'That makes sense. How many people are there in the first group?'

'About ten. Peter thinks we should find more. Knut too. But for this first run, I think we should be careful.'

'We might only get one go at it,' Peter says, joining Dina on the sofa. 'God, you stink.'

Dina smells her armpits and then laughs. 'Lucky I'm not trying to impress you.'

'Seriously, though,' he says, 'you should persuade Ulf to come on this first run. Just in case things go south. He can be your prize for all your hard work.'

'I'll think about it,' she says. 'You know, Jutta, it won't be long before West Germans are allowed to cross just like foreigners. Why don't you wait?'

It's something Karin's husband, Oskar, suggested when he got me my identity papers – papers that are a duplicate of Jutta's, his friend's sick daughter. She lives in the countryside and is too ill to attend school. Her misfortune has been my lifeline.

'We don't know how long that'll be.' I look down at my gloved hands. A hole is forming on the pinkie finger and I pick at the leather. Dina's music pauses, as if she knows there's something I'm not telling her. Peter asked me the same question when we first met, but the fact is that finding papers for a baby would be near impossible, even with Oskar's and Karin's connections. And I'm worried about Mama – she's waited long enough already.

'Right, back to work.' Dina stands up, stretches her arms and cracks her neck. 'By the way, my water bill was crazy last month. It's time you boys just cleaned your faces after a shift – you can wash properly at home. And, Jutta, I'm heading over to the East next week. If you write a note, I'll make sure it gets to your parents. Obviously no details or anything, just something to say you're safe.'

'Thank you. That would be . . . amazing. Thank you so much.' I'm so overwhelmed with gratitude I almost fling myself at her.

'Sure, no problem.' She shrugs and disappears down the hole.

Peter goes over to the pile of tools. He crouches down and begins to inspect each one meticulously, turning them over in his hands. Some – the damaged ones, I suspect – he separates into a different pile.

'The others,' I say. 'Why are they doing this?'

'We all have our reasons. I want to help my cousin. For Franz, it's a close friend. Dina, her boyfriend. Sebastian, Knut, Albert – they just want to help anyone who wants to be helped. Mainly other students we studied with, but families too. And teachers.'

He turns to look at me. 'Did you know that any teacher who lived in the East but worked in the West has now been barred from the GDR's education system for life? My favourite teacher is stuck over there. They've taken everything from him; he can't stay. And Knut has a friend who lives in the East but was studying politics here at FU. All he can do now is get unskilled work in a factory. He's been banned from higher education completely.'

When he's angry, Peter's music gets louder along with his voice.

'I know your plan is to go back to the East and stay,' he says. 'But I really hope – once you've reunited your brother with your family – you'll choose to come back here again. It's not a real life in the East. You get that, don't you? You're too young to be a voluntary prisoner over there. I'm offering you a key to get out.'

'I'll think about it,' I say. And I mean it. 'It will be discovered, though, eventually – the tunnel. Don't you think?'

'Probably. It only takes one Stasi informant to get a sniff of something and report it. But then I'll build another one. And another.'

'Aren't you scared?'

'Not really. It's more of a risk for those on the other side.'

I think of my family, the people I've put in danger by coming here. I thought I'd only be gone for a matter of days, but my continued absence won't have gone unnoticed. Have the Stasi already taken my parents in for questioning? Are they – right now – being tortured in a cell?

'Don't look so worried,' Peter says. 'We're safe here.'

44

LISETTE

Now – East Berlin, 9 December 1961

The aisles of Konsum are busy and I'm already regretting having left the apartment. Food shopping feels too normal – an act that shouldn't be done while Elly is missing and Axel is somewhere else being taken care of by strangers. That is what I have to believe – that Axel is at least safe, somewhere. But he should be with me, napping in his pram.

I needed to get out, though. I couldn't breathe; days have been bleeding into nights as if time is folding in on itself; even leaving the apartment hasn't stopped the feeling of claustrophobia. East Germany is still walled in and there's no way out.

I keep my head down, hoping I won't see anyone I know. Julius says everyone is preoccupied with their own tragedies – I'm not the only one who has been separated from someone I love – but if I hear someone else's pity, I will fracture like a bone.

I needn't have worried; the latest rules have locked people's heads together in gossip and they're blind to a slouching woman hidden beneath her hat.

'Surely they won't saw the antennas off?' one woman whispers, squeezing an orange as round as she is. 'My son will never give up RIAS. He lives for that raucous music they play.'

'Shh,' the woman's friend whispers back. 'They'll call him a mental border-crosser. The Stasi will be on him – and you.'

She catches me looking their way and her face pales, my grief mistaken for something more suspicious.

'Lisette.' I hear my name and I almost keep walking.

'Lisette,' the voice comes again and I find myself turning in slow motion. It's my friend Marion – sweet, young, unassuming Marion.

'It *is* you,' she says, lumbering towards me.

I try not to look at her pregnant belly or the small boy clinging to her skirt. Her hair is wild, her cheeks a healthy shade of pink. She pulls me into a hug and I can feel her belly pressing into my own shrivelled one. When she releases me, I struggle to breathe.

'Oh, Lisette.' She grips my shoulders with both hands, her eyes filling with tears. 'I heard about Axel. You poor, poor thing. It's so terrible. I can't even imagine how you are feeling.' At this, she places a protective hand on her stomach, as if to say she would never have let it happen.

'You'll get him back. I know you will. This barrier won't last, you'll see.'

She tries to look me in the eye but I can't meet her gaze. I will not cry. Not here in a supermarket aisle.

'Tell me, what can I do?' she says. 'There must be some way I can help.'

Even if I could speak, I wouldn't know what to say to this woman. She's much younger than I am – too young to remember the war properly and too pretty to have ever experienced true heartbreak. I hate myself for despising her in this moment. I want to shove her to the floor and run out of the shop. I want to open my mouth and scream. Instead, I pull out my pen and notebook.

I've lost my voice. A bad throat infection, I write.

'Oh, how horrible,' she says, waiting for me to write more.

Her son is staring at me.

'*Mutti*,' he whines, tugging at Marion's skirt. She strokes his head and I can't bear to stay here another second.

It was nice to see you. But I have to go. I rip off the page, press it into her palm and then run out of the shop, leaving my half-full basket blocking the aisle.

As I turn on to our street, a short Black woman brushes past me. She looks up, apologizes. Something about her makes me pause. She has the look of someone guilty. She backs away, her hands raised, the falling snow settling in her hair like dandruff. And then she's gone.

I half expect to see someone lurking in an alleyway or watching me from across the street. The Stasi are everywhere. This is the other reason I had to get out of the apartment. Right now, we can't draw any more attention to ourselves. We have to pretend that Elly is in Leipzig and everything is fine. Was that woman a Stasi officer? An informant? Is someone following me? But all I can see are Berliners trudging through the snowdrifts, their heads bowed against the biting wind.

The note is there when I come home, lying on the mat. A piece of white paper, neatly folded. I look around, expecting someone else to be here, but there's just Mother sitting by her window, staring blankly at the glass.

A is fine. I am too. Soon we'll be home. I promise.

I turn the note over but there are no more words, just these precious few. I hold the letter to my chest. I swear I can feel my children through the paper and tears spill from my eyes. They say it's the hope that kills you. But this note will keep me breathing. My children are together, alive, safe.

I have so many questions. Who delivered the note? How did Elly get Axel out of the hospital? Where are they staying? Do the Western authorities know Elly crossed the border? How are they going to get back? Elly has already risked her life once. What if her luck runs out? She'll be putting her brother in danger too. Part of me, the smallest sliver, wants them to stay in the West and start a new life, but the bigger – selfish – part of me needs them to come home.

Mother gets up from her chair and wanders into the kitchen. She runs her fingers over the mantlepiece on her way, checking for dirt.

'Is your father home yet?' she asks, opening the fridge. 'I must start on dinner.'

Not yet, I write, flashing my notebook at her. I used to try to explain the truth, but some days I don't have the energy. It's easier to pretend.

'What is wrong with your voice?'

A sore throat.

I've realized I now prefer the days when Mother is confused, when her thoughts are jumbled and she can't seem to anchor herself in the present. I know that's cruel, but on those days she doesn't mention Axel or Elly because, in her mind, they haven't been born yet.

I remember her confusion when Elly first appeared in her world. Back then, Mother was more active, her mind still clear at times. I remember finding her staring at the cot, her eyes wide, her mouth opening and closing as if she was trying to draw in more oxygen.

'Whose baby is this?' she'd whispered, looking from side to side. 'Have you *stolen* a baby?'

'No, Mother, I haven't stolen a baby. Why would I steal a baby? The baby is mine. Her name is Elly.'

Over that first year, we had this same conversation – or a variation of it – countless times. I was often tempted to reply, *Yes, I have stolen it; don't tell anyone*, just to break the repetition.

At times, I could see her grappling with the fact that she had no memory of me being pregnant. I felt sorry for her then. I was still suspicious of her forgetfulness, but sometimes, when her face twisted in confusion and her eyes became glassy, it was clear that her memory loss was real.

Now that her retreat into the past has become more permanent, I almost envy her. I know Julius does too. If only we could erase our memories as well, and wipe out all the pain with them.

45

ELLY

Now – West Berlin, 24 December 1961

I trudge back to Karin's through the snow, the smell of pine needles and roasted chestnuts triggering memories of Christmas that make my chest ache. Candles burn in windows and glittering lights decorate the streets with the promise of tonight's celebration. I let myself in and it's like being transported into the set of a Christmas play – the smell of sizzling sausages, the sound of children playing, the heat of a roaring fire.

'Elly, is that you? Come in.'

I take off my jacket, gloves and several layers of clothes, then poke my head around the living-room door. 'Are you sure? I mean, I don't mind if you just want a family Christmas?'

Karin jumps up from the sofa, sloshing wine from her glass on to the carpet, though she doesn't seem to notice. 'That's ridiculous. It's Christmas! And you *are* part of the family.' She grabs my hand, pulling me into the room, and motions to an armchair. 'Sit, sit. Do you want some brandy or a glass of wine? You're almost sixteen; a glass or two won't hurt. I've promised the children we'll open one present each before dinner.'

'Now?' Erich looks up from the floor where he's wrestling with one of his brothers. 'Please say now?'

'Ask your mother,' Oskar says. He takes a sip of his whiskey then turns his attention back to the newspaper on his lap. Wolfgang, the youngest of the boys, stands on the sofa examining his father's ears.

'You've got hair on your ears,' Wolfgang announces. 'Should we pull it out and stick it on your head? You've got a bald spot where there's no hair at all. I don't want you to get a cold head.'

Oskar glances at Karin, his cheeks reddening.

'Wolfgang, leave your father alone. He's perfect just as he is.' She picks Wolfgang up, places him on the floor and then plonks herself on Oskar's lap, giving him a kiss. I try to look away but I'm fascinated by the affection they share. I have a brief glimpse of a future me curling myself around my own husband. I try to picture Paul Newman's face but it warps into Andrei's. I push the image away.

'Right!' Karin says, jumping up. 'Present time. You can all choose one present with your name on it from under the tree.'

The children dive into the pile, squealing and laughing.

'Only one,' Karin says, but no one's listening. 'Erich, can you find one for Mila, please?'

I have never seen so many presents. They're stacked haphazardly under the tree but they are so numerous that they spill across the floor in every direction. Gifts have never been a big thing in our family. I usually get one at Christmas as well as something small on my birthday. I can't decide if the extravagance here is vulgar or one of the most wonderful things I've ever seen. Not for the first time, I wish this was my real home – my screeching, annoying, adorable siblings; my affectionate but scatty mother; my beautiful big house in West Berlin. The feeling that follows this thought is sharp and deservedly painful. I have a brother – one I don't know yet, but one who's helpless and needs me. And I have Oma Rita, my parents. There are cracks in every family – I just haven't seen them in this one yet.

I wander over to the window and look out into the darkness. Across the road two men stand under a street light, smoking. They're wearing hats so their faces are cast in shadow. They're both carrying bags as if they're on their way back from Christmas shopping, but it's at least minus ten outside and any sane person would be hurrying home. One of them looks directly at our house and I duck behind the curtain, my temples pulsing.

I return to the sofa, ignoring the tingle in my spine, and Karin hands me a present. 'For you.'

It's badly wrapped, the edges of the paper jagged and uneven, sections of the small box inside visible, and I suspect that one of the children might have 'helped' to wrap it.

'Go on,' Karin says, 'open it. Of course, there are more for you, but this one's just from me.'

She studies my face as I slowly pull off the wrapping paper. I attempt to fold it neatly in case she'd like to use it again but she grabs it from my hand, scrunches it into a ball and chucks it on the floor. 'You're a funny one. We don't save that kind of thing. I'll clear all this up tomorrow. Christmas Eve is about making a mess and not giving a hoot!'

I don't want to open the box in front of her. I can feel my eyes stinging. I don't want to embarrass us both if the inevitable happens. It's clear I don't have a choice, though – Karin's attention is entirely taken up by me and this little package.

I stroke the soft velvet lid. It snaps open to reveal a pair of gold button earrings.

'Do you like them? They're all the fashion. I have two pairs myself.'

Before I can stop myself, I wrap my arms around Karin's waist. Her dress is silky and I breathe in the faint lavender of her perfume. Her symphony is chaotic and yet it embraces me. It feels like home. And I hate what I'm about to do.

46

ELLY

Now – West Berlin, 6 January 1962

I pass the last bag of dirt to Knut, my shoulders aching with the effort, and clamber out of the hole. My entire body is encrusted with mud, somehow even beneath my clothes, and my eyelids droop with exhaustion, but I manage to crawl past the others and haul myself up on to the sofa beside Dina.

'Are you OK?' Dina asks.

I nod. 'Just . . .'

'Broken?'

'Exactly.'

She takes me by the shoulders and squeezes them. Then she brings her forehead to mine. It's such an intimate act, yet it feels completely natural. Even though my hands are weeping with blisters and my muscles spasm in unison, my mind feels a little less fuzzy in her presence.

'You're doing great.' They're only words but they give me sustenance.

'That's it,' Peter says. He takes off his glasses and attempts to wipe the grime away with muddy fingers. 'Only another metre or two to go.'

'I can't believe we've done it,' Knut says, shaking his head.

We're all wearing overalls and sweating rivulets of dirt but Knut looks immaculate in comparison. He's been hacking and digging and carrying just like the rest of us, but his smooth, pale skin seems to repel the dirt.

'So, tomorrow?' I ask. My tongue feels thick and my words seem to slur. 'We dig out the last couple of metres and then I make my way through?'

'Exactly.' Peter unfolds a map on the floor. 'If our calculations are correct, we should knock through into an old outhouse in the courtyard of an apartment building. Dina will cross the border with her passport in the morning – her visa's been approved. And, Jutta, after you've climbed out, Dina will give the signal to the people waiting. They'll follow her two by two, keeping their distance.'

'I should be the one who knocks through those last few metres into the East,' Franz says, picking dirt out from beneath his nails with a toothpick. 'I know you want to do it, Peter, but the space is too small for you. No offence.'

'None taken,' Peter says, clenching his jaw. 'But I disagree.'

'We can widen it gradually,' Franz says, 'but tomorrow, we just want to break through and get our first group out. We don't know how long we'll have until the tunnel is discovered. You've said it before yourself – tomorrow might be our only chance.'

Dina leans forward and catches Peter's eye. 'I'm sorry, but Franz is right. This is your project and of course it should be you, but this is bigger than any of us. We need tomorrow to go as smoothly as possible.'

'Fine.' Peter stands up abruptly and grabs his jacket. 'Meeting over. It's late and we all need to get some rest.'

He offers me his hand and I let him pull me to my feet. He avoids even Knut's gaze as we drag the mirror to the side, escaping into the adjacent basement.

'Are you OK?' I ask when we're out on the street.

'Of course I'm OK. Why wouldn't I be?'

For some reason, I expected it to be light outside. I've been underground for so many days I've lost all sense of time and space. I struggle to keep up with Peter as he strides down the street.

'Did you notice the way Knut didn't defend me?' he mutters. 'Though neither did you . . .'

'What? I mean, it wasn't an attack. Dina's right – of course, it *should* be you, but the last few metres of the tunnel are too small. There's no leeway down there. I'm sorry, though; I should have said something.'

He doesn't slow his pace and I find myself dodging abandoned Christmas trees that have been left to die on the street. Most are shedding needles the way dogs shed hair. The seasonal lights have disappeared and West Berlin has become dark and dreary and damp.

Most cars are coated with a dusting of snow while Peter's is blanketed with at least a foot. I glance up at the watchtowers. Have they noticed it too? We've been down there for days – working in shifts, only sleeping a few hours at a time in Dina's apartment. At first, we took it in turns to shower as well, but eventually everyone but Knut accepted there was little point in scrubbing off the dirt, knowing it would return. I'd had to lie to Karin, telling her I was spending some time with friends.

Peter wipes the snow off the windscreen but he needs a scraper to shift the ice. He shoves the key into the lock. It won't turn. Leveraging himself with one arm against the door, his feet slide on the packed snow as if he's doing a dance. Still it won't budge.

'Stop. It'll snap right off. Let me help?' I nudge him gently aside, pull out the key and rub it between my hands. I ease it into the lock and this time it turns, but the door is frozen in place. Together we yank at the handle. And then, as if someone has kicked it from the inside, the door flies open, throwing us backwards on to the pavement. Peter laughs but I swallow my own giggle.

I can hear music.

It's distant, like the rumbling of an underground train, but I can feel its vibrations. There's a menacing, echoing bass and a chilling, flat voice. Just then, Franz and Knut stumble out of Dina's apartment building. Behind them, high up on the watch-tower, there's a shadow. Whoever it is, he's watching us.

47

ELLY

Now – West Berlin, 7 January 1962

The car's engine coughs up the long drive. Peter has a cough himself and it's as if the two are competing.

'Did you say goodbye?' Peter asks. The car heater still isn't working properly; every so often, it merely burps some tepid air. My fingers are numb with cold and I have a sudden intense longing for summer.

'To Karin and the kids? No. You told me not to.'

'Good. It's better that way. Are you OK, though?'

'Not really. This is the second time I've disappeared on people I care about, but I know it's for the best. It is, isn't it?'

'Of course,' he says. 'It's about protecting them, but it's also about protecting the rest of us. The fewer people who know, the better.'

We pull into a parking spot and the car shudders to a stop. Snow drifts down, sugaring the windscreen, but there are pockets of blue in the sky.

'Once you're safely across, I'll let them know. I'll tell them you're safe.'

'Thank you,' I say, turning to face him. 'Thank you for every-thing.'

'Don't thank me yet. And remember what I said. Once things are settled, you should think about coming back. You don't belong in the East, you know that.'

'Does anyone belong there?'

'No, you're right. But tell me you'll think about it?'

'Yes.' I open the car door and brace myself for the cold. 'I promise I'll think about it.'

There's a lonely echo as I walk down the empty corridor and I'm relieved Peter decided it was best he stay in the car. His hulking frame would have drawn attention and right now I need to blend into the faded wallpaper. Thankfully the wards them-selves are busy and the nurses don't even glance at me as they rush about their business.

I've marked out my route and committed to memory the location of the supply room, but when I turn into the main cor-ridor I can't find it. It's supposed to be the third door on the left but I find myself in a bathroom instead. To my right I sense movement. I turn to see a face, ashen white with unruly hair and eyes wide and stricken. I stifle a scream moments before I realize it's just my reflection.

I take a few deep breaths, pull my hair into a ponytail, and then go back into the corridor and try the next door. It swings open and I slip inside, locking the door behind me.

The smell of bleach is overpowering and a wave of nausea passes through me. Closing my eyes, I find my song. I need to stay calm and focused; everything has to go according to plan. Slowly my heart falls into sync with the steady drumbeat of my music. I open my eyes. The uniforms are neatly stacked on a shelf. I shed my clothes and tuck them into a corner. I pull on the green-and-white outfit, then grab a mop and bucket. The door unlocks with a soft click and I make my way down the corridor, keeping my head bowed.

An old nurse with cloudy eyes and wiry grey hair is inside the nursery. She's standing by the large window, in a patch of pale winter sun, rocking a baby in her arms. She barely looks at me as I open the door, rolling the bucket in front of me. A dozen cots are lined up across the room and someone has painted some strange-looking rabbits on the walls – the heads are disproportionately large and the teeth much too long.

'Nurse Ilse is looking for you,' I say.

'Really? Why?' She doesn't look up, her attention too focused on the child in her arms.

I shrug. 'She asked me to find you. She says it's important. She's in Ward Fifteen.'

'Goodness, that's the other side of the hospital. Doesn't she know I'm on duty? I can't just leave the babies.'

'She said it was really important. I can keep an eye on them. I need to mop in here anyway.'

Reluctantly she places the baby in his cot. He stirs but she strokes his head and soon he settles once more. 'Hmm, well, I suppose. It's not like they can go anywhere. Are you sure you can stay here until I get back?'

'Of course.'

'All right, then. I'll be as quick as I can.'

The door swings shut and I hold my breath as I hear the click-clack of her heels retreating down the corridor. I give it one more minute then I move swiftly, scanning the cots for Axel. All the babies look the same and I'm terrified I won't recognize him – that I'll end up taking someone else's baby instead.

But then I see him. His wide brown eyes are the same as Papa's, the thin lips a copy of Mama's. He's awake, content, watching me curiously.

'There you are,' I whisper. 'I've missed you. Are you ready to go home?'

Gently I lift him out of his cot. He reaches up and touches my nose. I want to stay in this moment and cuddle him, but time isn't on our side. I snatch the blanket from his cot, wrap him tightly in it and then slip out of the nursery, my brother in my arms.

I force myself to walk slowly, even though my instinct is to flee. My whole body is shaking and I worry my arms will give way, dropping Axel to the floor. My plan was to return to the supply room, get changed and walk out with Axel tucked inside my jacket, but my feet lead me straight past the door. The corridor is busy now and no one looks my way but it feels as though there are a hundred hidden eyes watching me, waiting for the right moment to pounce.

Behind me, I hear footsteps.

'Excuse me!' The voice is clipped, authoritative. I have no idea if the man is talking to me or trying to attract someone else's attention, but I don't stop. The exit is only five metres away.

'Hey, you!'

Three metres.

'Young lady, I'm talking to you.'

One metre. I start running.

I fling the doors open. Outside, the raw wind almost knocks me over. I don't know if the man has followed me outside, or if he is at this moment calling the police, but I'm like a cannonball – I just keep moving, willing the ice beneath my feet to be kind. I hear an engine sputter. Then Peter's car appears in front of me.

'Get in,' Peter shouts and now I know I'm being chased. Whoever it is is about to dig his fingers into my arm, yank me back by my ponytail. I can almost hear my hair being torn from my scalp. But then I'm in the car and Peter starts driving before I can even close the door. There's screaming, too. A baby. My brother. I still have him, pressed against my chest, wailing as if someone has stolen him.

Which, of course, I have.

48

LISETTE

Now – East Berlin, 7 January 1962

I sit at the kitchen table and swallow the breakfast Julius has made for me. I look at the mound of unopened presents lying beside the Christmas tree. We have never embraced Christmas before – only giving one or two presents each – but this year I have overcompensated in the bizarre hope that it will bring my children home.

The tree is absurdly large and bushy and sheds a copious amount of pine needles. Mother is beneath it on her hands and knees, muttering as she picks them up.

A newspaper lies folded in front of me but I'm unable to focus on the words; they move around like a colony of ants. The bread tastes of nothing but I know I must eat. One day Elly and Axel will come home – I can't bear to think otherwise – and on that day, they'll need me to be at my best.

I look down at the paper and unfold it. The headline is a scream. *WAR CRIMINAL EGON WEBER CAUGHT IN ARGENTINA.* Below it is an old photograph of Egon, smiling widely in his Nazi uniform. The image catches me off guard and almost forces a sound from my lips, but not quite. My words are still hiding.

I glance over at Mother. She's physically here, but I don't know where her mind is. If I show her the headline, will she recognize the name? And if she does, will it only trigger bad memories, the ones we both want to forget?

After almost two decades, the article reads, *Egon Weber, a Nazi war criminal, was apprehended last night in Argentina. Between 1940 and 1945, Egon Weber worked as a prison guard at the notorious Ravensbrück concentration camp, where over 50,000 female prisoners perished. He will be charged as an accessory to murder and is expected to be sentenced to life in prison. The search is still ongoing for Egon's wife and fellow guard at Ravensbrück, Gertrud Weber.*

I rip off the page, scrunch it up and feed it to the fire. I watch as the picture of Egon melts away, the flames eating through his smile. Unlike Mother, I don't have the luxury of dementia. I remember sitting here in this very room eating chocolates and discussing working at Ravensbrück. If Gertrud was capable of this, was I? If I'd taken the job, would I have quit, horrified, when I learned the truth? Or does the potential for evil lie within us all?

49

ELLY

Now – West Berlin, 7 January 1962

'A baby?' Franz says. 'Absolutely not. This is insane.'

His cheeks and the tips of his ears poking out from his hair are bright pink. He glares at me with such anger I can feel it pulsing out of him. As he speaks, I rock Axel back and forth, my arms aching.

'For goodness' sake,' Peter shouts, 'keep your voice down. Let's sit and discuss this like adults.'

'Jutta is *not* an adult and nor is this bloody baby. What were you thinking? How could you agree to something without including the rest of us in the discussion?'

'This is my tunnel,' Peter says, his voice measured. 'The decision is mine.' He towers over Franz, but Franz won't back down.

Knut and I exchange awkward glances. He's against the plan too, I can tell. And so he should be. Axel's presence will put everyone at risk. I know this but I also trust that Axel will be quiet.

'I've given him some gripe water and filled him up with milk,' I say. 'He'll sleep. I promise.'

Franz is so angry his music has become a mess of sporadic

thunder and he won't even look at me. Axel is still awake but his eyelids are drooping and he seems calm snuggled against my chest. I sit down on the lumpy sofa – Axel is heavier than I thought and I need to conserve my energy. I move one of the cushions and a puff of dust rises. Axel lets out a surprised sneeze.

'Dina would back me up if she was here,' Franz says, pacing around the small basement. 'Waiting until the last minute is so incredibly deceptive. And risky.'

'If you want to back out, that's fine,' Peter says, crossing his arms. 'I can knock through the last few metres on my own. But it isn't really that risky. Jutta is going to the East, so it'll just be her and the baby on the way over. If she had been with the group coming back here, I wouldn't have said yes. Then everyone would be in danger. As it stands, it's just her and Axel who are. And that's her decision.'

'If that baby cries for a single second when she's in the tunnel,' Franz says, 'the whole mission will be in jeopardy. Fine – those on the other side may not be caught, but it will scupper their chance to escape. This is a selfish decision and you know it.'

'You've made your point. We don't have time to continue this argument.' Peter looks at his watch. 'Dina will already be over in the East. Are you in or out?'

Franz lets out a grunt and throws his hands up. 'You are infuriating.'

I wait for him to leave but he takes a swig from a plastic bottle, then turns to look at me. 'I want you to stay here until you see the flash of my torch. Understand?'

'Yes.' A dozen questions bubble up inside me but I keep them contained. The moment is fragile enough already.

He gives me a curt nod, ignoring Peter entirely, and then begins his descent. His face is a network of worried wrinkles and dirt has gathered in the creases. In his eyes, there's a flicker of fear.

Now all we can do is wait. The tunnel is less than two hundred metres long; it shouldn't take more than five minutes to crawl along it, but Franz needs to dig through the last few metres, avoiding any water pipes, and then break through the floor of the shed on the other side – all without making too much noise.

Peter crouches in the corner, meticulously checking and organizing the equipment. Knut leans against the wall, rubbing his hands together for warmth. A frown marks his usually smooth features and there's something strange in his song – a separate score of music hiding behind his symphony. I can barely hear it – it's like a whisper in a room full of shouts.

Axel squirms in my arms, a dream shifting across his face. I can't get him comfortable in my lap. He looks just as I remember him, but we don't fit together, not like a sister and brother should. I thought we would connect like two parts of a puzzle, but too much time has passed and I'm just a stranger to him.

There's a loud, distant bang. Not from below but above. Peter, Knut and I exchange worried glances. The banging continues – a broken shutter battered by the wind, perhaps. Or an army about to descend on us.

Knut goes over to the mouth of the tunnel and looks down.

'Anything?' I ask.

'Not yet.'

He sits down on the edge, his legs dangling into the hole. There's a pen on the floor and he swivels it on the concrete, round and round. The worm-like veins on his hand pulse with each twirl.

In my arms, Axel's eyes flutter. I pull the gripe water out of my bag, the words *No more fuss from baby* emblazoned on the front. I've already given Axel plenty but I can't risk him waking up. With my finger, I rub some more on his gums.

The banging above us stops as suddenly as it started, but my whole body is on alert. My heart slams against my ribcage and my skin burns, heat radiating off me as if I'm in the throes of a fever. With sweaty hands, I extract three scarves from my bag and wrap Axel tightly against my chest, just as I've seen Karin do when Mila sticks out her bottom lip and insists on being carried.

I struggle up from the sofa, my back pinching with the effort, and pace the small room, rocking and jiggling Axel the way Mama used to do.

'Any minute now,' Peter says, joining Knut at the top of the ladder. He turns to look at me. 'Are you ready?'

'As I'll ever be.'

'Peter . . .' Knut says, but Peter shuts him down with a look.

'Axel's asleep,' I say. 'He won't wake up.'

'And he's secure?'

'Yes.' I look down at Axel. He feels secure, the scarves' knots digging into my sides, but if one of them slips . . . 'I've practised crawling with him. He's tucked in tightly.'

I join them at the edge. We might as well be on the precipice of a cliff, staring into the abyss.

There is a flash of torchlight – three bursts, a short break, followed by another two.

'It's time,' Peter says.

He pulls me into a bear hug and a jolt of confidence moves from him to me. I can do this. Everything will be fine.

It's not until we separate that I notice the pistol tucked into his waistband.

50

ELLY

Now – West Berlin, 7 January 1962

There's a string of lights down here, guiding the way like stars in the night sky, but at intervals the darkness feels impenetrable. I slither on my hands and feet, the cold, damp sludge of mud between my fingers. I can hear water trickling and I'm sure it's wetter down here than yesterday. Have we hit a pipe? Is the tunnel slowly filling with water?

The ceiling is held up by timber supports, but I can almost feel the crushing weight of earth above me. Peter's an engineering student but I doubt tunnel building is on the curriculum. Could it collapse? Will this become my grave? Is there a death worse than being buried alive and killing your brother in the process?

I can feel Axel's gentle heartbeat, and the smell of his sweet, milky breath is somehow reassuring. While fear squeezes me, a boa constrictor around my neck, he's oblivious to the danger we're in.

The death strip must now be above us – a carpet of booby traps, landmines, patrolling guards and dogs. Dogs that will tear into your skin while their masters try to shoot you. If Axel cries . . .

Above me, I hear a muffled cough.

I stop crawling, hold my breath.

The tunnel must be only three metres deep at this point. Someone is standing directly above me. Someone who probably has a gun in his hands. And if I can hear him, he can hear me.

I lean back and sit on my feet; one of the swinging bulbs brushes against my forehead. My head is just half an inch from the packed dirt. I move my hand to my chest as if I could reach inside and stop my heart from thumping so hard.

The cough comes again. It's phlegmy and the man keeps coughing until his chest is clear.

I don't know how far through the tunnel I am. There's a pale light far ahead of me, one that perhaps comes from filtered sunlight rather than electricity, but I can't gauge its distance. It's the middle of the day – a group travelling through East Berlin at night would attract too much attention – yet down here it's the dead of night. All I know is that if the patrolling guards hear me beneath their feet, they'll shoot into the ground indiscriminately. They'll rip a hole in the earth and they'll keep on shooting until they're sure I'm dead.

I find my song. I want to sing it aloud or at least hum it, but I force myself to internalize it. It moves through my body like blood from a life-saving transfusion. I become the music and the music becomes me.

It's a long time before my body is capable of moving again. When I do, my foot spasms with cramp. I try to stretch it out by digging my toes into the dirt but it doesn't work. I bite down hard on my lip, shifting the pain, which somehow makes it more bearable. As if Axel can sense my discomfort, he stirs in his sleep and lets out a small, irritable cry.

There's a flurry of mumbled words above me. A dog barks. They've heard me. They must have. Should I scramble forwards? Backwards? Hold still? My limbs won't move. There's no music that will save me now.

Axel screws up his face and I can hear the cry before he opens his lips. I know it will be close to a scream. I press my hand over his mouth. I don't want to, but my hand moves on autopilot. We're so close. We can't be caught now.

'Move.' The words are a whisper but I recognize the voice. Peter. And he's behind me. Axel and I are no longer alone down here. Another life I'll be responsible for if we fail.

I can't move if my hand is still over Axel's mouth so I release it. I expect – deserve – a scream, but he's silent. If I had the luxury of time, I'd worry I'd killed him. Instead I scrabble through the muck, Axel a dead weight strapped to my chest.

I can see the light. It has the promise of a sunrise, a horizon I know is possible to reach if I just keep moving.

'Faster,' Peter says, his voice gruff. 'We're almost there.'

The dirty air burns my throat and clogs my lungs. And the ground is no longer sludge but a gloopy river. Water is coming in from somewhere and it's coming in fast.

The shaft of light is so close but a shadow falls across it like an eclipse.

'Turn around.'

It's Franz this time. He's in front of me. And in his hand is a gun.

~

'Oh God, Jutta, quick.'

It's so dark but I can see the terror twisting Franz's face. For a moment I thought he'd turned on us but the desperation in his voice is real.

'Turn around. They're coming.'

'Who's coming?' I meant to whisper but it comes out as a panicked shout.

'The Stasi. They know. And they're coming.'

There are only two options: paralysis or action. Being alone would have immobilized me but there are so many of us down here in this tunnel – Peter, Axel and Franz, but also Mama, Papa, Oma Rita and Andrei. Because they've been with me all this time, an integral part of every decision I've made. And I need to save them too. I need all of us to survive this.

This tunnel wasn't built for turning but somehow I manage it and, impossibly, Axel remains quiet. For Peter, it's more difficult. The last few metres are so tight, the earth presses in on him from all sides. He crawls backwards instead, his face so close to mine I can smell his sour breath. Franz is behind me now. Pushing and desperate.

The string of lights flickers. We drop into darkness.

A gunshot.

In this enclosed space it sounds like a bang followed by a whistle. I hear a yelp, but I don't know who it came from. Me? Franz? Peter? Does blood have a smell?

The tunnel widens and, though I can see nothing, I sense Peter is finally able to turn. As he scrambles ahead of me, he kicks muddy water up into my face. There's grit on my tongue and my trousers are soaked, so that I'm now wading rather than crawling.

Why is Axel so quiet?

There's another crack but this one is going in the opposite direction. The flash of a pistol, the grunt of the shooter or perhaps the one who is shot; later, I won't remember any of the details. I know that, but in this moment every second feels like it's being imprinted on my soul, every bullet ripping through my own flesh.

Another shot. And this time a scream. A rasping breath. The sound of someone dying.

~

We lie on the cement floor of the basement panting like dogs. Axel is still strapped to my chest. He lets out a small whimper and it's the most beautiful sound I've ever heard. He's alive.

'What happened?' I ask, my voice audibly trembling. We're safe but my body hasn't caught up with this fact.

Franz struggles to sit up. His dirt-streaked face is red, his eyes wide. 'I hit a water pipe. And then, when I knocked through, they were there. The Stasi. Waiting for me.'

'But how did they know?'

'They must have been tipped off.'

'But who would have done that? And why?'

'Knut,' Peter whispers beside me. 'It was Knut.' He's still lying down and his breath sounds ragged. His music is off-kilter and his song keeps faltering.

'Are you OK?'

'I think . . . I think I've been shot.'

The words seem to reach me as if underwater. They don't sound right and it takes me a moment to understand their meaning.

'What? No, no, you can't have been.'

I scramble over to him. His lips are white, his eyelids twitching. I lift the hand that's resting on his stomach and it comes away wet.

'Shit. Shit.' I unstrap Axel, hand him to Franz who's standing now, staring down at us, his lips moving but no words escaping his mouth.

I unbutton Peter's jacket, lift up his sweater and the shirt that lies beneath. I find a gaping wound pulsing with blood. I press my hands down and try to stem the flow, the blood leaking through my fingers.

'What do we do? It won't stop. What do we do?' I repeat the words over and over.

Peter mumbles something indiscernible. His eyelids flutter. Like a scratched record, his music keeps stuttering.

'An ambulance,' Franz says. 'I'll call an ambulance.'

I don't want him to leave me here alone but he's already ducking through the hole in the wall, cradling Axel awkwardly in his arms.

'Franz has gone to get help,' I say to Peter. 'You're going to be OK. It's not that bad, I promise.' My voice falters on the lie but I can't help but repeat it. He coughs and grabs my shoulder, drowning, clinging to me in the hope that I can pull him to safety.

'Hold on, OK? The ambulance will be here soon.' My face is wet and I can taste salt in my mouth. Maybe we're both drowning.

His music is fading; I strain to hear it. I tell myself his song is merely entering a ritardando, that soon the crescendo of the next piano riff will begin. But it's as if he's moved away from me into another room, another house.

'Please, Peter, don't go. Stay here with me. Stay.'

And then his music falls silent.

51

LISETTE

Now – East Berlin, 8 January 1962

Every day I go into Elly's room, hoping I will find her by her keyboard or splayed out on the floor reading magazines. But she's never there and, each day, her absence fragments me anew. It's been a month since her note. Where are they? Who are they with? Axel is six months old now and already I'm forgetting his face. He'll have changed so much. Are his eyes still like his father's or have they taken on the auburn colour of my own? I'll have missed so much. Soon he'll be crawling.

When I think about Elly, I get a ripping sensation in my chest. I flip between fury and devastation. How could she have been so stupid? I am so desperate for Axel to be returned to me but I can't see any real possibility of Elly achieving her goal. And in trying, she has put us all in danger, including herself. And yet, I know this is my fault. She has done all of this for me. If only I had loved her more, if only I had been a better mother.

There's a knock at the front door, a hard, determined rap.

'Lisette,' Mother shouts from her room, 'can you get that? It must be Frau Weber.'

I know it's not Frau Weber – she's buried in the park – but

now whoever is behind the door knows we're at home so I have no choice. I press my eye to the peephole. A smartly dressed man gives me a little wave and smiles. Even from here, I can see it doesn't reach his eyes. I take a deep breath and then lift the latch.

He has a thin moustache and is wearing an expensive-looking fur hat. His nails are clipped and neat but I can see remnants of his lunch stuck between his teeth.

I hold up my hand as if to say *Wait one moment*, and then I go in search of my notebook. I haven't invited him in yet, but while I search for my notepad in the kitchen, I feel the air in the apartment wrinkle with the sudden presence of someone new. I turn around to discover he's sitting on the sofa, his jacket folded neatly beside him, his hat atop it. He's examining a framed photograph he must have plucked from the mantlepiece.

'Elly, I presume?' He gestures to the photo – Elly as a chubby six-year-old with a gappy-toothed smile, sitting on Julius's lap.

I nod. My throat constricts. Even if I could speak, I'd remain silent.

'I'll have a coffee. Black, no sugar.'

I nod again and retreat to the kitchen. My hand trembles as I spoon coffee into a mug, the granules scattering over the damp counter. Behind me I can hear the man wandering around, picking things up, humming as he goes. The kettle takes for ever to boil but it gives me time to gather my thoughts and prepare what I'm going to say. When I return, I find him in front of the fire, jabbing the smouldering logs with the poker.

I've lost my voice, I write.

He takes the notepad from my hand. 'How awful for you.'

He tilts his head, smiles, then sits down again, lifting his trousers at the knees. He takes the coffee and blows into the cup. I can see the liquid rippling.

'Where is your daughter?'

I'm still standing and I don't know what to do with my hands. He sips his coffee but his unblinking eyes don't leave my face.

I take back my notepad and write, *Who are you?*

'I think you know who I am.' He smiles sweetly. He emanates a strange warmth, a kindness that feels almost palpable. But I know it's just a facade. These are the most dangerous men of all, Mother once said. Their charisma is like the flash of a camera – they blind you with it so you don't see who they really are.

'I know your son is in the West. That must be exceptionally difficult for you. But, let me ask you again. Where is your daughter? Where is Elly?'

Elly is staying with a cousin of my husband's in Leipzig. She's been unwell. Elly's gone to help.

'I see. I'd very much like the address of this cousin. Just to check Elly's OK. She hasn't called, has she?'

I shrug. And then I write, *You know what teenagers are like.*

Mother's door swings open and she strides into the living room wearing a black cocktail dress. Her hair is pinned into a bun and her neck is decorated with a pearl necklace – one of the few pieces of jewellery we had the forethought to bury during the war. Her mouth bleeds with red lipstick.

'Oh, who are you?' she says. 'I was expecting our neighbour.' She gives the man a dazzling smile. 'We are going to the opera tonight. My husband, Ernst, managed to get some excellent seats. Are you a friend of Lisette's? She does not often have male visitors.'

'You must be Rita,' he says, standing up and offering his hand. 'It's a pleasure to meet you. I'm Herr Winter, but you can call me Paul. We're all friends here.'

'Delightful. Has Lisette offered you something to drink? Perhaps a brandy to warm you up?'

I glance at the clock. It's not yet ten a.m., but the winter sun is low in the sky and believing it's evening isn't a far stretch for someone whose mind is upside down.

'I have coffee,' he says. 'Would you like to join us? I was just asking your daughter about Elly's whereabouts.'

'Who is Elly?'

I flip over a new page, unable to stifle a sigh. *My mother has dementia*, I write, careful to show only him.

'Gosh, how unfortunate.'

He seems bemused not suspicious, but I can't be sure.

'I won't take up any more of your time.' He drains the last of his coffee and sets the mug carefully on the table. 'I would like that address, though. We'll catch up again soon.'

He watches over my shoulder as I scribble down Julius's cousin's address. He folds the page neatly and then slips it into the front pocket of his jacket. I follow him through the apartment, knowing I need to see him leave with my own eyes. There is a rush of cold when he opens the front door, as if a ghost has pushed past me.

'Thank you for your time, Frau Lange. Until we meet again.'

He tips his hat and then he's gone.

52

ELLY

Now – West Berlin, 8 January 1962

'It needs to be tomorrow,' Dina says. Her skin is blotchy and there are red threads in the whites of her eyes, yet somehow she's managed to contain her tears.

I look down at Axel nestled in the crook of my arm, sucking lazily on a bottle of milk. Every few seconds he becomes distracted and turns his head to look at Dina or Franz and I have to tempt him gently back to the bottle.

The room feels achingly empty even though we're squeezed around Dina's kitchen table. I glance at the door, half expecting to see Peter lumber in and collapse on to one of Dina's wobbly wooden chairs. I try to focus my attention on Axel, not the door, and not Franz, who's using a fork to dig out dried blood from beneath his fingernails. Peter's blood.

'Jutta, are you listening?'

'It's Elly.'

'What?'

'My name – it's Elly. Not Jutta.'

'Elly. OK.' She tries to catch my eye but I keep my head down.

'Peter's idea, I suppose? To use a different name? Maybe he suspected one of us was . . . perhaps he knew.'

I shake my head. 'No, no, it was me who wanted to use a different name. If he suspected Knut before last night, he would have said something.'

'Are we sure it was Knut?'

'Of course it was Knut,' Franz says. 'I don't even think he was gay; I think he just led Peter on. And we didn't think why . . .'

'Stop it, Franz,' Dina says. 'We can't keep doing this. Assigning blame. Peter's hurt but he's going to be OK. That's what the doctor said. You know Peter – he'll be proud of his war wound. I know you both feel guilty but the tunnel was Peter's idea. None of this is your fault. Right now, we need to focus. We have to figure out what to do next.'

'There is no next.' Franz stands up abruptly, knocking the table with his knee.

Axel lets out a surprised cry but I quieten him with the bottle.

'It's over,' Franz mumbles. 'It's just too dangerous. Can't you see that?' He crosses to the window and presses one hand against the frosted glass. His shoulders begin to shake. I feel it too. The breathless horror of that moment when we both thought Peter was dead. I keep reliving it. Again and again. Dina wasn't there; she doesn't understand. But she *is* right. We need to focus on what comes next. I can't stay here; my time has run out.

Dina stands up and wraps her arms around Franz's waist, pressing her cheek into his back. I want to slide in between them but I have a strong sense of not belonging. Until a few minutes ago, they didn't even know my real name.

I blink away the image of Peter's lifeless body, the blood pooling on the floor. I look down at Axel and tighten my grip. Dina's right; it needs to be tomorrow.

'And your friend?' I say, my voice cutting into their embrace. 'She's OK with this?'

Dina gives Franz one last squeeze then returns to business.

'It's risky. But no riskier than what we did yesterday.'

'That's not what I asked.'

She hesitates, looks down at her hands. 'She's fine with it.' It's a lie, I know it is, but I choose to believe her. It's easier that way.

Franz turns to face me. He wipes his eyes and clears his throat, then sits back down, his spine straight. 'You'll have to cut and dye your hair,' he says. 'And we'll need to sort out your accent.'

'Do you really think this is going to work?'

Dina reaches out and squeezes my arm. 'It's going to have to.'

53

ELLY

Now – West Berlin, 9 January 1962

I don't recognize the girl returning my gaze in the mirror. It's not just the make-up and the new hair colour or the fact she looks older than me and more sophisticated. It's the look in her eyes I don't recognize. She's not a naive kid. She's looked death in the face and knows what's at stake.

'Just remember,' Dina says, placing a flamboyant yellow hat on my head and pinning it in place, 'it's about being confident, brash almost.'

The hat is excessively wide and hangs so low it obscures half my face, though I suppose that's the point.

'But don't annoy them either.' Franz stands in the doorway, Axel asleep in his arms.

'No, do annoy them,' Dina says, meeting my gaze in the mirror. 'Annoying them is better than acting suspiciously.'

'I disagree,' Franz says.

'Don't you always?'

His ears turn pink but I don't think it's anger that's making him flush. Why have I not seen it until now?

I take one last look in the mirror and then swivel around on the chair. Dina takes a step back.

'I'm ready,' I say.

'Yes, I think you probably are.'

Franz gazes out of the tram window. Axel sits on his lap wearing a frilly white dress, buckled shoes and a double-breasted blue coat with yellow flowers embroidered around the collar. He makes a beautiful girl; I don't know why I thought his real sex would be impossible to hide.

Since Peter almost died, Franz has insisted on carrying Axel whenever possible. It's only been two days but Axel seems equally attached. He sits now, his head resting on Franz's chest, his gummy smile a permanent feature while he takes in everything there is to see – the people outside wrapped up in winter coats, trudging through the snow; the commuters surrounding us on the tram, blowing on frozen fingers or reading newspapers with ink-stained hands. I forget that most of Axel's life has been limited to a hospital ward and everything he sees is a first. I wish I wasn't taking him from one prison to another. I wish there was another way.

'At least the broadcasts have stopped,' Dina says behind us. She sits with her knee up, one snow-encrusted boot resting on the edge of her seat. She ignored the elderly woman who commented on it when she first sat down and seems pleased the woman consequently switched places. I suspect that was Dina's plan all along.

'What broadcasts?' Franz asks.

'The Soviets have been playing music and hate broadcasts from loudspeakers at the border. You'll see them in a minute. There are dozens of them, all facing towards us, spewing their crap.'

I shift in my seat. 'Hate broadcasts? What exactly are they

saying? How long have they been doing it for?' It strikes me that this kind of conversation could only happen here in the West. We don't need to worry about who might be listening. When will I ever have this type of freedom again? The freedom to ask questions, simply to say what's on my mind?

I try to slow my breathing and think about something else. I pull at the collar of my jacket. The material is itchy and unfamiliar, the scent of someone else's clothes disconcerting. Dina says her friend Barbara was happy to lend me the jacket along with her baby daughter's clothes. But was she equally willing to lend me her identity? Dina is honest and righteous, but she's also determined, and morality is a blurred line when you think you have no other choice. I want to press her on this, but what does it matter now? It's too late to turn around.

'They've been doing it for a few days. They've been building more watchtowers, too, and putting up wooden screens at the few places where we've been able to wave to those on the other side.'

I look beyond the window and see that she's right. Loudspeakers have been erected on giant wooden posts – though, for now, they're silent – and dozens of new watchtowers have appeared. I can see the soldiers gathered inside them, their eyes trained not on us but on their own people.

We approach Bornholmer Straße. The Bösebrücke bridge and the checkpoint loom ahead of us. The voices around us fade and the grumble of the engine dominates. The woman in front of me, her hair greying at the temples, wipes her eyes. The man sitting beside her squeezes her arm and I wonder who it is they're missing. I doubt there's a soul in West Berlin who hasn't been separated from someone they love. Life goes on but it seems moments of mourning continue to take our breath away.

'This is our stop,' Dina says, her voice low.

I close my eyes for a moment and find my music. I wait for it to slow my pulse and then I let Dina help me up. My legs are shaking and I'm grateful that Axel is safe in Franz's arms.

We step down off the tram, careful not to slip on the icy steps. I can feel eyes watching me. It's clear I'm here to cross over and the passengers are probably wondering how I've secured a visa. It's still not a privilege West Berliners have been offered. Perhaps I shouldn't have spoken German on the bus. The moment I left Dina's apartment, I should have embodied the American woman I am pretending to be.

The tram trundles off towards the turning loop that's been built just short of the now-deserted bridge. Beneath it, I can see the wire-mesh fence marking the sector border. It runs directly along the Western track and is topped with glinting spikes and loops of barbed wire.

We move under the tram shelter and I perch on the bench, my legs still wobbly. The air is sharp and each breath stings my lungs, but my armpits are damp and this damn collar won't stop itching. I hate the hat, too. It flops from side to side and Axel keeps reaching for it.

'Do I really have to wear this?'

'Yes,' Dina says, tucking in a loose strand of my hair. 'But, listen, everything is becoming more permanent. You see that, right? This border, this wall – it's not going anywhere. This is your last chance to change your mind.'

I glance towards the checkpoint. On the Eastern side, it looks as though some kind of barracks is being built, and I can hear the muffled sound of drilling and hammering. It's not just more watchtowers and loudspeakers. These are permanent fixtures.

I look at Axel who's playing with Franz's nose, giggling each time Franz makes a honking noise when he squeezes it. Would a future here be better for him? Is this really the right decision? But then I think of Mama. Her baby is gone and with him her voice. If I don't bring Axel home, I'm not sure she'll survive it.

Above us a crack appears in the sky and the sun slips into it. A drift of snow by my feet catches the light and for a moment I'm blinded.

'We'll see each other again,' I say, shielding my eyes. 'I know we will.'

I reach for Axel and reluctantly Franz hands him over.

'You've got everything?' Dina says.

I nod. 'Let's not do a big goodbye. We don't know who's watching.'

She smiles at me and dips her head. I don't know how I'm going to do this without her. She pats Axel on his head, then thinks better of it and pulls us both into an embrace.

'I'll see you on the other side.'

~

The *VoPo* flicks slowly through 'Axel's' passport, his elbows on the counter. There's a toothpick in his mouth and he waggles it from side to side with his tongue. The guard on the Western side let me through without a single question but this one is more meticulous. His music is a repetitive bundle of chords broken sporadically by the eerie sound of a synthesizer. It's something I've never heard before. There's no harmony in his song, only dissonance.

'*Amerikanisch?*'

Axel reaches up to grab the rim of my hat and I shift him from one hip to the other. 'Yes,' I reply in English. Short and brash. Short and brash.

'*Vier Monate alt?*'

I keep my face blank and focus my attention on Axel. The room is small; there's nothing for Axel to see but the guard, and I can sense he's becoming restless.

'*Vier Monate alt?*' The *VoPo* repeats, slower this time.

I smile sweetly at him and point at my passport. 'American,' I say, pretending not to understand his question.

He holds up four fingers. 'Age. *Vier* – four . . . months?'

His eyes are the colour of a brewing storm and I try not to meet his gaze. 'Yes, she's four months,' I say. I bury my face into Axel's hair. He smells of formula and Dina's floral soap.

The *VoPo* looks at Axel then back down at the passport. He frowns, the lines on his face deepening.

'She's big,' I say, shrugging, then stop myself from saying more. I practised all night but the American accent is harder than I thought and if he detects a single hint of a German inflexion, he might not let me through. I tell myself I'm not escaping; they want to stop those going west, not the other way around. And yet, it feels as if my skin is crawling with insects, and the *VoPo* hasn't smiled once. Perhaps they're on high alert. They must know there was an attempted tunnel escape only two days ago.

'*Tasche* – bag.'

I slip it off my shoulder and hand it to him. There's nothing much in there and yet my heart expands in my chest. He rifles through it, takes out a lipstick, opens it and turns the bottom. The lipstick pokes out like a bloody finger. He sniffs it although I can't fathom why. Slowly, he takes out every other item and lines them up on the counter. The lipstick, my wallet, two cloth nappies, a bottle of formula and a dummy.

'*Sie wirken nervös*,' he says, glancing at me. I try not to register his words. I refuse to reflect on what he's hinting at.

'Nervous?' He tries to catch my eye, the toothpick flicking in and out of his mouth like a snake's tongue.

I shake my head, then start humming a melody into Axel's ear, although it's me who needs to hear it.

The phone on the desk shrieks.

I take a step back. Once more it strikes me that Dina's friend Barbara probably never did give her permission for me to take her child's passport and her own. Why would she? If it had always been an option, Dina would have suggested it from the beginning. Not only am I impersonating someone else, I'm doing so with something stolen, not borrowed. Perhaps Barbara has already reported it to the police – maybe whoever is calling is giving a red alert.

The *VoPo* lifts the receiver, his eyes never leaving my face. He says nothing, merely grunts several times in reply to whatever is being said. Slowly he replaces the phone in its cradle and removes the toothpick from his mouth. He picks up my passport this time and examines the photo. We tried our best with some home hair-dye but the colour isn't quite right – it's almost black instead of a chestnut brown. The other woman's lips are bigger than mine, too, and her nose is smaller. Why did I think this would work?

He gestures for me to come closer, then peers into my face. It feels like I've been stripped naked but I force myself to hold his gaze. His breath smells of onions.

He holds the passport up to my face, raises his eyebrows and shakes his head. He places it on the counter and stabs the photo with a yellow-stained finger.

'Not you,' he says. A fact not a question.

Breathe. Short and brash. Short and brash.

'Of course it's me.' I try to sound outraged but I can tell he's not convinced. 'I'm thinner now. I lost weight after the baby. The birth was traumatic. I ripped.'

He physically recoils as if I've vomited on the counter. Perhaps I took it a step too far, but men can't handle anything to do with women's bodies. His repulsion might distract him from his suspicion.

Unless, of course, he already knows.

He turns and raps his knuckles on the door behind him. It swings open almost immediately and another guard, older with a greying moustache, marches in.

'*Was?*' The man's voice is clipped. His dark eyes slide over me. His colleague whispers something in his ear and I can almost feel the cold metal handcuffs against the skin of my wrists. If I run, will they shoot me in the back, with a baby in my arms?

I hold my breath and focus on the older man's song. His music is impatient, each cymbal clash too fast, the rhythm off-beat. If I remain calm – and they don't already know – he'll let me go, I'm sure of it. His music tells me there is somewhere else he wants to be.

Then Axel begins to cry.

I've never been so thankful for such an awful sound. He goes from crying to wailing, the noise amplified by the smallness of the space. I will him to continue.

The older *VoPo* wrinkles his nose as if the scream is a smell. He grabs our passports and stamps them with purple ink before placing them in my outstretched hand. He nods his head towards the exit, giving me his permission to leave, and then turns on his heel and is gone.

I hurry out of the door and I don't look back.

54

LISETTE

Now – East Berlin, 9 January 1962

I wake to find winter's awful face pressed up against the window and Mother missing from the flat.

'I think she's in the courtyard,' Julius says, peering out of the window. 'Goodness, she's in her nightgown. Hurry.'

We find her knee-deep in the snow, her bare legs blue with cold. Her nightgown is practically see-through and I glimpse the outline of her sagging breasts, the shadow of hair on her pubic bone. She's not yet seventy but she looks a decade older. Small crystals of ice nestle in the strands of her grey hair, shimmering in the morning light.

In my hurry to get down here, I left my jacket and boots upstairs. My slippered feet sink deep into the snow, winter's white hands grabbing at my ankles.

Mother is holding a pair of garden shears. She looks around as if searching for something to prune but the ground is frozen solid and the shrubs are covered in snow. Half of me wants to seize her by the shoulders and shake some sense into her. The other half wants to tuck her into bed, stroke her brittle hair and read her a story until she falls asleep.

'What are you doing out here?' Julius says, his voice as gentle as a breeze. 'It's freezing. Let's get you inside, run a bath. Maybe a cup of tea?'

'Who are you?' Mother says. I can see the sudden shift in her. She grips the shears with both hands and clenches her jaw.

'I'm Julius – your son-in-law. It's OK, you know who I am.'

'I certainly do not.' She waves the shears like a sword.

'Lisette's here. You know Lisette. Please come inside, Rita. You'll get sick if you stay out here.'

He talks to her like a child. I don't know why but it makes me want to scream.

She doesn't answer him so he reaches out gently to touch her bony shoulder.

She lashes out.

The shears make contact with his arm, slicing through his shirt and the skin beneath. Bright-red drops of blood drip into the snow. The shock of the colour is as disturbing as the act itself.

'*Scheiße*,' Julius mumbles, but it looks worse than it probably is. And he should know by now not to touch her. He takes a step back and lifts his hands in surrender. I take his place and Mother's gaze falls on my face.

'There you are,' she says. 'Are you hurt? Did this man hurt you?'

I shake my head and her body relaxes, her arms dropping to her sides. I reach out my hand and she relinquishes the shears. They're sharp but flaking with rust and I make a mental note to clean Julius's wound so it doesn't get infected.

We get her upstairs and I usher her into the bathroom where I run the hot water. Her lips have turned blue and her teeth are chattering. I help her undress, stuff the wet nightgown into the overflowing laundry basket and offer to help her get into the bath. She ignores my outstretched hand but climbs in willingly. When I turn to go, she says, 'Please stay.'

I pull up a stool and watch as the colour returns to her skin. Tears begin to trickle down her face and I don't know what to do. My notepad is in the living room and I don't want to leave her, not when she's asked me to stay.

'I should have protected you,' she whispers, her words almost lost in the steam. 'As your mother, that was my job. I should have protected you, but I did not. The General has gone now, hasn't he?'

I nod but she's not looking at me. Her gnarled feet are poking out of the water and she looks at them instead.

'I thought it was the right decision,' she says.

Her voice is so quiet I have to strain to hear her.

'I offered myself first. Of course I did, but he did not want me. It was one or ten. He made me choose. I thought perhaps he would be kind, that maybe it would not be so bad for you. But he was not kind, was he? He took your voice and he took your music. You hate me for it and I deserve that. I should have said no. I should have killed him.'

She shakes her head and her tears drip into the water, causing miniature ripples across the surface. 'I have told myself so many lies. Admitting I failed you was too much to bear.'

She looks at me then and reaches out a dripping hand. I hesitate before taking it but her eyes implore me.

'I am so . . . so sorry, my beautiful daughter,' she says, looking me in the eye, her own a deep pool of regret. 'I will try to be better. I *will* be better. Do you think . . . do you think that perhaps – one day – you might be able to forgive me?'

It is not until she asks for my forgiveness that I realize I have been waiting for these words for over sixteen years. Back then, she did not have a choice. Not really. But I still needed her to recognize the part that she played, her failure to protect me.

My tongue feels thick in my mouth but my lips form a word.

It comes out as a croak, but it meets the world, strong due to its mere existence.

'Yes.'

~

Mother sinks into the mattress and I cover her with her duvet as well as my own – she's still cold, even hours later. We have spent the day together in mostly amicable silence. My voice has returned, but it's weak and sometimes stumbles. She seems to have found herself back in 1945 once more but I hope she'll leave it behind. As I tuck her in, she speaks of Father, wondering how long it will be until he returns. She continues to talk, but eventually her voice falls silent and her breathing turns heavy with sleep.

'Mama?'

My heart stops in my chest; my body freezes. I must be hearing things.

'Mama!' It comes again. My daughter's voice. I'm sure of it.

I stand on quivering legs. I force myself not to run. I must be mistaken. She can't be here. Can she?

I push the door open, just a crack.

Elly.

Axel.

I fall out of the room and rush towards them. I gather them into my arms, my whole body a sob, my whole world an explosion.

'You're here,' I say, my tears wetting their hair. 'You're here, you're here, you're here . . .'

55

ELLY

Now – East Berlin, 6 April 1962

We lie by the river, a blanket beneath us, above us only wisps of pink-tinged clouds. We're not touching but I can feel the heat of Andrei's body. The confident, steady beat of his music vibrates between us, converging with the rhythm of my own song. I'm no longer in denial.

I love him.

I don't know much but I do know this. East Berlin is synonymous with claustrophobia, yet when I'm with him, I can breathe. This small world we've been confined to somehow feels infinite when we're together.

His uniform jacket is tucked underneath my head. I resist turning and pressing my face into it so I can inhale his scent. Last year I would never have agreed to meet him here in full view of so many people. The air still nips, spring has yet to commit herself, but the park is full and I can feel the disapproving looks of others. It's strange how little I now care.

He turns towards me, propping himself up on one elbow. He takes the unlit cigarette dangling between his lips and taps it on the grass.

'It's good to have you back, Elly Lange.'

'It's good to be back, The Soldier Who Didn't Shoot.'

He reaches forward as if to stroke my hair. My breath snags in my throat, but he's just removing a twig.

It's been three months since I came back but he has yet to kiss me. Sometimes I question if that kiss above the sewer actually happened. But it did. I know it did. If I close my eyes, I can still taste his mouth, still feel his hands on my skin.

I focus my attention on the clouds moving swiftly across the sky. Insects buzz and blue-backed swallows dive and flap. Each time one comes too close, I can feel Andrei suck in his breath.

'I've been meaning to ask,' I say. 'How did you organize Axel's transfer papers?'

He shrugs. 'I asked my father to help. You don't get to his rank without getting your hands dirty.'

'And he was happy to do it?'

'Not exactly happy, no.' He laughs, but it's a short, humourless bark. 'I had to blackmail him.'

'What? You had to blackmail him? Your father? With what?'

'I told him if he didn't help, I'd tell my mother about his affair.'

'I don't know what to say. I'm so sorry.' I turn to look at him but his eyes are fixed on the birds above.

'It's fine. My mother knows anyway. She always knows.'

I reach out and brush my fingers against his. Just for a moment.

I sit up and wrap my arms around my knees, digging my toes into the scratchy blanket. On the other side of the Spree, the sun is beginning to dip behind the *Berliner Dom*. Papa says it used to be magnificent, and it still is; even if the dome is charred and most of the brickwork is black with soot, it still stands proud and resilient. One day perhaps they'll restore it to its original beauty but for now, it is what it is – beautiful, damaged and a reminder of the past.

Andrei sits up and takes my hand in his. Softly he traces each line on my palm. The intimacy of it sends tremors up my arm. I turn to face him and our eyes meet. The world falls silent – there are no barking dogs, no screeching children; even the wind stops whistling. Our music pauses, too, as if catching its breath. It's this silence in between the notes that stops my heart.

He strokes my cheek and I lean in to his touch. We're so close I can taste his smoky breath. He nudges his nose against mine as if to test the waters. I can now hear his music dancing with my own, twisting, teasing and twirling. I brush my lips against his, not a kiss but an invitation. Can he feel the way my whole body is trembling? When our lips finally meet, I don't know whether it is he or I who closes the space between us. His tongue is in my mouth and my hands are in his hair. He wraps his arms around my waist, pulling my body towards his, and who knew that kissing alone could be this incredible? All I know is that the people in the park, the Wall, Mama, Oma Rita – none of it matters. If Andrei is in the East, then this is where I belong.

And then our music stops. A voice smothers it. Mama's voice.

'Elly?' I push Andrei away from me and scramble to my feet.

'Elly.' She's standing on the path, one hand on Axel's pram, the other clenched at her side. 'What are you doing? Who's this?'

I look from Mama to Andrei and back to Mama again. For once I can't find any words. I have just turned sixteen – I'm not a child any more – yet I have never felt so small.

Mama pushes the pram on to the grass. One of the wheels gets stuck but I don't help her. She stops just short of our blanket. Andrei is standing now, too, his hat in his hands, his head a little bowed as if he's preparing to be told off.

'What are you doing here?' I say.

Ignoring me, she turns to Andrei. 'Who are you?'

'My name's Andrei,' he says. 'I'm a friend of Elly's.'

'I can see that.' She takes a step closer and inspects the green insignia on the collar of his uniform. 'You're *Grenztruppen*?'

'Yes, Frau Lange.'

She recoils as if she's been hit. Her face goes pale. 'You're Russian.' It's a statement not a question. Beyond her, the sun disappears behind the *Berliner Dom* and there's a sudden chill in the air.

Andrei hesitates and glances at me.

'I am,' he says finally. 'I'm Russian.'

Mama backs away from him, pulling the pram with her. Her heel sinks into the grass and she almost tumbles, but she clings on to the pram to keep her steady. 'Elly,' she says, but her eyes don't leave Andrei's face, as if she's afraid that, like a dog, he'll attack the moment she looks away. 'You're coming home. Now. I don't want you seeing this Russian again.'

My cheeks burn but I don't argue.

56

LISETTE

Now – East Berlin, 7 April 1962

'How did you do it?' The voice comes from behind me. I don't need to turn to know who it is.

The tram is busy but the space beside me is free and he slips on to the bench. He presses his shoulder into mine as if he's too big for the seat, which he isn't. He cracks his knuckles. Once, twice.

On my lap, Axel turns and looks at Herr Winter curiously. With a chubby finger, he reaches out to touch the man's thin moustache. It looks as though it's been drawn on with a pen.

'So?' Herr Winter says, moving his head just out of Axel's reach. 'Your daughter reappears, and your baby too. How did you get him back? I assume this is him?'

I hold Axel a little tighter and play the piano on his back. Outside, there's a traffic jam; horns are blaring, car fumes darkening the afternoon sky. The ride is bumpy; there must be gravel in the tram-rail grooves.

'My application for him was finally granted.' I shrug, but I hold my shoulders up too long – unnaturally so. 'I don't know why. We got lucky.'

'Lucky, yes. That's certainly one word for it. And it seems your voice has returned. That's also fortunate.'

He gives me his sickly-sweet smile. 'I went to Leipzig,' he continues, examining his shiny nails. 'I met your husband's cousin. She's not the best liar.'

'I don't know what you mean.' I stand up, move Axel to my hip, then slide down the window to let in some air.

'I'm sure you don't.'

Axel coughs – a small, painful bark. Just croup, the doctor said, but when Axel breathes in there's a high-pitched sound that scares me. He coughs again and spittle lands on Herr Winter's trouser leg. He takes out a pristine white handkerchief and wipes it away.

Then Herr Winter stands and yanks on the cord. The tram slows to a stop, the wheels groan.

'I'll be watching you, Frau Lange.' He tips his hat and then steps down on to the pavement. I don't look but I know he's still watching as the tram pulls away.

~

'That man, the Stasi officer – he was on the tram today.' My voice quivers with the memory.

'What did he say?' Julius asks. The newspaper lies in front of him; a cigarette smoulders in the ashtray.

'Not much. It must have worked, whatever Elly's friend's father did. I just hope he'll give up now.'

'He will. It's over.'

I rinse the cutlery and pile it on the damp dishtowel. The soapy water has turned cool and there's a film of dirt on its surface. I take a deep breath, tap my fingers on my thigh.

'I . . . I need to tell Elly what happened during the war, who her father was.'

'What?'

318

I don't turn to look at him but I can feel his eyes boring into my back. I know he heard me but I repeat the words, giving him time to let them seep in. I glance over at Mother. She's still dozing by the window, Axel asleep in his crib a foot away. She's calmer when he's beside her, less confused too.

'Why?'

It comes out as a deflated hiss, like a punctured tyre. I don't know why I thought this would be the easy part. I turn to face him, leaning my back against the damp counter.

'I need to fix my relationship with her,' I say. 'And I can only do that if she understands.'

'Understands what?'

'Why I have—' *Struggled to love her?* 'Why I am the way I am.'

'But ... what about me? What about my feelings?' His voice shakes with an emotion I've rarely seen in him before. 'I'm Elly's father. I have been since the day she was born. Haven't I loved her enough for both of us? We agreed we'd never tell her the truth.'

'I know. I'm so sorry, I really am. It's not fair on you and I understand that. But Elly's been seeing a Russian soldier. I saw them together in the park and I told her she can't see him again. She has to understand why. Also – if she knows, then maybe she'll forgive me.'

He takes my arm and pulls me into our bedroom, closing the door behind us. It's so out of character I'm momentarily disorientated. I've never seen him so angry. Not in all our married years. He's always been quiet, calm, steady.

'I can't believe you're saying this. You can't just—'

'She needs to know,' I repeat.

I walk over to the window and grip the curtain in one hand; the material is scratchy and gives little comfort.

'When Elly was born,' I say, 'I kept seeing his face in hers. She needed me all the time. And it was ... suffocating. There was never any respite. You knew I felt like that, didn't you? That's why you'd take her out, sometimes for hours. But even then, I couldn't breathe. Because I couldn't stop thinking about the fact that she'd come back. That I would never be free of her for long . . . That I would never be free of him.

'The more I pushed her away, the more she demanded my attention. Do you remember she used to cling to me? Like a koala bear? And in my head, I'd be screaming: *Get off. This is my body. Leave me alone.* That . . . man . . . he'd already taken so much from me, and she took the rest. I loved her, though. Of course I did. But sometimes I just couldn't find room for it.'

'You're being too hard on yourself,' Julius says. 'The past doesn't matter.'

'It does. I have to face it. I need to do things differently and that starts with telling Elly the truth. I need to fix our relationship. Start again. I need to do it with honesty this time.'

'She's home. Axel's home. Can't we just live? Can't we just be happy?'

'Are you happy, Julius?'

'What?'

'Are you happy?'

He hesitates. A beat too long.

'Of course I am. *We're* happy.'

I let out the breath I've been holding. It comes out with a whoosh and I sit down on the bed, as if my breath was the only thing holding me upright. Julius sits down beside me and takes my hand in his.

'Maybe it's time we *all* told the truth,' I say, my voice splintering.

He turns to look at me but I fix my gaze on our intertwined fingers.

'Maybe I've known this for a while . . . but you don't like women,' I say. 'You like men.'

The words hang in the air, silence holding them up for both of us to see them.

'I—'

'No, let me speak.' Now I've found my voice, I have to use it. 'You like men. I believe you loved Max. And he died. I can only imagine how awful that was for you. You came home and you found me – broken, pregnant, and in love with you.'

Julius makes a strange noise as if he's being strangled.

'It's OK. You don't need to pretend any more.'

It takes him a long time to speak but finally, his voice a broken whisper, he says, 'I'm sorry . . . I'm sorry for not telling you the truth. I'm sorry for marrying you knowing I would never be able to give you the love you wanted – the love you deserve.'

I look at him and we are both crying. I reach out and wipe away his tears, then lean my forehead against his.

'You have nothing to be sorry about,' I say. 'You have loved me in your own way. And together, we have brought up an incredible daughter. The day you came home, the day you proposed – you saved me. I would not have survived without you.'

'You saved me that day, too,' he whispered. 'Losing Max . . . I thought I would never be able to smile again. But you gave me Elly. You gave me something worth living for. I can never live freely, certainly not here, but it feels like a small sacrifice. I got to spend my life with you – my best friend – and I got to have two incredible children.'

He kisses my hair. My body feels light, lighter than it's ever felt. And I think maybe everything is going to be OK.

'When did you realize?' he says. 'That I'm . . .?'

'I don't know. Perhaps I always knew. I was wilfully blind, I suppose. Sometimes we just see what we want to see. I think you should tell Elly, but that's your decision. I *am* going to tell her about me, though.'

He nods and I know, from that simple movement, he's giving me his permission.

57

LISETTE

Now – East Berlin, 8 April 1962

The door jingles when I open it and the smell of wood polish and dusty leather washes over me. I close my eyes and breathe it in. It smells of the past but it smells of tomorrow too.

I see the one I want immediately. It catches me on a fishing line and I'm pulled towards it with only a little resistance. It's second-hand; I can tell from the faint scratches on the maple-wood lid – the previous owner probably rested ornaments on it. I lift the outer casing and glance inside at the soundboard – the piano's soul – and then I run my hands over the ivory keys.

The shop contains only a handful of grand pianos, a few key-boards as well as a dozen guitars hanging on a wall. How has the owner survived these hard times? I'm the only customer and the eagerness he greets me with suggests I'm the first he's seen in a while.

'She's a beauty,' he says, approaching me with caution, as if he's worried he'll scare me off. 'Would you like to try her?'

For a brief moment, the shopkeeper's face warps into the General's and my breath catches in my throat. I glance at the door. But if I leave now, I'll never come back. It's been so long – an entire lifetime. Perhaps it's too late to glue everything back together. But there's a fluttering in my stomach and my fingers tingle. It's time to live again and I know I can't live a full life without music.

I nod, then tuck in my dress and sit down on the brown leather stool. I move closer to the piano, elongate my spine and take a deep breath. I stretch my fingers and then begin to play. I don't know where the tune comes from. I don't think I know it; it simply spills out of me. My fingers move over the keys, gently at first, stroking and caressing them as if they're a lover's body. The sound is round and mellow and sweet. If it had a taste, it would be a rich cup of hot chocolate. And then my fingers begin to dance and the melody builds in strength, like a powerful storm rolling in from the sea. It shudders through me and I become the storm. I am indestructible. In this realm, I can exist as a whole, perfect person – one that doesn't need, doesn't want. All that matters is the music. As long as I have this, I can survive anything.

I play until my fingers ache and the muscles in my back begin to twitch with the effort. I finish off with Heller's 'Warrior's Song'. It simultaneously depletes and invigorates me. It didn't save me before but it will save me now. As I lift my fingers from the keys, the echo of the final chords fills the room, reluctant to leave.

Behind me I hear clapping. I turn to find not just the shop owner but a small group of people gathered in the doorway. The applause is not thunderous – they are only a few – but the feeling of elation that accompanies the realization I've been heard for the first time in almost two decades is electrifying. An old woman with pearl earrings and an oversized brooch on her lapel smiles broadly at me. The little girl by her side – her granddaughter, I presume – stands wide-eyed and open-mouthed.

I stand up, brush down my dress and remove an invisible hair from my cheek. Then I turn to the man by my side and say, 'I'd like to buy this one, please.'

58

ELLY

Now – East Berlin, 9 April 1962

I try to focus on my fingers and the music coming from the keyboard, but Mama's words keep repeating on a loop in my head. *I don't want you seeing this Russian again.* She can't dictate what I do. I survived four months without her, I crawled through a sewer of shit, I got shot at, my friend almost died in my arms. I'm not a child any more. And yet, things have been so much better between us since I returned. I have spent my life wanting her to love me and I've finally started to feel that love. But it's fragile. If I disobey her, I might risk breaking it.

'I like that song. Is it new?'

I turn away from my keyboard to find Mama hovering by the door, as if she needs my permission to enter. I don't think she's ever complimented my music before. She has only ever greeted it with a grimace. But a grand piano was delivered this afternoon and a rare, apprehensive smile has appeared on her face. Since I returned, something has shifted in her.

'Yes, it's . . .' I want to say *Andrei*. I've finally managed to capture his song. Not entirely – I don't have an orchestra of instruments, but I've found the piano, the heart of it all.

Mama picks at the peeling paint on the door-frame. Small flakes drift to the floor but she doesn't sweep them up. Instead her eyes glaze over as if a memory is floating just within her reach.

'You can come in, if you want?'

She nods and wanders over to my desk.

'There are ... some things I want to tell you,' she says, not meeting my eye. 'Is it all right if you just listen for a while? And don't interrupt?'

'OK.' I flick off the keyboard and sit on my hands. I vow not to butt in, but if it's about Andrei, I won't be able to stop myself. I can't give him up. I just can't.

'I want to explain why things have been the way they've been between us.' Her words are slow and measured. 'Why I've been such a terrible mother.'

I can tell she's practised this speech and my legs start to twitch. I've been looking for answers all my life but now the moment has come, I don't think I want to hear them.

'I don't talk about the war,' she continues. 'It's not just the collective guilt of our country that stops me. Yes, I bear the shame of all the horror that was inflicted by our people. But I also don't talk about the war because of the horror that was inflicted on me. And other women in Berlin. I was made to suffer for the deeds of others. I was just a young woman. I craved love and I just wanted a happy life, but I was punished all the same. Some days I'm angry because I didn't deserve it. But on other days, I think perhaps I did. I was a bystander. I allowed it all to happen. I *should* bear some guilt. We all should. I can't explain our lack of morality, the disregard we had for other people's pain. All I can say is that my world was small. And the plight of the Jews was too far removed from where my focus fell. But the fact is, we didn't ask enough questions. We didn't want to know the answers.

'When the Soviets came to Berlin – in those final days of the war – they raped as many women as they could find. I hid in the crawl space. But when they came for Mother I jumped down. It was one of the worst nights of my life. But that was only the start. Some welcomed officers into their homes to protect them. It was a choice between being raped by dozens or just one person. There was a man – a general. He became our protector, but he was . . . an awful man.'

She pauses and takes a deep breath. She rests one pale, delicate hand on the back of the chair. It seems as if she needs it there, not to hold her up, perhaps, but to feel something real beneath her fingers – a solid thing to anchor herself in the present.

'I'm so sorry, Elly, but Julius isn't your father.'

And there it is.

The room twists. A sentence struggles to form in my mouth and then dies before it's born.

'When Julius came back from the war, he found me pregnant and mute. I was completely broken. I used to play the piano; it gave me such solace. But the General took that from me too. He took everything from me. And if Julius hadn't come back, I don't know what would have happened.'

I know this is hard for her but I don't want to hear any more. I want to rewind the minutes, push the words back into her mouth. She must know I want her to stop but still she continues.

'When you were born, I could see his face in yours. And it destroyed me all over again. I struggled to love you.' Her voice is quiet, her words tiptoeing around me. 'I wanted to. I really did. But sometimes I just couldn't. A better mother – a mother that I'm not, a mother I wish I could have been – would have tried harder. Instead, I let Julius love you enough for both of us.'

She backs away from my desk and sits down on my bed, as if her body is heavy with the guilt she bears. Her shoulders slump, her body like a balloon slowly deflating. I should sit beside her, make this easier for her, but I can't.

She tells me everything and finally I understand. My face is a constant reminder of the monster who stole her music. I can't imagine living without the part of me that gives me most joy. I would die if it was taken from me or if it became tainted, like it has been for Mama. My heart stumbles when I think about everything she has been through, but it also falls over for me. The truth that Papa isn't my papa is like a thick smoke burning my eyes and scraping my throat raw. I'm the product of something evil.

'When you left,' she says, lifting her head and finally looking me in the eye, 'I felt another tear in my heart. I thought I didn't – couldn't – love you. But it's not true. I *do* love you.' She reaches out and takes my hand in hers. 'You're strong, brave, smart. Incredibly talented. And you're innocent of the crimes of that man. And Julius – he *is* your papa, in every way but blood. He has always loved you as his own.'

Tears spill from her eyes, but she doesn't wipe them away. My own cheeks are wet and I can taste salt on my lips.

'Are you in love with that boy? That . . . Russian?'

'Yes,' I say. Because I cannot answer her honesty with a lie of my own.

'OK.' She nods, swallows hard. 'I won't stand in the way. You shouldn't bear the guilt of your ancestors. And he shouldn't bear the guilt of his. It will be difficult for me, but for you, I'll try. I promise I'll try.'

She takes me in her arms. At first I resist – the feeling is too alien – but then I fold into her, resting my head against her chest. We sit together in our awkward embrace until it isn't awkward any more. As the daylight shifts across the room, I hear her music come back. It's been muted for so long and at first it sputters like a car engine in winter, but then it grows steady, more sure of itself. My own music converges with hers, the notes intertwining until a new melody forms. It's the most beautiful song I've ever heard. It's wild and untamed, swelling with promise. It's a song I've been seeking – one that has forever been dancing just out of sight. I've found it now. It was here, waiting for me all along.

Mama strokes my face, wipes the tears from my cheeks. She looks at me and I think it's the first time she's ever really seen me.

'I've spent my life pining for a man who never loved me,' she says, 'who could never love me, for reasons that are his to tell. It was all I ever wanted – a beautiful, perfect love story. It's taken me until now to understand that I already have one.'

She kisses my forehead and then her eyes lock on to mine. 'You are my great love story, Elly. You and Axel. I'm just sorry it's taken me so long to realize.'

EPILOGUE

ELLY

27 Years Later
9 November 1989, Berlin

It is Isabel who tells us. She stands in the hallway, bouncing on the balls of her feet.

'It's coming down.'

And even with those few words, I understand.

Andrei and I exchange the briefest of looks and then we leave our half-eaten stew on the dining room table and scrabble around for our scarves and coats. We follow our daughter down the stairs and out on to the dark street. Neighbours begin to pour out of the doorways near by. Some hover on the pavements, asking questions; others charge forward through the crowd, seeking out the answers for themselves.

Mama stands underneath a street lamp waiting for us, her silver hair dishevelled, her eyes wide. Isabel bounces over to her and plants a kiss on Mama's pale cheeks.

I don't know who called Axel but suddenly he is here too, his wife beside him and his newborn daughter in his arms.

'Come on,' Isabel says, turning her attention back to us. 'Hurry.'

We have waited decades and yet the thought of waiting another minute feels unbearable.

'He said immediately?' Andrei asks, softening his accent the way he always does in Mama's presence.

'Yes, that's what he said.' Isabel strides forward, nudging people out of her way. 'I heard him say it myself.'

'But it doesn't make any sense,' I say, hurrying after her.

'Why are you questioning it, *maman*? It's happening. It's finally happening.'

The crowd surges forward and we are swept along with it. My pulse is racing and my heart pumping with adrenalin. Beside me, Andrei squeezes my hand. Time seems to fold back on itself. I look up at the window, imagining Oma Rita looking down at us, but Oma Rita is long gone, Papa too. And now, just as I lived through an event that shaped my future, it is Isabel's turn. Just as it was then, the combined sound of everyone's music is deafening. Over the years of separation, the volume of the East Berliners' songs has been forcibly dialled down, but tonight they are no longer smothered; they are set free.

I look for Mama and find her beside me. She is watching Isabel, a frown deepening the wrinkle at the bridge of her nose. Will these actions have consequences? Has the shoot-to-kill order been rescinded? Isabel tries to steer Mama forward but Mama hangs back, each step laced with hesitation. I push through the throng and take Mama's hand; it's cold and clammy. She looks at me, her cheeks white, her eyes wide.

She's reliving it too.

I find Axel's face and he knows what I'm asking. His wife nods her permission and then he bundles his daughter into Mama's arms. This time they won't be achingly empty. This time she will have all of us here with her.

Trabant cars, belching smoke, roll through the streets, but

there are too many people and soon the drivers pull over and abandon them, joining the crowds on determined, marching feet.

At the Bornholmer Straße border crossing, the guards are outnumbered. They exchange glances but none steps forward and their guns remain by their side. They trade whispers while the mob chants, '*Tor öffnen* – open the gate. *Tor öffnen*.'

We edge forward and it's clear some people have already passed through. Now more are demanding the same.

We're right up by the Wall now. The closest I've been to it since I crossed back over with Axel, wearing a dress, pressed against my chest. I think of Peter, Karin, the children, Hannelore, Dina, Franz. I imagine them on the other side waiting for me. It has been so long. I feel dizzy, as if the world is spinning a little faster.

The news comes to us like a shiver through the crowd. The gates are open.

The Wall is coming down.

The seconds swell and become minutes, hours. Someone hands Andrei a sledgehammer. We move back, give him space, and he starts to swing. A chunk of concrete falls to the pavement. I pick it up, crumble it in my hands, watching as it turns to dust.

Around us people begin to dance and the music I hear is not just in my head. It ebbs and flows out of open windows and open mouths. And then, finally, we are released; the prison gates are open. I'm being crushed on all sides, yet my body feels lighter; the shackles I have worn all my life fall away.

We are free.

AUTHOR'S AFTERWORD

Writing historical fiction comes with a responsibility to accurately portray an important time in history and though my characters are fictional, they represent the many women who lived through both the Rape of Berlin in 1945 and the brutal division of Berlin in 1961.

There were so many books and articles that inspired me to write *The Silence in Between* and the research I have done has been extensive. I would like to acknowledge the part that some of my sources have played in the development of this story.

The War on Women: And the Brave Ones Who Fight Back by Sue Lloyd-Roberts and Sarah Morris

Sue Lloyd-Roberts's *The War on Women* is such a powerful, important book that everyone should find the time (and the bravery) to read. During her career as a journalist, Lloyd-Roberts documented the atrocities that have been inflicted on women worldwide. Though only one of the chapters focuses on rape as a weapon of war, the book examines everything from female genital mutilation to honour killings to Ireland's fallen women. It's a difficult read but the women Lloyd-Roberts met during her travels showed such courage in the face of the horrors inflicted upon them and it was this courage, this survival instinct, that I wanted to write about.

A Woman in Berlin by Marta Hillers (translated by Philip Boehm)

The memoir *A Woman in Berlin*, originally released anonymously but later confirmed to have been written by German journalist Marta Hillers, depicts the Soviets' occupation of Berlin with honesty and an admirable lack of sentimentality.

The exact number of German women raped during the dying days of World War Two is unknown, but it is possibly as high as two million (and many were raped multiple times). It's been estimated that in Germany 240,000 women died in connection with their rapes.

The awful truth is that civilian women in war are often overlooked victims, silenced by shame and the governments that should have protected them. In writing *The Silence in Between* I in no way wanted to diminish the horrors of the Holocaust and the suffering of those who were victims of it. I simply wanted to tell a story that has remained largely untold – the story of the German civilian women who were punished for the deeds of their country.

Berlin: The Downfall 1945 by Antony Beevor

This detailed, brilliantly researched account of Berlin's downfall was an essential source of information for me. Beevor sews together a catalogue of events and dates with eyewitness accounts to give an unbiased portrayal of the end of the war and Berlin's demise.

The Berlin Wall: A World Divided, 1961–1989 by Frederick Taylor

This book was another crucial source of information for me. It offers a comprehensive history of the Wall but also includes personal accounts portraying the devastating effects on those who found themselves in a fractured city.

Sigrid Paul

I researched countless heartbreaking stories of families separated by the Berlin Wall, but it was Sigrid Paul's story ('The Berlin Wall kept me apart from my baby son', printed in the *Guardian* in 2009) that stuck with me. Sigrid's son Torsten was a very sick eight-month-old baby when the border was closed. The hospitals in East Berlin were unequipped to care for him and, fearing he would die, one doctor organized for his transfer over to the West (transfers were only allowed for heart patients and so the doctor falsified Torsten's medical records). It was four years before mother and son were reunited.

Though the fictional story of Lisette is very different from Sigrid's, being a mother myself, her story struck a chord with me and it sparked the initial idea for *The Silence in Between*.

Roland Hoff

All the characters depicted are fictional, except Roland Hoff who was shot dead while trying to swim to freedom across the Teltow Canal on 29 August 1961.

BBC Radio 4's podcast *Tunnel 29*

Over the years, in the aftermath of the border being closed, East Germans attempted a variety of escape methods, from flying over the border in a homemade hot-air balloon to wading through the sewers.

Tunnel 29 is the gripping true account of a group of students who dug a tunnel under the Berlin Wall. Along with other sources, it gave me ample material to weave together Elly's story.

Elly's Music

In 2020 I read a fascinating article on the IFLSCIENCE website about the different ways we think ('People With No Internal Monologue Explain What It's Like in Their Head'). Some people have verbal thoughts, others experience visual thoughts and the majority experience both. My thoughts are purely verbal, and I couldn't get my head around the fact that some people don't have a running commentary accompanying their everyday lives. I'd heard of synaesthesia (those who experience a merging of senses) and I began to imagine a character who associated each person she met with music.

Some will dislike this part of the book, but I hope others will recognize that music is a language (one that heals), and my hope was to portray in Elly a quirky characteristic that would counter Lisette's mutism and the silence of those who suffered when the border closed between East and West Germany. The talented Micki Bonde has composed snippets of music for each character, and you can listen to these on my website: josieferguson.com.

Smaller details

Though this is a book of fiction, I have tried to incorporate not only big-picture facts but also smaller details not only to bring the story alive but to do this period justice. Some details may seem fantastical – like Hitler Youth members handing out cyanide pills and a hill in central Berlin made out of rubble – but are true nonetheless.

A friend who read an early draft of the book commented that the story felt too unrealistic. A border couldn't simply be closed overnight, a government wouldn't allow a mother to be separated from her baby, a rape victim would never offer herself to one man so as to secure her survival. Sadly, all of these things did happen. The border between East and West Berlin was secured in the dead of night; husbands were separated from wives, parents from their children; and at the end of World War Two women in Berlin did seek out Soviet officers to protect themselves from multiple rapes. These are stories from the past, but they are still echoing now, in the present. As I write this, Russian forces are using rape as a weapon of war against Ukrainian women; deported mothers are being separated from their children in the US; border walls are being built and fortified at an unprecedented rate across the globe (there are currently seventy-four in existence – though to my knowledge the Berlin Wall is the only wall that has been built to keep its people in rather than its enemies out). But this much is clear: when walls are built, people will find a way over or under them; when families are separated, they do everything in their power to be reunited; and when women are victims, they find the courage to speak up, to band together, to survive.

ACKNOWLEDGEMENTS

My journey to becoming a published author has been a long one. I started writing in my teens and the book you now hold in your hands is the fourth book I've written. In 2021 I signed up for the Curtis Brown creative writing course, where I met other aspiring authors and dedicated every spare moment to completing this book. I honestly believe that those who achieve their goals are the ones who never stop trying, but also those who are lucky enough to find a band of incredible people to support them along the way.

Discovering a small group of fellow writers was a turning point for me. Their critiques have made this book an infinitely better story than it was or could ever be. Oliver Bussell, Judith Pasztor Duffy and Claudia Turnbull – I know I would not have come this far without you and I will forever be grateful.

My incredible agent, Sam Copeland. I first met Sam in my twenties when I did an internship at Rogers, Coleridge & White. He was passionate about his work and he made such a strong impression on me that I remember thinking if I ever wrote a good-enough book, I would want him as my agent. Fifteen years later when he called to offer representation, it felt like fate.

An author himself and a champion for other writers, Sam is the best agent I could have hoped for.

My passionate and skilful editor, Kirsty Dunseath. Thank you for believing in this book. You made my dream come true and there will never be enough cake in the world I can offer to give an appropriate amount of thanks.

Alison Barrow, Milly Reid, Eloise Austin and the wonderful publicity and marketing team at Transworld. Thank you for your creative ideas and advocating this book. Beci Kelly, thank you for creating such a beautiful cover that evokes everything I hoped it would. And thank you to my copy-editor Eleanor Updegraff, and proofreaders Ian Greensill and Sarah Hulbert for spotting and fixing so many embarrassing mistakes. The sales team and the rights team, both home and international, thank you for your support and enthusiasm. Georgie Bewes, thank you for keeping the wheels turning behind the scenes. Your job is so important.

Laura Barnett and Lisa O'Donnell, my talented tutors at CBC – thank you for guiding me through the early stages of this book.

My family: Mamma, Pappa, Micki, Lotta, Kiki, Visan, Erik, Ted, Tom, Maja, Isla, Bailey, Nico, Theo, Trish, Gordo, Ian, Karolina, Tulle, Jonas, Neil and Carole. And my newly-discovered sister, Merete. Thank you for continuing to ask how the writing was going long after it was awkward.

Lotta, Visan and Micki, my first fans, thank you for being you.

Pappa, as I write this I'm the champion in backgammon. Now these words are printed, I'm pretty sure it means I will be the champion for the rest of time.

Jenny, Lauren, George, Wilton, Fifi, Booby, Jock, Charlotte, Louise, Suze, Jubes, Janet, Emily, Niamh, Annie, Lara, Irina, Holly. And Anna. Always Anna. I am so thankful that I have so many wonderful friends who have supported me through the years and across continents.

Jane. We still miss you every day.

My snygging, Douglas. Your unwavering belief in me has kept me sane. Without you, this book would have been a pipe dream laid to rest many moons ago.

Mia and Benji, my feisty, awe-inspiring children. I promise I don't have a favourite.

ABOUT THE AUTHOR

Born in Sweden, to a family of writers and readers, Josie Ferguson moved to Scotland when she was two. She returned to Sweden in her twenties, where she completed a vocational degree in Clinical Psychology (MSc). Upon graduating, she moved to London to pursue a career in publishing, something she had dreamed about since delving into fictional worlds as a child, hidden under the duvet with a torch.

She later moved to Asia in search of an adventure and a bit more sun. She currently works as a freelance book editor in Singapore, where she lives with her husband and two young children. While training to become a clinical psychologist, Josie learned about the complexity of human nature, something she explores as a writer. She believes books about the past can change the future and she aspires to write as many as possible. *The Silence in Between* is her debut.

Listen to music composed specially for this novel at josieferguson.com.